continued . . .

Haunting Warrior

Erin Quinn

B

BERKLEY SENSATION, NEW YORK

THE BERKLEY PUBLISHING GROUP
Published by the Penguin Group
Penguin Group (USA) Inc.
375 Hudson Street, New York, New York 10014, USA
Penguin Group (Canada), 90 Eglinton Avenue East, Suite 700, Toronto, Ontario M4P 2Y3, Canada
(a division of Pearson Penguin Canada Inc.)
Penguin Books Ltd., 80 Strand, London WC2R 0RL, England
Penguin Group Ireland, 25 St. Stephen's Green, Dublin 2, Ireland (a division of Penguin Books Ltd.)
Penguin Group (Australia), 250 Camberwell Road, Camberwell, Victoria 3124, Australia
(a division of Pearson Australia Group Pty. Ltd.)
Penguin Books India Pvt. Ltd., 11 Community Centre, Panchsheel Park, New Delhi—110 017, India
Penguin Group (NZ), 67 Apollo Drive, Rosedale, Auckland 0632, New Zealand
(a division of Pearson New Zealand Ltd.)
Penguin Books (South Africa) (Pty.) Ltd., 24 Sturdee Avenue, Rosebank, Johannesburg 2196,
South Africa

Penguin Books Ltd., Registered Offices: 80 Strand, London WC2R 0RL, England

This is a work of fiction. Names, characters, places, and incidents either are the product of the
author's imagination or are used fictitiously, and any resemblance to actual persons, living or
dead, business establishments, events, or locales is entirely coincidental. The publisher does not
have any control over and does not assume any responsibility for author or third-party websites
or their content.

HAUNTING WARRIOR

A Berkley Sensation Book / published by arrangement with the author

PRINTING HISTORY
Berkley Sensation trade paperback edition / May 2010
Berkley Sensation mass-market edition / March 2012

Copyright © 2010 by Erin Grady.
Excerpt from *Haunting Embrace* by Erin Quinn copyright © by Erin Grady.
Cover art by Tony Mauro.
Cover design by George Long.
Interior text design by Tiffany Estreicher.

ISBN: 978-0-425-24663-4

BERKLEY SENSATION®
Berkley Sensation Books are published by The Berkley Publishing Group,
a division of Penguin Group (USA) Inc.,
375 Hudson Street, New York, New York 10014.
BERKLEY SENSATION® is a registered trademark of Penguin Group (USA) Inc.
The "B" design is a trademark of Penguin Group (USA) Inc.

PRINTED IN THE UNITED STATES OF AMERICA

10 9 8 7 6 5 4 3 2 1

*This one is for my readers with heartfelt thanks for your support,
your letters, and your friendship. You know who you are,
and I am truly blessed that my journey has crossed paths with yours!*

ACKNOWLEDGMENTS

I would like to thank my wonderful editor, Kate Seaver, and incredible agent, Paige Wheeler, for their support and encouragement. I am so lucky to be working with you both.

Much gratitude goes to fellow authors Lynn Coulter and Kathryne Kennedy for early feedback on this novel and most of all for their friendship. Thanks to my sister, Bev Moriarty, and my mom, Betty Grady, for working their butts off at my launch party (and to Dad, who put up with all that female chatter for hours on end). Thank you Judi Barker for more things than I can list. Rebecca Goude, Julie Mahler, Jennifer Springer, and Jodi Springer, I send thanks for your proofreading skills and catching my million and one typos. Calista Fox and Sherri Knauss, *muchas gracias*, for the girls' nights that keep me sane.

And a special thanks to Sue Grimshaw, who has been incredibly supportive of me and my career! Words cannot express my appreciation!

Chapter One

"*H*URRY, Ruairi. Hurry."

The whispered command tickled the inside of Rory MacGrath's ear, featherlight and taunting. He brushed it away and rolled over, trying to block out what he instantly knew. It was the dream again—the one that felt too real to be just a dream. In a moment he would open his eyes and find the woman standing beside him. He wouldn't know if she was flesh or fantasy, wouldn't be able to distinguish imagined from reality. Not even in the morning.

He acknowledged this, tried to convince himself that he didn't believe her to be more than a projection of his own mind. A fantasy he'd conjured and spewed into this semisomnolence. He felt his heartbeat begin to race, his breath slow and deepen—combatant symptoms to the paralyzing awareness.

He thought he opened his eyes, but couldn't be sure anymore. Either way, he saw her waiting impatiently beside the couch where he'd fallen asleep watching ESPN. The apartment was dark, lit only by the flickering screen of the TV behind her. It cast her in gray and white, dreamscape shadows. Then the flashing screen went blank and they were both bathed in darkness.

This—of all that was about to come—it was *this* that he hated the most. The black-on-black void held him captive for interminable moments.

Sound came before the light was restored. It was rumbling, indistinct, but a sensory input that his panicking mind grasped gratefully. There was something out there. Something more than his fear. More than his sleep-deadened body.

A flicker heralded the flame of a candle. An instant later others sparked to life until boundaries of a room could be determined in the glow. He was no longer in his apartment.

He scanned his surroundings quickly before fixating on the woman again. It was impossible not to. She looked the same as she had last night and the night before and the night before that. She had dark hair—too burnished for black, too velvety rich for brown. It was full and silken and glossy as mink. It hung to her waist in a wave of body and bounce, gleaming with the flicker of the candlelight. Her eyes were brown, as dark as her glorious hair. They burned like the tiny flickering flames around her. Even his dream-self couldn't believe their luminescence. Her lips were full and soft, one corner caught between her teeth. She looked exotic, her skin dusky and her features fine.

She wore a blue dress with white sleeves—something that laced in places where there should have been seams or zippers. It bloused and flowed over her round shoulders, past hips that made him think of sex in a deep, drowning way. The hem brushed a scattering of twigs and straw on the floor. Not even her feet peeped out.

She stood in the center of a room with three stone walls. Behind him hung a thick woven curtain that served as the fourth. He knew it without turning to look. There was a table with a pitcher on it in the corner beside a lumpy bed covered by a scarlet blanket. The room was damp and drafty, making the tapestries on the walls billow, but the woman seemed oblivious to the cold.

As he watched, she began to untie the dress, letting it fall, revealing a white shift beneath it. The thin material silhouetted her body for a moment before she began to remove that, too. Even as some part of him shouted again that she wasn't real, Rory succumbed to the seduction. She was every fantasy he'd ever had, ever wanted.

Her skin was so smooth and hued it might have been carved from the waxed light that made it gleam. Her breasts were full and heavy, and he felt the air leave his lungs as she bared them. She glanced up then—every time, every night, at just that moment, almost as if she'd heard him. Her cheeks were flushed. Her eyes defiant. Anger bordering on rage filled their depths. So much of the dream made no sense, but that part—that look of fury mixed with consent—it bewildered him the most.

When she was stripped bare, she stood in the flickering light and stared at something just over his shoulder.

He turned—every time he turned, even though by now a part of him knew what he'd see. A tall man with overlong hair stood just behind him. A man dressed in a weird getup that looked like it had come from a movie set. Archaic, like the dress the woman had stripped.

His cloak was made of some animal fur—not politically correct faux fur, but the real thing, with paws stretched flat at four points and the stub of tail nearly dragging the floor. It was flung back from his massive shoulders, revealing a heavy circle of gold round his throat. An obscure word floated to the top of Rory's thoughts. *Torque.* That's what it was called. It was as thick as Rory's fingers and engraved with Celtic spirals. It looked heavy. The man's shirt had a wide slit for his head, boxy sleeves that fell to his forearms, and a front embroidered with more spirals and symbols in purple and gold at the hem and seams. It hung to his thighs, like a dress. Beneath it were short pants that gathered below his knees and leather sandals wrapped midway up powerful calves, Roman style.

But even his bizarre attire was not the strangest part. What made Rory gasp was more tangible, more figurative. It shook him no matter how many times he faced it.

The man looked exactly like Rory. He didn't resemble; he wasn't similar. He could have been Rory's reflection.

As Rory stared he became aware of the ebb and flow of noises coming from beyond the curtained wall, a rumble that now emerged as laughter and conversations he hadn't noticed while he'd watched the woman strip. He'd heard only the beat of his heart pounding in his ears then. Now sounds surged into the candlelit room, the drone of speaking men mingling with raucous hoots and jeering, an occasional giggle or shriek of mirth from the women. One man's words rose above the rest as the speaker threatened to come in and show Rory where everything went. The man used Rory's name, but pronounced it with the same Gaelic inflection that his dream-woman had used when she'd urged him to hurry. Ruairi.

Rory frowned, realizing he recognized the man's voice. He knew he'd heard it before. From their expressions, it was familiar to the naked woman and his identical twin, too.

A surge of lewd cheers followed the man's threat. Volunteers offered to help with the endeavor.

The taunts galvanized Rory's twin into action, and he began stripping away the strange costume with nimble, frantic fingers. He unfastened a gold chain holding the fur cloak at his throat and tossed the heavy garment onto the bed before bending to untie the sandals. Frowning, Rory went back to watching the woman as she watched his double. She stood straight and proud, neither hunching to cover her nudity or posing to flaunt it. She wore no expression, but her eyes sparked and flared with something Rory couldn't quite identify. It couldn't be longing. There was too much anger for that. Her fingers curled in on each other in a tight fist. Then they eased, then they contracted again.

But it was the way her gaze swept over his twin, the way her breasts lifted with a soft breath and her tongue moistened her lips that enthralled him.

He couldn't look away, though that distant awareness inside him was shouting again, warning him not to relax, not to be mesmerized by the rise and fall of those lovely breasts. But he couldn't stop himself as he stared at her, longing to touch her.

He knew the end of this fantasy dream was coming, as it always did just at this point when he felt he might explode with the want and need rising inside him. He braced himself for it, for what came after when he finally awoke alone and aching, still feeling that somehow it had been more than a dream, though he knew that was crazy. She would torment him during the wakeful hours afterwards. The sight of her, close enough to touch . . . to smell . . . to taste . . . He would imagine she was everywhere, just out of reach.

But this time the dream took another turn, veering unexpectedly. Shocking him.

Rory tensed, suddenly uncertain in unknown waters. What

next? Would his body double do what the real Rory longed for? Would he take her in his arms and bury himself deep between the woman's warm thighs? Would watching them be better or worse than always wondering what came after that heated look in her eyes?

Her gaze flitted over his twin's body, lingering on the bunched muscles in his shoulders, the tight ridge of his abs, sliding lower to the hard-on that stood tight against his belly. She flushed and turned away, moving to the table where she filled a cup with wine and gulped it down. Rory found himself entranced by the play of candlelight on the slope of her spine, the curve of her ass, the long length of leg. His body double watched with equal fascination.

She took another drink before facing his twin again, but whatever courage she'd gained vanished when she turned. She looked so vulnerable standing before the massive size and barely restrained power of his muscled twin. Rory wanted to intercede, not trusting his double with his dream-woman. Even now, a part of him caught the irony in that. Rory was no more trustworthy than this stranger who looked like him.

He watched with growing frustration as the two met in the center of the room. His twin reached out and touched her skin, slid his hands from shoulders to buttocks, pulling her tight against his body. It enraged him, watching. Confounded him, because he also felt some strange sense of participation. The old phrase *taking a shower in a raincoat* came to him. It fit exactly. He experienced some of what his twin must be feeling, and yet only through the thick layer of distance.

His twin and the woman backed up until they reached the crude bed and then fell on it. Rory's gut tightened as they came together in a tangle of limbs and passion. There was little love, that was apparent, but there was heat and need that perfumed the air and sizzled in the silence. The two seemed to clash in a battle for control, yet neither relinquished it and neither retained it. Rory could only ride the wave, dry and isolated, while his mind and his body yearned to take his twin's place, be one with the complex and fervent confrontation.

When it was over, he was twisted tight and hard as a rock. He cursed under his breath, damning this dream-world that had dominated him. Wishing to awaken but unable to bring his consciousness back to his sleeping body.

He heard a sound to his right. Confused, he looked at the stone wall and saw the woven banner with a crest at its center billow and then move. A man appeared—dressed like Rory's twin had been only not so fine, not so resplendent. This man's clothing lacked the adornment and embellishment, but it had the same ancient look to it. He was armed with a bladed weapon—too short to be called a sword, too long to be a knife. His manner said he knew how to use it.

What happened next came in a jerky blur—a film that jumped and dragged then sped forward without pause. His twin leaping off the bed, the woman sucking in a harsh breath that seemed to clog the scream she wanted to release. There was recognition on all their faces, and Rory understood that this intruder was no stranger.

Unfettered by the vulnerability of his nudity, his twin crouched in a fighting stance as the new man circled him with that long and wicked blade clenched tight in his hand. Then they charged one another, one naked, one garbed. The fight was quick, silent, and violent. Rory's twin overpowered the other but not without a struggle. He unarmed the attacker quickly, slamming him against the unrelenting stone and crushing his throat with his bare hands.

Stunned, Rory looked from the dead man now sprawled on the floor to his naked twin to the woman, who watched from between spread fingers. She rushed toward his twin with a look of horror on her face. Rory spun and saw that his double was on his knees now. His hands clutched his gut, and something dark and viscous ran through his fingers. *Blood.*

Rory crouched beside the woman as she stared at the gaping wound across his twin's abdomen. Blood gushed from it, splashing her bare skin, seeping into the straw and twigs covering the floor. There was so much of it. *Too much.*

"Why?" she breathed the question, those eyes scanning his twin's face.

Yes, why? Rory wanted to know as well. Why had the intruder attacked them without provocation?

His twin was bent with agony and didn't answer. As his twin reached out a bloody hand to the woman, Rory knew the life was draining from him. It was like watching his own death, unbearable and inescapable. The look in his twin's eyes cut him as deeply as the gash in the other man's flesh. There was rage and there was pain. Desolation. Realization. And something deeper, more agonizing. A wound more painful than the one emptying his life onto the floor.

"It's the both of us he's betrayed, isn't it?" the woman said, her words so soft Rory thought they were imagined.

His twin closed his eyes and nodded once. Then he looked up, and for a cold instant, it seemed he stared right at Rory. There was comprehension in the look—comprehension and shock. Then, relief. Rory felt the *how* forming on his lips, but he had no voice here, in this nightmare that had morphed into something no longer symbolic but terrifyingly real.

His twin stumbled to his feet and now he clutched an object in his hands. Rory gaped at it, reeling again from the shift this dream-world took.

It was the Book of Fennore. Rory would recognize it anywhere, even here, in this warped fantasy he couldn't escape.

The Book had a black cover made of leather, beveled with concentric spirals, and crusted with jewels, gold, and hammered silver that twisted and twined around the edges and corners. Three cords of silver connected in a mystifying lock fixed over the jagged edges of thick creamy paper. As old as the earth and sky, the Book was more than a bound text; it was an entity with its own consuming desires and twisted needs. Just touching it gave it access to the heart, mind, and very soul. Its call was irresistible. Its promises, unimaginable. Rory knew better than anyone.

A low humming had swelled around the three of them, a sickening buzz that lodged in the pit of his stomach and blocked out the sounds on the other side of the curtain. He felt hot and cold . . . and scared. The dream breached what little barrier remained between nightmare and terror.

The humming whine throbbed and pulsated—too low to be heard, too insistent to be ignored. With it came a blistering heat that burned like a coal in his head. A reasonable, alien part of him began to cite calming words—*It will be all right. It's just a dream. Just your imagination.* And once again, dream-Rory recognized that the input was coming from his wakeful self. Dream-Rory found that even more terrifying because that implied a plurality that went beyond the symbolic twin.

This can't be a fucking dream if I'm thinking all of that. . . .

Everything began to shimmer, became the stuff dreams are supposed to be—translucent, then transparent, then transcendental. . . . Before he could wrap his thoughts around it, the woman turned her head to where he knelt beside her. The cold fear on her face struck an answering chord within him. She saw him.

She saw him.

She lifted a hand that shook and set it against his chest, as if to test his solidity. Her eyes widened; her mouth rounded into an "oh" of disbelief.

And the shock of her icy fingers against his hot skin jerked him awake.

Chapter Two

I T was three A.M. the next night—morning—when Rory got off work at the Low Down Bar on Palm and Sonora. And it was dark like only the wee hours can be.

He'd stayed to help Martina clean after the club had locked its doors behind the last drunk, and he was dead tired. Night after night of chasing the dream-woman had left him gritty-eyed and short-tempered. He'd had zero tolerance for the punks who drank until they thought they were bulletproof, who were basically the only customers stupid enough to frequent the Low Down.

Once all the tables were wiped, floors mopped, and glasses washed and put away, he'd walked Martina, the bartender, to her battered Toyota—a heap of metal and rubber that had turned a hundred and seventy thousand miles but still managed to get her to and from work. There was an autumn chill in the air, and it mingled with the stench of garbage and smog and old grease. They were too far inland to smell the Pacific, not that the ocean breeze could have penetrated the borders of the barrio. Graffiti glowed neon on every surface in sight. The owner had finally taken down the sign that hung over the Low Down's door, tired of having it repainted after each tagging. Now the clientele found it by instinct—cockroaches drawn to trash.

"Your tires are low," he said as they approached the Toyota.

"And my *pompi*'s dragging," she said with a tired sigh.

He let his gaze run down her backside. "Your *pompi* looks fine to me."

She laughed and wiggled her ass for him, muttering in Spanish, *"not as fine as yours."* She didn't think he understood, but Rory had always had a way with foreign languages, an innate ability to interpret and even speak them. It wasn't that he was naturally fluent in so many different tongues; somehow he could grasp the meaning and intent of the words even when the sound and shape of them was unknown. With such an understanding, it took no time to master the new language. The skill came in handy more times and in more ways than he could count, but it wasn't something he broadcasted.

"Why don't you follow me home and find out just how fine it is, Irish?" Martina said in English.

She was only half kidding, and they both knew it. He grinned and raised his brows. "Ah, but then I'd ruin you for any other man, darlin'."

"I think you're afraid it will be the other way around, *mijo*. Once you've had a taste of some spicy *frijoles*, you'll be bored with your white potatoes."

He suspected she might be right, but he liked Martina too much to answer the invitation in her eyes. Besides, since the dream-woman had begun haunting him, he thought he might already be ruined for any other female. And that was just nuts.

Martina gave a derisive snort of laughter. "Don't worry, Irish, I won't want a wedding ring and three kids in the morning."

He took her keys from her hand and unlocked the driver's door, handing them back when she slid in.

"Drive safely, Martina."

"One of these days you're going to say yes, Irish."

"And that will surely be the day you change your mind to spite me."

She laughed at that. *"Sí."*

Her motor sputtered pathetically and then gave a half-hearted roar as she gassed it out to the deserted street. After her engine faded away, the crunch of his shoes against the loose parking lot gravel was the only sound in the night. Usually he liked the quiet, but tonight it played on his nerves. Made him jumpy.

There were a few other cars left in the lot. The cops cruised the three-mile area around the bar from ten to close, and those who still had licenses had learned to walk home after getting loaded. Most of them didn't have a pot to piss in, let alone a vehicle to worry about in the first place. Who knew where they went when their last buck was spent.

He crossed to his '81 Camaro, admiring the new paint job he'd had done. After driving around in gray primer for three years, he'd finally finished the restoration of the old car. The new black high-gloss was the crowning touch. He'd parked under the light where he could see it from the club's door while he checked IDs and bounced the stray unruly and obnoxious drunk. He probably put more care into the Camaro than he did anything else in his life. A fucking car.

The overhead light cast the inside in darkness, and it wasn't until he opened the door that he saw the old woman inside. Stunned, he stared, his brain stuttering and stalling as it tried and failed to put some kind of framework around what he saw.

The woman was Colleen Ballagh, his grandmother, and she sat in the passenger seat as if she had every right to be there. She'd seemed ninety when Rory was a kid, and she looked the same now that he was thirty. She sat calmly waiting, hands folded demurely in her lap, eyes sparkling like hell's fires burned within them.

In that one swift glance, he'd known, though there was no logical explanation for it. No sign, no telltale warning. But his gut knew what his eyes denied.

She was dead. A ghost, waiting in his Camaro. His certainty was ancient and superstitious, and it was complete.

Even as he acknowledged it, the concrete wall of reality fought to keep her out. If she was dead, then she couldn't be here. He shouldn't be seeing her. Ghost or not, she looked as solid and as real as the black leather of his seats and the shining chrome knobs on the dash.

"Boo," she said.

Rory staggered back a step and would have fallen on his

ass if he hadn't been holding on to the rim of the door. She laughed at that. Laughed, like it was a game.

He'd heard of it happening to other people, seeing the dead. Christ, where he came from people saw crazy shit all the time. That was Ballyfionúir—a town so small it could fit neatly inside any one of Los Angeles' mini-malls. It sprawled lazily on the Isle of Fennore just off the southern coast of Ireland. On the other side of the planet. May as well have been the other side of the universe.

The Isle of Fennore was more than an isolated community, "the last bastion of traditional Ireland" as the mainlanders liked to call it. It was shut off from the rest of the world, a satellite that had slipped its orbit and now ran counterclockwise to the expected flow of things.

His own family claimed they could trace their history back to the line of Heber, the same as Brian Boru, one of the greatest Irish kings of them all. But there was more than royalty in his family tree. Like many others on Fennore, Rory's family had special *gifts*. That's what they called it. *Gifts*. Whether it was seeing a visitor before he made it to the front door, or knowing a son or daughter had skipped school without being told, or having tea and a chat with a deceased relative on a bright sunny day—the gifts ran through Fennore like the rivers and the streams.

What people from the outside might consider supernatural powers, Fennorians viewed as normal. As expected as the flow of the tide and the rise of the moon—parts of the same great cycle. On Fennore, people knew things they shouldn't, saw things they couldn't, and did things ordinary people wouldn't.

But Rory wasn't on Fennore anymore—hadn't been since his mother sent him away to live with her sister in California when he was twelve. And if he'd ever had any of the *gifts*, it was so long ago he didn't remember. Didn't *want* to remember. It was why he'd never go back.

But here was his grandmother, smiling wickedly at him from the front seat of his Camaro in a deserted parking lot in southeast LA looking exactly as she had when he was a teenager and saying good-bye. Still, he had no doubt at all that she was dead.

"Are you going to stand there like a gobshite or are you going to say hello?" she demanded, and the sound of her voice washed over him in a wave of memory and pain.

Rory looked down, ignoring her. Hoping his disregard would send her back to where she'd come from. This was why he'd left Ballyfionúir and never returned—he liked his reality served up in inflexible, unconditional terms. He'd never been able to embrace the freak of nature that was his heritage.

"Is it afraid you are?" she quipped. "And you the size of Hercules. I'd never have guessed it."

His mouth was dry, and he knew she was taunting him. Nana had always known his weaknesses, what buttons to push, what switches to flip. She knew exactly what Rory Mac-Grath feared and how hard he'd fight to keep anyone else from finding out.

"What do you want?" he asked, sliding behind the wheel like he wasn't shaking inside. She was *fucking dead* and he was talking to her.

She smelled of lilac and scones, and the familiar fragrance made him want to scramble right back out and take off running—who cared what she thought. *Christ, ghosts shouldn't have a scent.* She wore a silky white flowered blouse and pale blue slacks that ended in bright white sneakers. *Go, Granny, go,* he thought.

"I've come to bring you home, Rory," she said, and it seemed she'd taken pity on him, because the fiery glee dimmed from her eyes.

"I am home."

"Oh aye, I can see that." She looked out the window. "And who wouldn't want to live here with all the lovely smog and asphalt?"

"It grows on you."

"Sure and it eats at you, too. Tell me it doesn't."

He didn't say anything. It was true and they both knew it.

"And that's not all that eats away at you, is it, Rory?"

"I like it here," he insisted, refusing to bite at the bait she dangled. Colleen Ballagh was a master at the lure and trap. It did no good to lie to her, and it was just as pointless to evade.

"Well," she said with a meaningful sigh, "you've always been a strange boy. Even before."

Even before what? Before he was sent away? Or before his father disappeared that night so long ago when he'd been five? He forced himself not to ask. If Nana planned to tell him, she would. If she didn't, no amount of pressure would get it out of her.

"Oh, and don't you think you're the smart one?" she said with a chortling laugh. "I used to tell your mother that you could outfox a fox. Of course, all she could see was the trouble you courted wherever you went. It's a mother's job, I suppose."

"Is there a point to this?"

"Watch that mouth with me, Rory MacGrath. I'm still your grandmother, dead or no."

That was funny, but he didn't laugh.

"Do you never wonder what happened to you?" she said softly.

He turned in his seat, wanting to see her face despite the way it made him feel. Or maybe because of it. Maybe he just needed to prove to them both that he wasn't afraid.

"Nothing happened to me," he said.

"Stubborn," she muttered beneath her breath.

She was one to talk.

"I've not time to argue it all out with you. I'm not on my own schedule anymore, as you might have guessed. And believe it or not, it's more than yourself I'll be needing to see."

"Who else are you going to haunt?" he asked.

"Haunting is it? Well I suppose I've been accused of worse. It's not your concern who else I'll be visiting. You'll find out when the time comes, if that's the way of it. For now it's enough to know that you'll be going home."

"I am—"

"Ach, and don't say it. You're far and away from home, boy. Far from your people and your purpose. You think all it takes to be a man is big muscles and a heart of stone? Living is about feeling. It's about risk and loss and having your soul torn out."

"Sounds like a great time," he said.

"You think I don't see how afraid you are?"

He clenched his jaw, staring at her coldly. "I'm talking to my dead grandmother and I'm not even drunk. I'm entitled to a little fear."

"It's not me that frightens you," she said, her tone so harsh it wiped any smartass reply right out of his head. "It's yourself, isn't it, Rory? You lost a part of yourself when you lost your father, and you're scared that it was the better part. I dare you to deny it."

For a moment, he could do nothing but stare. How did she know that? Her brows raised in challenge. How could he imagine she *wouldn't* know all his secrets, her look said.

"So, what?" he demanded. "You're here to give it back? Restore all my shattered little pieces?"

"Sure and hand over the world on a golden platter while I'm at it." Nana looked away in disgust, and despite himself, he felt ashamed. "I'm here to tell you that it's time to quit hiding like a child afraid of the dark. It's time to go back to Ballyfionúir and put things to right."

"Some wrongs can't be made right," he said softly. "It's too late for that."

She laid a pale and wrinkled hand over his where it clenched the steering wheel. The touch had no warmth and no weight, but the hand was so familiar, even after all these years, that it comforted him.

"No, child, it's not too late. But this is not a calling you can pretend not to hear. The night in the cavern, Rory, beneath the ruins of the old castle. The night your father vanished . . . You changed something."

Her words came at him like the tolling of a great bell. "What?" he asked softly, his mouth suddenly dry. "What did I change?"

She hesitated and for the first time since he'd opened the door, she looked uncertain. "You changed fate, Rory. And not just your own."

He stared at her, confounded. Torn between releasing a bark of incredulous laughter or a gasp of bone-deep fear. But the look in her eyes was too steady, too serious, too much of a contradiction to the bizarre words she'd spoken for him to do either. He changed fate, she'd said. What kind of bullshit was that?

"I cannot tell you all that I want to," Nana went on. "Oh, I know you think I'm enjoying myself, but that's not the way of it. I should have a fistful of years left to enjoy, but here I am as dead as this place you call home. The fault is my own, of course, because wasn't it me who toyed with fate from the beginning?"

"What the hell are you talking about?" Rory finally demanded.

His harsh tone stiffened her sagging shoulders and brought her chin up. The fierce sparkle was back in her eyes. "Sure and I'm a fool to think you'll understand what I say to you, but it is what it is. You *will* return to the land of your birth. And you *will* do what is asked of you. There's no choice. Should you deny your destiny, you will find that destiny is a whip with a backlash of fury. It will flay the skin from your bones."

"Christ," he muttered under his breath. She was not only dead, but she was crazy, too. "Well thanks for the warning, Nana."

He'd pissed her off now. She narrowed those eyes and pointed at him. "This is not a game. People will die, Rory MacGrath. People you care about, whether you'll admit it or not."

He stared at her. Again that conflicting need to either laugh or moan caught him in its grip. She meant what she said. She believed every single word of it, no matter how crazy it sounded. How could his going home now be connected to that night when his father disappeared or to the fate of his loved ones?

"When you get there, you'll find I've left something for you. Take it and keep it safe. You'll need it."

"What is it?" he asked, though he had no intention of going anywhere near Ballyfionúir.

She smoothed an imagined wrinkle from her pants and ignored his question.

"You're asking me to go someplace I don't want to go. I'm going to need a little more than 'destiny' to work with."

She looked at him for a moment, gauging the sincerity in his tone, and against his will he found a part of him rising up with earnestness. He could try to deny it, but some part of him wanted answers, wanted to know what he was supposed to do. Needed to know. Because somewhere in her crazy declarations, he'd felt that chill of truth.

He'd always suspected that he was somehow responsible for what happened that night his father vanished. But he'd never known how or why or even *what* he'd done. The idea that the answers to a riddle that had plagued him for twenty-five years were just on the other side of a page he couldn't figure out how to turn was a torment in itself.

"What do you remember about that night beneath the ruins?" Nana asked at last.

"Not much, just a few bits and pieces."

"But you haven't forgotten the Book, now have you?"

"The Book of Fennore? Is that what this is about?"

She only stared at him for a long, drawn moment, but her silence answered the question. What else would it be about?

"You're meant to find it, Rory."

"Why?" When she didn't answer, he tried again. "At least tell me what I'm *meant* to do with it once I figure out where it is?"

"You'll figure it out when the time comes." She cocked her head and smiled. "It's a bitter pill, I know. Would it make you feel better to know that you'll find the girl, too?"

"What girl?"

"Why the one you dream about of course."

She held up a hand, stopping him before he could respond to *that*.

"It's best you take care of loose ends before you go. That nice woman you walked out with should have a car she can depend on. Hers will finally quit running in a week or two and leave her stranded. I'll tell you now, it will end badly."

He scrambled to catch up with the subject change. "Martina?"

She ran a hand over the leather seat. "This one seems quite nice, and you won't be needing it where you're going."

"I'm not going anywhere."

"Of course you're not," she said.

"I mean it."

"Sure and don't I know it." But her smile contradicted her

agreement. "I've seen where you live. I've seen *how* you live, Rory."

She'd been to his apartment? He scowled, thinking of her wandering through the small rooms, trailing her dead fingers over his scant possessions. His furnishings were sparse—the main room dominated by his weight set and TV. Only a couch and a coffee table that more often than not served as the dinner table kept them company.

"I don't spend much time at home," he told her. "And when I'm there, I work out, watch TV, or sleep. What's the point in clutter?"

"Clutter?" she snorted. "Well you certainly don't have to worry about that. What do your lady friends say when they see how you live?"

"They don't see how I live. We go out, we go to their place. Keeps things simple."

Nana looked as if she didn't know whether to laugh or scold at that. "And tell me why is it that simple's the goal, Rory?"

"I've had complicated. It didn't work for me."

She made a derogatory sound. "Well I'm thinking you'll need a new plan, then, because things are about to get very complicated for you, darlin'. Very complicated indeed."

And she looked extremely pleased with herself about it. Apparently satisfied by his glowering face, she let out a deep breath and then nodded. "Well, that's it for me, then. I've done what I came for, and now it's time to go. I'll be seeing you at the wake no doubt. Be warned, I won't look as good as I do now, I'm sure. Your stepfather has taken it on himself to pick out my dress." She gave an exaggerated shudder. "Poor lamb, he's quite torn up over my passing. Good night, then."

Stunned, Rory realized she meant to leave.

"Wait. That's it? That's all?"

"Don't dally in coming. The wake is on Thursday. I'm sure they plan quite a feast in my honor, and you won't want to miss that."

"I don't give a damn about the wake."

She sniffed, insulted. "Well, have it your way. But you won't want to be late no matter. Even destiny has a schedule."

And with those parting words, she waved good-bye and simply disappeared.

"I'm not going anywhere," he said to the quiet that filled the spaces where she'd been. "You hear me? I'm not going anywhere."

Chapter Three

SARAID dreamed of the man again. A stranger whose features she could never discern, though he felt familiar and a part of her craved him. Like air. Like water. It made no sense, but then again, it was only a dream.

She sighed and rolled over onto her back. Her four sleeping brothers lay in a row beneath the open sky, next to a fire long since banked to ash. Above, the glittering stars were harshly bright in the deceptive tranquility of the night, and the moon glared flat and hard from the tapestry of the velvet sky. It cast writhing shadows into the trees and painted menace onto the most harmless bush.

There was no reason for it, yet something deep inside her tightened. Slowly Saraid sat up and stared from one twisting shape to another, her heart thudding like a *bodhrán* while the night became a swaddle, binding her fear tight against her. Nothing moved but the gentle rustle of branches in the light breeze; still the blackness of the sky pressed down and she fought the need to flee.

And suddenly she knew what was coming.

Wary, she stood, forcing the action, forcing herself to acknowledge that she was not trapped by anything more than her fear. Silently she left the warmth of her blanket and moved away into the deep and shadowed forest. It was not far from here that Cathán Half-Beard and his army of outlaws and

Northmen had carved out their small and violent empire. He'd conquered the peaceful inhabitants with brutality that had left them shocked and meek. Using a tactic of the Northmen, he'd then offered safe harbor to any who would pledge loyalty to him. The broken survivors either agreed or were slain. Generally, it did not take the slaughter of many to compel the others to bow their heads and swear fealty.

He'd wrought the same devastation on Saraid's people. He'd burned their *tuath* to the ground, slaughtered men, women, and children in a wave of terror that Saraid still could not comprehend. One moment they'd been sharing laughter and goodwill, and in the next they'd been under siege, running for their lives. Cathán Half-Beard's men had pillaged their harvests, plundered their coffers, and stolen their cattle. They'd been left with nothing to survive the coming winter, not even shelter.

Some of her people had gone into the Dark Forest with Cathán Half-Beard and served him still. It vexed him greatly that Saraid and her brothers had escaped with their handful of loyal followers. He hunted them relentlessly.

She did not like that her brother Tiarnan had chosen to camp so near to Half-Beard's forest tonight. He'd refused to answer her when she'd asked why, why he would risk such a thing. Tiarnan was her twin, but he was also the chieftain of what remained of their people. He did not answer to Saraid.

She paused, sensing something just ahead. As she watched, a hazy figure materialized like smoke taking shape and form. There was a leg, small and bent as if the rest of the person were sitting on the boulder behind it. A torso filled in, slight and short, then arms, neck, a head. Frowning, Saraid stared into the wrinkled face of an old woman she did not know.

Saraid had been visited by the dead before. It was her gift and her curse that their spirits sought her out. Many came before death even took them. Some came to warn her, some came to beg that she prevent it from happening. It didn't matter what their reasons—Saraid could not help them. She saw death's secrets, but she was never able to stop them.

She stared now at the old woman before her. She had dark hair, cut short to wave away from a round and lined face, tinged with silver at the temples. Eyes that looked black snapped with the reflection of moonlight. She wore strange clothing of a material Saraid had never seen. A weave of flowers covered the short tunic that fell just to the top of her hips, where it met pale blue leggings that draped her in a loose fit to the ground.

"Who are y'?" Saraid asked in a whisper, more startled by the fact that the woman was a stranger than that she was dead.

"Well isn't that the question?" the woman said with a smile. "I've not the time to answer you well, so I'll give you my name and you can do with it what you will. I am Colleen Ballagh."

The old woman spoke in a strange manner, but Saraid had no trouble understanding her. It made her even more uneasy to be talking to a spirit in its own tongue. "Colleen of the Ballagh," Saraid said. "What is a Ballagh? A place?"

"A thing, I suppose," the woman answered. "It means marked. My people are children of one who is marked."

Saraid nodded, though she didn't understand. "Why have y' come?" she asked. "I don't know y' and I couldn't change what will happen even if I did."

Colleen of the Ballagh laughed merrily at that. "Oh you couldn't, could you? I think you don't know the half of what you can do, Saraid of the Favored Lands, but that is as it should be. No gift given before it's wanted is worth its weight."

How did this old woman know her name? Before Saraid could ask, Colleen Ballagh pushed up from the boulder where she sat, moving with an alacrity that defied her age. On her feet were strange unnaturally white shoes with laces just as bright and glowing designs on the sides. Saraid had never before seen the likes of this woman's garb.

Scowling at the spry woman, she said, "Are y' from the Otherworld, then?"

"Most certainly I am."

"So yer not here to show me yer death?" Saraid asked.

"Ach, what would be the point of that? I'm already packed in a black box, wearing a dress I hate, I might add. My son picked it, God bless him. He should have left that for his wife, who has some taste at least, but there you have it. Once you're dead, you're dead, and no one cares that you never in your life wore a dress so ugly. No, all I've to look forward to is waiting for my family to weep themselves sick over the loss of me."

Her grin was wicked. "Quite a loss it is, I might add. But it was time and it was the only way."

Saraid didn't know what to say to any of that. This was the most perplexing visit she'd ever had.

"The only way for what?" Saraid asked.

"For my grandson to come home," she said simply. As if that should explain everything.

Frowning, Saraid tried to understand what the strange woman meant. "Come home from where?"

"California."

At Saraid's blank look, Colleen snorted. "Never mind that. Your life is about to change, Saraid of the Favored Lands. But you'd be knowing that without my telling you."

"I don't know more than life is a constant change for me now," Saraid answered, bristling at the woman's tone.

"Because of Cathán?"

Reluctantly, Saraid nodded.

"Aye, he's a devil, that one. Even as a child, he was more trouble than good. But I had hoped for him." She shook her head and took a few steps toward the camp where Saraid's brothers slept. Saraid moved to stand protectively between her brothers and the woman.

"Oh, look at you, the little she-lion protecting her cubs," Colleen teased. "It's no harm I mean for them. They have their roles to play, just as you do."

"What roles?" Saraid demanded.

"Sure and won't I be telling you soon enough. Don't get your laces knotted over it. In a few hours, your brother will be giving you some hard news, child. You'll not like it. Not a bit, I'll wager. But you'll see you haven't a choice and you'll do the right thing."

"What news?" Saraid asked, frustrated by the way Colleen seemed to talk in a whirl of unanswered questions.

"That I cannot say. Rules, you know."

"Rules?"

Colleen tilted her head and looked at Saraid. "Have you never tried to change something you know is going to happen? I can see that you have. Then you know it's like putting a stone in the flow of a river. It only diverts it. Trying to change one event in the course of the inevitable will only bring it about in another manner. Sometimes worse."

Saraid nodded despite her intent to give none of her thoughts away to this peculiar woman.

"This is what I can tell you, and I know it will make no sense to you now. But it will eventually, and it will help you when you come to it."

"What would y' say to me?" Saraid asked when the old woman paused reflectively.

"Here it is, then." Colleen cleared her throat and then pinned Saraid with a steady, black look. "A man will come to you in the guise of another. 'Tis the Book he wants—"

"The Book of Fennore?" Saraid interrupted.

"Is there another Book you'd be getting messages about?" At Saraid's silence, Colleen sniffed and said, "I didn't think so. Now, let me finish. It is the Book he wants; 'tis you he must have. He alone can save your people—my people, for somewhere down the line I will be born of your blood. You must learn to see beyond your eyes, or you and those you love will be no more."

Saraid swallowed hard as she sifted through the cryptic words, waiting to be certain Colleen had finished.

"Who is this man who comes?" she asked, grasping the one piece that had substance.

"Ah, that I cannot tell you. But when he comes, I suspect you will know him."

"But when will he come?"

"Soon." She smiled and devilment danced in her dark eyes.

"Well that helps not at all," Saraid said crossly. "Y' could have avoided waking me for all of the light y' shed on the matter."

Colleen laughed out loud. "And aren't you the little spitfire to be talking to one of the Otherworld in such a way."

Saraid felt her cheeks heat with dismay. The woman was right. The Others did not take kindly to impertinence. Were there not tales amongst tales of the wayward hero who had taunted the Others only to find himself transformed to stone or toad or flightless bird?

"Ach," Colleen said. "Don't turn into a fecking paranoid on me now. I'm not here to give you feathers. You think I wouldn't tell you more if I could? It's a risk I take telling you anything at all, but a risk worth the taking. Just remember my words. I came from far to tell you them, whether you get their meaning or not."

"A man will come. He wants the Book but he must have me instead," Saraid repeated woodenly.

Colleen rolled her eyes skyward. "That's not what I said. I said he would come in the guise of another. That's important. You understand?"

Saraid nodded.

"You cannot give him the Book, Saraid."

"I do not have it to give."

Colleen's smile made her uneasy. "Did you not hear me before? You don't know what you have. Not yet."

She moved deeper into the woods, and Saraid trailed her like a duckling its mother. "Y' think I have the Book of Fennore? Are y' Cathán Half-Beard's spy, then? Because if y' are, y' can tell him as I have before and again. I've no Book. I've never had it."

"I'm no one's spy, least of all Cathán's. But you believe what you want to believe. Either way it will be true."

"Why must y' speak in circles? I don't know what to make of yer message."

Colleen sighed, and turning, she reached out a small, wrinkled hand to Saraid's cheek. There was no feeling in the caress, and yet strangely Saraid was comforted by it.

"And sure, wouldn't I love to guide you?" Colleen said in a gentle tone. "But this is your path, and all I can do is done already. You must win him to your cause, child. Do you hear me?"

Slowly, Saraid nodded.

"Whatever it takes. You must beguile him, Saraid. Entice him, entrap him if you can. Make him think of nothing but you."

"Bewitch him? Is that what yer saying to me?"

"Aye. Win him over, and he will be your greatest champion. Leave him on his own course, and he will darken the skies forever."

Saraid's mouth pursed as she considered this, picturing the skies going black for all of eternity. She wanted to scoff. She wanted to run. Instead she stood there, waiting for the old woman to tell her how she would convince this man who would come. How she, Saraid, could seduce him away from the Book of Fennore?

"Would it help if I told you he's the man you dream of?"

Astounded, Saraid asked, "How do y' know of my dreams?"

"Otherworld," Colleen reminded her with a wicked smile. "'Tis no matter. Just know it is true. Now, you'll not be happy with my parting words, but I give them with my heart and I swear them to be true. Have faith in yourself, Saraid. Nothing that comes to you will come by chance. Not ever. Each gift has a reason, even this one that you hate. Only in death will there be resurrection. Only in trust will there be truth."

Saraid stared at her, feeling the words fill her like an echo in a chamber. Only in death will there be resurrection. Is this why she saw the dead? So that she would know the resurrected? Or did this woman speak of the Christ God? Was her message one of religion and faith?

"You'll find your answers in time," Colleen said. "And now the day is about to break. Best get back to your brothers. They are men, so sure enough they'll be wanting some breakfast. Some things don't ever change." Her smile was wistful, her eyes sad now.

"Will I see y' again?" Saraid asked.

Colleen studied her for a moment and then said, "One day, you will return this . . . favor. You'll come to me as I do to you. And rest assured you will confound me in the same way and leave me full of questions and anger at my own confusion. But I will tell you what you will tell me. Without questions, there can be no answers."

Colleen's smile changed yet again, and now the wicked glee was back in her eyes. "'Tis the chicken and the egg," she said with a laugh.

"What chicken? What egg?" Saraid demanded.

"Did I tell you first, or did you tell me? I guess neither of us will ever know, will we now?"

"I could make a list of what I don't know after this night."

"No, it's best you not write it down. That's not gone well for us in the past."

And what did that mean? Before Saraid could even sigh in exasperation, the woman began to fade, and she knew there would be no chance to ask. It was their way, the dead. They came for their own reasons and cared little for the unrest they left behind. As Saraid stood in the chilled darkness, she watched until even the strange shoes had disappeared.

Wide awake and full of thought, she made her way back to the camp and her sleeping brothers. Colleen of the Ballagh had spoken in riddles, but she'd delivered two very clear messages. A man was coming and with him, change.

Chapter Four

THE sun had broken the horizon when Saraid added small
bits of wood to the fire, blowing softly with each addition,
urging the cooling coals to spark and flame. Colleen Ballagh's
appearance still felt like a dream, but she knew it was nothing
so simple. Prophesy was never clear. Lore was as riddled with
cryptic messages as Saraid's visitor had been.

She wore her homespun dress, the wool warm against the
chilled morning. Beneath it her shift kept the gown from
chaffing her skin. Its sleeves billowed out at the arms and
down to her wrists. She'd strung a thin twine through both
armholes and tied it at the back of her neck to pull the sleeves
up and keep the fabric from dragging through the food she
prepared or, worse, the licking flames of the fire. She was
silent as she worked, preparing their meal without thinking of
the task. Instead, she dwelled on the message Colleen had
delivered.

A man would come disguised as another. Who could he
be? Someone Colleen thought Saraid would know once she
saw him. But who would he pretend to be? Someone looking
for the Book, it would seem. But Colleen had said it was she,
Saraid, he must have. Why would he think Saraid a good sub-
stitute for the Book of Fennore? She, who knew nothing of it
but that Cathán Half-Beard had ever been convinced Saraid's
mother, Oma, had stolen it from him.

She coaxed a bright flame into life and then built it up to a good blaze. Liam, the youngest of her stepbrothers, had risen early and killed and cleaned two rabbits for their meal. It was more than they'd had the night before, when only old bread and cheese had sufficed. The rabbits were now spitted and ready to roast over the fire. Her belly growled with anticipation.

"Saraid?"

Tiarnan's voice startled her, and she spun to find her twin brother standing in the shadows. He wore a tunic that covered his broad chest and hung almost to his knees, leaving his arms bare and unfettered. Once it had been the color of saffron and fine. Now it was ragged and patched over and again, faded to an unpleasant brownish hue. His belt was leather and supple, finely tooled, and a sword hung from it—not jeweled or graven as a king's should be, but honed and polished with care. It was a good sword, Tiarnan liked to say, and he used it like an extension of his own arm.

A cloak was draped over one shoulder, leaving his right free from any restraint. It was fastened with a brooch made of three connected spirals, seeming to have no beginning and no ending. His trews tied just below the knee, and Saraid knew a dagger was strapped to his thigh, high where it couldn't be seen but could be pulled in an instant from the slit in the seam. Leather sandals covered his feet. He would long for his boots when the cold set in, but they were gone forever, burned or ransacked from their *tuath* by Cathán Half-Beard's barbarians.

He took another step forward, and now she could see his unsmiling face. His expression made her uneasy, but she didn't let it show.

"Is it my heart y' would be trying to stop with yer stealth?" Saraid teased, releasing a shaky laugh. Colleen's appearance in the chill of predawn had disturbed her more than she knew if even her brother's familiar voice made her jump.

"We must speak, sister," Tiarnan said, his expression darkening even more.

Though they were twins, they did not much resemble one another. Tiarnan was tall and broad, as big a man as any warrior she'd ever seen. Saraid was the opposite—small, even for a woman. Their mother had been Saracen, their father an Irish king born of Irish kings. Of the two, Saraid had the look of her mother, or so people said. There were tales told of the exotic and mystifying beauty Oma had been. Saraid did not know what truth was in the tales. Her mother had killed herself when Saraid and Tiarnan were just babies.

When they'd been children, she and Tiarnan had been so close they could talk to each other's minds. Words were rarely used between them, and no emotion or thought was experienced alone. But Saraid couldn't remember the last time they'd shared themselves in such a way. She didn't know if they still could even if they'd wanted to. It made her sad, that loss, though she was thankful that he couldn't read her confused and anxious thoughts now.

"Well," Saraid said when Tiarnan shuffled his feet but did not continue. "I'm listening. What is it we must discuss?"

She set the skewered rabbits on the spit over the fire and turned to give him her full attention. Tiarnan was not one to easily show emotion. That his face bore such troubles concerned her. Colleen's words danced in her memory. *Your brother will bring you hard news. . . .*

"I have met with Cathán Half-Beard," Tiarnan said.

She felt the blood drain from her face. He'd met with Cathán? "And why would y' do such a thing? Is it a death wish y' have? Because sure enough if that's the way of it, I can brain y' with my skillet and take care of it cleanly."

His smile was tight and without a trace of humor. He was a big man, solid and banded with muscles hard as rock. Yet he looked very much a boy just then, standing uncertainly in the bright morning light.

"Are y' serious, then?" she said.

"It must come to an end, Saraid. We've not the men or the means to fight any longer. Winter is but a cold breath away, and if we doon starve first, then we'll freeze to death waiting."

"And what is it makes y' think talking to that monster now will do what it's not done before?"

"It was he who sent a messenger. A hostage to keep until after the meeting."

"A slave no doubt," she said, wondering how a messenger had come without her knowing.

"His son," Tiarnan said.

"The Bloodletter?" she gasped.

"Aye."

The conversation got queerer and queerer, but at least one question had been answered. This was the reason why Tiarnan had chosen Cathán Half-Beard's forest to make their camp. The risk of it still stunned her, hostage or no.

"And where is his highness?"

"I've sent him back to his father."

"In pieces I hope."

Tiarnan didn't answer, and that did not bode well with Saraid. So was this the news that Colleen had foretold? Or could it be something worse?

"Tell me why Cathán Half-Beard wanted to speak with y'," she demanded. "And how y' could meet with the man who has spilled the blood of our people like it was dirty water?"

"He made an offer of truce. It was my responsibility to listen to him."

What to say to that? He'd struck her speechless.

"Truce?" she repeated, feeling numb and giggly at the same time. "Did his tongue turn to stone when he spoke the word?"

Again, her brother remained stoic, and a spark of alarm hissed to life inside her. Above them, silent clouds slipped over the sun and dimmed it out. She did not need the omen to tell her that whatever her brother had to say next, it would not be good.

"He, too, wants to end the bloodshed," Tiarnan said, watching her.

"And what of his spawn? What of the Bloodletter?"

Tiarnan swallowed and looked down without answering. The spark of fear sputtered and then burst into flame.

"It's an alliance he proposes," Tiarnan said softly.

"What kind of alliance? One where we willingly lie down and let him put an end to us? I'm sure that would make him happy, but I didn't think y' such a fool that y' would agree to it."

That got a reaction, as she'd known it would. Tiarnan was many things that he did not like to admit, but he could not tolerate being called the fool. He glared at her, straightening his shoulders and raising his chin. Aye, he could intimidate the most fearsome of warriors with just such a stance, and she might be a fool herself for provoking him, but she would take the fierce warrior over the shuffling uncertainty. This, at least she knew.

"I'll not have that tongue flaying my hide, woman," he said in a tight voice. "Sister or no."

She bit back her scathing answer. Tiarnan would turn his back and tell her no more if she continued to goad him. It was unusual enough that he'd come to her in the first place. She dropped her gaze and spoke in a conciliatory tone. "And what is it he proposes, Tiarnan?"

"A match."

She pulled her brows in a frown, not liking the sound of that at all.

"A joining of our two people to make us one," Tiarnan went on. "A match between y' and Ruairi."

"The Bloodletter?" she said, the air leaving her lungs in a rush. Her short bark of laughter was high with panic, but she could not seem to control it. "And what did y' tell him?"

Tiarnan stared steadily back, his silence an answer in itself.

"Tell me y' did not agree to such a thing? Y' would not. Tiarnan, tell me y' could not."

"T'will end the fighting, Saraid," he said, his voice deep and angry. "We've little choice but to take the chance before he wipes us out completely. We're not far from annihilation now—y' know it as well as I."

She did know it, but knowing did not help her swallow the bitterness. Pledge her troth to Ruairi the Bloodletter? Cathán's murdering son? The man she'd watched strike down women and innocent children? Slaughter old men and green boys who'd barely learned to grip a sword . . .

"It will bring us peace."

"Yer worse than a fool if y' believe it, Tiarnan," she told him.

"And what am I if I do not? We've less than twenty soldiers, no allies that are left breathing. Just women, children, and old men who will starve or freeze before the winter is done. What of that do y' not understand? He has hundreds standing with him. Strong and seasoned men. Neighbors and allies—Northmen. Men who fight for him—"

"Out of their fear," she insisted.

"Does it matter? A blade to the heart is the same no matter what hand wields it. We're living in caves, like animals. And still he hunts us. We either join him or spend our lives running until he catches us. Which would y' have?"

She curled her fingers into tight fists. He spoke the truth again, but that made it no easier to abide. Had he said she was to wed the Christian's devil himself, Saraid would have taken the news better.

"Why the Bloodletter?" she demanded.

Tiarnan frowned at her in confusion.

"Tell the barbarians I will wed none less than Cathán Half-Beard himself," she said, turning her back and shielding her shaking hands in the folds of her skirts. "If I've to sleep with the enemy, it will be the chieftain and no less."

"Cathán? He's a wife already. Would y' be his second? Or is it his whore y' are thinking of becoming?"

What she was thinking of becoming was his widow, but wisely did not say so aloud. She had no power over who lived and died, of course. Still, her gift—her curse—to see a person's death before it came, was not something to braggart. Her efforts as a child to stop the inevitable had made people suspicious that she not only saw death's secrets, but that somehow she called them. Now she was careful never to mention death in any manner. Even the twin sister of a tribal king could be killed if her people suspected she not only heard death's secrets but controlled them.

People were like cattle and only knew the earth beneath their feet, the sky above their heads, and the wind at their backs. They could not understand the complexities of death, but they could fear it. As they feared Saraid, as they'd feared her mother. It was not by chance or choice she'd reached five and twenty years without a mate.

"Which is it, Saraid?" Tiarnan demanded, glaring down at her from all of his powerful height, but she did not flinch away. "A second wife or a whore?"

"Cathán's first wife is weak," she spat, fear and anger compelling her to break her own rule. "She will be dead with her unborn by full moon."

Tiarnan hissed in a breath and made the sign to ward off evil.

"They offer y' Ruairi to husband me," Saraid went on coldly. "Why do y' think, Tiarnan?"

Tiarnan glowered but could not answer her. He had not thought. He never thought. He led the men of this tribe by his passion, not his logic. The people loved him despite this fatal flaw, or perhaps because of it.

"I will tell y', brother. They give him because he is so vile even the people of the Dark Forest don't want him. Ruairi the Bloodletter. Why else has he been banished for all these years?"

"Not banished. He was fostered with relatives to the north. Had we more to our people, we would do the same."

Stupid fool. Saraid thought it, but did not say it. Tiarnan stood before her, convinced that he made the right decision. And perhaps he did, for it was nothing less than truth he spoke. They were near annihilation, those who had once been led by their father, Bain the Good, the Fair. Bain of the Favored Lands. Too few were left to carry the sword. If there was even a chance that Cathán offered truce, it was a chance that should be taken. In her heart, she knew it would pain Tiarnan to give her to Ruairi the Bloodletter, but if it saved what was left of them, he would do it. And he should.

But it was not the destiny she should have. It could not be. And what would happen if the man Colleen said would come, came too late and found her bound to the Bloodletter? What then?

"And why does he not offer a match between y' and Mauri?" she asked suddenly.

Tiarnan looked away, but not before his eyes betrayed him. She saw it all. Tiarnan had asked for Mauri and been denied. Cathán would not give his precious daughter to the likes of Tiarnan, but the Bloodletter he would willingly sacrifice. She turned away with a deep sigh.

"What does the Bloodletter think of this *match*?" she asked, giving her brother a cold glance over her shoulder. A dark flush colored Tiarnan's cheeks, and Saraid felt another wave of dread wash over her.

"He says he desires it." He lowered his eyes from the shock and disgust that no doubt showed on her face. "He says he desires y'."

"Me?" she repeated. "Y' know the truth of it, Tiarnan. It is not for me he lusts."

"Y' underestimate yer own beauty, sister."

She did not bother with that argument. Her brother wanted to believe Ruairi desired her, because that would be easier than the truth.

"And tell me, brother, once I'm wed are y' thinking they'll be having us all over for supper? We'll be a happy family sharing the lamb stew and bread even though we've spilled blood enough to fill the valley betwixt us?"

"I warn y', Saraid. Quiet that tongue."

She could not. "Will y' pledge yerself to a man with no honor, Tiarnan? For y' know he will demand it."

"I will do what I must to survive, the same as y'."

"Oh aye, easy words. 'Tis not y' who will lie down to be ravaged."

"And 'tis not y' who carries the yoke of our people. It is me."

"Yet I feel it all the same and will pay for it with my body and my soul. Take my tongue. It will not stop the lashing."

"He has given his word that I will still be tribal king. We can return to our homes, rebuild."

But she would not be going with them.

"I wish y' well then, brother. Y' take his word and use it to warm yer feet at night while yer sister suffers for all eternity."

He flinched, his face paling. "Have a care," he warned. "You do not see everything."

Saraid smiled coldly. "I see y'," she said.

Tiarnan stepped back. He could not help himself. She knew it and felt instantly ashamed. He did not want this for her, but his choices were as limited as her own. There were no other alternatives if any of their people were to survive. If she refused, he would force her. And if she made him do that, she would lose her only blood.

She touched his arm. "'Tis sorry, I am. I swear, I've never seen yer death, brother. I pray that I never will."

His eyes looked tortured as he nodded, staring into her face with such regret that it wounded her. He would carry the guilt for what he did until he died, and so it would be both his salvation and destruction, because if there was peace to be had, he might live for a very long time.

Saraid drew in a deep breath. "When?" she asked.

His gaze snapped up in surprise as if he'd already resigned himself to her rebellion. "Three days' time."

So soon. Colleen's words echoed in the quiet that followed. *Hard news*, she'd said. *Impossible, horrendous, unbearable.* Any of those would have described it better. But the old woman was right about one thing. Saraid now had a choice that was no choice at all.

Three days.

Sickened by the thought of it, she faced her brother and squared her shoulders. "Then we must prepare."

Chapter Five

R ORY didn't expect a welcome home when his plane finally landed.

When he'd left the tiny town of Ballyfionúir, Ireland, it was in a storm of controversy, chaos, and tragedy—the kind only a troubled twelve-year-old boy with too much time and too much rage can create. More than two decades had passed since then, but time didn't heal all pain. Not in the real world. And this was Ireland, where memories stretched beyond the days of yore. It didn't matter that his grandmother had said it was time to come home. He wasn't ready. He might not ever be ready.

Stepping into the cold, impersonal terminal at Dublin International Airport, following the crowd of tourists to customs, Rory felt like the boy he'd been when he was sent away to live with his Aunt Edel in America. He'd been scared, confused, alone, and pissed off at the world for all of it. He wouldn't be human if he didn't feel some of that now. The knot of it sat hard in his gut as the sounds and smells of the place brought back the memories like an old song on the radio.

He still couldn't believe he was here.

He kept his eyes forward as he walked, trying not to look around, not to seem hopeful that perhaps someone he knew awaited him in the sea of strangers. What would he do if a familiar face appeared? What would he say if his mother suddenly stepped forward with open arms and a welcoming smile?

He didn't know. His family had lived here since the beginning of time, like something out of a storybook filled with happily ever afters. They were loving, nurturing, caring. It had broken their hearts when he'd gotten himself into so much trouble that the only way out was to send him to his Aunt Edel. And they'd been devastated when his summer in California—a hiatus to get him away from a volatile situation and allow him some perspective—had grown from weeks to months to years during which they couldn't coax him back home.

But here he was now, and he hadn't even called first, even when he'd heard his mother's message on his answering machine, choked with emotion over Nana's death. He'd told no one of his plans to return. Another gray area he didn't care to illuminate. Was he afraid they'd no longer welcome him? Afraid they would? Who knew?

At baggage claim, Rory waited impatiently for his one battered duffle, scanning the crowd. His gaze skipped over unfamiliar faces and then snapped back to a woman hovering against the far wall. Irish from the set of her shoulders to the tilt of her chin, she nonetheless had a foreign look with her long dark hair and golden brown skin. Eyes so deep they sparkled like sable-hued gems.

It was the woman from his dreams, wearing the white shift that barely covered the swell of full breasts, the shadow of cleavage. She stared back at him with that familiar defiance, inviting and daring in the same ragged breath. He felt all the blood drain from his face. She was here and he was awake.

He rubbed his eyes, feeling the grit of exhaustion behind them. When he looked again, she was gone. But her image had seared into his jet-lagged brain like sunspots on a bright afternoon.

Christ, he was tired enough to imagine an elephant in Dublin Airport. Shaking his head, Rory hefted his bag off the carousel and strode to the door. Before stepping through, he glanced back and there she was again, standing not ten feet away, staring at him with an intensity that made him stop in midstride. A wiry man with a bald head and bad odor ran into him from behind, and Rory stumbled.

"Watch yer feckin' self," the smelly man said.

"Sorry," Rory mumbled, stepping aside.

He looked back, expecting her to have vanished once more, become the dream he knew her to be.

But she didn't waver.

Something hot and deep began to burn inside him. He took a step toward her, drawn like a lion to the scent of blood. Still she waited, watching him until he stopped less than an arm's length away. All around them, travelers swarmed, checking watches, hoisting bags, smiling their greetings. They jostled into Rory and bumped into the woman on the way to the door, but no one paused. No one seemed to notice the two of them standing like stones in a rapid river.

"Who are you?" Rory asked, feeling foolish and desperate in the same moment. *What are you*? he meant.

Her eyes rounded with surprise. "'Y' do not recognize me, Ruairi?"

The husky lilt roused every seductive moment of the dreams, though she never spoke except when she beckoned him to hurry.

"From my dreams," he answered. "Only from my dreams."

"Aye, the dreams." She nodded as if that held more meaning than it should. The harsh lights of the airport revealed the coarse weave of her shift, the grayed cast to the white. But it didn't detract from her beauty, from her allure.

She cast him a sidelong look filled with both question and promise, and he found himself reaching for her hand, taking it in his own. But there was no heat with the contact, no sensation of touching. The realization shouldn't have surprised him, but it caught him low and hard.

Christ. She was dead. Just like Colleen.

She shook her head, as if she'd heard. "Not yet, but soon."

Before he could ask how soon, the gray and white of the terminal began to flicker like the tail end of a reel of film flapping against the projector's bulb. Then it blurred, spreading out until the room, the counters, the windows looking onto the stark world, the friendly attendants and severe security guards, the other people—everything became a smear in the background.

But not the woman. She remained vivid and stunning,

emerging from the blur like a starburst of color. That hair, sunset-flecked midnight, and those eyes, dark and searching. They pulled him closer, towed him under until there was only the two of them, standing in a cloud of obscurity.

She lifted his hand and placed it over her heart. He stared at his fingers, spread across her flesh, his palm resting on the curve of her breast. Her skin was burnished, a hot and exotic silk against the swirling paleness surrounding them. And he couldn't feel any of it.

She smiled sadly and touched his face with her other hand. "Y' must hurry."

He bent his head, leaning closer to hear her words. Her scent was light and fresh, and he wanted to gather up the silken length of her hair and bury his face in it. Breathe her in and hold her tight inside. He cupped her face, willing himself to feel her. Needing to know she was more than his imagination.

"I'm to be wed in the morning," she said, her voice hitched with pain.

The idea of her married, of her with another man, caught him hard and low. Without waiting for her to say more, he pressed his lips to her mouth, expecting only air but hoping, praying for the sweet warmth of her lips. When it came, it shocked him. He jerked his head back an inch, stared into the velvet brown of her eyes. Questions formed in his head, clamored to escape, but he only cared about the feel of her in his arms, the taste of her lips on his.

"Hurry, Ruairi," she whispered against his mouth.

And then she was gone.

Chapter Six

R ORY stepped from the airport terminal and into the glow-ering gloom of exhaust fumes and thunderclouds bearing down on rush-hour traffic. As he moved toward the line of cabs, he heard his name and for a brief instant thought his dream-woman might be calling him; then he recognized the voice, but not from his dreams.

He hesitated, briefly toying with the idea of pretending he hadn't heard. Of jumping in the first cab and racing away— answering his own question of what he would do if someone he knew did appear. *Run*. He gritted his teeth against that disturbing insight.

"Rory," the voice called again, and he forced himself to turn, realizing that it was his sister's face he'd been searching for all along. He'd known—somewhere deep down, buried beneath denial—he'd known she'd be here. Returning home had opened the door to that other world, the one steeped in the mystery that was Ireland.

Bracing himself, he turned.

Danni MacGrath—*Ballagh now*, he reminded himself— stood next to a tan Volvo, her hair caught back in a ponytail, her gray eyes clear and insistent. No smile, he noted, but that wasn't a surprise.

"What are you doing here?" he demanded, not taking the step that would bring him closer.

"I could ask you the same," Danni said, still unsmiling. "But we both know you'll lie, so where's the point in it?"

She narrowed her eyes and cocked her head in a gesture that reminded Rory of their mother. Slowly her gaze took in the whole of him, from sun-bleached hair to faded, worn jeans. He didn't know what she thought of him. He didn't want to care. They were twins, he and Danni, and at one time in their lives they'd been so close they could read each other's thoughts. Rory had destroyed that tie over the years—at first out of anger and hurt. Then, later, out of necessity. He couldn't keep the barriers between himself and Fennore whole when his sister was around. He couldn't protect that core, that one true kernel of who he was, when she could look right into his soul. It was too painful playing nice with Danni, and so he played not at all.

But she'd still known he was coming.

She hit a button on her key fob and the boot popped open. Without a word, she yanked his bag from his hand, shoved it into the immaculate space, and slammed the door. "Get in," she ordered.

Irritated, he did as he was told and slid into the passenger seat, feeling strange and displaced on the wrong side of the vehicle. The wrong side of the world.

Two car seats were strapped in the back with two kids sleeping in them. One was his niece, Clodaugh—she'd be two or three years old now. The other was his nephew, Raegan, who'd been born just last February. He'd never met either one of them before and felt a wash of guilt as he stared at their sweet faces. On the seat between them a weird and ugly little dog sat straight and vigilant, watching Rory with cold eyes and a curled lip. It gave him an impressive growl.

"Easy, Bean," Danni said, sliding behind the wheel. "It's just Rory."

"Bean?"

Danni gave the mutt an indulgent glance. "Long story. She doesn't warm to strangers right away."

In response, the dog *gurred* at him again. Cautiously, Rory turned his back on the little beast.

"Does anyone else know I'm here?" he asked when Danni started the engine.

She shrugged. "Do you mean to ask if Mum is still by the telephone praying for you to call? No. I thought it best they prepare." She shot him a dark sideways look that was as full of reproach as it was apology. It caught Rory like a punch. He'd wounded his family in ways he couldn't even begin to imagine, that look said. He stared back, unblinking. Stoic. Finally she glanced away and pulled into traffic. When she spoke again after a few minutes, her tone was conciliatory.

"California has been treating you well, then," she said, and he wanted to smile at the familiar cadence of her speech, the dialect of the Isle of Fennore unique among Ireland. "Isn't it a movie star you look like? I don't think I've ever seen teeth so white."

She was one to talk. She'd gone to Columbia University in New York and picked up enough of the American ways to sport her own brilliant smile. The rest of her beauty was inborn. Their mother could have rivaled any movie star of her time.

Danni had made contact with him several times in the first year she'd been at school, but every meeting only seemed to magnify what he already knew. Rory didn't belong in her world anymore, and it hurt them both to face that monumental fact. In the later years, Rory had dodged her attempts to see him like an artist. By then it was shame, not remorse, keeping him away. Those were dark years, when he'd gone a little crazy, and even his Aunt Edel had wiped her hands of him.

"Uncle Frank had a go at me," Rory said now, answering her raised brows but ignoring the bitter question in her tone. "Thought to polish me up and make me respectable."

She gave a small snort of disbelief and mumbled something he didn't catch. When he'd been sent to live with Uncle Frank and Aunt Edel, the hope had been that they would straighten him out. What his aunt and uncle had done to deserve such a punishment, he'd never known.

He'd come to them with belligerence and rebellion. Aunt Edel had matched it with a darkness of her own that had cowed him when nothing else would. But Uncle Frank was an orthodontist from a long line of dentists and was considered a rebel by his own father for daring to branch out of the traditional field. Nothing in Uncle Frank's sheltered life had prepared him for Rory, and he'd been helpless in the face of his nephew's rage and resentment—an inept lion tamer with a broken chair and frayed whip he'd never had the heart to use. He'd long given up on Rory's black soul, but Uncle Frank had managed to triumph over his nephew's teeth. Rory's smile was perfect.

His sister stopped at a traffic light and looked at him. He could feel her gaze lingering on his nose. It hadn't been set straight the first time it was broken and was hopelessly crooked by the third. She seemed to be memorizing his face, reliving all the scrapes she knew about and seeking explanations for the ones she didn't.

A ragged scar nicked in over his brow from a knife fight in Compton that he was lucky to have survived, but he doubted she'd want to hear that tale. Or how he got the scar that caught his jaw low and near his ear. Of the two, the latter looked the most fearsome, but it had come from a game he'd played when he was seventeen and still trying to prove that he was the baddest badass of them all. That time he hadn't been in danger from anything but himself. Her gaze moved to his shoulders and chest as if she could see the scars there, too. Who knew, maybe she could.

"Nana said you still blame yourself for Trevor. Is it true?"

The question caught Rory off guard, and he looked away, not wanting Danni to see his expression. His stepbrother, Trevor, had been dead for seventeen years, but the sound of his name still made Rory want to wince. Yes, he blamed himself for Trevor's death. Everyone did. Why else had they sent Rory away?

"Nana was crazy."

"To her last breath," Danni agreed. "But that didn't make her any less right. His dying wasn't your fault, Rory."

"If you say so."

The truth was, Rory hadn't been shipped off to California without cause. For years he'd been a walking time bomb, and everyone around him had been listening to the steady, everlouder ticking coming from inside him. Finally they'd decided it would be best to be finished with Rory MacGrath before he decided to be finished with all of them.

"It's the truth," Danni insisted. "No one ever blamed you."

"Look, do me a favor. Let's just skip over the bullshit, okay?"

"It was a terrible accident, his fall. No one denies it. But not your fault."

He said nothing. These were platitudes he'd heard before. Trevor had been following Rory as he'd played amongst the castle ruins. It was a dangerous place, but Rory had grown up navigating the treacherous wall on the cliffs. He'd been showing off, making leaps he shouldn't have, taunting Trevor to keep up. . . .

"And you know," Danni went on, "Nana always said Trevor wasn't meant for this world and that we were lucky to have him the extra years we did."

And what was that supposed to mean? He'd had just about all he could take of Nana and her cryptic sayings. "Well thanks for clearing that up, Danni. It all makes sense now."

With a shake of his head, Rory turned back to the window. But he could picture Nana sitting at her kitchen table sipping cold tea from her favorite mug, the words *Que sera, sera* written on one side and the image of a saggy old lady about to be flattened by a speeding bus on the other.

Until his grandmother had shown up in his car, he hadn't spoken to her since he was twelve, when he left Ballyfionúir. But that didn't mean *she* hadn't managed to communicate with *him*. Notes would come, typically enigmatic messages that told him she knew what he was doing, though there was no way she could. For a while, he'd dropped off the radar so completely even Edel didn't know where to find him. He'd spent some time behind bars, but Nana had still tracked him down. She'd sent a packet of his favorite biscuits, which had arrived in crumbs with a note that simply said: *You are more than this*.

Danni's voice jerked him from the memory of clanging bars to the quiet hum of tires on pavement.

"How long will you stay, Rory?"

He didn't answer at first, thinking of Martina's expression when he'd left the Low Down last night, handing her the keys to both the Camaro and his apartment on his way out. He'd told her if he wasn't back in a month, sell everything—pocket the cash but keep the car. Nana's warning about Martina's Toyota breaking down and it ending badly had rung in his ears.

"Are you in trouble, Irish?" Martina asked, staring at the keys like they were poisoned.

He'd laughed. "Yeah. A helluva lot of trouble. Take care of my car. I'd hate to think of it stripped."

He said to Danni, "I haven't decided how long I'm staying. Depends on how things go."

"And how might they go?"

"Bad."

She nodded. "That's what I thought."

Disturbed by his own thoughts, by his own reluctant belief that Danni could see into the chaos of his psyche, he closed his eyes and tried to focus on the here and now. A crisp wind blew through the open windows, mixing with the purr of the Volvo's engine and the stilted silence in the car. Gradually his thoughts loosened and drifted.

He'd forgotten how the air felt here, how it smelled. How it tasted. The tight fist of nostalgia gripping his chest surprised him. He had no fond memories of home. After the night when his father had disappeared, life became a living hell for Rory. When he recalled the Isle of Fennore where he'd been born and raised, he did so reluctantly.

Yet here he was, drinking it in like a man dying of thirst.

Danni crossed over the River Liffey then out of the city limits and through pastures of emerald and soft rolling hills. In the distance he saw the Rock of Cashel standing stark against the green. The Volvo ate up the miles, bringing them through the wide-open thoroughbred grazing of Kildare. A few tiny towns still cropped up here and there, sporting bright doors and *Open* signs. This was a land of lore and it pulsed and breathed like a being of flesh and bone.

Danni remained silent the rest of the way and the kids in the backseat slept peacefully as they caught the ferry from the mainland at Youghal. While Danni waited in the car, Rory got out and moved to the railing, silently watching the sea of his childhood as it frothed and foamed beneath the boat. The shadow of a lone gull swayed across the undulating waves before swooping down for a fish.

Breathing in the scent of salt and brine, oil and burning fuel from the ferry's motor, Rory stared into the sea and pictured *her*. He still didn't know her name, but her scent, the velvet darkness of her eyes, the satin fall of her hair . . . it was all imprinted in his memory.

Who was she? And had Nana been telling the truth. Would he find her?

Chapter Seven

VERY little was different in Ballyfionúir since Rory had left. He wasn't surprised by it. He'd grown up thinking nothing ever changed here and resenting the fact. Now he was curiously grateful that it had not been transformed into something he no longer recognized. There was a comfort in that, and it caught him off guard.

"It's not all the same," Danni said, still reading his mind with annoying ease. "Lisa Ballagh married a Sicilian man and they've opened an Italian restaurant where Pete's Fish and Chips used to be."

"What happened to Pete's?" Rory asked, in spite of himself. He remembered the hot grease and crunch, the steaming white fish and chips so crisp and sizzling they seared his mouth.

"Pete went to Chicago to live with his daughter. I hear he opened up a business there."

Rory kept his face impassive, not letting her see how strangely betrayed he felt by this news. It wasn't right that a staple of Ballyfionúir like Pete's could suddenly pull up and move away—to Chicago no less.

The road took a wide turn and he stared out his window as the cliffs and the pounding sea danced just beyond. Farther south was the bay where his stepfather and the other fisherman anchored their boats. And up the hill from that was the street where his grandmother had lived. Something heavy pushed at his chest.

"Do you want to go by her house?" Danni asked.

Rory started to shake his head and then he stopped. "Maybe just for a minute."

She pulled up to the small cottage, and they both got out, but neither made a move for the front door. It would be unlocked, he knew. That much couldn't have changed. But he didn't have the heart to cross that threshold. As bizarre as the visit had been, it had awakened other memories inside Rory. His grandmother—step-grandmother, technically—had been the only person who'd ever known who the hell he really was. Himself included. And he'd loved her unconditionally.

The children continued to nap in their car seats, heads padded by soft doughnut-shaped wedges, but the weird dog bounded out and raced to Nana's porch, where it curled up on the *Welcome* mat with sad eyes and a sorrowful groan.

"Bean loved Nana at first sight," Danni mused, watching the dog. "It was the strangest thing the way they took to one another."

The news didn't surprise Rory in the least. She'd been as prickly as the little dog.

He shoved his hands into his pockets, afraid they might shake as they had last night. "She came to see me," he said softly.

Danni gave him a sharp look. "When?"

"Night before last." A part of him couldn't believe he was saying it out loud. A part of him wanted to laugh even as he remembered how it felt when he'd realized who was sitting in his car. "When I got off work, she was waiting for me."

Danni made a sharp sound of amusement. "Bet that scared you out of your knickers."

He forced a stiff smile.

"And what did she say?" Danni went on as if they were discussing the price of milk and eggs. "I've died, so come home?"

"Something like that."

"She wanted something, didn't she? She called you home to find the Book. Is that the way of it?"

He shouldn't have been surprised she'd know that detail, too, but he was. Reluctantly, he nodded.

"I can see there's no point in telling you not to do it, but it's dangerous seeking something that shouldn't be found. What did Aunt Edel say when you told her?"

"I didn't tell her. Why would I?"

Danni looked at him in shock. "You mean you don't know?"

"Know what?"

"Edel has used the Book, Rory. Did you never notice her eyes? How queer they are?"

Rory stared at his sister, open-mouthed. Edel had used the Book? Edel, who he'd lived with until he was old enough to move out on his own?

Suddenly it made so much sense. Suddenly he understood why his parents had sent him to his crazy aunt with her flat, dark eyes. Why she alone had been able to put fear into Rory's heart. They were kindred in more ways than blood.

"Why didn't anyone ever tell me?" he asked, angry.

She shook her head, clearly as surprised as he by this giant hole in his education.

"Who told *you*?" he demanded.

"I don't know. I've just always known."

If he hadn't hidden himself so far from home, perhaps he would have known, too.

"Rory," Danni said, and something in her voice had changed. He looked at her, found himself staring into those luminous eyes of hers—gray and stormy, like the Irish Sea itself. For one weak moment he'd wanted nothing more than to embrace his sister and tell her how much he'd missed her. How much she meant to him. How sorry he was for hurting her along the way to his liberation. But he didn't move and he didn't speak.

"I have something for you," she said. "In case I don't get the chance to talk to you alone later."

She pulled a small green box from her pocket. He stared at it curiously but made no move to take it.

"Nana wanted you to have this, and she knew Mum would keep it from you if she could, so she made me promise that I would give it to you."

She thrust the box out to him with a reluctance he couldn't miss. And suddenly he knew what was inside before he even opened the lid, knew what it meant that Nana had gone to so much trouble to make certain he received it. Knew this was what she'd told him he would need. Slowly he took it from his sister, his big hands dwarfing the tiny box. He hesitated, and then finally he lifted the lid.

Inside, nestled on a piece of cotton, was the pendant. The size of an old coin, the pendant glittered like something alive. A starburst of jewels fanned out from an emerald nucleus, sparkling diamonds, opals and rubies, woven silver and gold twined seamlessly into concentric spirals that had no beginning, no end.

"I know it's connected to the Book of Fennore, Rory, but I don't know how or why." She bit her lip and then blurted, "I'm afraid it's a key—a way to find it, use it. If it is, you mustn't do it. I beg you."

"Use it?" he repeated with a short bark of laughter. "How would I? Christ, I don't even know what *it* is."

"Not yet, but you will."

This simple statement hung between them. For a moment, Rory couldn't even breathe. He stared at her, unable to pluck even one question from the traffic jam of disbelief and confusion clogging his thoughts.

"That's bullshit, Danni."

But beneath his sarcasm, doubt lifted like smoke from a snuffed candle. He thought of the markings on his chest, just over his heart. A symbol he'd not just inked into his skin, but burned. Branded, because a tattoo wasn't permanent enough. He'd been fifteen, and he'd done it with a Bic lighter and the end of a metal hanger. He hadn't been drunk or high or even delusional. He'd been compelled, driven to desperation. His friends thought him a pain freak looking to get off on the self-mutilation. They'd only been half wrong.

He didn't know what the Book of Fennore was, but it had marked him in ways he still didn't understand. Now he realized that he'd been trying to make it a part of himself, wear it on the outside as he bore it on the inside.

Similar spirals marked the cover and spine of the Book of Fennore. And the lock that held the Book closed . . . the pendant was an exact duplicate. It wasn't a key in the traditional sense, but Rory was certain it was instrumental in unlocking the secrets hidden within the ancient Book. They were parts of a whole—the Book, the lock, and the pendant—a trinity in the same way a husband, wife, and ring were intrinsic parts of a marriage. But there was no power emanating from the necklace as there'd been from the Book, only a strange seductive light.

"If the Book is calling to you, there's a reason," Danni said softly. "And it's not your own, make no mistake about it."

He shook his head and took a step away. "Do you know why I left Ballyfionúir?" he asked her.

"Trevor," Danni said softly, without hesitation.

Just hearing his stepbrother's name made Rory's gut tighten. She was right. Trevor was at the heart of his leaving, but he wasn't the cause.

"I hated it here," he said. "I hated living in a world where nothing was ever what it seemed. I hated the superstition and the . . . the . . ."

"Magic?"

Angry, he gave a terse nod. "Dead people shouldn't show up in your car. Your sister shouldn't be able to see what's going to happen in the future."

Danni's eyes darkened with hurt, and he felt bad, but it was the truth and it needed to be said.

"Before she died," Danni said, her voice low, "Nana told me the past is only a version of what might have happened. She said life is like the spiral of that pendant. No beginning, no middle, no end."

"She liked to say things like that."

"'Tis a certainty. I know it. And yet that doesn't make what she said any less true, now does it? I think it's what she meant about Trevor. She said to me once that he'd died when he was only four or five."

Rory's gaze snapped up from the box. "He was fifteen when he died."

"But that's what she meant, when she said we were lucky to have him those extra years. That he wasn't intended for this world. Maybe she knew of another past where he didn't live so long. I don't understand it any more than you do, but somewhere in there is a kind of sense. I think the point is, what has happened in the past is not set in stone. It can be changed by the Book of Fennore. But you've no way of knowing what the change will bring. It may only postpone the inevitable. Do you see what I'm saying?"

He didn't answer, but inside him something dark and insidious slithered through his thoughts. A sibilant whisper hissed from the deep caverns of his mind, urging him to come closer, look deeper.

Was Trevor what Nana had been talking about when she said he'd changed destiny? Possibly, but he wasn't sure.

"The Book of Fennore, it's not to be trusted, Rory. You may think you want to find it to destroy it, but the truth is, if you're thinking of the Book, it's because the Book is thinking of you. Don't ever forget that."

"I remember . . ." He started and then paused, not sure if he should, if he could, share this piece of memory. "I remember touching it that night."

She gave a jerky nod, letting him know she remembered, too.

"I was scared. Ready to piss my pants I was so scared. But . . . but as soon as I touched it, all that went away. I felt, I don't know, at peace. I could see life ahead of me, and it looked like something out of a movie, you know? Grassy fields swaying in the breeze, laughter. Sunshine. It all came at me in this rush. And I wanted it."

He looked at his sister and shook his head, feeling foolish but unable to stop the words. "We'd been living on the wire for so long, what with Mom and Dad dancing around each other like boxers. We knew something was coming and it was going to be bad. And so that peace I felt—it was like a warm sun on my frozen face. It felt like heaven, and I never wanted to leave. I don't know what the me who was holding that Book was doing, but up here—" He tapped his head. "Up here, I was happy. I had no worries, no troubled past, no dismal future. I had everything I wanted."

"It was messing with you, Rory."

"I hear you, Danni. But it doesn't change a damn thing. This Book has fucked with my life long enough. First it was Dad, then . . ." He stopped before he finished the sentence. Then it was himself, feeling like he didn't belong. Filled with a fear he hated but could never quite escape. "Dad took it with him, wherever he went. Maybe if I find the Book, I'll find Dad, too." He gave his sister a quick glance, not confessing the other reason why he was determined to locate the Book. Not mentioning the dream-woman and Colleen's assurance that the Book would lead him to her. The need to find her had been building until now; he felt it like a weight on his shoulders. He didn't just *want* to know if she was real, he *needed* to know. Thoughts of her had begun to consume him.

"You haven't seen the Book lying around anywhere, have you?" he said in a poor attempt at humor that neither one of them found funny.

Danni looked at him for a long, drawn moment. Then she lowered her eyes and shook her head. "Finding it won't be the problem, Rory. It's looking for you, too."

Chapter Eight

T HE two kids awoke as the Volvo rounded the last corner. His niece did it quietly with a yawn and a stretch and a shy "Hullo." She was cute, with eyes like Danni's and rosy cheeks. His nephew chose to wake with an earsplitting howl and instantaneous tears.

"What's up with that?" Rory asked, looking back at the sobbing kid. The toddler's plump face was an alarming shade of red, his uvula waggling with distress.

"I think Raegan has nightmares," Danni said, reaching back to touch a flailing foot. "Dig around in my bag there and hand him that bottle, would you?"

Rory did as she asked, and Raegan took it with obvious suspicion, but then he jammed the nipple in his mouth and began to suck furiously. The dog gave Rory a warning growl as he pulled his hand back.

"There are crackers in the other pocket for Clodaugh," Danni said.

"Your dog's going to go piranha on me if I reach back one more time."

"Don't tell me you're scared of a harmless little thing like Bean?"

Okay, he wouldn't tell her. Nervously, Rory rummaged for the crackers and then reached over the snarling dog's head to hand them to his niece. She dimpled with delight and scolded the dog. "No no!"

Grinning, Rory sat back in his seat just in time for his first glimpse of home. Shocked, he stared for a long, silent moment.

It came in sight all at once, like a masterpiece painting suddenly unveiled. There was the sea, harsh and unrelenting in the background, the violent green of never-ending fields and hillside. Trees, seeped and soaked with the oils of the earth, trunks brown, black, and yellow, leaves spanning the spectrum from emerald to army. Yews and alders, oak and pine. The colors and scents assaulted him, welcomed him.

At the far edge of a cliff that scarred the horizon, a castle now stood where once only ruins had lain in decay. The collapsed spires and tumbled bastions had been the playground of his youth. Before he'd turned his attention to the demons inside him, he'd slain many a dragon in the ruins of the stone keep.

Danni had mentioned that she and her husband, Sean, had renovated the castle on the cliffs of Ballyfionúir, but she hadn't prepared him for this. Where there'd been only crumbling stones to hint at a fortress that was surely grand in its day, now a towering structure stood whole and breathtaking, as austere and formidable as his imagination had always pictured it. Restored in a way Rory never would be, never could be.

This was no Cinderella's castle; this was a stronghold, built to defend people against their enemies. Built to protect all the secrets behind its walls.

Danni steered the car over the cobblestoned drive and parked. Rory took a deep breath before he opened his door and stepped out. Once there'd been a house perched in the shadows of the ruins like a boil on the face of perfection. It had always looked like the afterthought it was, built where it didn't belong, destroying the mysticism that lurked in the air here. Now the house was gone, bulldozed and cleared away. Not even a foundation lingered to hint that it had ever stood in that awkward place. He'd lived in that house when he was a boy. His family had moved somewhere new, apparently. He hadn't even known.

Before he could assimilate this information, a strangely small door at the side of the castle opened and a man stepped out. Rory swallowed hard as he recognized his stepfather, Niall Ballagh.

"And didn't our Danni tell us you were coming?" he boomed, striding up to Rory and pulling him into a smothering bear hug. Niall smelled of ocean and the salty tang of fish and fresh air. During the years Rory'd been gone, Niall's dark hair had silvered and the squint lines at his eyes had deepened to grooves in a face turned copper by years on the deck of a fishing boat. But the bright eyes hadn't changed nor had the welcoming smile. It brought an unexpected lump of emotion to Rory's throat. Somewhere in his plans, he'd thought to remain aloof during this visit. He realized now that—as usual—he'd been a fool.

"Let me see you, then," Niall said, standing back to eye Rory.

A gentle giant, that was Rory's stepfather, and the sound of his voice, deep and cajoling, brought Rory back to his heritage in mere seconds. When Rory's real father had disappeared and Niall stepped in to care for his mother and her two children, Rory had been filled with resentment. Who was Niall to think he could take Cathán MacGrath's place?

Rory hadn't wanted him to even try and he was never shy about making it known. He'd treated Niall like a disease to be overcome only through great suffering. The shame of it rose up in Rory now, but he fought it back. He was not here to revisit his childhood or analyze his failures as a man. He was here to bury his grandmother and, for better or worse, find the Book of Fennore.

"Jaysus, I knew you'd be a man, but didn't a part of me expect to see the boy in you?" Niall exclaimed happily. "And isn't it a movie star I thought you were?"

Rory wanted to squirm under the scrutiny. He'd been gone a long time. Not long enough to forget he was Irish, but long enough to become Americanized. His hair had been bleached by hours in the sun, his skin browned by the same. He probably looked every bit the California boy they'd all thought he'd become. Either they didn't know he'd spent more time running from trouble than he had chasing the waves, or they were pretending he was a normal kid come home to the bosom of his family. His money would be on the latter. They were all good pretenders.

Niall gave him a playful slap on the shoulder. "Mr. Hollywood is what you look like. Isn't that right, Sean?"

Niall turned to the younger man who'd come to stand beside him. Rory and Sean were stepbrothers as well as brothers-in-law. No blood relation of course, but they'd lived in the same house for a time before Sean had gone off to university and Rory to California. Sean was as big a man as Rory, hard with muscle and steady of gaze. His smile was welcoming, though, and Rory shook his hand.

Niall beamed at them before wrapping his fingers around the solid muscle of Rory's bicep.

"Are you doing the steroids, then?" he asked.

"What?" Rory demanded. "No."

"Don't get your fecking knickers in a twist," Niall said, laughing. "We hear about those Americans and how they like their steroids. What about that baseball player?" He looked at Sean with a frown.

"Which one?" Sean asked.

"I can't remember his name, but they say he liked the steroids more than he did breakfast."

What happened to the good old days when everyone thought that all Americans drove Mustangs and wore aviator sunglasses?

"I don—" Rory began, but Niall wasn't finished.

"And doesn't he look big enough to heft a building, Sean?"

Sean grinned, enjoying Rory's discomfort, though not with malice. "That he does. Don't pick a fight with him, Dad. He'll mash you like a potato."

Rory didn't know whether to smile or frown. He settled somewhere in the middle and said nothing.

Danni moved to stand beside her husband, Raegan in her arms and Clodaugh wrapped around a leg. Sean scooped up his daughter and held her high until she giggled.

"Ah, well, it's good to see you and have my family together again," Niall said. "Come on now. Your mother's waiting."

His mother. Rory sighed as he imagined the meeting with his mother. He'd hurt her the worst by staying away, and he dreaded seeing that in her eyes. Aunt Edel had accused him of punishing them—maybe he had. Maybe he'd just been punishing himself for not being one of them. For never wanting to belong to a world where fathers could disappear like smoke in a windstorm and sisters could read your mind. A world he feared, and like a coward, because he feared it, he'd taught himself to hate it.

Feeling like a man condemned, he followed Niall into the keep through the same little door he'd used earlier. As he entered, Rory realized the door only looked small, set as it was in the towering side of the castle. In truth, it was easily ten feet tall. It opened onto a mudroom, where benches ran along two sides, boots tucked underneath and raincoats hanging on hooks above. A counter lined the wall by the door, filled with pots and gardening tools. At the end of it was a sink for washing off mud and muck.

Rory trailed Niall to a hall that opened onto the heart of the castle. In the original keep, it had probably been a banquet room or the like. His mother stood waiting in the center of the enormous room.

She was a small and slender woman who still looked young despite the fact that her children were grown adults. She'd always been graceful, soft-spoken, and poised. As a kid it bugged Rory, her tranquility. He'd made it a personal mission to rile her whenever he could and had succeeded on quite a few occasions. Yet his victory had never felt good.

"I wondered" was all she said when she saw him.

Left without a response, Rory stood silently, letting his eyes take in the grand hall that had been converted into a massive sitting room with large, comfortable furniture and an immense fireplace, framed with shelves of books. For all its size, it was a warm room, decorated with hanging tapestries and marble statues. Rugs covered the wooden floor and flowers brightened the tables. He wouldn't have believed it if someone had told him, but it was homey. He tilted his head back and looked up at a ceiling thirty feet high. A tiled mosaic mirrored the spiral designs of the pendant, of the lock on the Book of Fennore. Of the brand seared over his heart.

"How long will you be staying?" his mother asked, and reluctantly he pulled his gaze from the mesmerizing design and looked at her.

"Just a few nights," he said softly.

"Are you nutters?" his mother exclaimed. "You came all that way for just a few nights?"

At the moment, he felt like a raving lunatic, but kept it to himself. He didn't mention that the quick turnaround was all he thought he could take. All he thought anyone would want. But Danni caught her lip between her teeth, and his mother looked like she might cry.

"There, now, Fia," Niall said to Rory's mother. "Let's just be happy he's here now."

A girl who Rory hadn't noticed before stepped forward to stand just beside Fia. She watched him with huge gray eyes and a small frown.

"You remember your sister Meaghan sure enough?" Niall said, smiling happily, oblivious to the tension that radiated off the young woman.

Meaghan had only been a little girl with skinned knees and no front teeth when he'd left. Now she would be twenty, a woman. Beautiful, like Danni and their mother. But there was something more than just beauty here. Something ethereal, something otherworldly. She was breathtaking, so lovely she didn't seem real. But the unwavering stare she gave him was tangible, and it made him want to squirm. Irritated, he stared back without a word.

"Is it the Book you're here looking for?" she demanded without preamble.

Niall sucked in a breath, and his mother made a shushing sound. As surprised by the vehemence in Meaghan's tone as the question, Rory raised his brows and shrugged. Meaghan wasn't old enough to have any bad memories of him—not of her own anyway, but who knew what she'd been told over the years. She'd been sweet and uncomplicated as a child and she alone had been exempt from Rory's rage. She'd followed him like he hung the moon and he'd let her. But the woman staring him down now had no hero worship in her eyes.

"Good to see you again, too," he answered with a curious smile.

"I've spent three years searching for it, you know. It's not here. You won't find it."

She glared at him defiantly, as if she'd thrown down a gauntlet and dared him to pick it up. He might have laughed if the tension in the room hadn't been so high and tight. Why had his youngest sister been looking for the Book of Fennore? And if it was true, then why did it evade her? Danni had said the

Book knew who was thinking of it, looking for it. He wanted to ask, but the expression on his mother's face made him remember that Nana had thought his mother would keep the pendant from him if she'd known about it.

"Meaghan, leave him be," his mother said, interrupting Rory's silent questions.

"But—"

"You heard your mother," Niall told her. "Now, who's hungry? The least we can do is feed our Rory, aye?"

"It's okay. I ate earl—" He stopped at the look on his mother's face. He didn't have the heart to dim the hopeful sparkle in her eyes and so he said instead, "Food would be good. Haven't eaten since some peanuts on the flight."

She smiled and it nearly broke his heart. "I've salmon cooking with potatoes and your favorite soda bread."

Another wave of nostalgia sucker punched him. Niall was a fisherman, and salmon was as much a staple at mealtime here as fast food was in the States. He'd decided he hated the fish by the time they'd sent him away. But the savory scent that came from the kitchen and the thought of this meal, prepared by his mother as she'd prepared so many others, was enough to make his stomach growl and his heart ache.

"Sure and we didn't know when you'd get here. . . ." Or if he was coming at all, Fia's pause said. "But it should be ready by now."

She led the way into a huge kitchen where an enormous table was set and ready. In his mind, Rory heard the echo of Nana's voice.

People you love could die.

I'm here, okay? he silently answered.

He sat with Sean, Niall, and the toddlers while his sisters and mother moved food from oven to table. When they were all seated, his mother took one hand and Niall the other and they all bent their heads in prayer that felt familiar and alien at the same time.

His mother ended by thanking God for bringing home her son. She had tears in her eyes when she finished, and they'd all turned to Rory expectantly.

"It smells great," he said, and his mother beamed as she passed him the platter of salmon.

"Hope you're not too tired, Rory," Niall said with a big smile as they all began filling plates. "But friends and family will be stopping by later to pay their respects to Mother."

Niall's eyes looked suddenly glassy, and Rory thought of how selfish he'd been not offering his condolences. But it seemed too late now. It occurred to Rory only then that the wake might be tonight. That somewhere in this castle Colleen Ballagh was laid out for the viewing as tradition warranted. Hell, people would be coming from far and near to see her.

Rory was pretty sure his expression said exactly what he thought of facing all those *friends and family*. "I don't think there's anyone I want to see," he said.

Sean laughed at that. "You're in Ballyfionúir, Rory. When has anyone here ever cared what you do or don't want? It's not in their genetic build to have concerns outside of their own."

A truer statement had never been made. Still, Rory tried. "Let's not play this 'we're glad to have him home' game, okay? No one was sorry to see me go. I don't want to make nice about my being back. It's just for a few days and then I'll be out of your hair."

"I was sorry," Danni said softly.

"Aye, me, too," Niall offered.

"Is that what you think—" his mother began.

Rory stood so suddenly his chair shot out from beneath him. They all stared at him with startled eyes. He wanted to shout—say something so obscenely offensive that they would stop looking at him like he was the returned messiah. He didn't know how to cope with this benevolence. They were all so good, so *caring*. Why couldn't they see that Rory was everything they weren't? That he didn't belong here with them? Didn't they remember what he'd been like before they'd sent him away? Didn't they remember Trevor and how Rory's negligence had led to his death? Had he been given time, Rory would have eventually self-destructed and taken down anyone in his path as he went.

"I'm not glad to have him back," Meaghan said, and the shocked gazes all turned to her. "Fecking look at him," she went on mildly. "All my girls will be wanting to snog him, won't they? And he may look like a fecking Superman, but I'll doubt he can do twenty of them in one night."

Still no one said anything. Rory's mouth was open. He shut it.

"I'm just saying. They'll be pissy about it."

Sean was the one who finally laughed, though he fought it valiantly before losing. To Rory's amazement, Danni joined in and then his mother. His mother, for Chrissakes. Niall was laughing so hard he started to cough. Even the little ones giggled, though it was obvious they didn't have a clue what everyone was laughing about.

"I don't know what's so damned funny," Rory said, trying to look fierce. But the laughter was contagious, and he found himself standing like a fool with a bewildered expression and a stupid smile on his face. To cover it, he turned away, silently retrieved his chair, and sat down.

"Pass the potatoes, please," he said, and this elicited a howl from Meaghan that nearly rattled the hanging light.

His mother had tears in her eyes as she passed the bowl to him, planting a kiss on his cheek as she did. Dazed, Rory loaded his plate with food he doubted he'd get past the lump in his throat.

Chapter Nine

THEY had come, people he hadn't seen since he'd left.
People he never wanted to see again. Each face was a
memory he'd worked hard to forget. Each friendly smile a
poisonous reminder of how little he deserved it. Each black
scowl a welcome landmark on an uncertain path.

They'd filed by, seeking out the family members to offer
condolences. Seeking out Rory because now he was a novelty
and they wanted to know how he'd changed. How he hadn't.
In a haze of grief and confusion, he'd managed to keep it
together. Barely.

And through all the long hours, he'd seen *her*. The woman
from his dream, flitting in and out of the sea of memory. As
she had in the airport, she'd appeared amongst the mourners,
a seduction in motion, always out of reach. No one else took
notice of her, and that was the only way Rory knew she wasn't
really there. Because she looked every bit as real as the others.
She'd drawn him from the fringes of the gathering and into the
thick of it, then vanished, leaving him at their mercy.

He drank way more than he should have, but only managed
to feel stupid instead of numb. And then morning came, greeting him with a hellacious headache and a queasy stomach.

He'd almost lost what little he'd eaten for breakfast when
he'd learned the price he was expected to pay for the pendant.
With Nana, nothing came without strings attached, so he

should have expected it. But still, her decree that Rory would be one of her pallbearers caught him like a blade to the throat. Nana knew better than anyone what it cost him to enter the house of God, a place he'd been forced to spend many hours as a child and a repenting adolescent. Undoubtedly she was in heaven—or hell, knowing Colleen Ballagh as he did— laughing her fool head off.

The sermon went on for eternity, moving some in the congregation to tears, sobs even, and others to stifled yawns and a deep desire for drink. The entire ceremony left Rory feeling like a tightrope walker balanced over razors. When at last he stood with Sean, Niall, and Ronan McCourt, who'd always been sweet on Nana, he felt the weight of finality that lodged between his heart and throat. He put his shoulder to the task of hefting the coffin, grateful to be exiting the church, even with death on his shoulder. The casket felt unbearably heavy, her remains somehow larger than life itself. Nana in a nutshell.

In small groups they followed the hearse to the gravesite where Nana would be buried next to her late husband. It was a silent time for reflection. Rory didn't want to think, but he was thankful he wasn't expected to talk instead. Now he stood awkwardly away from the others, outside the shade cast by the canopy sheltering his family from the relentless sunshine.

He'd forgotten there were days like this in Ireland. Days when the sun brought a vengeance with it, turning the humidity into baked wool that weighted his steps and chaffed his skin. Morning had dawned with bright rays and wispy clouds, and he'd hoped for rain—prayed for rain that would bring relief to the sullen heat, but the gray cast had merely gathered like a gang over the choppy seas and waited for a better opportunity to bully.

A storm would have been fitting weather for Nana's funeral. She herself had been a tempestuous woman—a microburst of allegiance and fervor. Small and spry, never above spite, never below malice. He'd loved her, more than anyone else. She'd understood him in a way that mystified him, even now.

He shifted his weight, glad he'd spurned decorum in favor of a simple button-down shirt and his best jeans. Niall wore a suit that must feel like a fur blanket about now. His mother, stepfather, sisters, and brother-in-law sat in the front row, only moderately cooler in the shade provided by the canopy. His mother wept uncontrollably, though Nana had been Niall's parent, not hers. Niall stared at the small black coffin impassively, but Rory saw the tick in his cheek and the burning red rimming his eyes. Meaghan's grief mirrored her father's with uncanny accuracy. Beside them Danni and Sean held one another, quiet in their sorrow as both said good-bye to the woman who'd been so much to all of them. Father Lawlor picked up where he'd left off in the church and droned on about the virtues of Colleen Ballagh and the waiting arms of Jesus, the Lord.

Rory wanted to laugh. She'd been many things, but Nana had never been virtuous. And never without motive. In one of his earliest memories, he'd had a dawning awareness of being a pawn in a great, but gentle manipulation only Nana understood.

He reached in his pocket and felt the pendant he'd stuffed there this morning. Older than anything he could imagine, the charm was probably worth thousands—maybe more. He rubbed his fingers over the jeweled face, the leather thong it dangled from. The desire to pull it out, to put it on here and now was nearly overwhelming. He looked back at the casket, knowing she'd intended that. Even from the grave, she manipulated.

Father Lawlor began his closing prayer. Soon there would be doves bursting from their cages, and the mourners would adjourn to the castle to eat and drink and carry over the celebration of Colleen Ballagh's life and death that they'd begun last night. Rory's gaze traveled over his family again. Niall's solemn calm had crumbled and now he wept. He turned into his wife, holding her tightly as they grieved. Sean passed a tissue to Danni, and as she wiped her tears, she glanced up and her eyes met Rory's. For a moment—a flashing instant—Rory felt the soft brush of her thoughts against his once more. Her need for him to move into the circle of family. Her wish for him to belong again.

Then her gaze shifted to something just over his shoulder, and the connection was lost. He saw her eyes widen and the blood drain from her face. All the hair stood at the back of his neck, and slowly he turned to see what had put that fear in his sister's eyes.

The woman of his dream was standing in the meadow beyond the family cemetery. Still dressed in the white cotton shift that whipped about her legs, she could have been the infamous white ghost of the valley that Ballyfionúir was named after. But there was nothing ethereal about her. She was too solid for that.

He cut his eyes to Danni, grappling with the fact that she saw the woman, too. There was no mistaking her fixed attention.

He looked again, expecting his dream-woman to have vanished. But still she stood, her long, dark hair making a gossamer frame of her pale oval face. She lifted an impatient hand and pushed the heavy weight of it back before gesturing to Rory.

Come with me. . . .

From the corner of his eye he saw Danni start, her head shaking as she turned a panicked gaze on him and reached out in a gesture opposite of the dream-woman's. *Don't go.*

But he was too far away to touch, and nothing his sister or anyone else could say or do could stop the step he took toward the woman. Who was she? Was he about to finally find out?

He heard a rustle come from the mourners as he started down the hill. Father Lawlor paused, and his mother called out Rory's name. He didn't stop. He didn't answer. The woman moved faster and so did he.

A strong wind had stirred up from nowhere and now gusted over the swaying emerald grasses and shushed the leaves in the ancient alders and sagging yews. Rory gratefully turned his face into its coolness, letting it dry the sweat on his brow as he followed the woman across the meadow toward the castle. Behind him, Father Lawlor's commanding voice faded and disappeared altogether.

She'd reached the jagged edge of the cliff that dangled above the sea. To his left the castle stood whole and strong, lording over the island. It was like an optical illusion, seeing it there now when it had always been just a crumpled and desecrated ruin before. The woman up ahead paused and stared at the structure with wonder. She glanced at Rory then back to the castle before turning to navigate the eroding stairs leading down to the cove. Either Sean hadn't gotten around to repairing them, or they were meant to disintegrate like the stones and gnarled driftwood on the beach.

If he had to guess, Rory would say it was the latter. The stairway led to a place that should have been sealed up long ago. A place he remembered with trepidation. With icy dread.

The woman gave no quarter to caution as she descended, and he struggled to keep up, his larger feet finding only treacherous footholds leading down. He slipped several times and almost made the journey ass over elbow. At last he reached the shell-strewn bottom, crunching the broken fragments beneath his shoes. If he'd harbored a hope that she was headed anywhere but the cavern, he gave it up.

The air carried a heavy scent here, seasoned with fish and salt and the cold depths of mystery that were the sea itself. The tide thundered in and out, spewing white foam and mist that clung to the shoreline. Lithe and agile, the woman moved through it undeterred, unconcerned with the danger inherent in this place. People had died here, Rory knew. Sometimes he suspected he was one of them.

"Wait," he shouted over the crash and crescendo of the waves.

Without even hesitating she hiked up her shift and climbed past the rounded boulders that blocked the entrance to the cavern. Cursing under his breath, Rory scrambled after her.

It took a moment for his eyes to adjust to the dark interior of the cavern beneath the fortress. The tide was high and the surging sea swelled up, nearly blotting out the entrance, but once it reached inside, the waves were subdued by massive boulders until they lapped against the stone basin, black as obsidian and glittering from the thin shaft of sunlight that followed them in. On every wall the same triple spiral that locked the Book of Fennore was carved into the stone. It was everywhere, the designs as ancient as the waters that lapped at the edge of the pool.

He knew on the far side of the cavern there was a doorway to stairs that spiraled up into the castle. At least that's where they'd led when he was a boy, but Sean may have had them sealed off. Rory certainly would have. Enormous rocks made irregular sentries around the tide pool, some set back against the jagged walls, others teetering close to the edge. The woman hovered beside one, watching him now as she had in the dream.

Her dark hair gleamed like the sparkling water, alive with light and energy. It fell in a shining curtain around her shoulders and down her back. He imagined it would feel like silk against his fingers. Her dusky skin, long slender throat, and the bare expanse of chest that showed above the line of her shift seemed luminescent in the darkness. As always, he wanted to touch her. To pull some of that radiance into the black of his soul.

"Who are you? Why are you here?" he said, meaning it as a demand. But even he didn't have the stones to make demands of an angel. And that's what she looked like to him. A dark and iridescent angel.

His voice echoed in the chamber, distorted by the lapping waters and the concave walls until it bounced back at him, a stranger. She gave a small shake of her head, nearly imperceptible but for the movement of her hair. He couldn't take his eyes off her, didn't want to look away.

The string that held the front of her shift was loose, making the gown gape. Teasing him with glimpses of the swell of her breasts. The mist from the tide had dampened the fabric and he could see the deep rose of her nipples, the dark shadow of cleavage, the seductive line of her hips and the enthralling vee at the juncture of her thighs. Everything inside him hardened and tightened until he felt like a coil twisted to the point it would spring free.

At last he braved a step closer, watching as she hovered there. Her eyes were huge, deep, and compelling, and he felt himself pulled into the mystery of their swirling depths. He stopped a few feet in front of her, almost close enough to touch. Almost.

"Are you real?" he asked.

She tilted her head, as if trying to hear the words he spoke clearly.

"Of course you're not real," he muttered.

She answered with a step forward, shortening the distance between them, stunning him with her closeness. She smelled

of the sea and of heather. The scents mingled on her skin and
became fresh and exotic, more intoxicating than any drink
he'd ever consumed. He couldn't stop himself from reaching
out, from trailing his fingers through her glossy mane, letting
the long strands slip across his palm. It felt like silk, just as
he'd imagined. It was warm from her body and alive with
color. He stared, fascinated, as the light caught auburn and
sable, ebony and russet.

When he looked up, she was watching him, her expression
wary and wanting. There was an intensity to her gaze that
unnerved, that made him feel as if she was looking deep inside
him, shining a light on everything he didn't want her to see.
For a moment he was afraid she'd find him lacking and turn
away. Who would blame her? Rory MacGrath was a fuckup.
It was no secret. He always had been.

Neither of them moved for several long seconds punctuated
by the soft splash of the water and the ragged sound of his
breath catching and releasing. He bit his bottom lip, wanting
more than anything to make her stay, frustrated by the sense
that she never would.

Then suddenly she glanced over her shoulder, as if she'd
heard something else, something that frightened her. When she
faced him again, her chin was raised. Not in challenge, not in
fear, but with pride. Slowly she reached for the neck of her shift,
pulling the tie completely free before tugging it over her head,
and letting it drop to the rocks at her feet. Rory's mouth went dry.

He'd seen her perform the same actions in his dreams night
after night, in his fantasies day after day. Now he didn't know
which it was—dream, fantasy, or real. It didn't matter. She
stole all ability to breathe, to move, to care.

She was magnificent, burnished satin skin, slender limbed
and grace in motion. She was breathing heavier, and her chest
rose and fell, drawing his gaze. He couldn't stop staring at her,
drinking in every feature, every dip and valley. Every shadow.
He wanted to touch. God help him, he wanted to touch.

Forgotten was the funeral, the reason for his being here,
the inky waters that instilled cold terror in him. All he knew
stood like an ethereal shaft of clarity in a land of sin and
disillusionment.

She took another step closer and her heat reached out like a caress, welcoming, inviting. Torn between his fear that she would vanish and his fear that she might simply realize she had the wrong guy, Rory touched her face, letting his fingers cup the curve of her jaw, the softness of her cheek. Her lashes fluttered for a moment and her lips parted, then she was leaning in, coming up on her toes, resting her hands against the solid wall of his chest. Her mouth was just inches away, and he closed the distance, but not his eyes. He watched her features blur as his mouth settled over hers.

Her lips were soft, sweet like cream, and he shivered at the feel of them against his own. Every muscle in his body clenched with the hot need rising inside him. Slowly he dragged his mouth over hers, reveling in the friction, the small breath she gave and he took. He used his tongue to tease her lips open and let him in. In all his life, nothing had ever felt as stunning as the hot velvet of her mouth, the dark seduction of her kiss. He realized that he was losing something of himself in that intimate touch, something he might miss, something he might never want to find again.

She swayed against him, lost her balance, and he used the movement to pull her tighter, pressing her body to his, feeling her soft breasts flatten against the muscles of his chest, wishing he was as naked as she. Her hands circled his neck, fingers digging into his hair.

Christ, it was like falling into a blazing inferno. He felt the heat all around him, coming from within, from without, singeing his fingers, his heart, his soul. She made a sound that licked the flame through his blood. Then she eased back, trailing her touch over the hard muscles of his chest, her fingers lingering on the spiral scar for just a moment before dragging down the flat dip of his belly. He caught his breath, waiting for her to go lower, praying she'd go lower. But instead she dipped into his pocket and pulled free the pendant his grandmother had given him. She dangled it between them, her body angled away from his, forcing him to focus on what she held until at last he reached for the glittering object. She pressed it into his hand, curling his fingers around it.

And then she whispered the words he knew he'd been waiting to hear. The words he'd fled from in his dreams. The words that had lured him here, to this place with her. Now.

With her lips against his once more, she said, *"Hurry, Ruairi. Hurry."*

Chapter Ten

Rory had the sensation of floating. He was neither here, nor there. He was trapped between the two.

The cavern was gone; the woman, too. He was outside again, in fresh air beneath a rising sun. All around him was open land, green and lush as only Eire could be. But there was no trace of the sea, no scent of the ocean lapping damp shores. He might still be in Ireland, but there was no place on the Isle of Fennore where he wouldn't smell the salt and spray of the rolling waves. And the landscape was too wild and too hostile for it to be the island he knew.

He was moving with a steady, rolling gait. *Horseback?* It fit, and yet a part of his brain rejected the idea as quickly as it came. The sensation was there, but incomplete in a way he couldn't explain. He looked to his left, and the twin he'd dreamed of so many times before emerged from a blurred silhouette into crisp clarity. As if it had taken Rory's attention to bring him into focus. Rory filed that away in his too-weird-to-contemplate compartment and studied his body double.

The other Rory rode a mighty black horse with ribbons braided into its mane and tail, coat gleaming and adorned with bright silk scarves. It was dressed up for something and excited. It tossed its head and lifted its hooves high in an agitated prance.

His twin looked confident in the saddle. His fur cloak was

flung back from his shoulders and draped over the horse's hindquarters. The dead paws still attached to the skin flapped in the breeze and made a parody of petting. As he had in the dreams, Rory's twin wore a long blue shirt embroidered at the hem and seams with spirals and symbols in purple and gold. On the chest was the intricately woven triple spiral, the pattern exactly like the pendant Rory's grandmother had given him. Rory looked down, realizing only then that he still held the pendant. His fingers were tangled in the leather cord, the hard metal and jewels pressed into his damp palm.

He thought to return it to his pocket, remembering how his dream-woman had pulled it out and pressed it into his hand before he'd suddenly fallen into this crazy quasi dream.

It was only then that he made another realization.

He had no pocket. He had no clothes. He was stripped. Stark naked and hovering beside his twin like some wacked cherub in a celestial painting. Rory's body rocked with the sensation of riding the horse, mimicking the movements of his twin, but there was no animal beneath him.

He tried to get his mind around what he was feeling, seeing . . . experiencing. It wasn't Rory astride the great beast, but he shared the sensation of it. The steady roll of its gait, the feel of its barrel chest expanding with each huge breath, the toss of its head. He felt his twin's admiration for the spirited mount. The sparking satisfaction that he and he alone had broken the stallion into submission. His pleasure mingled with a churning tension and anger that roiled just beneath the surface.

The dreams of the woman had been strange, erotic, disconcerting. He'd felt a similar sense of participation in them. But this . . . what he felt now . . . this was something altogether different. Rory couldn't explain how or why, but it was. Definitely it was.

"Quit your brooding, boy," a voice commanded.

Startled, Rory snapped his attention from his twin to the man who'd spoken. Like an optical illusion, his shape and form burst from the smear of colors and became suddenly clear and vivid while his voice roused some slumbering recollection that splintered the surface of his mind but did not emerge enough to grasp.

The man rode a horse to the twin's right. Behind the two of

them were others who seemed to materialize only as Rory's gaze passed over them. A long line of others, to be exact. Men, striding in formation, two abreast and no less than fifty deep. A pair in front carried banners with the same tri-spiral image that marked the pendant and the twin's tunic. The procession twisted and snaked over the hillside, following the two on horseback with the kind of subdued obedience that made Rory think of disciplined Nazis marching in perfect precision. Questioning nothing as they moved as one. Wondering at his own snap judgment, he noted how their eyes tracked the man riding beside Rory's twin as he swayed in the saddle, waiting for the tiniest shift of movement to guide them.

No one seemed to notice Rory was there. He was invisible, as he'd been in the dreams. But he wasn't dreaming now, was he? He'd been wide awake—standing up even—when this . . . this vision or whatever the hell it was had taken him. And where was the woman he'd followed? She'd disappeared again and left him here like a clown with his balls hanging in the wind.

Frowning, Rory turned his attention back to the man riding beside his twin. His voice had been familiar, but Rory didn't know why. He'd spoken in a strange archaic language that Rory had never heard before, and yet he understood what was said. He'd never been more grateful for his natural ability to comprehend the meaning of a language before he even grasped the mechanics. It was the only gift of his heritage that he'd never rejected.

The man's hair glinted golden and red, salted at the temples with gray, a sign of age that was not mirrored in his youthful face. More gray flecked his neatly trimmed mustache and goatee, but few wrinkles creased the sun-browned skin or fanned from the bright blue eyes. He had an open face. Friendly. And yet there was something hidden in his expression that contradicted that impression in the same way the gray contrasted with the young-looking face. Rory couldn't say just what it was.

He was heavyset and solid, clothed like Rory's twin in bright blue and purple with a replica of the spiraled image woven into the front. His fur cloak was white, amazingly bright in the crisp morning sun. Rory couldn't hazard a guess on how many animals had died to make the garment. A gold chain held it in place, and it didn't surprise Rory in the least that the clasp was yet another jeweled triple spiral.

The black horse his twin rode tossed his head again, and instinctively Rory tightened his thighs, holding on when the horse reared in agitation, understanding how stupid it was even as he did it.

"Control that beast," the man beside them said. He flicked a quick glance over Rory's twin, and there was a perplexing mixture of contempt and regard that caught Rory by surprise. And strangely enough, that unfathomable look brought with it absolute recognition. Rory hadn't seen this man for twenty-five years, but he knew instantly and without a doubt who he was. Impossible, unbelievable, and yet undeniable. The man was Cathán MacGrath. Rory's father.

A wash of incredulity stole his breath and filled his lungs even as tears burned his eyes and blurred his vision. How many childhood fantasies had included moments like this when Rory would single-handedly find the man he'd loved more than anyone? The man whose loss he felt responsible for?

Memories came at him like lightning in the thunderstorm of confusion. The last time he'd seen his father had been that night beneath the ruins when they'd both held the Book of Fennore between them. When they'd fought each other and the demons inside to control it. How was Cathán here, in this bizarre fantasy that continued to warp and race to inexplicable ends? And did his being here mean the Book was, too?

"I don't like it," Rory's twin said angrily. "We can call them out and stomp them to dust if that's what yer wanting, but this skulking y' have us doing is not right."

"Christ, but you're like your mother." Cathán spoke in the same strange tongue, only betraying himself by drawing out his "yous" instead of clipping them short.

Rory's twin obviously found this offensive, and the simmering rage Rory sensed in him boiled into festering fury. "If the men knew of yer plans, they'd be of the same mind," he insisted coldly.

"Which is why they don't know of it, you fool. We've been stomping Bain's fucking people to dust for ten years and still they defy us. I see them gaining power, working the sympathies of others against us. This will take the heat from their flame. They will be powerless."

"They'd be powerless dead," Rory's twin insisted.

"No," Cathán said, his tolerance departing with the one word. He reached over and grabbed Rory's twin by the front of his tunic, crushing the fabric in a tight fist. "They'd be martyrs, and there's no worse an enemy than a martyred one. Now shut it and do as you're told."

"Wed the witch."

"Aye. Wed and bed her, you pathetic imbecile. Get her with child and be quick about it. Only then will we own her. I wish to Christ I could do it myself."

Rory stared at his father with disbelief, trying unsuccessfully to put his memory of his father into this sharp, hard mold.

"I give you this chance to be a man, Ruairi. Do not fail."

"I am a man already and y' give me nothing," Rory's twin said angrily, jerking away.

To that, Cathán's response was cold, mirthless laughter. "You are what I say you are. A beast as sure as the one you sit on. I mean what I tell you, boy. You'll not harm her. We've tried the whip, now it's time to try the honey."

Rory's twin clenched his jaw on whatever he wanted to say, but his ire shimmied around him like a silent windstorm. Rory recognized it. Saw it in the taut line of his shoulders and the dark scowl on his face. He'd worn that expression himself, felt that smoldering anger waiting to ignite and explode. Felt at once comforted and distressed to see it now.

He exhaled, felt his twin do the same. He wanted this . . . this *episode* to end, but he couldn't make himself wake or come to or whatever the hell it was he needed to do to end it. He felt like he was drowning in it and he couldn't find the surface.

"I still don't see how this is the answer," Rory's twin blurted, as if he couldn't help himself. "Marriage or no, Bain's people will never be our friends."

"No, they'll not be friends, but a man thinks twice before killing his family. And a mother will do anything to save her babe. You get the girl with child, son, and I will take care of the rest. Do you think you can manage that or will I have to help you there as well?"

The insult did not go unnoticed. Rory's twin leaned forward and glared at Cathán, and for the first time Rory noticed a flat gleam to the blue eyes that were so like and so different from his own.

"Watch yerself, old man," he said in a tone deceptively soft.

For a moment, Cathán looked uneasy—frightened even—and Rory viewed his twin with new eyes. He was massive and armed to the teeth. But what made him truly terrifying was the rage on his face and the pitiless well of those eyes.

"Once we have the Book, you'll thank me for this," Cathán said, spurring his horse forward, bravely giving Rory's twin his back.

The Book . . .

He heard the capital *B* in his father's tone, knew it could be none other than the Book of Fennore.

He leaned forward, hoping to urge his twin to catch up to Cathán and ask more about the Book. But whatever signal connected the two of them didn't seem to work both ways. Rory felt the churn of frustration inside his twin, but he was unable to convey his own needs.

Ahead, Cathán came to a place where their path was met by another and he stopped. The procession came to a halt behind him and waited for Cathán to tell them what to do next. The horses shifted and snorted, the men scanned the clearing and the forest line on either side with anxious eyes. Rory felt his gut tighten. What were they waiting for?

He joined them in scrutinizing the horizon, searching for movement and finding none. A dark, dense forest crowded up to the road on the right, and the branches waved in the breeze, leaves shushing the birds that twittered and cawed.

Uneasiness moved through the men like a wave and drew Rory's attention to a small party of four cresting the hill. He felt his twin's tension as he spotted their horses, felt the expectant hush as the small group drew closer. Among them was the woman who had haunted his sleep, haunted his thoughts, brought him here. Rory felt the breath leave his lungs.

She was as beautiful and seductive in this fantasy as she'd

been each night she'd tormented him. Dressed now in more than just a shift, she wore a blue gown that shimmered in the clouded sunlight. Her hair had been braided into an intricate pattern and then coiled around her head. The dark gleam of it caught the sun and reflected it. Her skin looked golden, eyes almost black and tilted at the corners. Her nose was a little long, her mouth a bit too wide. But the small imperfections somehow balanced her face and made it all the more perfect. She was as exotic and magnificent as an orchid in a bed of roses.

He closed his eyes against the memory of her lips on his, her breasts pressed against his chest.

She wasn't real. *This* wasn't real.

A light flush covered her cheeks, as if she'd heard his thoughts. His twin shifted, and Rory glanced at his face only to find an expression that was most likely a reflection of his own. A word brushed the back of Rory's mind. *Besotted.* They were both of them, besotted.

Was it she who Cathán—*his father*—had said to wed and bed? This woman? A strange emotion welled in him at that, an unsettling sense of jealousy, of thwarted possession. She was *his* dream-girl, not this imposter's.

He didn't believe in fairy tales, but if he did, he would say he'd been caught in her spell. The look on his twin's face said the same thing. As Rory watched, his twin angrily narrowed his eyes at her. Instinctively, Rory understood that his twin feared her in some way and that anger was his only defense. He didn't like anyone having power over him, and especially not a woman. There was suspicion and barely suppressed violence in his bearing, and Rory suddenly feared what he might do, this man who could be a walking, talking photograph of Rory. Fear was like an enemy to Rory, and when cornered by it, he came out swinging. Was it the same for his double? Surely he wouldn't hurt this woman . . . would he?

His twin dismounted, and Rory followed, feeling foolish as he pulled his legs from around his nonexistent horse and stepped down, painfully aware of his nudity, though no one took note of him. His annoyance at being ignored conflicted sharply with his desire to remain invisible and his fear that he would suddenly appear naked to all. The woman glanced his way, did a double take, and then looked again.

Rory stared in shock. Had she seen him?

The idea that she had, even if only for an instant, spurred him forward. He tried to get between his twin and the woman, feeling the rising rage from one and the terror from the other.

Rory clenched his fist, reaching for his twin. The flash of gems in the sunlight reminded him again that he still clutched the cord that dangled the pendant in his other hand. It swung back and forth with hypnotic intent. For a moment, everything froze as Rory stared at it. The woman, his twin—all of the others—once more became smudges against the backdrop of the forest.

Rory had the sense of a vortex spinning toward him, sucking him up, spewing him out. In a blink, his mind whirled through the chain of events leading to this moment, examining, discarding. Seeking the significance of his hand clutching the pendant and the weight of its swing.

He felt like a boat, listing out of control, adrift in the rolling tide. The sense that this was a dream, an illusion, couldn't breach the barrier that the pendant's solidity suddenly created in his mind. Because the pendant *was* real. And it was here, with him.

Nothing else had followed him through to wherever he was now. Not his clothes. Not his watch, his phone, his wallet, or the change in his pocket. But this, this pendant . . . it had. This one thing his grandmother had said he would need was still in his hand when everything else was gone.

So what did that mean? What did that say about what would happen next?

He looked from the pendant to the frozen images of the woman and his twin, understanding what some part of him had known from the start. There was only one way to find out—there was only one way to *get out* of this in-between state of mind that had trapped him.

Slowly, filled with foreboding mingled inexplicably with excitement and release, he did what he'd wanted to do at Nana's graveside.

The leather cord was long enough to fit over his head. He slid it down, over his ears to his neck and then let it go. The pendant fell heavily against his breastbone, the branded scar over his heart an exact replica of its shape. It bounced once with a weighted jolt that seemed to ricochet through him and then expand outward. It rumbled like thunder, like a sonic boom, like a quake.

Suddenly everything was moving again and moving lightning fast. He stepped between his twin and the woman, bracing himself for what he didn't know. He felt the first brush of contact, and then a sickening plunge as his twin slammed into him. For one screaming second, Rory felt like he was being ripped apart, stretched wide to accommodate the insertion of a mass too large to absorb. Like lungs filled to capacity but still inflating until the air seared and split the walls of tissue.

And then everything snapped back, and he was left standing in front of her. The woman stared at him with wide, shocked eyes. Rory wasn't sure what had happened, couldn't hazard a guess at what it was she'd seen. It felt as if his twin had been wedged beneath Rory's skin. He could feel him there now, fighting to get out. But the men standing beside her had no reaction at all. Rory glanced over his shoulder, feeling awkward in the solid form, feeling another's thoughts moving through his mind. His father stared at him with expectant eyes.

Not knowing what was real, what was imagined, what else he should do, Rory faced the woman again. She'd composed her features into a calm mask, making him think he'd imagined her reaction before. Slowly, she slid from her horse.

With a deep breath, she squared her shoulders and lifted her chin in a gesture he recognized. Defiant and yet vulnerable. She stepped forward and put her hand in his, and Rory knew without a doubt, there was no turning back.

Chapter Eleven

SARAID looked upon the giant man she was expected to wed feeling weak and sick and angry all at the same time. He stood no taller, no broader than her brother Tiarnan, but somehow the Bloodletter seemed twice again his size. Perhaps it was the tight coil of his muscles, the hard planes and defined ridges of his massive shoulders and chest, the bulge of strength in his bare arms. Or maybe it was as simple as the cold flatness in his gaze and the sneer on his face that made him seem so much larger, so much more formidable that for a moment she could only stare at him.

Fair skinned, with eyes that rivaled a clear sky for the blue, he had a jaw set and stubborn, a mouth full but hard and cruel. There was no warmth when he looked at her. That was fair, she supposed. There was no warmth when she looked at him.

They'd met before, when he'd been a small boy and she a little girl. He'd seemed all eyes and fear then, and she remembered that she'd felt sorry for him. But now he was a man, a very solid and imposing man, and there was nothing about him to inspire her compassion. She could not look at him without seeing the stain of blood from all of her slain people.

During the three days Saraid had been given to prepare for this moment, she'd prayed that the man whom Colleen of the Ballagh had foretold—the one she'd said would come in the guise of another—would appear and save her from this fate.

But he had not, and now here she stood, trapped by her twisted destiny.

Her stepbrothers had been angry when Tiarnan told them the news of her joining with Ruairi the Bloodletter. But Tiarnan was trying to prevent the obliteration of their people, one good and noble cause for this monstrous marriage. Neither she nor her brothers could dispute his reasoning—even if she wasn't sure she believed in it. Unhappy, but resigned, they'd drawn around her in support, and she'd held her head high, not letting them see the absolute terror she felt. They'd left Cathán Half-Beard's forest that day and made the journey home in silence to tell their people what was to come. It cut her to see the hope on their faces, the shocked horror that lingered in their eyes.

"Who can trust such a man?" one of the elders had demanded.

Tiarnan did not explain his reasons a second time; he rarely explained his reasons a first. He'd said only, "They will marry in three days. My brothers will go with me to witness. If it is a trap, only we will fall into it."

"And then who will lead us?" the elder asked.

"If it is a trap, I will have led y' to death," Tiarnan answered simply. "If it is not a trap, I will have led y' to salvation."

Saraid gave him a sideways look, his self-important tone astounding her. Colleen said they all had a part to play. Perhaps ignorance and arrogance was Tiarnan's. Yet something in his commanding tone seemed to calm the agitated elder.

"When we know what is to be, we will come for y'," Tiarnan went on. "Until then, trust no one outside of yerself. Do not answer the summons of anyone else or believe if they say we have sent them—it will be one of us or no one at all."

He looked each of the small group in the eye and received a solemn nod in response.

"That is all. In three days' time we will know the outcome."

Each had come to Saraid then. They'd kissed her hands, whispered blessings at her feet. Wept for her. She'd met them resolutely. What other choice had she? Over the next days, she found gifts of berries and soap, a ribbon salvaged from the ruins of their old lives, a hammered gold pin to wear at her waist. When they had so little, these gifts were treasure.

She and her brothers had managed to save only one small chest of possessions from Cathán's destruction. A chest that held her father's tunic—made of king's colors—and his long sword, which Tiarnan now carried as his own. There were other items as well, tiny bits and pieces of who they once were, but what Saraid cherished above others was a blue gown that her mother had been wed in. She would take her own vows in it, regardless of the mockery her joining would be.

She could understand her brother's motives, but she could not come up with a reason why Cathán, Ruairi's father, had proposed this union. It was not for peace—she knew this without a doubt. Cathán Half-Beard did not care if her people lived or died. Dead they posed less of a problem. So he wanted something else, something she suspected had as much to do with the Book of Fennore as it did with Saraid herself. Cathán had always believed Saraid's mother stole the Book from him. He'd convinced many that her daughter hid it even now. It was certain he thought once he had Saraid, she'd lead him to it.

He was more than a fool. Even if she knew where the Book was, she would die before she'd give it to him.

You don't know the half of what you know. Wasn't that what Colleen of the Ballagh had said? Difficult woman.

That morning they'd ridden to the place they'd lived as children, before Cathán Half-Beard had driven them out. There was a waterfall, sheltered by the forest. Here they would leave Liam, who had been chosen to stay behind at the camp and wait for word on the outcome. The youngest was most unhappy about this, but the decision had been made and, as with Saraid, made without him. If no word came, he would take it to mean the worst and ride in warning to the others.

Poor Liam could not even look at her as she said goodbye, so great was his grief. He'd fought Tiarnan's decision to give her to the Bloodletter the hardest. But Tiarnan would not be moved. And certainly not by a boy.

"Do not worry so, Liam," she'd said gently. "T'will be fine, ye'll see."

He did not believe her, but he put on a brave face. All of her brothers did, and her heart swelled with pride. This was why she'd taken the first step to go through with the marriage.

These four boys—men now. Somehow they would be the future if she could just help them survive.

Silent after parting with Liam, Saraid and her older brothers returned to the place where they'd camped three nights before and prepared to meet their destiny. Saraid had gone to the stream, where she washed the dust from her hands and face with the lavender soap she'd been given, and tried not to think of what she did. Alone, she'd stripped her traveling clothes and donned a crisp white underdress and then the lovely blue overdress. She smoothed the gown with loving fingers, admiring her mother's dainty stitches and the soft spun fabric. The kirtle hugged her breasts and dropped in a soft haze to her feet. A shimmering thread had been woven into it and it sparkled like fairy dust. Before she'd left that morning, one of the women had done her hair, twisting it into a braid that wound around her head and down her back with flowers bound into the intricate pattern.

And then she'd heard the familiar melody drifting on the breeze from a *cruit* and accompanying *buinne* and she'd known it was time. Cathán and the Bloodletter had come. The thrumming tones of strings and flute wrenched at her heart. It should be a joyous morning, this day she would wed. But how could a union to Ruairi the Bloodletter be anything other than a tragedy?

Her brothers had come to stand beside her, Tiarnan, Eamonn, and Michael. They'd bathed and put on their best trews and tunics—Tiarnan in her father's king's robe, she noted with ill humor.

Her brothers looked very handsome, and if not for the wear of their garb and the darkness that lurked in their eyes, Saraid could almost imagine them the royal family they'd once been. She'd smiled at them, wanting to banish the fear in their eyes and the worry in their hearts. Whatever this fate, it was sealed.

She'd nearly turned back when she saw Cathán and the Bloodletter waiting at the bottom of the hill with his long line of men at arms. Fear swallowed her whole and left only the shell of who'd she'd been behind.

Now she stood close enough to touch the Bloodletter. She trembled despite her effort to be as brave as her brothers and not shame them. There was a strange expression on the Blood-letter's face as he silently gazed at her, and she saw to her horror that it was desire. She looked away, unable to stomach the thought of his hands on her, touching her. But from the corner of her eye, she saw a flash of something that drew her attention and for one strange, tilting moment it seemed there were two Bloodletters standing before her. She blinked hard and there was only one, yet the sense of that other did not so easily vanish.

Apprehensive, she allowed the Bloodletter to take her fingers in a rough clasp. His hand was big and scarred from battle, and hers looked like a trapped bird in his grip. His touch felt like flesh and blood, bone and sinew, like any man's would. But Saraid wasn't fooled. Ruairi the Bloodletter was a monster, not a man.

She fell into step beside him, knowing he could quite easily drag her if she'd dallied. Was that not what they did in Rome? Capture their brides and haul them over the threshold of their new *homes* so that no risk would come of them tripping and bringing bad luck?

The walk to the church was long, as was custom. She looked the part of a bride, but there were no bridesmaids dressed in matching gowns to confuse the evil spirits who might try to snatch her on the way. There were too few women left of their people to risk jeopardizing any of them in such a pointless way. The evil spirits could not destroy Saraid's happiness as they were wont to do. There would be no happiness for her—not today. Not ever. Nor would there be honeyed mead to last the first month of their union and assure the birth of a son. Saraid hoped there would be no children of this vile match at all, but what would be would be.

It seemed to Saraid that their steps became a march, a trudging climb that hammered home the dread in her heart. She felt the Bloodletter watching her as they went, and once he snared her glance in his. The eyes were no longer cold and the sneer did not curl his lip. Instead, his expression seemed stunned, bemused. Again she saw that glimmer of desire, only now it was mired by the clearness of his eyes, and it did not make her skin crawl.

This unsettled her even more. Did he think to lure her with

false kindness? It would not work. She knew that at the heart of him was only cruelty and mercilessness. She'd seen too much evidence of it, the bodies cut in two, the eyes gashed out with his blade, the entrails twisted and eaten by the birds. This man was an animal, and she would do well to remember that when she stared into his guileless eyes.

At last they came upon the deep trench that circled Cathán's *rath* and crossed over the bridge into the circular settlement. She'd heard that Cathán aspired to build a keep of stone, a strong fortress that would safeguard all who lived within its walls. For now, he'd taken over what had once been the village of her cousins. Saraid remembered happier times when they'd come here to visit friends and family. It looked much as it had then, and Saraid swallowed hard, realizing that for others, Cathán's invasion had not been so devastating. The sound of a blacksmith's hammer rang out, mixing with the shouts of children running to and fro. They moved past granaries, stocked for the winter, and armorers' sheds, which no doubt bulged as well.

Cathán Half-Beard was a believer of the Christ God and he kept a priest at the *rath*, but he'd been called away on God's business and Cathán had not wanted to wait for his return. In his stead, a young monk with clear eyes and a peaceful smile would perform the rites.

"You'll be priest-wed when he returns," Cathán declared. "Until then we'll make do with the old ways."

She and her brothers had no say in it, though Cathán knew well enough that their beliefs were of the old ways—the Gods of earth and water, fire and air. Being priest-wed would be no more binding to Saraid than the words they spoke in the simple handfasting ceremony. She only wished that the year and a day that the handfast signified would bring her freedom, though she knew that was a fool's thinking. She'd call herself fortunate if she lived to draw breath when that day came.

The rest of Cathán's people, men, women, and children dressed in their drab undyed homespun, waited beside the small stone church. What did they think of this union? Their faces were bright and expectant, but a wedding was cause for feasting, and that alone would bring joy to these poor folks.

There were too many to fit into the tiny church, so they

gathered on the pathway before it. For a moment, no one moved or spoke. Then Cathán pulled a blue ribbon from his tunic and stepped forward, giving them both the signal to face one another. On wobbly legs, Saraid turned to the man she would wed. The monk in his long, coarse robes emerged from the small gathering and stood patiently waiting for Saraid to put her right hand in the Bloodletter's left. Her left in his right, wrists crossed. With a satisfied grunt, Cathán began to twine the ribbon around their hands, over and under until the knot of eternity was complete. She was numb through the monk's speaking of the vows. If she did not know better, she would say the Bloodletter was feeling the same. There was a gleam of something that might have been panic in those blue, blue eyes. Did he dread this as much as she? But that would mean Ruairi the Bloodletter had feelings, and that could not be true.

She took a deep breath when he lowered his head to kiss her, feeling dizzy and sickened and something else she could not define. As if sensing the turmoil inside her, he caught her gaze and held it for a moment, his searching, probing. She felt as if he were trying to say something with those enigmatic eyes, and for a flashing instant she felt again that sense of another lurking behind the sky blue of them. What a frightening mystery this man was, she thought.

And then his mouth settled over hers and thought fled. His kiss was warm and soft when she'd expected cold and hard. The touch of his lips gentle and coaxing when she'd prepared for rough and invasive. The kiss was brief, and yet it felt that time stopped for the length of it, giving her the chance to feel every nuance, every unexpected instant. It seemed he tried to pull back and then hesitated, allowing just another moment of the contact that shocked her like a hot ember popping from a blazing fire to burn her. With their hands bound and trapped between their bodies, Saraid could do little more than allow it. She'd be allowing so much more later, when they were alone.

He pulled away, just enough so that he could look into her eyes again, and she saw something there that she did not understand. Confusion that matched her own. A need—but not the kind she'd expected. Not lust, but longing.

Then he was stepping back and a mask came over his features once more. His father stared at him for a moment, the look hard and warning, the message unmistakable. It was only then that it occurred to her that the Bloodletter might be as much a pawn as she.

Around them the people of the Dark Forest sent up a cheer that made her want to cover her ears and scream. Her brothers were somber and quiet, gazes moving warily over the jostling crowd. Once again she gave them her brave smile, but inside she was quaking.

She'd imagined the moments of this ceremony to be frozen and unfeeling. She'd imagined herself shielded by her own hatred. But she'd seen something in the Bloodletter's eyes that had stolen that from her. He'd seemed a man awakened from a nightmare to find he was still fighting for his life, only now the dream-pain was real. It unsettled her, this glimpse that made him more than an effigy for her contempt.

Still bound by the ribbon and its symbolic eternity, the two followed the procession for what seemed miles, though in fact it was no distance at all. A large thatched dwelling stood in the center of the *rath*, and it was big enough to hold them all. As they made their way, more people joined, laughing and teasing and talking of the pig, the deer, the swans that had been prepared for the wedding feast. Meat pies and tarts, sweetmeats and candied fruits. In spite of herself, Saraid's mouth watered at the thought of the banquet. She only wished she could let herself believe, as these people did, that this union meant peace.

Inside the long house, clean rushes had been spread on the floor mixed with flowers that released a sweet scent as they were crushed beneath the tromping feet. Dogs darted around the edges, and children scampered away from their parents. People laughed as they found seats, unaware of the spiraling tension inside Saraid and her brothers. The setting felt bizarre—as displaced as the visit from Colleen she'd had only a few nights before. So long had it been that carefree chatter had abounded around her that now it seemed contrived and jarring.

Servants and slaves hurried to bring out the platters of roasted meat, placing trenchers to be shared at the tables. All had brought their own eating knives, for not even one as wealthy as Cathán Half-Beard had enough for a crowd this size.

Saraid noted all the empty seats as the guests quickly lined the tables, and she realized they'd been set for her people—the people of the Favored Lands. So Cathán Half-Beard thought there were still enough of them to fill those places at the tables. He knew not at all how few were their numbers. If he had, he would not have offered this match.

"Where are your men? Your women and children?" Cathán demanded, hefting a mug of ale at her brothers. "Is my food and my ale not good enough for them?"

Eamonn and Michael stared straight ahead without answering, leaving Tiarnan to speak for them. They looked young and uncertain, and not one of Cathán's men failed to note it.

"They'll be along," Tiarnan said, head held high and gaze level. He made her proud, the way he stood as if their very lives were not dangling over disaster. "They come from far and with many."

Saraid might have laughed had her insides not been icy with fear. Tiarnan had also noted the empty seats and was smart enough to take advantage of Cathán's ignorance. He'd steadfastly clung to the idea that once the marriage was consummated, the risk would be gone, but he would not send for the others until he was sure they would be safe. Saraid thought that would be never.

Cathán scowled, and for a moment the laughter and good wishes of the gathering waned. Noticing, Cathán lifted his mug again.

"Then you'll have to drink their share until they make it here, won't you now?" he said.

The threat held little disguise, but to his credit Tiarnan showed a face as calm and unconcerned as any Saraid had ever seen.

"That I will, Cathán Half-Beard. And with pleasure."

He and her brothers accepted cups from a servant and lifted them in toast. Saraid doubted anyone else saw the guarded flicker in Tiarnan's eyes.

Chapter Twelve

"To the happy couple," Cathán called, and the men all lifted their mugs.

Cathán drank to his own toast and then caught the bound hands of his son and his new wife and used them to tow the pair forward, hauling them across the floor to a curtained area just behind the head table. Saraid's panic increased with each stumbling step she took. Something was not right here. She looked at the Bloodletter and he, too, had an expression of bafflement.

The people gathered on the floor beneath them and watched with interest, as if she and the Bloodletter were mummers about to perform. Saraid's brothers shifted uncomfortably, glancing around with suspicion.

Cathán pulled back the curtain with great flourish and a smile that turned her blood to icy water. Beside her, the Blood-letter sucked in a surprised breath.

Behind the curtain was a wooden bed with leather stretched over the frame. It held a mattress that looked soft enough to be down with a bright crimson blanket topping it. There was a table in the corner with two cups and a jug. A tapestry hung on one wall and a banner with Cathán's spiraled insignia hung on another. There was nothing else in the room.

"What is this—" Tiarnan said angrily.

"There'll be no talk later that this is not a real marriage,"

Cathán told them all, his voice booming with authority. He turned that raw anger and power on Saraid. Putting a finger beneath her chin, he tilted her head until she was forced to look at him. "You understand, Saraid of the Favored Lands? You will do your wifely duty and get yourself with child by my son. The sooner, the better."

The threat had no veil or disguise.

"And you," he said to the Bloodletter, "will do as you're told. You'll fuck the girl and do it prompt."

A dark red flush crept up the Bloodletter's face, but he gave a quick, jerky nod. Apparently satisfied, Cathán turned to the assembly and raised his hands, signaling silence. He spoke loudly, his words reaching every ear in the room.

"I'll have this wedding consummated now. There'll be no call that it's not legal later."

The Bloodletter cast a look at his father that spoke of a hatred deeper than the dark of the forest—as deep as her own, but Cathán Half-Beard did not even acknowledge the glare, which surely burned where it touched.

"Get to it," he said jovially. "I'll be expecting my grandson in nine months."

This brought laughter from the avid onlookers. Without a word, the Bloodletter urged her behind the curtain as best he could with their hands still bound together. Cathán followed them, pushing his face between them until his hot breath made Saraid want to fight her way free. He took Saraid's chin in a rough grip and twisted it until he was nose to nose with her. "I'll be back for the sheets, and do not think to fool me with fakery. I'll know if it's a woman's true blood."

Saraid stared back with cold eyes and said nothing, but her heart pounded against her ribs like a wounded bird in a cage. Could he really know a woman's virgin blood?

As soon as Cathán disappeared on the other side and drew the curtain shut, a raucous cheer went up from the men. No doubt he'd emerged with some crude and blatant gesture.

The Bloodletter cursed under his breath and struggled to free his hands from the knotted ribbon, but Cathán had tied it unusually tight. At last he used his teeth to loosen the knot. The feel of his lips against the sensitive underside of her wrists sent a tremble through her. Soon that mouth would be touching her in other places, those hands roaming at will.

How would she endure it?

Finally free, he stepped back, and so did she, their silence made louder by the ruckus on the other side of the curtain. Ruairi looked as if there might be something to say, but he did not speak. He appeared suddenly as young and as uncertain as she felt.

"I don't hear the sound of rutting," Cathán shouted. "Or do I need to show you how it's done?"

Bawdy laughter erupted from the room, and it was not just the men enjoying this bit of sport. Saraid felt strangely betrayed that the women had joined in.

"This is not our agreement," Tiarnan said angrily, his voice lifted to be heard above the commotion. "She's a king's daughter, a king's sister. She's a princess and she should be treated with respect, not like a cow yer going to milk."

"I think it will be her highness who is milking this eve," Cathán said. "And she better be at it quickly or I'll know why."

The words filled Saraid with a dread that went deeper than her soul. This was her fate. She'd known it, had accepted it. But she had not understood how it would feel to be standing on this cusp. A choice that was no choice, Colleen of the Ballagh had said, but it was only now, in this moment that Saraid fully understood.

The Bloodletter watched her warily, not daring to reach for her again. But soon he would, and she could do naught but let him.

The breath she released hurt as it burned its way from her lungs to her throat to the tight, sooty air around them. She looked down at the lacings on her dress and slowly began to untie them. Knowing modesty was a fool's luxury, she wished she could turn her back to him all the same. But he would see her bared soon enough, and she was determined to show no fear. Gently she tugged the lacings free, noting her trembling fingers as if they belonged to someone else. She bit down on her lip, cursing the weakness that held her in its grip. She was Saraid of the Favored Lands, Saraid, daughter of Bain. A chieftain's daughter and she would not shame herself. Not this day.

The lacings at last were free and with a feeling of surrendering a piece of herself that once lost could never be regained, she pulled her overdress off and stood in her thin white shift. Mustering her waning courage she lifted her gaze and stared defiantly into her husband's face, a man she hated with every part of her soul.

The Bloodletter said nothing, but he caught his breath—a quick, sharp sound that danced over Saraid's taut nerves. She shuddered, at once humiliated and strangely exhilarated by his light gaze stroking her body. It drifted from her eyes to her heaving chest, lingered on the shadow between her breasts, slid down to her ribs, brushed past her waist to settle at her hips and the shadowy outline of her legs.

Colleen of the Ballagh had said a man would come. A man in the guise of another. Saraid held tight to that thought, imagining him bursting through the long house doors, rescuing her from this fate. Was that why the old woman had appeared to her? To give Saraid heart at this time of darkness?

Praying it was so, Saraid vowed to keep fear and doubt from her heart. She would not give the Bloodletter that power. Still, her mouth was dry as she forced her shaky legs to the table, where she found wine in the jug and poured it. Her hand trembled so badly, she sloshed it as she lifted the cup and drained the bitter-sweet contents.

Behind her, the Bloodletter shifted suddenly, a restless noise that alarmed her. Had he removed his clothes? Would she find him stripped, engorged, and waiting to destroy any romantic illusions she might have? Well he would be disappointed, would he not? Because Saraid knew him to be a barbarian and she expected nothing less than agony and degradation at his hands.

As she turned, again something caught the corner of her eye. For an instant she thought once more there were two men waiting and her heart jumped in fear. But as she looked fully, there was only the Bloodletter looming large and fierce in the center of the room.

He had, indeed, removed some of his clothing. He stood stripped from the waist up, muscled and hard from the corded sinew of his neck to the solid strength of his broad shoulders.

A light dusting of golden hair covered the hard bulges of his chest, leading down over a rigid, flat abdomen before disappearing into his trews. His was the body of a warrior, honed like steel, rippling with strength. She'd never seen a Roman, but she imagined Ruairi the Bloodletter would have fit among their ranks.

A long, nasty scar rippled the flesh of his ribs. Another puckered like silk at his shoulder, battle wounds survived.

She shuddered, slopping more of the wine onto the thrushes covering the floor.

The Bloodletter took an aggressive step forward, purpose darkening his eyes as well as something else. Was it anger? She'd done nothing to incite it, but then the Bloodletter rarely required provocation for his cruelty. She'd seen it enough times.

He reached for her before she could move back, and she braced herself not to cringe, not to anger him beyond whatever rage it was she saw simmering in his eyes. He took her wine, drained the cup, then tossed it aside.

"Have y' bewitched me?" he demanded, his voice hoarse.

Saraid looked into his eyes and saw torment in them and a part of her swelled with the knowledge that she was not powerless after all. Let him think her a witch. Let him fear her magic.

"Aye, I have."

He jerked as if stung and took a staggering step back.

Cathán's voice boomed from the other side of the curtain, ridicule heavy in his tone. "'Tis much too quiet in there. Do you need me to warm her up, then? It would be a sacrifice to leave my good neighbors, but I'm willing to help if I must."

Though spoken lightly, Saraid knew it was the last warning they would get. The threat spurred her to action and she advanced, taking the Bloodletter's face in her hands, becoming the provoker herself, stunning him as she pressed her mouth to his before he could guess what she intended. The shock of his lips against her own nearly turned her to stone, but if she did not consummate with the Bloodletter, she had no illusions that Cathán Half-Beard would restrain himself from finishing the deed.

She moved her hands from his face to his hair, surprised by the soft feel of it against her fingers. It seemed everything about this man should be hard, and the silky strands were a contradiction that shook her. His neck was solid with muscle, the skin cool and smooth to the heat of her touch, but she was not fooled. There was nothing about Ruairi the Bloodletter that did not burn.

As if of their own volition, his hands circled her waist, their span nearly wide enough to meet thumb to finger. She drew him forward, feeling his shock, his resistance, his defeat. Even as he made to pull away, his hands were sliding down the slope of her spine in a warm and possessive stroke. Her legs bumped the bed and then they were both falling onto it, and once again she thought she saw two men where there was only one. But her sharp gasp was quelled by his heavy weight bearing her down into the soft ticking. There was only the Bloodletter crushing her beneath him.

She wanted to shift, to put some space between them, though she knew it was pointless. There was not time when at any moment Cathán might barge past the curtain and demand his chance. Perhaps that was Cathán's motive for taunting them—for certainly he had one. Pressure them with his mockery . . . intimidate his son to the point where he could not perform his husband's duties . . . or did he hope Saraid would deny the Bloodletter his conjugal rights because of the crude circumstances? For all his jibes to the contrary, did he want the union to be declared unlawful because she refused to bed her husband?

The outcome would be severe if he could prove such a thing. Women had power by their own rights, but a husband or wife who refused to couple with their partner was scorned by both Christian and pagan laws. How else would children be conceived? It was a sin to deny the act.

And how better to prove that this crime had been committed than with an audience eagerly awaiting the outcome? Cathán would cry foul, claim his offer of peace had been rejected along with his son, and the people would believe him. They would not stand in the way when he moved again to destroy them.

The Bloodletter shifted his weight, and she took a deep and grateful gulp of air. He propped an arm on either side of her and rose up to look into her face. The muscles of his arms and shoulders bunched with strength and suppressed power. She lowered her lashes so he wouldn't see into her eyes, but he took his weight on his elbows and cupped her face in his palms, forcing her to meet his steady gaze. She saw what she expected in the glittering blue. Cruelty, rage, simmering resentment that he could barely contain.

But his hands gentled even as his eyes did not, and his fingers moved softly over her cheek and down to her throat. She sensed warring desires within him—one wanted to hurt her, the other to caress. His touch was tender, but beneath it was a violence she could taste.

He made a deep sound—not a growl, not a moan, but something of each—and his mouth followed his stroking fingers. He'd confused her and now she lay trapped in the snarl of his conflict. He touched her as if he'd waited his whole life to feel the softness of her skin, as if he hated her for the weakness it showed in him. Not for the first time since she'd looked upon his face this day, she had a feeling of duality. There were two men behind those blue, blue eyes, unaware of each other. She felt them converge with each caress, and the feeling went beyond superstition, beyond fear, and beyond comprehension.

He didn't ask questions, didn't hesitate. His fingers were in her hair, pulling it free from the braids, scattering flowers around them. Stroking it, fanning it like a halo. Then he was wrapping it around his hand, holding her captive as he covered her mouth with his own. His kiss was fierce, consuming. He used teeth and tongue, wielding intimacy like he would a weapon. There was no resisting; there was no surrender.

And beneath the onslaught she felt that yearning again, that need that he emitted like the hum of a bee. It lodged within her, finding some piece of herself that understood it when the rest of her could not. It caressed and coaxed and lured her to respond.

Her fingers spread against his back, her legs twining with his as she moved without thought, tempering his assault. His lips softened, enticed where they had punished. He kissed and nibbled, teasing her with his tongue until she opened for him, laying herself bare to his gentle onslaught. His hands moved over her as if he knew exactly where to touch, how to touch. As if he'd lain with her a hundred times before. His fingers were beneath her shift, inching it up until he pulled it over her head, leaving her stripped and vulnerable. Quickly he shed the remainder of his own clothing and then pressed his body to hers.

She made a soft sound in her throat that embarrassed her, but it came unbidden and unstoppable. They lay chest to chest, her belly flat against the hardened slope of his, his hips falling between her legs, making her want to lift them and wrap them around him, making her want to shift and wiggle and open her thighs as she had her lips. She'd prepared herself for violence and degradation. This seduction disarmed her completely.

She pulled back and stared into his face, and once again there was the shadow of another in his eyes, and suddenly Colleen's words took on a new meaning.

He comes in the guise of another. . . .

Who are you? she thought, for surely what she saw in his eyes could not be Ruairi the Bloodletter's soul.

He shifted, moving his mouth down her throat to her breasts, dragging his fingertips gently over her ribs, past the softness of her belly to touch her with bold and demanding strokes. He found her wet and ready and pulled back to look into her eyes with something akin to pride. She was scared and trembling and furious and wanting.

"Who are y'?" he whispered the question she'd not had the courage to ask him herself.

Was it she who'd been bewitched?

"I am yer wife," she said, and the words seemed to fill the oily smoke in the air.

The simple truth started a war behind the Bloodletter's eyes, a host of contradictory reactions. He gripped her face, all tenderness gone. He could snap her neck without any effort and the both of them knew it.

He drove into her then, without warning, without care. With brutal force, he pushed himself deep inside her. She threw back her head and let loose a sharp cry at the invasion, at the betrayal of the harsh violation. Her eyes filled with tears she could not control.

He stilled as the sound of her pain washed over him. Buried deep within her, he hung his head so she could not see his face.

"I did not mean . . ." he whispered.

What he did not mean was unclear. But again, his touch was gentle, apologetic as he brushed his lips against the hammering pulse at her throat.

Gooseflesh broke out on his shoulders and arms as he held himself motionless in the strange union of tenderness and cruelty. He looked at her then, pulling her into the swirling color of his eyes like a bird to the sky.

"God's blood," he groaned, dropping his chin as he sucked in a shaky breath. Her own chest heaved with the effort to breathe as slowly her muscles expanded to accommodate him, this foreigner, this pillaging warrior.

Carefully, little by little, he began to move. He eased his hips forward, watching her for a sign to stop, to go, to give, to take. How she knew was a mystery, but somehow in this strange act they'd reached an understanding. He felt enormous, alien, and yet fitted in a way that mystified her.

She held his gaze as he pushed in and out of her, seeding a bond she neither understood nor accepted. She could no more fight it than ignore it. She felt his tension increase and an answering tightness in herself and then he shifted, bringing a hand down between them to stroke her as he slid in and out. It felt like something inside her exploded, something bright and hard and glittering. And then he was tensing and driving into her and she heard him make a sound so deep in his chest that it felt like it came from his very soul. He buried his face in her shoulder, his breath a burst of warm air, his scent, hot and clean, enveloping her.

Slowly he relaxed his grip on her, easing back to stare into her eyes. There was grim satisfaction in his face and something else behind it that she could not interpret. But there was no time for that, because as he stilled, propped up above her, a sudden movement came from behind the huge crest that covered the wall opposite the bed.

As she looked, her emotions a bewildering infusion of

admiration and abhorrence, she saw the blur become a solid form in the gray room. She hadn't the time to even understand what she saw before a man with a mask over his features and a long wicked blade in his hands leapt straight at them.

Chapter Thirteen

RORY was in sensory overload. There was the vertigo that came from being forged to his twin by the heat of the woman's body beneath them. The wild frustration of feeling that layer separating him from her flesh when he was desperate to experience every part of her. The bizarre sense of sharing his thoughts and his feelings with the stranger-twin, coupled with intense awareness of being in a place and time that were both intangible and unreal. Each sensation, each friction-filled movement came to him from a maddening distance he could not overcome.

He looked into the woman's face—they called her Saraid—wanting to express something—anything—of the chaotic emotions inside him. She stared back at him, confused no doubt by his bipolar behavior. Still she looked as if she wanted nothing more than to hear what he had to say.

Then a sound distracted her, and a flash of color caught the corner of his eye. The twin inside him bounded from the bed before Rory could even look twice.

A man emerged from an alcove that had been hidden by a huge tapestry. He hovered at the end of the crude bed, a scarf tied over the lower half of his face like a bandit out of a western. Above it, muddy eyes scanned the room before settling on Rory and watching warily.

It was the man from the dreams. : . .

On the tail of that recognition came the lash of what his appearance might mean. In the dreams, this man killed Rory's twin. And right now, that twin was beneath Rory's skin or perhaps it was the other way around. He wasn't certain. But clearly the twin and Rory shared a body, and if this man succeeded in killing that body, what then would happen to Rory? Would he awake as he always did, at home in front of the flashing TV, disoriented and freaked out but otherwise whole? Or would he return to that naked, floating nonexistence that had greeted him when he'd followed Saraid to whatever place and time this was?

Or would he simply die as his twin did?

The man glanced from Rory to Saraid and back. She sat on the bed with the blanket pulled up over her bare breasts. Her eyes were wide with fear and something else. It took an instant to understand. Saraid knew this intruder.

"What is it you're thinking, Stephen?" Rory heard himself ask in the archaic language his father and the others used. "You mean to kill me, is that it?"

"And aren't y' the fool for not seeing it coming?" Stephen sneered, though there was bluster in his tone that his tough guy act couldn't quite conceal. So he was afraid of Rory's twin. He should be. Rory could feel the tension coiling inside his twin, the aggression that threatened to explode any minute. The body they shared was every bit as big and as cut as the one Rory had left back in the cavern beneath the castle—if, in fact, that's where it was. . . .

From beyond the curtain wall, a loud cheer went up followed by laughter and applause. Then the sound of lively music began, and it seemed everyone started to sing along.

"What is it y' think my father will do with y' once this business here is over?" the twin's words rumbled from Rory's lips.

The shock of what he'd said hit Rory hard. *His father? Cathán?*

It made him dizzy, this feeling of being plural. This sense of another inside him—of being inside another. He wondered for a moment if the twin was feeling it, too. Did he sense Rory moving beneath his skin?

"What did my father tell y'?" his twin went on.

"He's my father, too," the man called Stephen said angrily. "And he loves y' just as well as he loves me, I'm sure."

Those words hovered between them, and Rory could see this Stephen guy making connections that he hadn't linked up to that point. But Rory still wasn't clear how going from point A to B suddenly led to his father. Did Cathán know this Stephen planned to kill Rory?

No. He couldn't.

His twin took a deep breath and smiled. Yet the tension in his body ratcheted up a notch. When he spoke, his tone was hard and derisive. "Are y' thinking ye'll find a reward waiting for y' when I'm dead?"

Stephen's chin rose, and Rory knew that was exactly what the younger man thought.

"Surely y' can't be such an idiot to think that is how it will be. He's betrayed one son, has he not? What would stop him from turning on another?"

Stephen's face grew red above his mask, and before Rory could fully process the words that had come from his own lips, Stephen lunged. He thrust out with the glinting blade. Rory hadn't expected it, but his twin had. He jumped to the side so quickly, Rory was only aware that they'd moved after it happened. In the next instant, Rory's twin charged the masked man, catching his blade hand by the wrist and spinning to slam an elbow hard into Stephen's spine, splaying him on the floor.

Saraid gave a choked gasp that distracted Rory for an instant. He looked up to find she'd moved from the bed, red blanket tucked around her, and stood watching a few feet away.

"Careful," she breathed, and Rory turned again to find Stephen scrambling to his feet, sword still clutched in front of him. Stephen jabbed, anticipating Rory's evasion this time. He wasn't graceful, but he was deadly accurate. The blade connected, and a lancing pain seared from Rory's hip to his gut and the hot spill of blood ran down his naked legs. The cut was deep. Rory didn't have to look to know.

His vision blurred for a moment and his head felt light and heavy at once. Suddenly what had seemed a vivid fantasy, a 3-D illusion that he would eventually emerge from, became real. Very real. And the idea that he might die here hit him like a hammer swung fast and hard.

This was not good.

His twin's reflexes slowed and his movements became sluggish. Rory felt his twin's grip on consciousness dwindle, his control over the body they shared slip. Panic caught Rory in a scorching rush.

So not good.

Come on, he silently coaxed. *Get a grip. Fight.*

But the twin was faltering, and Rory realized he was on his own. He took a deep breath, braced himself. And then, without even knowing how he did it, Rory took over.

He'd been caught off guard, off-kilter in a world he didn't know, but Rory was no pansy. He may not know swordplay and fancy footwork, but he'd fought for his life enough to know how to scrap.

The pain in Rory's side felt like someone had crammed a burning torch into his gut, but that feeling of distance that had frustrated him while he'd held Saraid in his arms now came in handy. If he could just put that same distance around the fear that his life was draining onto the straw-covered floor, he'd be good to go.

Stephen crouched low, weapon ready, circling Rory as he looked for an opening.

"Not going to happen, buddy boy," Rory muttered as he weighed his options. Stephen looked at him sharply and with a glimmer of fear. Rory realized he'd spoken English, a language Stephen obviously didn't understand. It had broken the other man's concentration.

Rory flashed a smile. "Bugs you, doesn't it, not knowing what I'm saying." He stepped forward, and Stephen scuttled back a hasty step. "I could be telling you exactly what I'm going to do." He lurched again, his grin cold as he watched Stephen's defensive retreat. "Like I'm going to take that knife and shove it up your ass. I could even tell you how I'm going to do it, and you'd still be staring at me with that same stupid look on your face, wouldn't you?"

Stephen responded by doing just that, and Rory laughed, liking how Stephen's eyes went wide with dread. He glanced quickly at Saraid, as if to ask, "What the fuck?" but Saraid didn't have a clue what Rory said, either. While the two shared their bafflement, Rory went for Stephen's feet, swiping them out from under him with a low kick that had Stephen on his ass before he knew what hit him.

"Whoops," Rory said.

Stephen scurried back like a crab as Rory bounced on the balls of his feet, arms loose and cocked. He kicked the sword away, and it slid across the floor to where Saraid stood. She picked it up without hesitation.

"Good girl," he said, then repeated it in her own language like he'd been speaking it his whole life. He didn't know how, he just did. Her gaze was startled, but her hand steady as she held the weapon.

Rory turned back to Stephen. "Okay dickhead, whatcha gonna do now?"

Stephen raised his hands in surrender—a fake that Rory didn't fall for. "Try again, asshole."

Stephen did, springing up and away with speed Rory wouldn't have given him credit for. He pulled another blade at the same time, this knife smaller and tucked in his boot. When he charged, Rory braced and curled, protecting vital parts as he hurled himself forward to meet the attack. But Stephen went past him, catching Saraid unprepared and knocking the sword across the room. With a brutal twist, he wrenched her arm behind her and held it pinned while he laid his blade to her throat.

Rory stared for a shocked moment, stunned by Stephen's precision and speed. He'd underestimated the man. He wouldn't make that mistake again.

"Let her go," he said in Stephen's language.

"I don't think so, Bloodletter. I think I'll just hold on to the lass until y' drop dead. It shouldn't take long now."

His words drew attention back to the pain throbbing and burning in Rory's side, compelling him to look at what he didn't want to see. Blood spilled from the grisly wound at an alarming speed.

"It's beyond me how yer still standing," Stephen said with a complacent smile.

As if the words were blades themselves, the pain swelled, penetrating that distance that had cocooned him. Seeing it had made it all the worse. All the more real. Christ, even if there was an ER around the corner, a wound like that . . .

Rory swayed on his feet, sudden sweat stinging his eyes, blurring his vision.

"It won't be long now, will it?" Stephen said, twisting Saraid's arm higher on her back, making her yelp with pain. He pressed his lips to the skin behind Saraid's ear. "I think I'll share yer rewards before I tell Father the deed is done, though." With a hard smile, he bent and nibbled at the silky skin of her shoulder.

And made his first deadly mistake.

Saraid bucked her body away and the knife slipped, leaving a thin red line on the pale column of her throat. As if in slow motion, Rory watched a scarlet droplet fall from the shallow cut onto the dusky skin of her chest.

The rage that came over him was instantaneous—hot and red and all-consuming. He could feel his twin rousing inside him, a sleeping dragon who raised cold eyes and snorted a breath of fire. Together, they fought back the dizziness, the sweat of death, the taint of weakness. And before Stephen had a clue that his last breath was about to be drawn, they charged.

Rory grabbed Stephen's blade with a bare hand, oblivious to the edge that lacerated his fingers as his pulled it away from Saraid's throat. Given that inch to breathe, she dropped to her knees and out of Stephen's grasp in a graceful move Rory had only a split second to admire. Still fueled by the fury within himself, within his twin, he tossed the knife aside and grabbed Stephen's head between his hands, crushing his skull and grinding his eyes into the sockets with his thumbs.

Stephen's scream was muffled by the merry shouts and singing booming from the other side of the curtain. He tried to pry Rory's hands free of his head, but Rory and his twin were too strong and too far gone. Stephen's eyes bulged and then popped like grapes, leaving a hot ooze that made Rory's stomach roll even as something dark and barbaric inside him howled with joy.

No longer sure if the chaotic rage fired from his own synapses or from his twin's, no longer certain where one ended and the other began, Rory spun Stephen's unresisting body, locked his fingers around Stephen's throat and squeezed with all his strength, all his wrath.

Blood streamed down Stephen's face, and he made a gurgling sound that finally penetrated the fog of rage consuming Rory. For a moment, one simple sane thought emerged.

I am not a killer.

But it was too late. Stephen's Adam's apple collapsed with a grotesque sound and a last hopeless gasp escaped him.

Horrified, exulted, Rory staggered back and let the corpse fall to the ground. He heard Saraid catch her breath as she stumbled forward, turned, expecting to see her disgust and loathing at what he'd done, but she spared not a glance at the dead man. Her attention was on Rory, and he had a moment to revel in the fear on her face—fear for him, not of him. Then he collapsed to his knees, hands gripping the wound on his side.

Pain defined the moment. It seared and twisted until blackness swam behind his eyes and death seemed like a blessing. Whatever barrier had existed between himself and the twin was gone, and he experienced the full brunt of agony. And then suddenly Rory was free of his twin, free of the anguish, standing once more beside him, naked and invisible, watching as the blood poured from his body.

Saraid reached out to Rory's twin but there was nothing she could do. The blood gushed, staining the straw strewn over the floor, pooling beneath it. Rory could see gore in the gaping wound.

Saraid snatched Rory's cloak from where he'd dropped it and struggled to staunch the flow. Blood smeared her body as she tried futilely to hold back the deluge of his twin's life.

"Do something," Rory said, pacing around the two.

"I cannot make it stop," she answered. For a moment he thought it was in response to his demand, but she remained blithely unaware of his presence.

His twin was dying, right here, right now, and there wasn't a damn thing he could do about it.

And where would that leave Rory?

"This can't be happening," he said.

Saraid faltered, and he thought once more that she'd heard him.

"Did you?" he said, kneeling beside her. "Can you hear me?"

But again she wasn't listening to him. She was staring at

his twin as his skin turned ashen and the once-invincible body withered with weakness.

Rory's twin lifted a bloody hand and brushed back a stray wisp of Saraid's hair. All around him, the rage that had sustained the battle with Stephen still hovered and sparked in the air, diluted now by the excruciating pain that lingered in Rory's memory though not in his now-invisible body. But there was something else in that look, and Saraid seemed to realize it. He saw some shift in her thinking, some acknowledgment he didn't understand.

"He's betrayed us both, hasn't he?" she whispered.

Rory's twin closed his eyes and nodded once.

"Who's betrayed us?" Rory asked. *His father?* He didn't want to believe it, but he'd be a fool if he chose to be blind to the facts. The man in the banquet hall looked like his father, went by his father's name, but he wasn't the same man Rory remembered. Could he, like Rory, be existing in a twin? The idea was so abstract that even after experiencing the phenomenon himself, Rory could not wrap his mind around it.

"Y' must go," the twin said, his voice no more than a breath in the stillness.

"Go? Where can I go that Cathán will not find me?"

The confirmation that whether true or false, these two believed Rory's father had planned the attack filled Rory with pained bewilderment. *Why?* How had his father become the kind of man who would plot the murder of his own son? And why today, his wedding day?

In this world his father wasn't the nicest guy, but he wanted this marriage. He wanted Saraid pregnant for reasons Rory still didn't know. He didn't want her dead. He didn't want his own son dead . . . did he?

Rory moved to the curtain and peered through the gap where it met the wall. On the other side, musicians played a loud and jaunty tune. Tables had been pushed back, and dancers circled in the clearing. Against the far side of the room by the door, Saraid's brothers stood alert and watchful, troubled eyes moving from gathering to curtain. Cathán's men were three deep everywhere he looked. Their mass and power on grim display around Saraid's brothers.

"He means to use y', Saraid. Do not let him," Rory's twin

was saying, his breath coming in a wet rattle of agonized breath. "Go, now."

It was sound advice, but Rory knew without being told that she wouldn't leave her brothers out there, surrounded by the enemy. With one last glance at the three of them, Rory came back to her side and knelt down.

"You should listen to him, princess," Rory said. "It's going to get ugly." He looked at the bloodied version of himself on the floor. "Uglier."

But she didn't hear him. Of course she didn't.

"He wants the Book from y'," his twin was saying. "Do not give it to him. It is all that keeps y' alive."

Rory snapped his gaze to Saraid's face, shocked by the words his dying twin had spoken. "You've got the Book of Fennore?" he demanded, thinking back to the dreams he'd had of Saraid and the Book. Suddenly it made sense. Nana had sent him here for the Book, using this woman, Saraid, as bait. All he had to do was get her to give it to him and then he could go home. "Where is it, Saraid? Where is the Book of Fennore?"

His twin's eyes had shut, and Rory waited, fearing the next rattling breath would be his last, trying to ignore the insistent question in his head—what happened to Rory when the twin died?

Then suddenly his twin's eyes snapped open and he slowly turned his head. For an instant Rory thought he might be seeing angels coming to take him—or the devil more likely, coming to bring him home to the fire and brimstone that had spewed him into the world. But then his eyes seemed to focus, and Rory realized with a chilling certainty that his twin was looking at him.

His twin's expression changed from horror and fear to utter surprise and then . . . relief. Frowning, the woman followed his seeking gaze with her own, her face paling, her breath coming in soft, frightened gasps. Every hair on Rory's body stood on end.

"You see me. . . ."

Rory held his breath as it seemed she stared right at him. He looked down, the feeling of being invisible—though he couldn't even say just *what* that feeling was—had waned. There were his hands, resting on his knees as he knelt beside his dying twin. Solid. He was naked, stripped down to flesh and bone. Only the pendant hanging on his chest.

He lifted his hands and saw there was blood on them. Whose blood, he didn't know.

Into the silence came a new sound, a humming deep and insidious emanating from all around them. He recognized it, the feel of it worming its way under his skin, pulsing at his ears, thrumming through his heart. The Book of Fennore. Only the Book of Fennore made that kind of rumble, that earthquaking tremble of heart and soul. Where was it?

He'd barely thought the question when he saw his twin holding the Book in his bloody hands. *How? Where had it come from?* The question was mirrored on his twin's face and on the woman's. The three of them stared at it in shock, while that drone became a sickening disease that tainted the air. The black-covered Book gleamed in the flickering light, beveled leather writhing with concentric spirals and crusted jewels. The gold and hammered silver glowed with an eerie light at the edges and corners, all leading to the three strands of silver woven into a lock that held prisoner the rough-edged parchment inside the covers.

Rory reached out as if to touch the Book, but his twin pushed his hand away. "It lies," he rasped. "It lies."

What that meant, Rory didn't know. His twin now pointed to the pendant hanging from Rory's neck, swinging back and forth above the leather Book, its intricate pattern a perfect match for the mystifying lock. "Keep it always, wear it always. Do not let him have it. Ever."

Then the Book fell to silence and vanished as quickly and ominously as it had appeared. The three remained motionless, staring at the place it had been, doubting that they'd seen it. In the next instant the air seemed to shift and become gritty, like sandpaper, and now his twin began to fade—there was no other word for it. In the same way Rory had become substance, his twin began to crumble, layers blowing away and taking with them years until a boy stood where his twin had slumped.

Stunned, Rory stared at the child while his mind whirled through possible explanations and found none that made sense. The boy stared at him and Rory couldn't help the feelings washing over him. Once again, he looked into his own eyes. This was Rory. Rory as he'd been twenty-five years ago, that night in the castle ruins when his father had disappeared.

Saraid was making a small hiccupping sound as she stared, and he knew without a doubt she saw the boy, too. Knew she'd seen the unbelievable transformation of his twin to this child, but could not begin to understand what she'd witnessed. From the gritty air there came a voice, calling out Rory's name. As he had at the airport terminal just the day before, Rory recognized who spoke. It was his sister, Danni, calling him home. The boy turned away and in a blur of color and motion, he was gone.

"Fuck me," Rory breathed.

On the wall behind Saraid a candle guttered and smoked. The slight hissing sound it made seemed unnaturally loud in the sudden silence. Slowly she lifted her eyes and stared into his.

"You *can* see me now, can't you?" he asked and then said it again in her language.

She stared at him, her eyes wide and shocked, her gaze traveling slowly over his features, erasing any doubt that he was still invisible. She saw him. That was good. But there was terror in her expression, panic that seemed to swallow her whole. That was not good.

"Hey," he said, gently touching her hand. "Breathe, princess, breathe."

She did as he told her and took a great, gasping breath.

"That's it," he said, watching the color return to her face. She was shaking from head to toe. Not surprising—so was he.

She gulped another breath and said, as if reciting some memorized script, "A man will come. A man in the guise of another."

He didn't know what to say to that, but she seemed to expect a response. Mutely he shook his head. Her dark gaze raked his features.

"It is y' she foretold. It was always y'."

The baffling statement came with a tone of accusation and another expectant stare that made him feel stupid and hopelessly inadequate.

"What are you talking about?" he said. "*Who* are you talking about?"

"Colleen. Colleen of the Ballagh."

Colleen of the Ballagh.

The name pushed him back and he sat hard, the stone floor jarring his bones, the straw scratching against his bare skin. He stared at the woman, remembering Nana's words as she'd sat in his Camaro. She'd said Rory wasn't the only one she had to visit that night. Had she come here as well? To the woman from his dreams?

"Colleen Ballagh told you I was coming?" he repeated slowly.

Saraid nodded. Then she lifted her hand as she'd done so many times in his dream and reached out, touched him. Her fingers were icy against his chest. It made his heart stutter, that frozen contact.

"Colleen of the Ballagh told me y' would come to save us."

Chapter Fourteen

SARAID stared at her splayed fingers, feeling that the freezing hand must surely belong to someone else. Not her. Not Saraid. Yet she could feel the coldness of it pressed against the burning heat of the Bloodletter's chest. Feel the fierce pounding of his heart beneath her palm. She was numb and raw at the same time. Her mind felt dull, and yet every pore of her skin was sensitive to the slightest shift in the air. The draft coming from beyond the curtain chilled like a blustering wind. The voices in that other room boomed loud and jarring. How could they still be laughing? Playing music and dancing? How could they not know what Saraid had witnessed? The impossibility of it felt as enormous as the sky, the sea, the very earth beneath her.

It is you she foretold. It was always you.

Saraid had spoken the words before she'd even realized their truth.

But somehow her eyes and her mouth had accepted what her mind still rejected. This man staring at her from behind the Bloodletter's blue gaze had changed—pulled himself in two and . . . and . . .

She moved her icy fingers, trailing them over the heated muscle to the rippled pucker of a scar just over his heart. Slowly she traced the outline while he remained perfectly still, barely breathing. Watching her with the same shock she felt inside.

The scar was as big as her hand, spread wide over it. It was shaped in three continuous spirals that had no beginning, no ending. She knew them, recognized the symbol from the ancient stones at Tara, from the countless mounds and dolmens scattered throughout Éire. It was the triple spiral that represented life, death, and rebirth. The same symbol that she'd just seen locking what could only be the Book of Fennore. The spirals had been burned into this man's flesh so long ago that the skin was now white and silky. But the scar hadn't been there before, when he'd stripped his clothes. When he'd taken her on the bed.

She might have overlooked it—doubtful as it was—but even if that was the case, she knew that such a symbol would have been noticed before. Stories would have circulated about the warrior marked by the mystical Book of Fennore. Legends would have been told. Songs written and sung for the tribal kings and their people. It would have been known by all. And yet not once had she heard even a whispered word about it. Not once.

Slowly, she raised her gaze to his face, watched emotion play over his features, tried to understand what went on behind those bottomless blue eyes. What was he thinking?

It is you she foretold. It was always you.

They were her own words, but could they possibly be true? Was Ruairi the man Colleen had prophesized? Saraid had seen him dying on the rushes, she'd seen him fade into a boy and answer the voice of the goddess who called him home. Yet here he was, kneeling next to her. Strong and whole. Had he been thrown back from the Otherworld? Rejected by the gods and goddesses? Or could it be that what she'd just beheld—Ruairi, pulling himself in two—was what Colleen had meant when she'd said he would come in the guise of another?

He'd recognized the dead woman's name, Colleen of the Ballagh. There was no mistaking that. But beneath his reaction, she saw misgiving and distrust. No longer did she have the sense of another within him, but no longer was she sure who this man was at all.

He made a sound that might have been anger or might have

been fear. Could he be as frightened as she by what had just happened? Or was that simply some wishful part of herself trying to make him more human than the Bloodletter could ever be?

But he wasn't the Bloodletter anymore . . . was he?

The question crystallized like a sharp icicle in her mind. It pierced the fog surrounding her thoughts and sent her scurrying backward, finally breaking the contact of her hand on his chest. She gulped a huge breath and let it out with a shudder.

As if her withdrawal had released him from his own inertia, he stood suddenly and paced a few steps away. "Nan— Colleen," he corrected himself. "She was here? She told you I was coming? Here?" He said it as if of everything else that had happened, this event was the strangest.

Saraid scrambled to her feet and nodded.

"Well where the hell *is* here? Where am I?"

The question shot a flame of alarm through her body. How could he not know where he was? And what had made him so suddenly angry? He reached for the fur cape she'd used to staunch his twin's blood and laid it over Stephen's dead body before facing her again. His brows rose as he waited for her to answer his question.

Feeling foolish, she chose her words carefully, "We are in the Favored Lands. At least that is what this place was once called. Now it is part of the Dark Forest, part of Cathán Half-Beard's kingdom."

"Kingdom," he repeated. "My father has a kingdom?"

"Yes," she said, and her voice tightened with anger. "A kingdom built on a river of blood. A kingdom he conquered with his son, Ruairi the Bloodletter. That would be *you*, in case y' were thinking to pretend y' didn't know that already."

He blanched and pushed agitated fingers through his soft golden hair. Again, his reaction made no sense. Nothing about him did.

Saraid shifted her eyes and watched him warily. He was built like a god, hewn from hard muscle, sinew, flesh, and bone that bulged and tapered as a man should but rarely did. He was the Bloodletter in every way. Yet, he was not. It was there in his troubled eyes, in the revealing vulnerability of his mouth. Her gaze moved to the wound on his side, which was barely a scratch now. As if the blade had cut through a shielding layer before it nicked his skin.

And there was the pendant, hanging on a leather cord from his neck, power pulsing off it that she could feel, though he seemed oblivious. Where had it come from? Like the scar on his chest, she knew he'd not been wearing it while he'd lain with her on the bed, pounding heart pressed against pounding heart. She flushed, remembering the intimacy they'd shared, the way he'd made her feel passion when she'd been so determined to feel nothing but contempt. That alone was more convincing than all the other signs.

"You said Colleen told you I would come to save you. . . ." He spun and faced her. "Save you from what?"

For a moment, she couldn't think, couldn't understand what he asked. And then she remembered her own words, the sound of her voice as it hung in the sudden quiet.

Colleen of the Ballagh told me you would come to save us. . . .

It wasn't exactly what she'd said. Colleen had said he had the power to save her people, not that he would necessarily use it for that purpose. She'd said he was looking for the Book of Fennore, and if he found it, he would darken the skies. She'd said Saraid must bewitch him. Beguile him. Do whatever she must to keep him from finding it.

But she had not said he would help her.

"Save you from what?" he repeated, letting the sentence fall short, underscoring the doubt Saraid could hear in his voice.

"Save *us*," she clarified, compounding her lie with another. "My people. She said y' would come and save my people."

He shook his head, gave a soft bark of laughter that held no humor, and then looked at her again. She could see the battle going on behind his eyes to look stern, but there it was again, that vulnerability that was so at odds with the familiar face he wore.

"And just when did she tell you this?"

"Three nights past," Saraid answered with a shaky exhalation. That much was the truth.

"Three nights? What would you say if I told you Colleen died five days ago?"

She raised her chin and gave him a hard stare. "I would say she looked very good, if that is the case."

He paled at that, and she had a moment of satisfaction, but it only lasted until his next words.

"Okay, I'll give you that one. A little thing like being dead wouldn't stand in her way if she wanted to talk to you anyway. So what am I supposed to save your people from? The end of the world? The great flood? Maybe I'm supposed to part the seas and usher all of you to the Promised Land?"

Perhaps it was the sarcasm that even his strange accent could not conceal or perhaps it was simply her own dread snaking through her heart, coiling around her chest until she felt she couldn't breathe. Whatever the cause, Saraid had had enough. He wasn't the only one to have his world turned on end. He wasn't the only one to be afraid.

Anger made her jaw tight and her blood hot. "Save them from the murdering lust of y' and yer barbarous father, as y' well know."

Again she saw that queer mixture of distrust and fear shift through his eyes. In the great hall, the music rose to a booming crescendo. The Bloodletter froze for a moment and both of them stared at the curtain until another song began on the trailing notes of the last.

He took a deep breath and let it out. "Listen, if you say Colleen was here, then she was here. But if she said that I was coming to save you, she was spiking your punch, princess. I don't know what the hell I'm doing here. I don't even know where here *is*. But I can pretty much guarantee that it's not to help you or your people. Sorry. I'm not that guy."

She stared at him like he'd sprouted another head—which still wouldn't have been as strange as what he *had* done.

Was she a fool to think what she'd seen made him the man Colleen prophesized? Whatever had happened in this room, it could all be a part of some bigger plan Cathán had devised. Perhaps it was all an illusion—even Stephen's dead body lying on the floor beneath Ruairi's cape. Cathán was a worshipper of the Christ God, one who scorned the old ways, the Druid ways. But he would not be the first to proclaim one faith and exploit another to his own advantage. Only someone with mystical powers could make it seem that one man had become two. Could Cathán have found someone who possessed such capabilities?

Ruairi snapped his fingers in front of her face. "Earth to Saraid. That's your name, right?"

"How can y' pretend not to know my name?"

He flushed at that and shot a quick glance at the bed, and she saw a reflection of her own surprised wonder that two strangers had shared something so . . . incredible.

He paced a few steps away and then turned to face her once more. "I'm sorry. I know this isn't going to make a damn bit of sense, but I don't know who the hell you are. I don't even know how I got here."

"Y' walked," she said, lifting her chin. "Beside me. Our hands were bound."

"Yeah, I got that much. But I don't know why . . . before that I . . ."

He shook his head with frustration, those blue eyes wide and bewildered. For a moment, she almost wanted to aid him, might have if she wasn't feeling so lost and helpless herself. He let out a deep breath and raked his hair with his fingers again. Watching him with all the trust she might give a loosely tethered bear, she kept her tongue and waited.

"I'm not who you think I am," he said at last.

She knew that to be true, but she said, "And who are y' then if not Ruairi the Bloodletter?"

Though she'd meant for her tone to ring with scorn, something inside her cracked and her voice wobbled, revealing more than she wanted. He heard it, that weak flutter, saw it in her eyes . . . the same scared child that seemed to lurk in his. He lifted a hand, let his knuckles gently brush her cheek, and for an instant, she wanted to turn into the warmth of that caress. Stunned at her own thoughts, she quickly looked away.

He paused and she felt his gaze searching her face, but she wouldn't—couldn't look up.

"I woke up this morning and went to my grandmother's funeral," he said at last.

That did get attention and drew her startled gaze to his. "Y' lie."

"No, I swear it. My grandmother was Colleen Ballagh, and we buried her today."

Colleen of the Ballagh. Saraid narrowed her eyes and waited for him to continue.

"In the middle of the funeral, I saw you."

"Me? I witnessed no funeral."

"I followed you," he went on as if she hadn't spoken. "Into a cavern beneath my sister's . . . house. It's a castle really."

If she hadn't seen him split into two men, seen him become a child and then disappear at the same time he became a new man at her side—if she hadn't seen the unbelievable, she might think it was madness that afflicted this man. But she had seen it. No matter that it was impossible, *she had seen exactly that.* And as crazy as he sounded, she felt that he spoke the truth.

"Come closer to the light," she said, managing to make her voice commanding, though her knees shook and inside she was quaking. Could it be true? Had he seen a vision of Saraid?

He resisted, but only for a moment before moving to stand before her. The light cast by the flames seated in sconces about the room flickered shadow and illumination on his features in alternating patterns. He was still naked, unabashed as he stood before her a mighty warrior. But now that the immediate danger had passed, there glinted in his eyes an awareness of her that suddenly surfaced above the confusion she saw there . . . a spark that her own awareness turned to flame. Feeling the heat rise up her throat, she tugged the red blanket she'd wrapped around her tighter.

Cautiously, she took his face between her palms and stared into his eyes, looking for that wildness that came to those who'd lost their senses. The impossibly blue eyes that stared back held a myriad of emotion—but no madness. She saw intelligence, and she saw fear, hovering in the shadows. She felt it humming beneath his skin.

His face appeared just as it had when he'd taken his vows. Strong, lean, sculpted. Eyes like the sky on a winter's day, lashes long and curling, feminine but for the masculine features surrounding them. But the cruelty that had gleamed in those eyes . . . that was gone. So, too, was the cruel line of his sneer. Now those lips were soft, parted as he silently watched her.

"I saw you in my dreams," he said softly. "You came, every

night. And I saw this." He indicated their surroundings with a lift of his chin and a glance of those blue eyes. "Every damned night."

Saraid was shocked by the confession, for she had dreamed of a man as well. A man whose features she could never make out . . . a man whose touch had awakened a yearning she hadn't understood.

His voice took on a seductive pitch that played along her senses as he went on.

"Then this morning, there you were at the funeral. My sister saw you, too. You motioned for me to come"—his voice dropped lower and he leaned in—"and I followed you to the cavern."

His face was still cupped between her palms, his skin warm to her touch. She thought she should let him go, step away. But she didn't do it.

"Then you kissed me. You told me to hurry."

The breath of his whisper teased the hair at her temples, sending chills down her spine. His lips were only a heartbeat from touching her and despite logic, despite fear and suspicion, she found herself swaying forward.

"Hurry, Ruairi," he murmured. "That's what you said. The next thing I knew, I was here, just before we walked to the church."

He frowned, as if he was trying to work it out in his own mind, but he didn't look away from her eyes.

"You couldn't see me at first, but there were moments when I felt like you knew I was there. It was like I was inside his"—another gesture, this time to the place where his crumbled body had bled into the rushes—"inside his skin. That's how it felt."

Her startled gaze widened and she couldn't deny that sense of duality she'd felt when she first saw him. As if there were two men inside the one. He saw it all in her expression now and it seemed to fill him with satisfaction—with comfort, as if it was important that she saw him—saw *through* the man he wasn't to the man he was.

Hope gleamed in his eyes for a moment, hope that she believed him. That she understood. She could feel it reaching out, begging her to accept what he said. But she didn't know what she believed. Her own eyes? Or the face of the man who'd butchered so many of her loved ones? Which was real?

She tried to turn away but he gripped her arms, holding her so close she could feel the hard ridges of his body through the blanket. He smelled clean, spicy with a scent she didn't recognize, a scent as indefinable as the mysterious man she'd wed. Layered over that intoxicating scent was her own fragrance, which had rubbed into his skin where it had touched her own. And they'd touched in many ways and in many places. The memory of it made her sway.

"I am not the man you think I am," he said, his voice low and rumbling with emotion.

"Nor I the fool y' take me for," she whispered back.

He exhaled heavily and slowly shook his head, making her feel exactly the fool she claimed not to be. She'd disappointed him, and for a moment, she wished she could unsay those words. At last he released her, and she felt strangely bereft. Colleen said she should bewitch this man, but it felt that *he* had cast a spell on *her.*

He took a step back and then another. His eyes were dark with frustration and something else, something wounded and exposed. The mismatch of those emotions playing across the face of a killer shook her.

"Okay. So we agree to disagree. Let's just say, for the sake of argument, that I got hit in the head during the fight. Or maybe someone back home slipped a Quaalude in my tea. Maybe I am a fucking nut case. I don't know. But I swear to you, I'm telling the truth. I shouldn't be here. I'm not this Bloodletter guy that you think I am. I can't even guess what my grandmother has to do with this, but knowing her, it's just a twisted joke she's playing on everyone. Maybe we'll all wake up in the morning and realize it was a bad dream. However it is, I didn't know a thing about your world—about anything until I saw you on the hillside waiting for me."

Saraid swallowed hard, both pulled and repelled by his fervent speech. She believed him, but she wasn't ready to admit it. Not yet.

"What is a *kwaylood*?" she asked in the deafening silence that followed.

"Never mind," he said with a shake of his head. "Whether

you believe me or not is the least of our problems. Right now, we're in a whole world of hurt unless you think it's normal for a father to send one son to kill another."

He reached down and scooped up the clothes he'd shed earlier. She watched as he fumbled to put them on, like he wasn't sure where all the pieces went or how they should be bound. He managed to get his trews up and laced before he looked at her. His eyes darkened as he caught her staring, and his gaze skimmed over her heated cheeks to the bared flesh of her shoulders and chest. Then he was gazing deeply into her eyes once more, and she felt as if he knew every crazy, unpredictable thought that was in her head.

"So what's it going to be, princess? You going to blow the whistle and tell the world I'm a whack-job?"

"If by that y' mean will I tell them y' are mad, then the answer is no. I will not. Even if they believed me, who would care? We've all thought y' mad for a long, long time."

She lifted her white undergown from the rushes and shook it free of straw before stepping into it. Only after she'd pulled it up and slid her arms through the holes did she tug the blanket free and let it fall at her feet.

She glanced up to find his attention fixed on the rise and fall of her breasts. Slowly, his gaze moved up to her face, to her lips in a caress she couldn't help but feel. Agitated, she reached for her overgown, shaking it free of the straw that clung to it. She didn't want to pull it over her head and leave herself vulnerable even for a split second, but the neck was too narrow to step into as she had the underdress, so she tried working it over her arms first but only managed to become tangled in the fabric. After a moment of watching her, making her more nervous by the moment, Ruairi strode to her side, took the dress from her hands, and tugged it unceremoniously over her head. She poked her arms out, shooting him a dark look but feeling better for the garment.

He gave her a crooked grin that did strange things to her heartbeat and rubbed the pad of his thumb over her bottom lip in a gentle caress. Stunned into silence, she could only stare as he went back to his own garments and pulled on his tunic, at last covering the brawn and breadth of his bare torso. She took a deep breath in relief and looked away.

"So, what do you think? How the hell do we get out of here?" he asked.

"And how would I know the way out of this place?" Saraid said, her voice wry. "Is it a regular guest y' think I've been?"

"No, I guess that would be too easy. But he"—Ruairi pointed at Stephen's body—"had to have had a way in. That's going to be our way out."

She was surprised that he'd said *our* way out. Did he mean to take her with him, wherever it was he thought they would go?

"And where is it we will go? My brothers are in that room surrounded by Cathán's men. I'll not be leaving them."

"It's just the three of them, right?" he asked, striding to the far wall and running his hands over the surface.

"Aye, three brothers in that den of wolves."

Her entire family . . . save her youngest brother, Liam, left behind for his protection as a safeguard to their complete destruction. Three to more than a hundred of Cathán Half-Beard's men—and those were just the ones she could see. Others guarded the doors outside and more walked the grounds of the *rath* and beyond. She saw the Bloodletter—Ruairi—considering this as he searched the room. In the chamber behind them, Cathán's voice rose as the music ended. He proposed another toast, laughing at the stamina his son was displaying and the length of time that had lapsed. The gathered people cheered and drank to Ruairi's sword and the sheath that harbored it.

Both Ruairi and Saraid held their breath, waiting for what came next. Ruairi's eyes darted to the body lying on the floor. What if Cathán pulled back the curtain now?

Then, in the sudden quiet a voice rose in song and a flute answered with a delicate melody.

Both Saraid and Ruairi let out a sigh of relief, but she sensed their time was running out. She'd thought marrying this man was the worst thing that could happen to her, but now she wasn't sure. For whatever reason, fate had put them here, now. None of it made sense and yet one thing was clear as the waters that ran through the Favored Lands: Their destinies were linked together in the same way night was linked to dawn.

Ruairi might still be an enemy, but chance had conspired

to put them on the same side of Cathán's injustice. That made him an ally—granted one that couldn't be trusted, but perhaps one that could be used.

And if he *was* the man Colleen of the Ballagh said would come, then he was here for the Book of Fennore. Marked by it. Colleen had been very clear that Saraid must convince him to help her. How had she phrased it? *Win him over and he will be your greatest champion.*

She stepped closer to Ruairi and lowered her voice so as not to be heard beyond the curtain. "Cathán expected the rest of our people to come and join in the celebration. It's tradition. But we knew more than to trust his pledge of truce and bring the others to his slaughter."

"Wait," he said, frowning. "You knew he'd betray you, but you married . . . me anyway? Why?"

She shifted nervously, feeling her face heat again. "A chance at peace, no matter how small, was better than no chance at all," she said simply.

"So you sacrificed yourself."

"I hoped it would be a worthy sacrifice." She looked into his eyes with that, letting him see that she had not yet made up her mind whether wedding him had been a disaster. Letting him know that judgment could still be turned.

He shook his head in silent response. "I told you, princess. I'm not that guy."

"In that case," she said coldly, "then yes, I sacrificed myself."

He flushed, still shaking his head, a curse on his breath. "The rest of your people . . ." he said. "Are they somewhere safe?"

"Until Cathán Half-Beard hunts them down. And with me and my older brothers gone, there will only be Liam to carry on the name. He's but a boy, not yet twelve. They'll have no trouble wiping him out and with him, the line of the king will die as well."

He paused in his perusal of the stark chambers and stared at her. "I heard your brother say that. You're the king's daughter?"

"My father was Bain the Good, a tribal king, not a High

King, but yes, a powerful man before Cathán Half-Beard struck him down."

"And that's what all this is about? If my da—Cathán—if he wants you dead, why didn't he just kill you and your brothers at the hill where we met up? He had an army with him. It would have been easy. Why send someone to take me out instead? It doesn't make sense."

"Cathán cannot kill us outright," she said, choosing her words with care. "Not now."

"Not now?" Ruairi asked. "Why? Has something changed?"

"There has always been unrest on Éire. Tribes fighting against each other, raiding, stealing. But until Cathán Half-Beard, there were rules that were followed, and my father kept peace whenever it could be had. But Cathán waged his war without conscience, certainly without mercy. The more he has, the more he wants, and there are few who could oppose him, few that do."

She paused and Ruairi waited patiently for her to continue.

"Now in the north there is another who marches on his neighbors—not with the ruthlessness of Cathán, but with an invincible arm. Word has reached him of Cathán's conquests, and he has sent warning."

"And Cathán heeds this warning?"

She nodded. "For now. Brian of the Dal Cais—"

"Brian . . ." Ruairi interrupted, looking stupefied. "Brian Boruma? Brian Boru?"

"Do y' know him, then?"

Ruairi gave an incredulous laugh. "No."

Frowning she went on. "He has Cathán worried."

"I'll bet he does."

Irritated, Saraid glared at him. "Do y' know this man or not?"

"I know *of* him," Ruairi said. "And Cathán is right to be afraid."

Grimly pleased by that statement, she went on. "Before this warning, Cathán was able to lead his armies to every *rath*, every *tuath* in the south and overrun it. He destroyed their homes, pillaged, raped. Offered shelter only to those who pledged fealty to him after they were broken. But now with Brian of Dal Cais watching, he must change his tactics. I think Cathán planned it to look like I murdered y'. That would be justification enough to rise against us in vengeance."

"But he said . . ." Ruairi hesitated, and she would swear that he blushed. "He said he wanted you pregnant. Sounded to me like he meant it."

"Perhaps he did. What better way to control a woman than through her babe?"

As soon as she spoke, she wished to call the words back. She knew, even before he asked, what his next question would be.

"Why would he want to control you, Saraid?"

"I told y'. He thinks I have something of his," she hedged.

"I'm going to take a wild guess and say it's the Book of Fennore."

Saraid stared blandly back, neither denying nor agreeing with his conjecture.

"Cathán must be pretty certain to go to such lengths," Ruairi said.

"Do y' think so? Are y' really so blind about yer own father?"

"So you don't have it? You don't know where it is?"

You do not know what you have. . . . Colleen of the Ballagh's voice spoke in her head.

"No," she said. "I do not."

He looked like he might say something to that, but her tight expression stopped him. Still, he searched her face, seeking her secrets. For once her eyes did not give her away. At last he turned, surveying the room. Giving her a moment to gather herself.

He moved to Stephen's body and hefted it up. "Pull that back," he said, nodding at the tapestry where Stephen had hidden. She hurried to do as he said and he stuffed the broken and lifeless body into the alcove hidden behind it. He had to bend the legs and fold him, but when he was done, the tapestry fell smoothly into place and there was no sign that the body was behind it.

He handled his half brother's body efficiently, but she saw a haunted look in his eyes as he turned away. Remorse, regret . . . guilt, she realized. He felt guilt over the murder.

Catching her stunned gaze, he quickly bent and hid the dark stain of blood by scattering fresh rushes over it. Saraid still couldn't believe Cathán had thought Stephen would be a match for the Bloodletter. She caught her lip and chewed it.

"What is it?" Ruairi asked.

She shook her head, not liking the thought that blossomed like foxglove in her mind. What if Cathán had known the Bloodletter would not be defeated by Stephen? What if it was further deceit designed to make her trust this barbarian she'd wed? But no, that thought had no place in light of what she'd seen. Cathán might be able to mask his son's body, but not his eyes. And whoever was behind those blue eyes, it was not the Bloodletter.

Ruairi came to a stop in front of her and tilted her chin so he could see her face. She met his gaze, refusing to let any of what she felt inside show.

"What are you thinking?" he asked.

"That we are doomed."

He exhaled a soft laugh. "Yeah. Well, it's been a long time coming for me."

He kept a wary eye on the curtained area as he went back to searching for the passageway he thought Stephen had used. Taking his lead, Saraid began on the other wall, slowly feeling her way, seeking a latch or a crease that would not be apparent at first glance.

When Bain's people had still lived in their keep, her father had a secret door off the main hall that led out through a tunnel. She would be surprised if there was not one here. But even if they found it, to what end would it serve? She'd meant what she said. She would not abandon her brothers.

She reached the bed and saw the small gap between the stones beside it.

"'Tis here," she said.

Ruairi ran his hands down the wall until he felt the small finger hole. She heard the soft *snick* and then he pushed it inward. The space was just large enough to crawl through. No more than that.

"Bingo," he said, turning to her. "Let's go."

"Were y' not listening? I'll not leave without my brothers."

"They're big boys," he said. "They'll find their way out."

"And how will they do that? Cathán will be in here again as he was before. He'll see what is about, and if we are missing, he'll use my brothers."

"Use them how?"

The simplicity of the question drove out any lingering doubts she might have retained that Ruairi was telling the truth about himself. The *real* Bloodletter would know exactly how her brothers would be used.

"The youngest he will kill outright, just for the pleasure of it. The older ones he will torture until we're found."

"And if you stay?"

"Alone? I'm sure the men will have their pleasures with me before the night is through."

Ruairi's eyes darkened, and he shook his head slowly, cursing again beneath his breath. "Couldn't be easy," he muttered. "Never easy."

She waited, wishing she could send him on his way, wishing she didn't need his help.

"All right," he said. "You go through this way. I'll get your brothers and meet you on the other side."

"Will y' now?" she said. "Yer not known as the Bloodletter for yer honor. How will y' get my brothers? How will y' know where the other side is? Could be no more than a crawl space to hide." And she'd rather die in blood than be sealed into something so tight and dark. It was the stuff of nightmares.

Her scorn was ill concealed and only a fool would not have felt it. Angry himself, he stood, backing her up a step despite her determination to hold her ground. His size was overpowering, but she refused to let him break her will. He might well leave her here to meet her fate, but he would know what that fate was and she would make certain the knowledge haunted him.

She stared him down until at last he shook his head again and muttered, "Complicated. Can't say she didn't warn me."

"What was that?" Saraid demanded.

"I said, okay. We do it your way. We go out the front door. Together."

Her soft snort of laughter brought him up short. "Stroll through the front door, will we?"

"Do you have a better idea?"

She didn't, curse his beautiful blue eyes.

He gave her a sideways look, as if he'd heard her thought.

"What happens next?" he said. "I mean, what would a . . . normal couple be doing after . . . um . . . ?" He waved a hand over the bed, avoiding her eyes.

After the marriage had been consummated, he meant. She felt yet another hot rush stain her face. A normal couple would not have been expected to consummate in such a way. A *normal* bride would not have felt she bore the weight of two men at once.

"After a Christian wedding, the bride is expected to prove her purity to the groom's father."

Ruairi's jaw dropped. "How does she do that?"

Saraid moved stiffly to the bed and began to gather the sheets, both proud and humiliated by the smear of blood on them. Ruairi's eyes followed her actions, his brows drawn close in a frown.

How could he not know that she was expected to bring them out and deliver them to her new father by marriage? Cathán would hold them up for his brutal soldiers to jeer at. It should be a rite of happiness and pride, this symbol of their union. Instead, it would be filled with shame.

"Yer father will acknowledge that I came to y' untouched and that our match is done."

"And then?"

She frowned, not understanding his question.

"Will there be more partying? Dancing?"

Partying? Such strange expressions this man used. She said, "There will be merriment, yes. Music. The men are half in their cups now. They will plunge all the way as the night goes on."

He nodded, sucking in a deep breath and slowly letting it out.

"Good. So this is how we play it. We're going to go out and smile and act like we've done our duty—accepted our fate. Whatever you call it here."

It was her turn to stare openmouthed.

"We're going to move through the room like we don't have

a care in the world. When we get to your brothers, if you can, you're going to tell them what's up. Do you think you can do that without being noticed?"

At one time, she and Tiarnan had been able to communicate without words at all. That gift had been trampled with their innocence years ago and she no longer knew if it was still possible. She could only pray it was.

Before she could answer, he pointed at her hair. "And you might want to do something with that first."

She reached up, finding the braided glory had been reduced to a snarled mess. Amazed that she could still have a sense of vanity in these circumstances, she felt yet another flush heat her skin. Quickly she began to pull the tiny braids that had survived from the rest and unravel them. After a moment, Ruairi moved to her side and started doing the same thing. His hands were big and clumsy, but his touch was gentle, his fingers warm as they brushed her nape. His nearness made her clumsy, her stomach jittery. His hands in her hair seemed almost as intimate as the joining they'd shared.

Once all of the tiny braids had been unraveled, her hair hung in a rippling mass to her waist. He held it then, running his fingers through the silky curtain, separating the strands, watching the play of candlelight gleaming through it. Then he brought it to his face and inhaled the scent, seeming unaware of what he did. Saraid, however, was all too aware of his every single move.

"God, your hair is beautiful," he said so softly she wondered if he'd meant to speak aloud. "It smells like heaven."

His gaze snagged hers and she felt the fire of it to her toes.

Quickly she finger-combed it back, divided it into three sections, and braided it into one thick rope that hung down her back. She used her blue ribbon to secure it. Ruairi watched the whole process with a hungry look in his eyes that stoked the embers still burning inside her.

Swallowing hard, she said, "I'm ready."

He nodded, reluctantly pulling his gaze away. "All right, then. Let's do this."

She gathered up the sheets, feeling another wave of hot embarrassment at the memory of what they'd done. His blue eyes tracked her movements, and not for the first time, she had the unnerving feeling that he read her mind.

With the bundle in one arm, she settled her other hand in the crook of his elbow. He hesitated at the curtain, and she heard him say something under his breath. It sounded like "show time."

Chapter Fifteen

DOUBT had become Tiarnan's trusted friend.

It wasn't always that way. Once he'd been bold and decisive, leading his men in battle, guiding his people to salvation. But that was so long ago, Tiarnan himself half suspected he'd imagined it. Perhaps he'd always been plagued by the gnawing gnats of uncertainty. Even now he wanted to turn to his younger brothers and beg them for reassurance. Ask them, *Did I do the right thing?*

But he knew what they'd say.

Only Liam, the youngest, had been brave enough to tell him he was a fool when Tiarnan presented his plan. Just as Eamonn had surprised him with his loyalty, agreeing wholeheartedly that it was the only way, standing beside him and offering support. Tiarnan had been grateful for that, but he knew that the others believed what Liam did—Tiarnan was not capable of leading them to anything but destruction.

He'd given his sister to a man who—even as Tiarnan bemoaned his own insecurity—raped his sister. Had the right to do whatever he wanted with her, a right Tiarnan had gifted him. If not for the music, they would all be hearing her cries, her sobs. He'd condemned Saraid to this fate, and she would never forgive him. Yet she'd gone to it with her head held high. Her courage, her sacrifice, only enlarged the feelings of failure within him.

All around him the festivities surged as the wine and mead flowed with the music. Looking at the happy faces—many familiar from the times before Cathán had come and wreaked his havoc on their lives—he felt destitute. How could he hope that Cathán would keep his word?

There were more strangers than friends in the room. Most were Northmen with their blond hair, icy eyes, and conquering ways. Cathán's wife's people. Everything they did was bigger, grander than any ordinary man. They ate like each meal was their last. They laughed like laughter might be snatched away if not enjoyed to its fullest. And they whored like their seed was a gift of the gods.

It could have been worse, Tiarnan told himself. It might be a Northman behind the curtain with his sister. But the voice of doubt jeered at even that. Nothing—*no one*—was as bad as Ruairi the Bloodletter. Not even a Northman.

Scowling, he shouldered his way past the revelry to the head table where Cathán sat like the king he'd proclaimed himself to be.

"Ah, Tiarnan of the Favored Lands," Cathán exclaimed loudly. His tone mocked, his eyes scorned, yet his face split with a grin that would certainly fool anyone who might be watching. Tiarnan glanced over his shoulder. That would be nearly everyone in the room.

"Sit," Cathán boomed in a jolly voice all could hear. "Eat. Enjoy yourself for once."

He felt his face burn at the laughter that came from the last. Damn Cathán Half-Beard. Tiarnan had no desire to eat or drink in this man's presence. And there would never be enjoyment for him here.

"Where is the treaty, Cathán?" he demanded. Their agreement was that the treaty would be signed once Saraid was given to the Bloodletter, reinstating his rights over the *tuath* his people had once called home. The treaty would legalize his claim to property, proclaiming Cathán's intentions to be peaceable.

Cathán's emotionless eyes glittered hard and flat even as his smile broadened. He knew it irritated Tiarnan, this gleeful front he presented. "All in good time, my boy."

Tiarnan placed his palms on the table and leaned closer,

towering over the seated man in a manner he knew would aggravate. Two of Cathán's men took a step forward, but Cathán shook his head, unconcerned by any threat Tiarnan might pose. But the pulse beating at his temple gave him away. He was not so calm and at ease as he wanted to appear. Yet as much as he wished to be the cause of Cathán's stress, Tiarnan sensed his agitation came from something else. *What?* Curious, Tiarnan narrowed his eyes, watching the older man as he pretended that all was well.

He shifted his gaze to Cathán's wife, who sat at his right with her nose in the air and her horseface scrunched up with distaste. She made a dismissive noise as she looked away. To her right their daughter, Mauri, lovely in a dress of ivory and lavender with tiny woven flowers at the sleeves and neck, watched him with her doe eyes. For her, he checked his anger. Still it burned deep inside him.

Tiarnan eased back and motioned to one of the serving-women hovering at each end of the table. She scuttled forward, eyes downcast and tray with mead in front. He took a cup, drank, forced himself to smile.

When he spoke, he was glad to hear his voice sounded calm. It would benefit no one to lose his temper now, and his interest was piqued by the tension emanating from Cathán. What would make such a powerful man nervous on a day like today, when everything seemed to be stacking up exactly as he planned?

Pushing, Tiarnan said, "Our agreement was that papers would be signed after the joining. The deed is done. The papers should be signed."

"So they will be. But not now, when everyone is having their fun. Look at them, Tiarnan. Look at their happy faces. They're hopeful."

Reluctantly he glanced back at the gathering. It was true. Those people who had lived through the long years of bloodshed now believed that peace was coming and they danced with joy and hope, unaware of the mockery in the flat gaze of their leader or the cold, calculating attention of the Northmen who viewed them all like tasty morsels to be devoured later.

With all his heart, Tiarnan wished he could trust that the

peace he himself had bargained for with this marriage would actually come to be. Perhaps having the treaty signed and in hand would color this picture in a different way. Perhaps it would make what Saraid endured worth the sacrifice. Perhaps it would slow the flood of self-loathing that threatened to drown what was left of his self-respect.

"They've not been priest-wed yet," Cathán reminded him now. "That will make it official."

"And what of this?" Tiarnan demanded, pointing to the curtain where his sister was even now being ravaged. "A priest will do no more than consummation."

"But I've seen no proof of that yet, have I, boy?"

Tiarnan's jaw set hard. "I am not yer boy."

Cathán's smile broadened. "No, I don't suppose you are. You're a man. A big man, aren't you?" He paused only long enough for Tiarnan to feel the salt in his scorn. "But I don't see that you've held up your end of the bargain. Where are your people? You've brought only your brothers and none of the rest. Do you not trust me?"

"Like a rabbit trusts a fox," Tiarnan said before he could stop himself.

"The treaty will not be drawn until I see the evidence of consummation. And until you bring your people to witness."

"That was not our agreement."

Cathán raised his brows and stroked his half beard. "Fine, then. Go and gather your sister and be gone."

Tiarnan felt his face burn hot with rage and humiliation. Cathán had him by the stones, and they both knew it.

The smile he forced felt like it might crack his face in two. "We will wait for the proof but no more than that. Do not think to betray me Cathán Half-Beard."

"Or what?" Cathán demanded, leaning forward until his face was close to Tiarnan's. "What will you do?"

"Whatever I must," Tiarnan said with more courage than he felt.

Because in truth, what *would* he do? What *could* he do? What had he been doing since Cathán's first, brutal attack years ago? Fighting, running, losing everything he loved . . .

Cathán's smile told Tiarnan his thoughts had been read,

and he cursed himself for the fool he was. They'd been right—all who had questioned his decision. Angrily, Tiarnan looked away and found himself staring into Mauri's beautiful eyes. It should have been him behind the curtain with Mauri, not Saraid and the Bloodletter. Cathán's daughter smiled at him, the gesture tremulous and hopeful, and Tiarnan felt another wave of despair.

Before he could gather his thoughts, he saw Eamonn and Michael shouldering through the crowd to his side. One quick glance and he knew they'd sensed the tension and were here to stand or die with him. They were good boys, nearly men, and their loyalty felt like a noose, ever tightening.

He gave the two a quick shake of his head, letting them know there was no cause for alarm. Not yet anyway. Eamonn looked almost disappointed, but Michael let out a shaky breath of relief.

Tiarnan returned his attention to Cathán, the bastard, but just then the curtain drew back and his sister stepped out with the Bloodletter at her side. The crowd behind him quieted before turning as one to gaze with open curiosity at the pair poised behind the long table. Cathán's brows came together in a quick frown and then he spun suddenly, looking at his son and new daughter-in-law with shock that he couldn't mask quickly enough. It darted through his eyes, a dark question that Tiarnan could not read. But it momentarily froze Cathán's triumphant features into a harsh mask that Tiarnan would have sworn was fear. Or could it be anger? Or a snapping banner of both? Regardless, it was gone before Tiarnan could understand more, or what caused it.

But why was Cathán surprised to see his son and Saraid?

The question boomed in Tiarnan's mind, the echo a forewarning he couldn't quite grasp. Something was happening. Something bigger than the monumental joining of Saraid to Ruairi the Bloodletter. . . .

"God's blood," Eamonn exclaimed softly as he, like the others, watched Saraid move into the room as graceful and proud as a queen.

The Bloodletter laid a proprietary hand at the small of her back, and his gaze settled on her features in what looked for an instant to be tenderness. *Tenderness? From the Blood-letter?*

As quickly as it appeared, it was gone, and the Bloodletter's blue eyes moved away as he scanned the room with purpose. What was he looking for? Yet another question Tiarnan had no answers to. At the Bloodletter's side, Saraid was pale and tense, but she didn't falter.

No other woman would have been able to hold her head high as she entered a room such as this—especially given the manner in which she'd left it, chased by the raucous laughter and crude comments of the people before her. Sent to be defiled by the man at her side. But Saraid looked regal, brave, and Tiarnan's heart swelled with pride in her. Her gown was wrinkled, her hair hanging in a simple braid, and yet she still managed to look like royalty ready to address her kingdom. Scared royalty, for certain, but regal all the same.

The Bloodletter said something softly in her ear, and a sudden smile spread across her face. It didn't make it to her eyes, though. Those were guarded, watchful. When she saw Tiarnan standing by the table, they widened for a telling moment. In her hands, she clutched her bundled wedding sheets. The proof Cathán required. For a moment, he allowed himself a glimmer of optimism that he had done right by his people.

He heard his name and it pulled his attention from his sister to see who had spoken. Beside him, his two brothers stared back with blank expressions. No one else was close and the voice had been a woman's.

"*Tiarnan*," it came again, this time loud enough to make him jump.

"What is it?" Eamonn asked, staring at him.

The hairs on the back of Tiarnan's neck stood on end. He recognized the voice now. Slowly he looked back to his sister. She stood stiff as a stone pillar, chin up, eyes forward. Not even looking at him. Yet it had been her voice. He'd swear it.

When they'd been children, when they'd felt safe and cherished, they'd talked to each other with their minds. The memory of it hit him now, hard and low. He'd all but forgotten about it—when he did remember, it was with a sense that perhaps he'd imagined it. Dreamed it up like fairies and magical horses that could fly them away. And like their imagined fantasies, the ability had waned with their youth and disappeared forever.

At least that was what he'd thought.

"Tiarnan, if y' can hear me, nod."

Feeling the fool, he did as she bade.

"Cathán has betrayed us all. He tried to kill Ruairi."

Tiarnan frowned, unable to wrap his thoughts around what she said. No, it wasn't shocking that Cathán would betray them. Hadn't they planned for it, laid in wait and dread for it? Hoped they were wrong? But why would he try to kill his own son? Ruairi was the power of his right hand. The force that drove them. Why—

"I cannot explain it, brother. Know that if ye've ever trusted me, now is the time to do so again."

With a cautious glance to make sure all eyes were still on the Bloodletter and his bride, Tiarnan nodded once more.

"You must take the boys and escape. Now."

He opened his mouth, but whether he intended to speak or not was unclear to even himself.

"Do not worry for me. Ruairi has vowed to help me escape."

He heard the doubt in her voice and yet layered over it, there was hope and truth. It made no sense. None at all. And since when did she call Ruairi anything but the Bloodletter?

He coughed into his fist and gave a violent shake of his head at the same time. Beside him, Eamonn helpfully thumped his back.

"I know it is hard for y' to believe. I scarce believe it myself, but there's no time to explain it. I will see y' on the other side of these walls. At the waterfall, where Liam awaits."

He shook his head again, trying to shoot his thoughts into her head the same way she'd done to him. But if he'd really ever had the skill, he had it no more, because she stared serenely forward and his protests went unanswered. If what she said was true, how could he leave her here? How could he trust the Bloodletter to see to her escape?

The answer was clear. He couldn't.

And yet as he looked around, he could not ignore his limited choices. Either die fighting his way to her side and bring about the deaths of all of them, or do as she said. *Trust.*

"Make haste, Tiarnan. There is no time to doubt."

Chapter Sixteen

Rory could feel Saraid shaking as they moved to the curtain. Or maybe it was him. He gave her one last glance, noting her brittle composure. Wondering if his own was as transparent. Any of the women he'd known before her would have been hysterical by now. But not this one. She held her head high, her expression blank and her eyes watchful.

Already the memory of her lying beneath him had joined the surreal realm of everything that came after. But her scent was on his skin and it teased him, even now as his mind quaked at the brink of shock. It kept him from catapulting into the dark world of insanity.

Crazy. Crazy with icing on top, but crazy all the same.

He fought to keep the images, the shock and gore of what he'd done to Stephen out of his head. But it was there, buried beneath the motor commands that kept him standing, walking, reacting. The feel of Stephen's eyes as they'd caved beneath his thumbs, his throat as it collapsed in his tight grip. The cry of vengeance that had pumped with Rory's blood.

He'd killed a man. In self-defense, yes, but that didn't make the finality of it any less severe. Nor could it dilute the horrifying thrill of victory he'd shared with his twin. The shame he bore alone.

He'd done a lot of things he wasn't proud of in his life, but he'd never killed. He'd never murdered . . . until now. He took a deep breath and forced that back. This wasn't the time to feel remorse over what he'd done. It wasn't the time to feel at all.

The smoky chamber they entered seemed filled beyond capacity. He estimated eighty to a hundred men were there, but it felt like ten times more than that. Big men, though some were more mass than muscle. They were a filthy lot, and the stench of them was overpowering. The women and children matched their number, but the kids were at a constant run, racing between tables and darting beneath them.

A fire raged hot and fierce in the huge hearth, and serving-women hustled back and forth with platters of food and pitchers of ale or wine or whatever it was that this motley mix imbibed. Dogs snarled and snuffed at the droppings in the straw on the floor, fighting for bones and scraps. He didn't have a sense of how much time had passed since they'd entered the curtained bedroom. Forty minutes? An hour tops? Not that time was even relevant. Getting out—that was the only thing that mattered.

"Smile," he said softly to Saraid as he led her into the room. Her lips turned up as if on wires. The smile looked fragile to him, and he doubted it would fool anyone.

For a moment, their entrance went unnoticed by all but Saraid's brothers, who saw them immediately.

Her oldest brother tracked their progress with hard eyes. He was tall, taller than Rory, who topped six three. He was a solid wall of muscle, ripped from his neck to rock-hard pecs to bulging biceps. A human tank. If this guy had been sent to kill him instead of Stephen, Rory would be dead.

He stood in front of the long table where Rory's father sat with a posture of indifference that belied the sharp look in his eyes as he surveyed the room. Cathán MacGrath. His father. Even though Rory had seen his father during the rite, he still couldn't believe it was him, and yet, there was no denying it. His father looked like a shiny nickel in a jar of old and tarnished pennies—as much an anomaly as Rory himself.

Earlier, when Rory had hovered over the processional, the impact of his father's presence had been somehow diluted. Now he felt the full force of it, the pain and memory. The grief. The rage. Rory had worshipped this man as a boy—mourned his loss for his entire life. Nearly self-destructed under the weight of responsibility that came from knowing somehow, in some way, he'd been the cause of Cathán's disappearance.

A thick knot of emotion caught Rory low and hard. He'd been just five when Cathán vanished from the cavern beneath the castle ruins, and over the years, his memories of his father had become a pain that never left him. Or his *absence* of memories might be a better way of putting it. He couldn't recall playing ball or chase with his father. He couldn't be sure he remembered the timbre of his father's voice or even the way he smelled. But some twist of his psyche had given his need for those memories a substance, and the lack of them as he grew older became a sharp-edged hollow inside him. A chunk of himself that was always missing—leaving the rest of him to fester and rot. The hurt child that lurked just below Rory's skin wanted to throw himself in his father's arms and cry like a baby. Ask his dad if he'd missed Rory as much as Rory had missed him.

But there were far more important and disturbing questions that Rory needed answering. Like why did he send Stephen to kill Rory's twin? And did his father know that the man who'd looked like Rory, talked in Rory's voice, stared from behind Rory's eyes was not really his son—was not wholly his son. . . .

He shut down the rampant thoughts—shying away from his fear of that answer. Saraid's fingers tightened on his arm, bringing him back to the moment. But Cathán looked so much like Rory remembered that it both filled him with longing and unsettled him. As he'd noted before, the face was still youthful, unmarred by the ravages of age and harsh living. The only sign that time might have touched Cathán MacGrath was the gray at his temples and that had an illusory look to it, as if he'd colored it for effect. Millions of women in the twenty-first century would kill to know what fountain of youth he'd been drinking from.

Except perhaps his Aunt Edel, he realized with a start. She had always seemed ageless, too. With her, Rory had chalked it up to expensive cosmetics and a good plastic surgeon. Now he wondered.

A woman sat beside Cathán. Dressed better than those

assembled in front of them, she was obviously someone important to be perched up here at his father's right hand. She had long blonde hair that showed more gray than Cathán's and a broad face with high cheekbones, sharp nose, and a square chin. The word *Nordic* came to his mind. She was heavy boned with thick wrists and broad hands and he guessed her to be about forty, but wouldn't lay money on it. There was a weariness to her that spoke of trials and failures. The kind that aged a person beyond their years. She shifted back from the table and revealed a swollen belly. She was very pregnant. Was she Cathán's wife? Stephen's mother? If so, he tried not to think of her face when they discovered her son and what Rory had done to him.

At her side, a younger woman shifted nervously on her seat. She bore a slight resemblance to the first, but tempered in the hard high plains of her face were traces of Cathán. The full lips, the aristocratic nose. The pale eyes. A half sister? Stephen's sister? If so, did she know what Stephen had been up to? What their father had sent him to do? The girl stared at Saraid's oldest brother, her eyes huge and soulful, gleaming with youth and innocence. Innocence Rory figured had no place in this hellhole where they stood. For a moment, Saraid's brother gazed back and there was a raw hunger in his look, mingled with anger, disappointment, and unquestionable longing.

Interesting. Rory filed that away for future reference.

The older woman—Cathán's wife, he guessed—leaned close to say something to her husband just as the crowd below noticed Rory and Saraid hovering outside the curtain. She quickly glanced back and sucked in a breath. In that instant, Rory realized that she'd known Stephen's plans for the night. As the understanding hit him, Cathán spun as well. Shock flashed in his cold eyes as he stared at his son. It was gone just as quickly, but Rory had seen what he needed to know. There was no doubt in his mind that this man was his father—that somehow, Cathán had traveled through time after that night in the cavern when they'd fought over the Book of Fennore just as Rory had done after he'd followed Saraid from his grandmother's funeral. But whatever honor and moral fiber had made Cathán the man he was twenty-five years ago no longer existed in the man he was now. This Cathán MacGrath was not the father Rory remembered him to be. This Cathán had sent one son to murder another. . . .

His thoughts tangled over that, but Rory fought to keep his expression composed, blank, while inside a knife sharper than the one Stephen had used to carve Rory's twin slid deep and hard between his ribs. Pressing a hand to the small of Saraid's back, he moved forward. The man they'd called the Bloodletter, Rory's twin, wasn't one to smile, and for that Rory was grateful. He couldn't have faked joviality if it had meant his and Saraid's lives.

Saraid dropped a stiff curtsy in front of the older woman, who looked at them both as if they were rats who'd suddenly scurried across the dinner table. If she was Cathán's wife, then she was also Ruairi's stepmother. But there was no love between them. That much was very clear.

Cathán stuffed an enormous bite of what looked like bread soaked in greasy gravy into his mouth and spoke while he chewed. "Took your time with it, didn't you?"

Rory doubted anyone else could see the small flare of alarm in Cathán's eyes as he looked past Rory and Saraid, trying to see through the drawn curtain. Looking for Stephen? Wondering why his other son had not taken care of business?

"Was it to be a race, then?" Rory responded, still trying to match the cadence of the strange accent and coming close, but not exact.

His father's eyes hardened, and Rory knew Cathán heard something off in his dialect.

"Not a race, but we are waiting for the proof," Cathán said.

With quiet dignity, Saraid stepped forward, bowed her head, and handed him the bundled sheets she held in her arms. Cathán stood, shaking them out and examining the small pinkish stain in the center. Rory felt the burn of humiliation rising off Saraid's skin, shared it even as an act that had been intimate despite the circumstances was now paraded in front of a horde of unwashed men and eager-eyed women. Cathán sniffed the sheet and Rory wanted to punch him. Instead, he jerked it from his father's hands, balled it up, and thrust it back at Saraid. He knew anger etched an outline around him, but he couldn't hide it. Thought it best that he didn't try.

"It's done," he said, and this time he nailed the accent. With Saraid's hand clasped tightly in his own, he faced the room. "She is my wife and will be treated with respect or you will answer to me."

The threat and wording of it came instinctively, and he suspected the line was from some old movie he'd seen, but they didn't know that, and he saw that he'd captured the essence of their customs and delivered something that met their expectations. There followed a brief moment of uncertainty in the room, and then two men went down on bended knee in a gesture of submission. Like copycats in a game of Simon Says, others soon followed. Not all, though. The larger men gathered at one side of the room just watched with bright eyes and interest. If Rory had his history right, he'd guess those were Vikings, and they bowed to no one. The biggest of them bore a strong resemblance to Cathán's wife. Something else to file away.

Still acting on instinct, Rory said, "I will drink now."

Like magic, a woman appeared at his side with a tray and a cup. He took the mug, catching himself before the automatic thank you escaped. The woman hovered there for a moment, her expression one of terror. At first he thought it was him— the Bloodletter—that had her looking like a frightened mouse, but then he saw her watching Saraid and realized for whatever reason, the servant feared his new wife.

Wishing he had the time to unravel all of the strange undercurrents and emotions surging through this room, he turned away. He lifted his cup first to his father, then to the waiting men and women.

"To my bride," he said and took a drink. The contents of the cup were dark, the color vile, and the smell sweet and cloying. The taste wasn't much better. He swallowed and handed the cup to Saraid.

She stared at him in surprise, but quickly recovered. "To my husband," she said in a clear and steady voice. "May he be blessed with long life and prosperity." She put the cup to her lips and he found himself momentarily distracted as he watched her drink.

Then Cathán lifted his cup and the woman beside him did the same. The signal sent a rumble of relief through the gath-

ering. Others toasted the happy couple and in the corner of the
room the man with the fiddle began another lively tune. Someone else joined in with a song, and the gathering once again
became the loud rumble of drinking and merriment that had
accompanied Rory and Saraid earlier in their strange rite of
marriage. Yet Rory felt the fine thread of tension that held the
entire gala together, invisible shackles stringing ankle to
ankle, man to weapon.

Beneath the laughter and song, they were watching. Waiting. But for what? What did they know and what had they
merely surmised? Was it dread or anticipation he tasted in
the air?

Before his father could say another word, Rory pulled
Saraid from the dais and toward the blazing fire against the far
wall. He stopped in front of it and gave her a nod when he saw
the startled question in her eyes. Her brows came together and
she cast an uncertain look back at his father and stepmother,
but then with a gleam of defiance he recognized from the
countless nights she'd haunted his dreams, she tossed the
sheets into the flames. He heard his stepmother gasp and
assumed sheets in whatever time period he'd entered were not
so easily come by as a quick trip to the mall. Burning them
was a direct offense to the hostess.

He smiled for the first time since stepping out from behind
the curtain.

Back straight, shoulders squared, and gaze level, he moved
Saraid through the room, picking out bits and pieces of the
conversation, gathering names and committing them to memory. He'd always been good at that.

He met a man called Gormán with a hulking mass of wild
hair and too many chins to count. He had eyes Rory didn't
trust. The string bean at his side answered to Albert. Rory
sized him up and thought him the type of man who followed
the leader—whatever leader had the best chance of surviving.
Someone who might be swayed from one side to another. And
so it went as they made their way through the room. They
stopped occasionally to accept congratulations and blessings
from those brave enough to speak, which fortunately, were
few. Several times he intercepted strange looks directed at
Saraid—once again, there was fear. He even caught one man

making a covert hand sign with middle fingers down and pointer and pinky up. Wasn't that what they did to ward off evil?

It confused him, but there was no way to ask about it, so he added it to his mental file and moved them both through the room. All the while, Rory kept his attention divided between his father, who tracked them with the flat glitter of his gaze, and Saraid's brothers, who stood in front of Cathán's table waiting for their sister to complete her circle of the room and come to them.

Saraid was no longer trembling, but he could feel the apprehension rising in her. It hummed over her skin and gripped him tight. Several times he caught her staring intently at her oldest brother, who stood as alert as a cop patrolling a dark alley in the middle of the night. It seemed some silent communication went through them both, but Rory couldn't be sure. Certainly he and his own sister Danni had been able to talk without words, but was it crazy to think Saraid and her brother could do the same?

He leaned in, putting his mouth near the silky skin of her ear. "What are you up to?" he asked softly.

She startled, but didn't pull away, and for reasons he didn't want to explore, that filled him with a fierce satisfaction. But she didn't answer him, either, and he couldn't press without drawing attention.

The great hall was not only filled with Cathán's men and the people who lived nearby. As the conversations surged, he learned others had traveled days to get there. He thought of Brian Boru and his campaign to become the one King of Ireland. And that wasn't even the most bizarre thing he'd learned today. Hilarious if the situation had not been so terrifying. Were some of them here to witness the ceremony? He glanced back at the dais and caught his stepsister gazing at Saraid's brother again. It was obvious she had a thing for him. Why hadn't this marriage been between those two? Why Rory and Saraid, when it was obvious Saraid had no such feelings for him?

Saraid squeezed his arm where her hand rested lightly at the crook as she stopped in front of her brothers. She embraced the two younger ones under the spotlight of attention, and a rush of possessiveness washed over Rory as other men in the room turned to watch her. The feeling was Neanderthal in intensity. It made him want to spin in rage and snarl until they lowered their eyes. Christ, had being around all these barbarians turned him into one? He needed to keep his head in the game. Get himself, Saraid, and her brothers out of here and then he'd be on his way. However he'd come to be in this place, his goal had not changed—it had only become more imperative. The Book of Fennore. Somehow it was the reason he'd come to this place. He had to believe it was his ticket out as well.

Saraid spoke each brother's name as she embraced him, and Rory added them to the running list in his head, playing word associations in an attempt to keep them straight even as he tried to follow every nuance of what went on in the room. The tension had reached a screaming pitch, though Rory had yet to discern the source.

The brother with the dark hair and bright blue eyes was Eamonn. Next to him, with burnished red curls and freckles, was Michael. The last brother, the giant, was Tiarnan. Rory smelled Tiarnan's fear as he watched the room. Knew without looking that Cathán did as well.

Saraid stepped back and returned to Rory's side. Despite his intentions not to, Rory took her hand and curled her fingers around his arm, once more anchoring her to him. All three brothers watched the small, telling gesture with narrowed eyes.

"It is done, Tiarnan," she said, and the simple statement seemed to have so many meanings. "Ruairi is my husband now. We've given proof."

Her husband. In a million years, Rory never thought he'd be married. And he wasn't now, he reminded himself. Yes, he had a hard-on the size of Texas every time he touched Saraid, but that didn't make him her husband.

"Proof," Tiarnan spat. "Y' had a fooking audience."

Rory watched Saraid fight a wave of shame that crept up her chest to her face and he wanted to step forward and back Tiarnan down. Without being told, he knew that Tiarnan was responsible for Saraid's being here at all. That his own guilt made him want to punish her for it. Saraid went on in a calm and soothing voice before Rory could react to that bit of insight, but it did crystallize something else. Though Saraid might not be leader of her tribe, she was the voice of reason that moved them.

"That may be so, Tiarnan," she said, speaking as if Cathán were not there to hear every word. "But there can be no doubt now that we are joined."

Joined. Fused together by the heat between them . . .

Cathán shifted in his seat and made a small noise of irritation.

"I've not seen the treaty yet," Tiarnan said. Then, turning to Cathán, "Y' have yer proof. I'll have our agreement now."

"You are one to rush things, aren't you, boy?" Cathán replied mildly. "I have told you already, I want witnesses and not just my own. I've been betrayed by your kind in the past. I won't stand for it again."

Tiarnan looked like he might jump across the table and rip Cathán's head from his shoulders, but once more, Saraid calmed with a touch.

"We understand yer terms, Father," she said in a sweet voice. The casual "Father" tightened the corners of Cathán's mouth and made his wife flinch. Rory knew speaking it left a bitter taste on Saraid's tongue.

Behind Cathán two men built like matching brick houses waited for a command. Throughout the crowded room, Cathán's men appeared to be drunk and happy, but mixed with the genuinely buzzed, there were eyes that watched, sober and alert. Those men were poised, each an arrow nocked and ready to fly. It was clear Saraid's brothers would not be strolling out the front door. And how long before someone decided to look for Stephen?

Tiarnan cleared his throat and stepped forward as if he'd been nudged, though no one had moved. "Yer right, Cathán," he said in a commanding voice that probably fooled no one. "Ye've proven yer honor. Now I will do the like. My brothers and I would ride out to bring the others to the feast."

Cathán's eyes narrowed. "Leave?"

"We are not free to do so?" Tiarnan asked calmly, and though Rory was still pissed at the way he'd embarrassed Saraid, he felt a hint of admiration at his composure. The man had stones.

"Yes, you're free to come and go as you please," Cathán said with a merry snort of laughter. "But it's a celebration of the happy joining of our two beloved families."

"And like y', I would want more than my brothers to enjoy yer hospitality."

"I'll send a runner," Cathán offered. A wave of his hand and a man was ready to do his bidding. "He can deliver your message and guide your fair folk safely to our door."

"It must be me who goes. Our people have been hunted by yers for too long to trust yer man."

Cathán nodded slowly, obviously knowing this was true. After a long moment, he said, "I see your point, Tiarnan. Since this is the case, you may go, then. But alone. Your brothers will await you here."

Tiarnan's mouth twitched, as if he'd found humor in that idea. "Nay. We three go together or not at all."

"Perhaps you plan not to return?" Cathán's wife said, her tone snarky, her face red. Cathán gave her an irritated glance.

"My sister will remain here waiting," Tiarnan said, still keeping his cool, but Rory could see his hold on it slipping. "We'd never abandon her."

At that, Cathán's eyes became lasers, inspecting Tiarnan like an engineer looking for the fissures in a dam. Knowing somewhere there must be a crack, knowing just the right tap with just the right tool would be all it took to bring the whole thing down.

"Of course you'd never betray your sister," Cathán said with a wry smile. "Not you, Tiarnan the Good . . . at least the Good's son."

Rory frowned, trying to put that comment into context and failing. Then he remembered. Saraid's father had been called Bain the Good.

"You three may go and retrieve your faithful people. But your youngest brother, he will stay and keep your sister company. What is his name?"

"Liam," Tiarnan supplied helpfully. "But he is not here."

This brought a scowl that Cathán couldn't hide. He scanned the faces in the room, apparently stunned that he had not noticed the absence before. "Where is he?"

Tiarnan raised his brows. "It was not a sure thing, this

union, and all of us know it. Liam was left to send word—good or bad—when the deed was done."

"Left where?" Cathán asked.

"What does that matter, Father?" Rory said, stepping in, hoping to bring the game of bait and trap to an end. "They will bring him back with the others." He turned to Tiarnan. "Isn't that right?"

Tiarnan shot him a poisonous look, but Rory didn't flinch. He owed these people nothing, he reminded himself. He was here for the Book, not to save Saraid's arrogant brother.

"If you like," Rory continued, "Saraid and I will accompany them."

Cathán's brows came down on a black scowl. "No, I don't like. You will stay."

Rory had known he'd get that response. Waltzing out the door with Saraid and her brothers was too easy. But it was worth the try.

"Our people will not believe it is safe unless they see me and both of my brothers," Tiarnan said.

"And why is that?"

"Because y' might easily be holding the others captive, or murdered. It wouldn't be the first time such a ploy has been used to draw out the unwary."

Tiarnan smiled then, an easy smile that fooled most of the men in the room. Most, but not all. Not Rory and not his father. Still considering that smile, Rory watched Tiarnan give another pause that struck him as dramatic. What was he up to?

"An escort would be a fine gesture on yer part," Tiarnan said.

Cathán couldn't keep the shock from his face and neither could Rory. Rory had made the jump—the wild guess—that somehow Saraid had been communicating with Tiarnan, sending thoughts or images or however it worked between the two of them. But now he wasn't sure. If Tiarnan planned to escape, he wouldn't be asking for an escort—which Rory would lay money translated to armed guard—to go with him.

Rory shifted his gaze to his father's face, watching him make the same assumptions. For Tiarnan to ask for men to accompany them, he must be sincere in his intentions to go and return. He meant to bring the others back with him. Then

Cathán glanced at him and quickly away, but that look was all it took to give Rory another flash of comprehension.

Cathán thought Stephen had yet to make his move.

The Ruairi they knew here was a hothead, a violent man who would've come out swinging if he'd survived the attack. No way could he have kept his cool and sauntered out with his new bride. At least that's what Cathán was banking on.

Rory rocked on the heels of his stiff sandals and considered that—tried to get into Cathán's head and put the pieces together in the same way his father would. To have all of Saraid's people here when Stephen did make his move . . . that would be a crowning moment, wouldn't it? Rory's murder, made to look like it was done by Saraid would prove that she and her people deserved to be wiped from the face of the earth. And here they would all be, just as he'd hoped. Sitting ducks waiting for the hunt.

Cathán signaled to one of the men standing behind him, stiff and ready to do his bidding. "Have twenty of your best escort our honored guests to their destination and back."

"Twenty?" Tiarnan said. "To escort me and two boys?"

The two "boys" stiffened in resentment but neither said a word.

"I wouldn't want anything to happen along the way," Cathán said with an innocent smile.

"And I appreciate yer concern, Half-Beard," Tiarnan said smoothly. "But that would seem more a guard than a courtesy, wouldn't it, then?"

And Rory finally saw the light. In that moment, he realized he hadn't given Tiarnan near enough credit.

Saraid's brother had known that Cathán wouldn't let them leave with a kiss and wave. By asking for the escort, he'd diffused Cathán's objections and undermined any attempts to send the whole fucking army out with him.

Cathán couldn't argue it, not in front of the people who watched with avid interest, not without showing his hand. But he considered Tiarnan, his piercing eyes searching for lies and deceit. Slowly he moved his gaze to the younger brothers, who stared back with open mouths. They obviously didn't have a clue. At last Cathán's gaze lit on Rory and watched him for long, drawn moments. He could feel his nerves stretching tight beneath that steady scrutiny. Feel the rising apprehension of the spectators as he stared calmly back. What chance did he stand if he was attacked now? And what would happen to Saraid after they brought Rory down?

At last Cathán looked away. "A dozen men, then," he said and snapped his fingers at his captain.

A dozen put the odds four to one against Saraid's brothers, but it was still better than twenty, and they might just stand a chance if the three were as capable as they looked. Rory let out a held breath, but then Cathán played one last card—one no one could have guessed.

"Mauri," he said, turning to his daughter. "Would you care to accompany Tiarnan and his brothers?"

Cathán's wife gasped, and the two guards behind Cathán stiffened with shock. Saraid's brothers did the same.

Mauri looked anxiously from her father to her mother to Tiarnan as if she couldn't believe what she'd heard. It was obvious that she wanted nothing more than to go with Tiarnan.

"No, I won't have it," Cathán's wife exclaimed hotly.

"Be quiet," Cathán snapped. To Mauri he said, "Well, what's it to be? Would you like to go?"

"That would be wonderful, Father," she said with a tremulous smile. "I would like to very much."

Cathán ignored his wife's sputtered arguments, but Rory figured she'd give him hell later if her red face and clenched fists were anything to go by. Mauri flung her arms around her father's neck and hugged him. Cathán's flat eyes never changed as he patted her back and pushed her away.

Without being told which twelve, the party gathered by the door. They were big men, all armed to the teeth, and the panic in Tiarnan's eyes glimmered for a hot second before he managed to hide it. They might have had a fighting chance standing united as three brothers against Cathán's men—some of whom looked a little worse for the drink. But throw Mauri into the mix—Tiarnan would be divided between his need to fight and protect.

Odds were, they'd be cut down before they could get their swords drawn if they tried anything. Saraid's grip on Rory's arm tightened, and her expression told him she'd come to the same conclusion.

"See that no harm comes to them or their people," Cathán told his men. "And have a care that my daughter enjoys herself. We are all family now."

In a matter of moments, Tiarnan, Eamonn, Michael, and Mauri were flanked by Cathán's meat-suits and escorted out of the hall. Tiarnan gave a last, troubled look back at his sister as he went. Saraid tried to keep her expression blank, but there was no disguising the fear in her eyes. She thought this was the last time she'd see them. She was probably right.

Not my problem, Rory reminded himself, but he couldn't meet her eyes, not when he knew the pain that would darken their velvet depths.

He'd told Saraid he would see her brothers out of the great hall and he had—not how he'd hoped, but they were out. Now he just needed to get the two of them back to the curtained room and through the hidden door. Then he could wipe his hands of the whole mess.

Really? a voice in his head jeered. *Really?*

"Christ," he muttered beneath his breath, giving Saraid's hand a pat that did nothing to reassure her.

"They'll be slaughtered," she breathed, turning her face to him so that no one else could hear.

"You don't know that," he said softly. "Tiarnan seems like a resourceful guy. He'll figure something out."

"Does that make it easier for y' to accept?" she demanded, keeping her voice down, but the anger in it cut sharp all the same. She acted like this was all his fault. It wasn't his idea to send Tiarnan out with Cathán's henchmen. That was all on Tiarnan.

He said, "Well, hanging around here isn't exactly the key to eternal life either, is it?"

"I do not care for this new man ye've become," she hissed. "At least the old Bloodletter looked his victims in the eye when he killed them."

Her words brought an instant visual of his hands around Stephen's throat, crushing. Stephen hadn't had eyes to look into. And now, apparently, he'd have the blood of her three brothers on his hands as well. He shook his head, searching for options. Finding none.

Without a word, he turned, pulling Saraid along with him,

avoiding the sparking temper in her gaze. Beneath his tunic he felt the pendant hanging from the leather cord around his neck, hot to the touch, burning his skin.

Life is about to get complicated, Nana said in his head. Jesus H. Christ.

He wanted to bolt, right then. Get the hell out of Dodge and figure out how to get back to his own world, but Saraid's hand on his arm anchored him in more ways than one. He might have failed her brothers but he'd be damned if he'd fail her, too.

He took a deep breath, and, as if they had all the time in the world, Rory guided Saraid to the head table and took seats beside the woman he guessed to be his stepmother. Her cold glare let him know he wouldn't have to worry about small talk.

A servant brought out strange, rectangular dishes that Rory surmised were the time's version of a plate. To him they looked like miniature troughs. A greasy slop was ladled into it and warm bread placed beside it. One trough was set between Rory and Saraid, apparently to share. He watched as platters were passed their way, laden with cheeses and fruits, meats and fowl, breads and sweets. Saraid took some of the cheese and set it at the edge of the trough. He did the same.

Mimicking the manners of those around him, Rory dipped his bread into the mess and ate it. It was salty and thick, but not as bad as it looked. After the first few bites, he realized he was starving, and he reached for some of the bird and the rib of something that might have been pork. He paced himself though, not wanting to have a lead stomach if he needed to move fast. It seemed Saraid was of the same mind. She nibbled at the roasted goose or duck or whatever in the hell it was.

As they ate it became clear to the crowd that the new bride and groom weren't going to do anything more exciting than feed their faces, and their attention finally moved on to the music and dancing. Cathán slumped in his chair and scowled at the party. Rory suspected he knew that in some way he'd been duped by Tiarnan, but he just wasn't clear on the how of it or what he'd missed.

Did he realize he'd sent his innocent daughter into a potential bloodbath? Did he care? Or was his daughter only a pawn to be used like Stephen? Like Ruairi?

With a deep breath, Rory leaned into Saraid, breathing in her scent of lavender and something else that was all her own. His hand at her back brushed the thick rope of her hair and he remembered what it had felt like in his hands, heavy and silky. He wanted to feel it brushing his chest as she leaned down to kiss him.

She'd been seducing him in his dreams for weeks. It should come as no surprise to him that she had the ability to do it in the flesh. The sooner he got away from her alluring presence, the better.

With his mouth close to her ear, he spoke softly. "It's time, princess."

Chapter Seventeen

R ORY felt like a two-bit actor performing in a really bad dinner theater. The lights were dim, the walls close, and the audience was near enough that he could smell their foul breath from his and Saraid's place at the head table. When he stood and pulled his bride to her feet, all eyes turned toward them. "We'll say good night now," he said woodenly.

"Good night? And where is it you think you're going?" Cathán demanded.

"No so far," Rory answered, forcing a smile. "I want to be alone with my new wife."

The words were forced and yet they started a flood of heat in his body. He did want to be alone with her in spite of everything going on. That had not changed a bit.

Though they'd spoken in low voices, they had the attention of those close enough to hear, and a knowing rumble spread through the room as those who watched put their own lewd meaning to Rory's desire for alone time with his bride.

"No. You will stay," Cathán said. "After Tiarnan has returned I will consider allowing you to go, but not until then."

"I wasn't asking for permission," Rory said.

Cathán's mouth tightened, though Rory could hear caution enter Cathán's tone when he spoke. He tried to exude congeniality and goodwill for the avid spectators. "But how can you think of depriving us of your lovely wife's company, especially when her people have not yet arrived?"

"Let them go," someone called in a jesting tone. "They are young. T'will not take so very long."

Laughter followed this, and Cathán forced a smile that gleamed hard from his eyes.

All the rage that Rory had managed to control since Stephen bounded from behind the tapestry and tried to murder him on behalf of his *father* surged within him now. But like his father, he treaded cautiously. Too many people were watching.

"We'll be back by the time her brothers get here," Rory said, stiff and formal. Unable to look full on at his father. Unable to reconcile this man to the memory he'd held for so many years. He had a good idea about the real reason Cathán wanted Rory to wait until Saraid's brothers returned. Cathán thought Stephen still lurked in the tunnel or somewhere in the curtained room and he had no way to tell Stephen to wait before he attacked. Wait until everyone was in place to witness Saraid emerging covered in Rory's blood.

Another voice jeered from the gathered people and others chimed in, shouting bawdy comments about Rory's speed and a woman's needs—and just how each should be handled. Saraid turned a deep shade of red, and Rory was pretty sure his face matched hers in color. Well they certainly looked the part of blushing bride and groom. Surprise, suspicion, and calculation darted through Cathán's eyes as he watched, and Rory cursed the reaction he couldn't control.

"You seem changed, boy," Cathán said softly.

Slowly, Rory looked into his father's face, wishing that Cathán would really see him. See who it was beneath the skin.

"What man isn't changed by marriage?" Rory asked, amazed at the words that came readily to his lips. Once again, it was the right thing to say and it left his father with no response. Cathán's wife didn't buy it, though. She made a soft sound of disbelief, drawing her husband's disapproving glare. Rory gave his father a quick bow that probably looked as stupid as it felt and then ushered Saraid behind the curtain.

Once on the other side, he and Saraid stood frozen for interminable minutes, waiting for his father to burst in, waiting for another of his minions to appear from nowhere and finish the job Stephen had started. The sound of heckles and laughter told Rory that though Cathán may have tried to come after them, the guests had thwarted his attempts. Cathán walked a fine line—he didn't want to misstep and act out of the ordinary, not when there were so many people here who might point it out later.

Thinking they were as safe as they were going to be—at least for the moment—Rory took Stephen's scabbard and blade from beneath the red blanket where it was hidden and belted it at his waist. He felt both comforted and awkward with it on. If he was attacked, could he pull it out and use it with any skill? Or would he only end up lopping off his own balls in the process? He hoped he wouldn't have to find out.

With a deep breath he moved to the hidden door. The latch popped quietly and he opened it. He took a candle from one of the sconces and poked his head inside the dark cavern. The tunnel was small and tight at the entrance, but up ahead it seemed to fan out and become wider and taller. Saraid might be able to stand straight at that point, though it looked like he would have to crouch the whole way.

"Come on," he said, moving aside so she could enter first.

Saraid hesitated, and he caught the shadow of fear in her eyes. Was it the dark and closed space or was it Rory that scared her? He didn't ask. Where was the point? It was this way or no way.

Silently he handed her the candle.

"You'll have to crawl at first," he said. "Just for a while."

She gave a short, jerky nod and went down on her knees. He could hear her breath coming in short bursts, almost feel her heart pounding with fear as he waited.

"I'll be right behind you," he said softly.

She looked at him over her shoulder, her eyes round and frightened, making him wish there was another way—but there wasn't. It was this or nothing. "I don't like small spaces," she said, her voice hitching.

The confession seemed to pain her, but even now, defiance glittered in the mahogany depths of her eyes.

He smiled gently and crouched down beside her. "I'm not so crazy about them either. But I'll take this tunnel over what Cathán has planned. How about you?"

"Yes."

But she didn't move. Didn't start down that dark and winding passageway. He brushed his fingertips over her brow, down the satiny softness of her cheek. Her lashes fluttered for a moment and it seemed she leaned closer. He forced himself not to test the waters, not to reach for her. This wasn't the place. There wasn't the time. But she was like a trip switch in his head, blocking logic and flooding him with thoughts that went no further than the feel of her, the taste, the need.

"I'll be right here," he said, his voice deep and husky, even to his own ears. "I won't let anything happen to you."

She licked her lips, drawing his gaze with the small gesture. "It's not that . . . it's . . ."

She looked into the gaping hole, and a shudder went through her. He felt the vibrations of it and wanted to hold her, reassure her. He moved his hand to the tense muscles at the back of her neck, rubbed softly, waited for her to reject his comfort.

Instead she looked at him with those velvet eyes and whispered, "What if we can't get out?"

He hadn't wanted to think of that—of what would happen if they got to the end of the line to find a rock wall waiting. By then turning around and coming back might be just as wrong. And if Cathán realized what they'd done, where they'd gone, he'd need only to close up the tunnel exit and let them die a slow and torturous death sealed inside until they rotted away. . . .

"I told you I'd get us out of here," Rory said, trying to sound confident. He couldn't tell if he failed or succeeded. "And I will."

Her eyes seemed huge and endless as they scanned his face. She wasn't convinced, but she lifted the candle and with a deep breath, crawled into the tunnel. He joined her in the cramped space, hesitating a moment before pulling the door shut behind them. Only the weak pool of candlelight broke the thick wall of darkness that descended. Saraid sucked in breath that sounded harsh and thick with anxiety.

"Easy girl," he murmured. "Just start moving. It'll be all right."

"I do not think I can," she said, her tone angry and helpless at once.

He touched her shoulder, feeling the stiff posture, the rigid muscles frozen with fear. She wasn't going anywhere.

"Okay," he said. "It's okay. Look, why don't I move around you, go first? Would that make it better?"

She didn't answer, but he thought she gave a small nod. Her skin looked pale and waxy in the flickering gloom. A fine sheen covered her face and the hand holding the candle trembled, splashing the walls with a writhing glow.

Carefully he moved forward. The space was tight, barely wide enough for one of them, let alone both. He had to pull her into him, wrap his arms around her quivering shoulders and shift, inch by inch, to get by. He could feel each ragged breath she took, smell the heat of her skin, her fear, her awareness of every shifting shadow. It seemed to take a very long time to maneuver around and all the while he was aware of how close to the door they were, how at any moment his father might yank it open and catch them. And then what would he do? Skewer them like a couple of pieces of meat? They were wasting time—time they didn't have.

"Cool it," he muttered to himself, trying to keep his head. Now was not the time to freak out.

Saraid almost set him on fire with the candle as he finally eased his body around—and wasn't the idea of burning in the coffin-sized space enough to make him panic—but somehow he managed to reverse their positions without dying a terrible death.

"There," he said, still speaking low, as if to a wild animal caught in this trap. He shot an anxious glance past her to the door. "We're all good, right? Give me your hand."

He felt her startled gaze, her embarrassment, her discomfort with her terror. She was used to being strong, in control. But the clenching black of the tunnel had reduced her to jangling emotions. She put her hand in his, her trust in him, and the weight of that small gesture settled uneasily on his shoulders. He wasn't used to people depending on him. He was Rory MacGrath, the hell-raiser who'd been banished from his home, not the guy you turned to when you were in trouble.

He crawled awkwardly, one hand reaching out to feel what was ahead, the other reaching back, holding hers. His shoulders and body blocked the candlelight from reaching the crevasses in front of him, so he moved blindly, trying to remember the path he'd seen when he'd looked in. The tunnel floor was rough, with sharp edges and hard surfaces. His hands and knees were raw by the time they'd made it to the place where the twisting tunnel sloped sharply down before leveling out and becoming bigger. He'd been right. Saraid could stand straight here, but he had to bend to keep his head attached to his shoulders. Still, it beat crawling, and he was grateful to get off his knees.

He rose, pulling her up with him, bending to brush off the pebbles that clung to her skirts. She held the candle between them, watching him with eyes that seemed to have swallowed her face.

"You all right?" he asked, when he finished.

"Yes. Thank you."

He smiled at her and pushed a lock of hair behind her ear. "Good. Let's keep moving."

They could walk side by side now, but Saraid kept hold of his hand. Her fingers were as small and fine-boned as a bird, and more than once he caught himself running his thumb over the softness to the erratic pulse at her wrist. The caress felt as natural as the heat between their palms. Did she feel it, too, that current that seemed to travel between them when they touched? Or was she oblivious to it, to him?

Feeling like a fool with his first crush, he turned his thoughts back to the banquet hall, to his father's eyes as he'd watched him. Cathán knew something wasn't right, just not what. How long would it take before he pulled back the curtain and discovered them gone? And what would he do then? Where would the attack come from? Behind them, in the tunnel? Or ahead, where it came out? Both? His tension increased as he worried it, playing in his mind possible scenarios. None ended with him the victor, though. Finally he shut down his thoughts altogether and focused only on putting one foot in front of the other, making sure Saraid did the same.

He couldn't have said how long they were in the tunnel. It felt like days of straining to hear anything beyond the sounds they made themselves, anything above the hammer of his heart in his chest and the roaring of his blood in his ears.

After what seemed an eternity, Saraid said, "I smell fresh air."

Surprised, he paused and took a deep breath. It was there, a breeze, redolent and fecund, thick and damp. Hunching to avoid whacking his head on a low-hanging stone, he pulled Saraid forward, and at last, the pale glow of moonlight hovered just ahead. They'd hit the other side.

He wanted to whoop with relief, but caution kept him silent. He inched closer to the end of the tunnel, feeling the brush of cool air against his skin—the relief of knowing he wouldn't have to face Saraid's worst nightmare with her.

A few feet from the opening, he suddenly stopped, putting a hand out to still Saraid before she bowled him over. Slowly he touched her lips with his finger and shook his head. A playful breeze blundered into the tunnel and doused their candle.

Without the hiss and flicker, they both stilled, straining to hear beyond their isolation. Chirping crickets mingled with the creaks and groans, and rustling leaves. The seesawing harmony went on, unbroken until the howl of a wolf pierced the night. A second later the clatter of rocks skittering against one another cracked the quiet, but the tunnel distorted the sound and they couldn't tell if it had come from near or far.

Then silence settled again, hushing even the crickets.

"What did y' hear?" Saraid whispered, her lips to his ear, her warm breath a fan against his skin.

He wasn't sure, but something had triggered a flush of adrenaline and rush of tension inside him. He shook his head, alert and listening, straining to dissect the silence. And there it was. A soft jingle, so faint it might have been imagined except for the deep exhalation that followed. *A horse?* Instinct told him he was right.

So was it Cathán's men, then? Waiting to pick them off as soon as they stepped out?

He made a hand motion for Saraid to stay put and quietly pried her fingers from his own. He slipped from the tunnel into the deepest shadows, crouching and rolling under a bush as he did, bracing himself for the slicing pain of a sword piercing his body. Surprised when it didn't come.

Slowly, carefully, he peered out from the concealing foliage. Ahead was forest, dark and intimidating as anything God had ever created. The trees stood like giants, branches twisted and stark in the moonlight, trunks twice again the span of a man's arms, roots thick and bubbling up from the ground. To the left and reaching out behind him was a wide swath of dirt road cut into the forest. And there at the edge was a horse standing placidly beside a jutting boulder.

The horse snorted and shifted its weight with restless boredom. It had been here a while. Rory knew it with bone-deep certainty, but he couldn't say just what made him sure. It felt like more than a guess, but there was nothing to back that up, just the weird feeling that he was right.

Warily Rory lifted his head to see over the bush, looking for a rider. As far as his eyes could penetrate the moonlit darkness, nothing moved but the branches swaying with the breeze. He ducked back down, turned, and looked in the other direction. Nothing there either.

What did that mean? That the rider was off taking a leak somewhere? Or that he was hiding, waiting for the idiots in the tunnel to step out? The second seemed most likely, and Rory looked again, scanning every shape, every shifting shadow. Not a damned thing moved.

He eased silently back into the tunnel where Saraid waited.

"What did y' see?" she asked in whisper.

"There's a horse, but no rider."

She pulled her brows together, thinking. "Just one?"

He nodded.

"And what color is it?"

The question caught him by surprise. What did that matter? "Brown."

"Does it have markings? White stockings?"

Yes, it had four white socks. He nodded again. "Why?"

"That would be Stephen's horse. Left here to take him away after . . ."

After he murdered Ruairi the Bloodletter. She didn't have to finish the sentence.

It made sense, and he should have thought of it himself. But hell, this world had him turned inside out—literally. He was lucky to be thinking at all.

"That's good," he said, giving her a weak smile. "Good thinking."

She looked flustered by the lame compliment, and he found his smile stretching. It was cute how tough she played and how easy it was to ruffle her feathers. In another time, another world, things between them might have been so much different.

She took two steps toward the tunnel opening, instantly wiping the smile off his face.

"Hang on," he said, stopping her just before she made it into the open. Good thinking didn't make her right for God's sake. "You wait here."

He strode out a little bolder now, but still expecting that bite of metal cutting through his skin. The memory of being gored like a pig was too fresh not to worry about a repeat performance. The horse looked up with interest when he appeared and whinnied in greeting, but nothing else moved save the leaves in the trees and the second hand ticking away in his head. As if waiting for a cue, the crickets began to chirp once more.

"It is his horse," Saraid said, standing at Rory's elbow.

"I told you to wait."

She raised her brows, back to her cocky and defiant self now that he'd saved her from the tunnel monsters.

"And why would y' be thinking I'd take orders from the likes of y'?" she asked, brushing past him with a haughty tilt of her chin.

He caught up with her as she approached the horse. It was agitated now, dancing on the end of its tether, eyeing Saraid with distrust. Making soft hushing noises, she reached out and took the reins that were looped around a low branch.

"Shhhh, Pooka. 'Tis just me," she murmured, stroking the horse's neck.

"How do you know this is Stephen's horse?" asked Rory, more than a little ticked off but not sure if it was because of the woman, her attitude, or his own timidity, which seemed like cowardice now that they were out in the open without any immediate threat materializing.

"Because Stephen stole it from my brother," she answered. "This is Pooka. I helped raise him."

Pooka breathed deeply, and Rory felt the recognition of Saraid's scent register with the animal. It calmed instantly and nuzzled her ear with a soft grunt. Another besotted male. Just what they needed.

Rory took a step forward, placing a hand gingerly on the horse's haunches. The skin beneath his palm gathered in tension and the big stallion turned and looked at him, assessing. Rory stared back, feeling a queer sense of communication passing between him and the animal. It tingled over all his senses and left him charged with static electricity. After a long moment, the horse gave him a dismissive grunt and went back to nuzzling Saraid. The two were engrossed in their happy little reunion and neither seemed to care whether he stayed or left. Well that was fine. It solved a big problem.

"Can you ride?" he asked, and Saraid gave him a distracted nod as she rubbed Pooka's long nose.

"And you know where your brothers will go? You know where to meet them?"

Another nod, this one with some hesitation, as if she knew what was coming. He checked the saddlebags on the horse, found a leather pouch filled with water, took a drink, offered some to Saraid.

There was hardtack in the bags, a blanket tied to the back of the saddle. *She will be okay*, he told himself. This was her world and she'd survived the last twenty-five years without him.

"Then it's here we go our separate ways, princess," he said.

Her startled gaze snapped to his face, those eyes big and clear. "And which way will y' be going?" she asked calmly.

"South," he said, and turned to face that way.

"Alone?" she asked, her voice curiously light and unconcerned.

"That's right. You'll be better off without me. You can ride back to . . . to where you came from in half the time it will take if there's two of us. And I've got business of my own to take of."

"Aye. Of course."

He took his first step away from her, then another, finding it harder than he'd imagined to keep going. All those nights of chasing Saraid and here he was walking away.

"Fool," he muttered to himself, but what else should he do? If the Book had brought him here, it had to be the way to get back home. And getting back was more important than staying with this woman who obviously didn't want him . . . wasn't it?

She said nothing until he was several feet gone, and then she asked, "Is that where y' think ye'll find it?"

He turned. "What did you say?"

"I said, is that where y' think ye'll find it?"

"Find what?"

"The Book of course. Is it not why ye've come?"

He stared at her in silent surprise, feeling again that she'd cast a spell on him, because he wanted to say *no*. No, he hadn't come for anything but her—a woman he'd thought a dream until just that morning.

She crossed the distance that separated them and looked deeply into his eyes. Hers were a dark glimmer surrounded by thick black lashes. He couldn't read what was in them, but she seemed to have no difficulties seeing what was in his own.

"Do y' think it will give y' what yer looking for?" she asked softly.

"What do you mean? I'm not looking for anything but a way home. I don't belong here."

"Are y' sure about that, Ruairi?"

Perplexed, he shook his head, wondering why he didn't just laugh. Wondering why he felt he *needed* to hear her next words.

"I only ask because it seems to me that y' are here for a reason. Perhaps yer not meant to leave."

He wanted to say something sharp and smart, but he could only watch as she took another step closer. A shaft of moonlight caught her unaware, and now he saw something in her eyes that set off a small jangling alarm in his head. Her hands settled on his chest, and he felt a tremor go through her.

"Have y' thought," she said, and she licked her lips, glancing up and quickly away as she did. Gauging his reaction. "Have y' thought that maybe y' were meant to be with me?"

She came up on tiptoe and pressed her mouth to his. For a moment, that light touch was the answer to every question he'd ever had. Maybe he *was* meant to be here, with her. Then it hit him, what had started that alarm inside him. Colleen had told

Saraid that he would save her people, and she wasn't about to let him walk away if there was a chance it was true.

She was playing him.

She didn't care about Rory. Hell, until a few hours ago, she'd thought him a bloodthirsty killer. He was someone she'd hated for years. The duplicity in her kiss hit him harder than it should have. He grabbed her arms and backed her up, torn between the desire to kiss her until she forgot about everything but him or push her away and turn his back forever. It seemed she saw the flash of hurt, of anger in his eyes, and she couldn't hold his gaze. Flushing, she looked down, her shoulders hunched in defeat.

Before he could even think of what to say, he felt a hint of fear sparking against his senses.

Not his fear, not even hers.

He looked around just as the horse raised its head and swiveled its ears. A fine shiver of alarm ran through its thoughts and broadcasted out like a radio signal to Rory.

"Shit," he muttered, shaken by the realization that he'd somehow heard the horse's thoughts. "They're coming."

Chapter Eighteen

THE night was sharp and crisp as Tiarnan and his brothers left Cathán Half-Beard's keep. Above them a hard, flat moon bore down from a speckled sky, both witness and illuminator of the tragedy that was sure to come. As they moved through the still and silent compound, Tiarnan tried not to think of the songs the bards would sing of this night, or the fool's part he played in it. But he could hear the notes, tittering with the forest sounds, taunting, jeering . . . truthful. He had no one to blame but himself. From the moment Cathán had sent Ruairi the Bloodletter with his proposal for peace, Tiarnan had played the ultimate fool.

Cathán was not a man to make peace when he could take control. Nor did he ever forgive and forget. There was always a plan. Always a step and counterstep. Always an outcome in his favor. The old ones—those who'd survived Cathán's first attacks and the years of flight that followed—had warned Tiarnan. But he hadn't listened. He'd wanted to believe the unbelievable, and when word had reached him that Cathán would meet in a public place, a neutral place, Tiarnan had gone with hope building in his chest.

They'd come together at the keep of Big Calhoun, an honest man who believed as Tiarnan did that peace could be made. Calhoun was a shared ally, someone Tiarnan had known since he was a babe, someone so powerful that Cathán had not dared raid him. In front of Calhoun himself, Cathán had gifted Tiarnan with food, cattle, supplies that they desperately needed and proposed the match between Saraid and the Bloodletter. The offer had seemed sincere, heartfelt even, and both he and Calhoun had taken it for truth.

They'd both been fools.

Now Tiarnan looked around him with despair that bordered on complete desolation. Cathán Half-Beard's men rode three in front, with a point man centered in the lead. To the right and left of Tiarnan and Mauri, two more guards made brackets, holding them in formation. Four others hemmed Eamonn and Michael in just as completely. And following behind, the last three. Tiarnan noted that the rear guard was composed of the biggest men, and they rode straight and silent. Alert to every shift, every thought that might flit through their doomed hostages' heads. Of the dozen guards, only a few were worse for the wear of too much drink and food—something Tiarnan had counted on afflicting them all. The rest were ready for battle.

No, the rest were hoping for it. He could see it in their eager eyes. In the casual caress of their weapons, in the tight clench of their fists.

"This is very exciting, isn't it, Tiarnan?" Mauri said, mounted on a docile white mare beside him. She spoke in the same refined manner as her father, reminding him of the vast differences between them. "First Saraid and Ruairi . . . I confess I did not know such a match had hope, but to look at them this eve, they seemed happy, did they not?"

Her eyes sparkled with pleasure, and the brisk night air had made her cheeks rosy. The smile she gave him was open and without guile, and his heart crumbled beneath the weight of it. She had no idea her father had used her in his deceit, used them all. There was no happiness in the match of Saraid and Ruairi just as there was no desire to please in his offer to allow Mauri a journey with Tiarnan.

"Must we go far to reach your people?" she asked. "I do hope so. I hope we will ride for the entire night. I feel more alive here and now than I have for all of my life."

The blurted declaration ended with a shy giggle, but she looked deeply into Tiarnan's eyes as she spoke, and he felt the passion behind her words. If only this crossing was what it appeared to be. A token of acceptance for both their people. Cathán, allowing his daughter to accompany them. Tiarnan, bringing his lambs into the pen, not the slaughter.

"It will take us some time to reach them," he said softly.

"I was surprised when my father suggested I come, Tiarnan. But I am filled with hope now. He would not have sent me if he didn't trust you. If he did not believe that perhaps there might be another union between our families."

She looked away, and Tiarnan watched with fascination as she caught her lip with her teeth and waited for what he would say.

"Y' know I would do anything to make that so, Mauri."

She nudged her horse closer to his and touched his arm, her hand featherlight, her skin warm and silken. "You must ask him again, Tiarnan. He will say yes this time. I know it."

Tiarnan swallowed the hot ball of fury and shame that lodged in his throat. Cathán would not say yes, even if Tiarnan lived long enough to ask, which was highly doubtful.

Eamonn chose that moment to spur his horse forward so that he rode on the other side of Tiarnan. "What now?" he asked beneath his breath.

Tiarnan glanced at their flanking guard, noting the one to his right had fallen into a limber sway that matched the horse's gait. He'd seen that rhythmic motion before, ridden in the same unbroken patter. That guard dozed in the saddle. The one behind him was alert, yet Tiarnan sensed he was more attuned to the forest surrounding them than the three men they escorted. These woods were filled with deer and boar, rabbit and quail. He'd hunted them as a youth, depended on them now for the livelihood of his people.

"Does Eamonn not know where the others are?" Mauri asked innocently, leaning forward to smile at Tiarnan's brother.

Disconcerted by the angelic look she gave him, Eamonn blushed and scowled at the same time. "I know," he said gruffly.

Eamonn nudged his horse closer and lowered his voice more so that Mauri couldn't hear. Hurt at being excluded, she looked away.

"Well? What now?" Eamonn urged again.

Tiarnan had no answer. What could they do? Make a run for it? Hope that at least one of them survived? Stand and fight, knowing they would surely die? Tiarnan was a warrior, fierce and feared on the open battlefield. He could draw his sword and be done with the two on his right before the men even knew he'd armed himself. He could whirl and take out the next two or three that came at him. But could his brothers do the same? Eamonn, yes, but Michael? Michael would be cut down before he could fumble his sword free. And what of Mauri? How could he protect both his younger brother and her at the same time?

Mauri touched his arm again, drawing his attention back to her. "Will you dance with me when we return, Tiarnan?"

He felt like bait dangling between two fish, each jerking him to their side as they nibbled, devouring the bits and pieces of him they tore free, both just short of swallowing him whole.

"I would love it so if we danced," Mauri went on.

"If your father will allow it, that would make me happy as well," he said woodenly.

In his head, he played out every possible scenario that might result with the two of them dancing. But it was no use. In all likelihood, he would die tonight. It was a truth that could not be denied.

So that left one option. Fight. To the death if necessary.

He sat straighter, putting shoulders back. Throwing off that weight of inevitability that had near crippled him since he'd seen his sister emerge in her gown of blue, eyes wide and brave. Facing the fate he'd brought her without tears, without recrimination. He could do the same. He *would* do the same.

It would be crucial that he get to the three men in the back first. But to do that, he would have to spin and cut a swath through the guards on the left. If Eamonn could be counted on to move right and take out that flank, it just might work. That would leave both Mauri and Michael in the middle where they might be caught in the cross fire, though. But if Cathán's men tried to defend Mauri, she might be just as much a liability to them as she was to Tiarnan. He nodded to himself, working out how that could be used to his advantage.

Then another thought came as he remembered the words Saraid had spoken inside his head. Cathán had already tried to kill his son. What if, like Ruairi the Bloodletter, Mauri was expendable to her father? What if Cathán had plotted this whole night with the cold-blooded brutality he had his own son's murder? If Cathán was willing to sacrifice his son, why not his daughter as well?

Had he given instructions to his guards to kill her? Make it appear that Tiarnan and his brothers had slain the girl?

Could anyone be that ruthless?

Tiarnan was not one for strategy—he knew this. Knew he was out of his depths trying to guess what a man like Cathán Half-Beard would do. It would only tie him in knots trying to unravel the long rope of his plan. All he could do was act on what his instincts told him to be true. Mauri being here was an impulsive decision on Cathán's part. He had not been prepared for the Bloodletter to emerge from the curtained chamber, not been prepared to let Tiarnan and his brothers go, and so he had improvised and thrown his daughter into the mix of his deceit.

"Mauri," Tiarnan said, keeping his voice soft so the guards couldn't hear. "Has yer father never talked of other matches for y'? Someone"— *better*—"more suitable to marry the daughter of a king?"

"Who more suitable than the son of a king?" she asked sweetly.

"I'm serious."

Mauri sighed. "He has talked of wedding me to Thorgils, but it's not what I want."

Thorgils was fifty if he was a day and he looked every minute of it. The Northman was gnarled and chewed, missing bits and pieces of his fingers and ears, leaving behind a disjoined visage that frightened children. Tiarnan's gut clenched at the thought of gentle, kind Mauri mated with the scarred warrior. It was unthinkable. But not to Cathán.

"Tiarnan, this is not the time to woo your love," Eamonn said, anger in the tight, clipped words that were spoken no louder than a whisper.

"What do y' suggest?" Tiarnan breathed back, watching the guards flanking them from the corner of his eye. The one still dozed, but the others rode backs straight and attention forward. He knew they strained to listen.

"Something," Eamonn insisted. *"Anything."*

As it always had been. Eamonn expected him to make an impossible situation into something that it wasn't. It's what all of his people wanted from him.

Ahead, Gormán, Cathán's lead man, pulled up on his reins and halted his horse. One by one, the rest of them did the same. They'd come to the point where the road branched off, and the time to make decisions could no longer be avoided. All around them the night sucked in a breath of anticipation, silencing the squawking and chittering, muffling even the rustle of leaves.

"Which way?" Gormán demanded.

Michael nudged his horse forward and came abreast of Tiarnan. The three of them sat in a straight line, Mauri between them. Tiarnan felt the weight of expectation, of their hope as they waited for him to speak again. Couldn't they see he had no choices? Couldn't they understand that all directions led to disaster?

"North," he said at last. "We go north until we reach the river."

Tiarnan felt Eamonn start as he heard the truth spoken. He hoped his brother would be aware of what it meant that he hadn't lied—there was no way he'd take these marauders to where their people waited. That meant that somewhere between here and there, they would have to be stopped, no matter the risk, no matter the outcome. Tiarnan chanced a glance at Eamonn and caught the widening of his eyes.

Yes, he understood.

Michael, however, looked only stunned. As he'd feared, Michael would not be of use when the battle came . . . and it would come. Tiarnan could feel the back and forth of destiny's sword as it cut the air above his head, each swing bringing it closer to his scalp.

As they started again, Tiarnan frantically struggled with their dilemma. There had to be a way, some weakness to be used to the advantage. . . . Twelve men to their three and one woman . . . Tiarnan scanned the forest, desperately searching for an answer.

When it came, it was like a knife to his heart.

There was only one weakness, and it was one they all shared.

Mauri.

If Cathán was planning on marrying her to Thorgils, then perhaps he didn't mean to sacrifice her here at all. Which meant the men would do whatever it took to protect her. Tiarnan must use that loyalty to defeat them.

He nodded, feeling the weight of his decision settle heavily around him. "Mauri?" he said softly.

"Yes, Tiarnan?"

"We have a way to go still. Would y' like to rest a moment before we continue?"

She gazed at him with trusting eyes. "Aye, I would like that."

He called to Gormán. "Mauri needs to rest."

Gormán reined his horse around and stared suspiciously at Tiarnan. "Is it so much farther?"

"For a delicate girl like Mauri, yes," Tiarnan answered. Dutifully, Mauri nodded.

Their winding trail had led them to a spot Tiarnan knew very well. Low and flat, it opened on one side to a grassy meadow that swayed in silent commune with the white moonshine. Surrounding it was a steep crag that rose up like a sentry to a point that was home to an old monument, shaped like a finger pointing to the sky. Its long shadow tracked the rising and setting sun as it circled the mound built around it. At its base, huge boulders lay in a tumble of sharp edges and unmovable surfaces, as if a giant had cracked the top of the peak and everything had toppled down but the sharp spire.

"Come," Tiarnan said cordially, taking Mauri's arm. "Sit over here and I'll bring y' water."

Gormán laughed at his manners, but Tiarnan ignored him, knowing—hoping—he'd be the last to laugh. "Michael," he called. "Bring my flask."

Michael did as he was told and, as Tiarnan had expected, Eamonn followed him to the largest of the boulders where he waited with Mauri. Taking the flask from Michael, Tiarnan let his gaze roam over Cathán's men. They stood in a half circle, talking amongst themselves, keeping a watchful eye on Tiarnan and his brothers. One of them stood off to the side, holding the reins of their horses.

The situation would not get better.

Feeling like his limbs were made of lead, Tiarnan moved close to Mauri, leaned down and whispered in her ear.

"Forgive me."

"Forgive you? Why, Tiarnan, whatever for?" she began just as Tiarnan grabbed her and jerked her back against his chest, one arm clamped across her small, soft breasts. Her body fit snuggly to the length of his, all curves and yielding flesh. They should be joined like this in love, not in war. Not in betrayal. He held her tight when she tried to squirm away, and using his free hand, he laid his knife to her throat.

With speed that would have filled him with pride had not the circumstances been so shameful, Eamonn and Michael drew their weapons and moved in beside him. The three of them stood with their backs to the towering crag, facing twelve furious men with only Mauri in between.

"Tiarnan? What are you doing?" Mauri cried. She tried to jerk free, and his blade nearly nicked the silky skin of her throat.

"Hold still, damn y'," he growled in her ear. "Do not make me hurt y'."

"Yer a fool, Tiarnan," Gormán said, taking bold steps forward.

"Aye, I've heard that before. Drop yer weapons, right there. Now."

"I don't think so."

Tiarnan tightened his grip on Mauri, dying inside as she whimpered. "Y' test me?" he shouted with far more conviction than he felt. "You'd rather face Cathán with his daughter in pieces?"

"Y' won't hurt the girl."

Tiarnan didn't bother to answer. Instead he pressed the point of his knife into her throat until he pricked the skin and a trickle of blood spilled over his blade.

Mauri cried out with fear and pain.

It was wrong. It was so very wrong. Inside him, pieces began to fall away, like the great stones from the spire, tumbling down, down until his soul was left in ruins.

Gormán ceased his advance. "Y' have bigger balls than I gave y' credit for," he said with grudging admiration. "But I will kill y' nonetheless."

"Perhaps. But not this day. Weapons. On the ground."

Gormán gave a nod and slowly, reluctantly, the men began to strip their weapons. Gormán bent to toss his sword into the pile and shot a quick glance to the man at his left. It happened so fast, Tiarnan barely had a moment to register what had transpired before a blade was sailing toward him. He shifted, instinctively twisting to shelter Mauri from the attack. In the same instant, the man on the right charged and everything seemed to slow to a painful stop.

The knife flew toward him like a hawk made of silver. Michael lifted his sword and brought it down, fiercely cleaving the man just in front, wrenching the blade free and slicing through to the second. Tiarnan had underestimated his younger brother's reflexes. On his other side, Eamonn plunged his blade into the man who'd thrown the knife and then pressed forward to the next. And as Tiarnan spun to avoid the flying blade, he tripped and slammed back against the wall.

He saw the blur of silver and then heard the sickening sound of it hitting flesh, then bone. He jerked, instinctively bracing for the searing pain that did not come. His shocked brain registered the flow of hot blood splashing his face, the wheeze of Mauri's breath as she fainted away. The sight of the knife protruding from her shoulder, buried deep in a ghastly wound filled him.

It was all he needed to see. The searing heat of a warrior's rage washed over him, turning everything red and black and fierce. The cry that broke from his lips as he charged pierced the night like a banshee's scream, hurting, tearing. Knife in one hand, sword in the other, Tiarnan leapt into the fray.

Chapter Nineteen

CURSING under his breath, Rory strode past Saraid, untied Pooka's reins from the tree branch, looped them over the horse's head, and secured them to the strange saddle it wore on its back. The animal had become more agitated by the moment, and Rory soothed it, running his hands down its sleek neck. He cleared his head of the emotional tangle he felt over Saraid's deception and tried to think calming thoughts. He pictured the stables he'd seen as they entered the village with the wedding party, thought of oats and hay and the boy he'd seen mucking the stalls. The horse's ears perked and swiveled and it gave him a soft whinny and head toss that looked suspiciously like a nod. There was intelligence in the dark brown of its eyes. Intelligence and understanding that disconcerted Rory as much as the knowledge that danger was coming and coming fast.

"Go on now," Rory murmured, giving the horse a gentle swat on its rump.

With a toss of his head, Pooka took off in the direction of the keep, gaining speed as if compelled.

"What are y' doing?" Saraid demanded, watching the horse gallop away with wide, shocked eyes.

Without answering, Rory took her hand, pulling Saraid in the opposite direction, into the thick growth of trees and undergrowth. "One of two things is happening here," he said softly as he stepped off the worn path and into the dense foliage. "Either they figured out we're not coming back and they sent someone to get us, or they're here to kill Stephen when he comes out."

She said nothing, but he heard the sharp intake of breath.

"Whichever it is, we don't want to be around to find out. If we take the horse, they'll have a better chance of tracking us. With a little luck, they won't think we'd head into the woods."

"No, they won't think that," she said. "Only someone brainsick would head into these woods."

With that she paused to hike up her gown and wrap the extra material around her arm. He waited, unabashedly taking in the flash of creamy thigh and long calf, remembering the feel of all that skin sliding up his own legs, wrapping around his back . . . would it be so bad to be stuck here with her, no matter her reasons for wanting him? He'd already had a taste of what she'd do for duty and it had been very, very sweet.

She looked up, caught him staring, and for a moment their gazes held. There was something earthy in the look that passed between them, something as dark and sensuous as the lush scent and rich fertility of the flora surrounding them. Was it real? Or was it just a renewed effort to seduce him into being the savior Colleen had told her was coming?

Blushing, but steely eyed, she gave him a brisk nod to continue. Without a word, he took her hand again and they moved silently through the deep and dark woods that exploded with chirping, scratching, rustling, and angry cawing as they approached and then fell into a midnight quiet as they were upon it. Rory had the sense of undulating corridors that stood opened behind and ahead of them, echoing with a clamoring ruckus of wildlife. But in the circumference of their presence not even the whispering sigh of the leaves in the breeze could be heard.

"Why would they kill Stephen?" she asked in a low voice after a few moments of dodging fallen logs and half-submerged stones.

"If he'd done his job, he'd be the only witness other than you. The only one who could tell the truth about what happened behind that curtain. No one would believe you without someone else to support your story."

"Y' think Cathán would kill both of his sons? But he would be wiping his own seed from the earth. There would be no heir left to take up his holdings when he's gone."

"Does he look like he's worried about getting old and dying to you?"

He could see her thinking over that one, picturing Cathán's youthful face and fit body. He should be in his fifties, but look close and he didn't appear a day older than Rory.

As they moved deeper into the woods, the branches overhead grew so thick that they blocked out the bright moon and stars. Beneath, it was almost as black as the tunnel had been and twice as treacherous. Each step had to be taken with care. As near as Rory could tell, they were headed east, northeast most likely. Certainly away from the Isle of Fennore, his destination, the last place he'd seen the Book of Fennore.

When they were far enough from the tunnel that he felt safe stopping for a moment and regrouping, Rory pulled out the flask he'd found on the horse and took a drink before silently handing it to Saraid. She stared at it for a moment before finally taking it from him. Even in the darkness he could see that her face was flushed, her eyes bright. Even knowing she'd tried to manipulate him, he couldn't look away.

"Where are you supposed to meet your brothers?" he asked softly.

"There's a waterfall north of here, tucked back from the forest. It can only be seen from the hills above."

"How far is it?"

"Half a day on horseback. Not far."

He would have laughed, but she looked so serious he didn't. They'd be lucky to make it by sunset tomorrow and that was trudging on without a break. He looked down at her slippers. If they were half as uncomfortable as they looked, midnight might be closer to the mark.

"Do not worry over me," she said sharply. "I'll not slow y' down."

He might have told her that wasn't what he was thinking, but instead he shrugged and let her believe what she wanted.

The going was slow and difficult the deeper they went into the wooded area. Roots seemed to snake out and snag their feet, stones lay hidden under leaves only to thrust up and trip them. Vines tangled around their ankles and branches barred their way. It felt as if the plants had become living beings determined to keep them captive. He figured they'd been trudging through the darkness for just a few hours, but it felt like days.

"'Tis a fairies' woods," Saraid said softly, her strange statement somehow a reflection of his thoughts.

He glanced back at her just as she stumbled over a root as thick as his arm and caught her before she went face-first into the foliage. The action earned him a hot look that made him think of pulling her closer, of holding all that heat against him.

"What's that supposed to mean?" he asked. "A fairies' woods?"

"Only that people get lost in such places, and if they are so lucky as to escape, they are forever changed."

"Changed? In what way?"

"In the most important way, of course," she answered, her voice low. "Sometimes it is their minds that go. Sometimes their youth and others times it's their senses. Fairies are fickle creatures."

Her eyes glittered darkly as she watched him and for a moment he suspected she was one of the fairy folk and he'd never escape her spell. Where was the point in resisting? But she'd hurt his pride when she'd faked the attraction that he couldn't seem to control, even when he was pissed off at her.

He still held her arm in his hand and he could feel the warmth of her skin through the thin fabric of her gown. He could still picture her stripped and gleaming in the candlelight as she'd moved beneath him. But if he was honest, he'd have to admit he'd been thinking of her like that for much longer. He'd been ensnared since the first time she'd stepped into his dreams.

"Y' can release me now," she said, and pulled her arm free, yet even as she did it, he felt the reluctance in her that was at odds with her words and her actions.

"What? You don't want to convince me to stay anymore?"

She narrowed her eyes. "I'm no seductress, obviously. It was foolish to think it would work."

"Oh it would work," he said. "You just have to try a little harder."

"Do not play yer games with me," she said sharply.

"Sorry. I didn't realize you had the monopoly on that."

"It is not a game for me. It is life."

"Back atcha, princess."

Her expression might have been funny if he'd felt better about it. Could he really blame her for using every weapon in her arsenal to convince him to stay when she thought he would be their savior? It was ridiculous to think he was anything more than bad news, but she'd had a visitor from the dead deliver the message and then presto-chango he'd appeared like clockwork. Of course she believed it, and he was a jerk to hold it against her.

They walked for a while longer in quiet dark. The forest surrounded them with sibilance and shadow, nothing quite what it seemed in the faint glow that struggled to penetrate the phantom cloak of branches and leaves. Each step made him feel like he moved through barriers, thick and unrelenting. He was so tired he wanted to lie down and sleep for a year, but her comment about fairies, ludicrous as it was, seemed unnervingly possible in this protean world. He'd lived in the States for most of his life, yet he was still Irish enough to feel the trill of superstition dancing down his spine.

Irritated with his own susceptibility, he said, "We can rest for a while if you need to."

"Did y' not hear what I said?" she exclaimed. "This is not a place to dally."

"You don't really believe there are fairies?" he replied, pleased that he sounded strong and sure and not the least bit worried.

She wrapped her fingers around his arm, forcing him to stop and look at her.

"I believe a lot of things, Ruairi," she said.

There was more to that statement than the words she spoke, and he couldn't pretend otherwise. Hadn't they both seen the unbelievable—lived the unbelievable? How could he question something as minor as the reality of a fairy woods when his own existence in this place and time was itself impossible?

He heard all this in her tone and with it, another message. No matter what had happened between them, no matter what Colleen had told her, Saraid still didn't trust him and she certainly didn't feel safe following him through the unknown. Good, he told himself. He didn't want her dependent on him. He only wanted her out of his way so he could get on with his life, find the Book, and hope that it would return him to his own world, his own life.

But if that was what he wanted, why did he feel like slamming his fist into a tree? Why did it bug him that she didn't believe he could keep her safe?

"I don't care where we are, princess," he said. "I need a breather. And so do you."

He moved to a fallen log, plopped himself on it, and stretched out his legs. Reluctantly, she followed and perched next to him.

"Tell me something," he said, watching the way the filtered moonlight shimmered over her hair, trying not to be too distracted by the midnight sheen. "Why is my dad so convinced you have the Book of Fennore?"

She considered his question before answering, and he wondered if she meant to lie to him, but when she spoke, her voice was steady and low.

"He thought my mother stole it from him," she said at last, meeting his gaze.

Truth, then.

Encouraged, he asked, "Did she?"

"No. At least not that she ever confessed."

"So why does he think you have it?"

"It would be more likely that *you* would know the answer to that," she said, raising her brows.

"If it happened before you and I met on the hillside, then you can pretty much assume I don't know it."

She stared at him thoughtfully and he wished he understood what went on behind those dark, mystery-filled eyes. It was clear she was uncertain about what to believe, and Rory didn't have the words to convince her. What would she say if he told her that before that moment when they'd met, he'd been in another century and place, watching people on a flat screen and drinking water from a magic spout over a porcelain sink? These things would sound as strange to her as her fairy woods sounded to him.

Finally she said, "There are stories about y' and Cathán

and yer strange ways. They say the two of y' came from nowhere. You just appeared the night y' stumbled into our *tuath*."

"When was that?"

"The night Tiarnan and I were born."

"Let me guess. Twenty-five years ago?"

She nodded. "It was storming that night and the pair of y' were stark naked, or so the stories go. Yer father said y' had been wandering for hours and y' were both fever sick. My father took y' in and later my mother nursed y' to health. They offered friendship." Her voice hitched over the word. "And for a while, yer father accepted it."

Her pause lasted a long time, but Rory waited, knowing there was more.

"Then for some reason, Cathán became convinced she'd stolen the Book of Fennore. He had no proof that I ever heard spoken, but he would not be swayed otherwise."

"So what made him so sure she'd taken it?"

"I've never known. There was gossip, of course. People said Cathán had the Book of Fennore with him when he arrived. They said *It* brought him to us."

"Still not seeing the connection to your mother."

"He thought she stole it from him while he was senseless with his fever. But she didn't. I'd swear to it."

"Where is she now?" he asked.

Saraid shrugged and her voice came soft and hurt. "She killed herself. Tiarnan and I were not even a year old when it happened. I've no memories of her."

"I'm sorry," Rory said and meant it. She might not have been old enough to remember her mother, but the loss was no less devastating. He could hear that in her voice.

"It was a long time ago," she said.

"Your father married again?"

"Yes. It was years later and I don't think he ever stopped loving my mother. The boys' mother—Eamonn's, Michael's, and Liam's, I mean—had been widowed in Cathán's attacks and I was old enough to help with them. She needed a man to protect her and her children, and Bain needed a mother for me and Tiarnan."

"And where is *she* now?" he asked, though he knew the answer even before she spoke.

"Dead."

The finality of that single word brought home as nothing else had just what Cathán had done to Saraid's people. Just how much hatred she must have for his father . . . for the man she knew as the Bloodletter.

He took her hand in both of his and held it. "I'm sorry, Saraid. For everything he's done."

Surprised, her gaze moved over his face, searching for the truth, searching for the lies. She'd find only honesty this time. He was sorry. He'd been responsible for what happened that night in the cavern ruins—responsible for his father coming here and destroying all that Saraid held dear.

"Y' believe me, then?" she asked softly. "Y' believe that I don't have his Book? That until tonight, with y', I'd never seen it before?"

He nodded and she let out a breath that she seemed to have held for a very long time. He did believe she was telling the truth, but he knew there had to be a reason his father was so convinced her mother had stolen it. Whatever that reason was, Saraid must know it.

He wanted to press her, but an uneasy alliance had somehow been struck between them and he hadn't the heart, the energy to break it. He exhaled, trying to release his frustration with the air. Maybe he needed to give something to get it. A trade of secrets to seal their pact. Only Rory didn't give his secrets easily. He couldn't remember the last time he trusted someone enough to tell them what he really thought . . . what he really felt.

Stiffly he stood and took a step away, unwilling to show her his face when he spoke again. "I've seen it before tonight," he said softly. "Once, when I was a boy."

He could feel the burn of her gaze on his back, but he didn't turn. He didn't want to face what might be in her eyes when she finally connected the dots and realized Rory had brought hell's fires to her doorstep on the day she was born.

"Twenty-five years ago," he finished.

There was a rustle of skirts and the soft pad of her steps on the spongy earth. She came to stand in front of him, refusing to have this conversation the way he wanted it—with his back to her. He felt open and vulnerable as she stared into his eyes, powerless to look away.

"Tell me how y' are here, Ruairi who is not the Bloodletter. Who are y'?"

He swallowed, his throat suddenly tight and dry. "I don't know if I can answer that. I don't know who I am anymore."

She could have laughed. If she'd lived in Rory's time, she might have. She'd have called it a cop-out. No one in the twenty-first century knew who the hell they were.

But she didn't laugh. She waited patiently, her face turned up to him like a flower, her eyes open and watchful. In his entire life, he'd never felt so unworthy—and that was saying something, because for all of his life, he'd never felt worth a damn.

Saraid might have secrets, but she'd had the courage to face them. She'd married a man she thought a cold-blooded murderer to protect her people, her family, from harm. She'd done it with grace and pride, even when it came to screwing a man she'd obviously hated.

Rory, on the other hand, had run away from his family, his people. He'd left them far behind and never looked back. Never delved deep enough to know why. He'd lived with his aunt—a woman who might have answered all of his questions—and never seen outside himself enough to know to ask.

That night beneath the castle ruins had changed him, molded him into something he wasn't. And he'd been running from it ever since. Afraid of what it was he'd become. Maybe now, knowing about Ruairi the Bloodletter, he was right to be afraid. And to run.

She took his face in her hands and forced him to look at her. To let *her* look at *him*.

"Who are y'?" she asked again.

He still couldn't answer her, but he tried. "Evidently, I came here with my father when I was five and I grew up here—grew into this Bloodletter guy you married. But the life I know—" He shook his head. "It wasn't here. It wasn't in this time, this place."

Her hands moved from his face to his chest, one resting over his heart where the scarred spirals puckered his skin.

"When I was boy," he said, "there was a fight in a cavern beneath an old castle ruin."

"Yer sister's house," she said, surprising him. "Y' told me about it, that I led y' there after the funeral."

"That's right. This cavern, it's connected to the Book somehow. At least that's my guess. There are spirals engraved on all the stones and walls. It's the kind of place you can't wait to leave."

Her fingers traced the outline of his scar, and a shudder went through him. She felt the vibration but she didn't move away. He wanted nothing more than to pull her closer, to bury his face in the sweet scent of her hair and forget the rest of the world existed. Hide from the truths he didn't want to tell. Let her use him, if that's what she wanted.

"That night, when I was five, my dad and I fought over the Book, at least that's what my sister told me later. She said we disappeared for a few minutes and that somehow, she brought me back."

Saraid stared into his face, and he could see her trying to discern truth from shadow. He knew she was remembering today, when his twin had faded into a boy and a girl's voice— Danni's voice—had called to him just before he disappeared.

"She brought me, but not my dad."

"Why? Did she not love yer father?"

Rory blinked, surprised that the question had never occurred to him before. He and Danni never talked about their dad, and he really didn't know why. Maybe, some part of him had always associated his father with a night that had traumatized them all. Maybe there was another truth deep in the pit of denial that he couldn't ever face.

"I don't know if it was intentional—not bringing Dad. But . . ." He moved away, unable to continue with her peering into his very soul. As if he hadn't a care in the world, he sat on the soft mulch cushioned by dead leaves, using the fallen log as a backrest. Quietly she sat beside him, her body close enough to feel, close enough to touch. He couldn't have stopped himself from reaching for her, from pulling her to his side, even if he'd tried. She stiffened for just an instant, and then she let herself relax into him, taking his warmth, giving some back.

"What happened then, Ruairi?" she asked softly. "What happened when yer sister brought y' back?"

His mouth worked for a moment before words emerged. They came slowly, painfully, clawing his throat as they fought to stay inside.

"She left part of me behind."

Saraid said nothing, but he felt her attention, her absolute focus zeroed in on him.

"I mean, hell, I don't know what I mean. But somehow I have—*had*—an identical twin living here with my dad at the same time I was living there, with my mom and my sister."

"Like you were split in two?" she said simply.

"Like I was split in two," he repeated, finding a strange relief in speaking the words he'd always felt. "I was just pieces of a person." Never whole. Never complete.

"Do y' think the Bloodletter felt the same?" she asked.

"I don't know. Maybe."

"Perhaps that is why he was so vicious and cruel. Like a wounded animal."

She spoke so matter-of-factly, unaware that her words cleaved something open inside him. Something hard and festering, something that needed to be chopped to bits and vanquished.

She shifted, lifting her head from his chest to look at him. "What we saw earlier, when yer . . . twin . . . died. We saw him become a boy. Was it yer sister who called to him?"

Rory nodded. He couldn't have spoken, not when he felt like everything he was, everything he'd believed himself to be, had just been overturned.

"Do y' think he switched places with y'? That he is now in this cavern y' talk of? Living yer other life?"

He hadn't considered it for an instant, though it made sense. He shook his head and said, "I don't think so."

"Why, Ruairi?"

The answer formed like a blinding message written on the darkest screen, rolled off his tongue before he'd even acknowledged what it said. "Because I feel whole again."

It had been coming to him in stages, incomprehensible but undeniable. And now that he'd shone this light on it, he could see that it was true.

Saraid stared at him, her dark gaze glittering over his face. It seemed she saw it, too, everything he'd spent his life hiding. And he was embarrassed by how raw and exposed it made him feel. He took a deep breath, looking away.

After a moment, she said, "I've not met yer sister, but she sounds very powerful. Powerful enough to take on a force so dark and immense that it's survived hundreds upon hundreds of years."

Rory frowned, not liking the turn she'd just taken. "I don't know that I'd call her powerful. She's not a witch."

"Isn't she? Well, that may be a matter of words, not deeds. But for all I do not know about the Book of Fennore, one thing is thought to be true by all. The Book does no good. I don't know why yer set to have it, why Cathán has destroyed so many to find it. But do not let it fool y' into believing it can be used like a tool. It has no purpose but to serve itself. Whatever promises y' made it, it will expect to be fulfilled. No matter if it takes a second or a thousand years."

"I didn't promise it anything. And I'm not here to use it."

Her gaze was skeptical. "Have y' ever thought that while yer sister was pulling y' back, the Book was holding on? That the reason y' were torn in two was because y' were in the middle of a battle of rights? And in the end, each side won only a piece."

The blood drained from his face, but he said nothing.

"And yesterday, when y' returned to this place, the two halves were made whole." She paused, watching him closely.

"And you're wondering whose side I'm on now, is that it?"

"I don't know what to wonder when it comes to y', Ruairi who is not the Bloodletter. Y' are a mystery to me, but I no longer think y' are a monster."

He snorted a breath of laughter. "Well thanks for that, I guess."

She smiled back, though he saw the shadows in her eyes. "As y' say, now y' are whole."

Again, there was subtext in her words that he heard but could not understand. He stared into her eyes, feeling as if he fell into them. Feeling that he would never find his way out.

"You're pretty much a mystery to me, too, Saraid who is now my wife."

He'd meant to play on her own words. He'd wanted to lighten the mood, to tease a real smile from her. To turn that torch she'd shone on him another way. But somehow his voice hitched with emotion and it came out as a declaration. A pledge.

She stared at him, her expression one of shock, confusion . . . acceptance . . . all of it there in fleeting glimpses. And then he was leaning closer, her features blurring as he neared, hoping she wouldn't pull away.

He felt her soft breath of surprise and then the silky warmth of her mouth beneath his. Their first kiss had come through the shield of his twin and had not prepared him for the blast of heat that jolted every sense, every nerve ending now. His arms closed around her, binding her to him even as hers curled around his neck in the sweetest surrender he'd ever known.

She wasn't shy or coy, nor was she brazen and bold. This time, there was nothing practiced in the brush of her lips as they moved over his mouth or the slide of her fingers through his hair as she pressed closer. Nothing contrived about the sound she made when his hand trailed from her jaw to her throat to the fine bone of her chest, his palm just over the swell of her breast. Her heart pounded furiously beneath it.

She was everything and nothing that he had expected, perfect in her simplicity, pure in her complexity. She'd had him in knots for weeks, and now he was taut and drawn and in her hands, willing to let her mold whatever shape she desired.

He kissed her mouth, the hollows of her eyes, the sensitive skin between her brows, the satin slope of her cheek. Then her mouth drew him back and he cupped her face so he could deepen the kiss, die in the sweet taste and wonder of her. Her lips were soft and full and when he ran his tongue across them, nipping gently at the corners, she opened for him, shy but willing. He became completely absorbed in the sensations, the heat of her mouth, the velvet softness of her tongue, the intimacy of exploration. It seemed so much more than just a kiss and he thought that if all they did for the rest of his life was this, he would be satisfied. But even as the realization filled him, he knew he wanted more—more of her, more from her.

He shifted, urging her onto his lap, straddling his outstretched legs. Through the tangle of her skirts he felt the soft heat of her against the hard length of him and he shuddered. His hands searched for the hem of her dress, seeking a way under the garment to the warmth of her skin. Her fingers tangled with his as she tried to help him. Still the kiss went on like a dream, taking all his fears, his pointless insecurities, his selfish and destructive tendencies and turning them into something so insignificant they could blow away.

He heard the voice from somewhere in the distance and tried to block it out. Wanted to pretend it was only he and Saraid left in this crazy world. But he knew that was foolish. This was a dangerous place, and he should never have let down his guard, never given into his need to touch her. He should have known he'd never want to stop.

Saraid lifted her head, her face level with his, and stared into his eyes. For a moment their breath mingled in the small space between as they each strained to hear beyond their labored breathing.

The man's voice came again and others responded. Rory thought there were three, maybe four of them. He listened, but now their conversation grew fainter. They were moving away. A few more minutes and they were gone.

"Jesus that was close," he murmured, resting his forehead against hers.

Whoever was out there, it was doubtful they were friends. They could have easily stumbled over Rory and Saraid making out like teenagers in the backseat of a car.

As if reading his mind, Saraid slid from his lap. Her face was red, her eyes averted. He wanted to pull her back, to say to hell with the consequences. Instead he tilted her chin and gave her one last, gentle kiss. Her lips clung to his when he pulled away.

"Probably not the best time and place for that, huh?" he said.

"I don't suppose it was," she murmured.

"We better give whoever that is a chance to put some distance between us before we start moving again," he said. "Why don't you close your eyes and try to get some sleep."

"I could not sleep," she said.

"Then just close your eyes and pretend."

She shot him a startled look, but before she could argue he tugged her hand, pulling her back down against his thumping heart.

"Just for a little while," he said, his breath fanning the silky hair at her temple. "I'll keep watch. I'll keep you safe."

For a moment, he thought she might argue, might point out that he was the last person she'd feel safe with. He braced himself for the rejection, knowing it would cut deep. But instead she gave a tight nod and obediently closed her eyes, trusting him to take care of her in the big, bad fairy woods.

Chapter Twenty

SARAID felt the shift in the air and recognized it for what it was even before she came awake. Someone was coming. Someone not of this world. Would it be Colleen of the Ballagh again? Returning to finally answer the questions that had plagued Saraid since her first visit?

Slowly she sat up, realizing as she glanced at Ruairi, that it was only her dream-self who moved. Her body still lay sleeping in the circle of his arms.

Her face looked peaceful, secure in sleep. Sure that this man she barely knew—this man who had kissed her until she had no awareness of time or place—would protect her. He was awake, as he'd promised, though he looked tired. He scanned the woods around them, ever vigilant.

She stood, leaving her slumbering self behind, and Ruairi's head suddenly turned and he stared right at her. For a moment she froze, watching his gaze shift back and forth from her corporeal body to the ethereal one that stood beside it.

He could see her. The realization frightened her at the same time it brought a queer sense of comfort. Ruairi could see her. She wasn't alone.

She heard her name called from somewhere deep in the forest and she turned to it, wanting to deny the summons even as she heeded it. Surprised, she realized that she didn't want to leave Ruairi behind, that somewhere, sometime in this long arc of sun to moon, she'd begun to feel safe with him.

But the dead did not like to wait, and so she forced herself forward, carefully picking her way through the underbrush, compelled to keep moving through the bracken and thorns that tore at her gown. She looked back at Ruairi and found him scanning the woods, searching for her. Most likely thinking he'd imagined seeing her step from her body and move into the forest.

Around her the thick trunks of oak and elm crowded close, heavy branches jostling to touch her and tear at her clothes. In the heart of the Dark Forest, Cathán had cleared hundreds of trees to build his fortress, but he'd left the surrounding woods to act as sentries. His men were known to be agile climbers, and they trained to use the forest as an ally when they fought. The strategy had proven effective.

Saraid hesitated now as the glimmer of moonlight vanished beneath the impenetrable wall of bough and leaf. Ahead a wraithlike form separated from the gloom, and she held her breath as it slowly took shape. There was a head, a torso, arms thick and corded, barrel chest, legs. As the features of his face filled in, she clenched her eyes and prayed it would not be one of her own brothers.

When she looked again, a man stood before her. He was older than her brothers, older than many of the men who had survived Cathán's attacks, bigger and stronger than any of the elders. A stranger, then. That surprised her even as relief tingled through her limbs.

The dead were particular about who they spoke to, though, and the last stranger had brought change that Saraid had been ill prepared for. Her chest tightened with the certainty that this one brought an omen, as well, and not a good one.

The man's features were obscured by shadow, but she could make out a thick and lush beard of copper streaked liberally with gray and waving hair the same shade. There was more gray at his temples, not so much to make him look ancient, but enough to speak of maturity and wisdom. He wore a cloak that hugged his broad shoulders and fell gracefully toward the ground in a weave of blue and green, so artful it tempted the hand to stroke it. Beneath the cloak was a scarlet tunic that bore an intricate design of spirals, lines with no end and no beginning, linking without touching, turning with just a shimmer of thread in brilliant gold and silver, rich green and blue, startling purple. Cathán had tried to duplicate this very garb, but had failed in a way she knew mystified him. He had not earned the seven colors of a Celtic king. But this man, obviously, had.

A king. Her mouth went dry.

Strapped to the stranger's hip was a sword with a long blade and a silver hilt. It bore the impression of a human head with dark gems glinting in the eyes. She'd heard legends about this sword and knew the skull topping its hilt was meant to hold the souls of its conquests.

The king stared at her long and hard, his gaze a glowing force in the darkness. It moved over the fall of her dark hair that had escaped its loose bind and now danced about her shoulders in the cool breeze. Her tattered wedding gown whispered against her ankles and fluttered in a sudden gust. Most certainly she was not dressed for a royal visitor, but he had chosen the time and place and would have to be satisfied with what he saw. He scrutinized her face, staring at each feature with a look of loss in his expression that bewildered her. It seemed that he knew her and she felt the first brush of recognition.

"Come," the man said before she could dwell on it.

He reached out his hand and reluctantly Saraid took it. She couldn't feel his fingers wrapped around her own, but the strange king managed to pull her forward, tromping over the undergrowth of the forest floor with little care, keeping ahead of her so that she couldn't see his face, couldn't place why he looked familiar. As the king led her deeper into the darkness it began to feel as if she merely skimmed the surface. She couldn't see where they were going, and then the world tipped and it felt like they flew for a time, like birds soaring through the Otherworld. She clenched her eyes and fought back her fear.

At last the king slowed. She felt her feet touch ground and she could see again. They stood before a corridor made of twisted vines and gnarled roots that wove together in a living tunnel that beckoned them forward. She didn't want to go in there.

The king tugged on her hand and, ducking low, he stepped into the long passage. The need to keep his head down slowed him, and Saraid was able to follow without stumbling over the uneven tangle. It seemed the tunnel went on, unending, and panic minced her fear. Were they going down, deeper into the Otherworld where she would never escape?

She pulled at his hand, trying to stop him, but he moved steadily forward, hauling her like a cantankerous goat on a rope. And then she felt fresh air and they were stepping out on the other side.

Saraid sucked in a deep breath as she looked around. Here the moon shone bright as the sun and banished the darkness with its odd radiance. The strange and eerie passage had opened onto a cove surrounded by a wall of ancient trees. They seemed to sprout from the mossy rocks that hunkered on the other side of the still pool of water. Branches grew like mangled limbs sprouting from gnarled trunks. Some kind of nut grew in clusters between the shivering leaves, but they were unfamiliar to Saraid.

Her sense that she'd crossed over into the Otherworld grew into terrifying proportions. The king watched her, his face still obscured but for the glittering gaze. Again she felt recognition in his look and remorse in his study but couldn't fathom the source of either.

"Who are y'?" she whispered, her voice uncanny in this nowhere land.

He didn't answer; she hadn't really expected him to. Instead he moved to the soft bank beside the water. He knelt. Saraid did as well.

One of the trees released a nut and it plopped into the pool. In a shiny flash, an enormous fish arced from the water and caught the bobbing nut in its gaping mouth. Saraid realized she'd begun to make a small, whimpering sound deep in her throat. She clenched her teeth and silenced it.

This wasn't like the visitations she'd had before. There'd always been a set purpose to the other visits. They came to her for one reason—to show her the death that would soon be theirs and then leave her with their terrible secret. Terrifying though that was, she'd known what to expect. But first Colleen had broken that mold, and now this king seemed determined to fashion a new one. He'd taken her beyond her boundaries of knowledge.

He set his palm against the ripples in the pool left by the jumping fish and pushed away, creating a small wave that rolled with a glow emanating from his touch. It rose as it crossed the water, spreading out like magic across the surface. The trees shuddered when the wave crashed against the mossy stones and more nuts fell, plunking into the pool like hail. Hundreds of fish bounded from below, churning the water into a tempest. The man nodded with satisfaction and then he pointed at the choppy surface and Saraid was compelled to look.

The stars and moon glinted in the water, their shimmer and sparkle seeming to suck her down, below the surface where everything was dark and murky. Then the sparkling glimmer drew in tight, creating a white reflection on which a scene gathered and began to play out. Saraid gasped as she plunged forward, no longer inside herself, no longer crouched on the soft bank of the pool. She was floating through the swirling current. She was falling through to the other side.

She came to a sudden stop that snatched the breath from her lungs. Shaken, she looked up and found the pool of water suspended over her head, giving her a warped vision of the cove above, of herself bent over and staring back.

"What have y' done?" she asked the king, who was once again beside her.

Without answering, he stepped into a round lodge that appeared in their path. Saraid had no choice but to follow. Inside was a large circular room with a roaring fire in a brazier at its center. She felt the heat coming off it in waves, smelled the scent of roasted meat that hung heavy in the air. A man sat on a dais in a chair built for a leader, a chieftain, a king. There'd once been such a chair in the *rath* where her people had lived.

She stared at the chair, knowing suddenly that it was the same chair, the same round lodge where her people had once brought their grievances to be arbitrated by the chieftain. Now a younger version of the king standing beside her paced the floor in front of the chair. Suddenly the glimmering tendrils of recognition slammed into Saraid and she gasped, looking from the younger version of the king on his throne to the elder version at her side.

"Bain," she whispered. This man—both of them—was her father. She'd been only eleven when he'd been murdered, and his beloved face had faded in her memory, but she knew now, it was Bain beside her.

There were others in the room. Some stood off to the side or sat at the long tables arranged in the center. The younger Bain wore a tunic of dark blue and red, more simple than the one the older king wore now, but bright in comparison to the gray and yellow tunics the others wore. It wasn't just the colors that told her he was a man of power, it was the air about him, the presence of authority in his stance.

An old woman entered the lodge. She had long gray hair caught back in a neat braid then twisted around her head. Her skin looked thin and withered, but her eyes were bright and sharp. She moved quickly, for one so bent with age, and approached the younger king who'd turned to face her.

"Is it over?" he asked her in a low voice. "Is the babe come?"

The woman looked uncomfortable as she shook her head. "There will be more than one, Laird. I fear the worst is yet to come."

Saraid watched the young king absorb this information. His brows drew in concern, his eyes narrowed. "More than one. Twins, is it?"

"Perhaps."

"She will bear through it well, though?"

"Perhaps," the woman said.

"Will she or will she not?" he demanded impatiently. "Doona speak in circles to me."

"She is having a time with her trials, Laird Bain," the old woman said. "More than that is not for me to know."

Though she'd made the connection herself, hearing her father addressed so, hearing the confirmation that he was, in fact, Bain the Good, stole her breath. She stared at him in silent awe. Her father. She shifted her gaze to the older king standing silently beside her and she saw pain in his eyes. Deep, scarring pain. He said nothing.

The old woman hesitated, as if there was more she wanted to say, but then turned and left as silently and quickly as she'd come.

Saraid frowned, looking at the older king, the older version of her father. "Why do y' show me this?" she asked, but he didn't answer.

Time passed in a strange blur, and she didn't know how much, how long they'd waited. They were still in the room with her young father—though he was alone now, pacing the room, pausing every few steps to look to the door. At last the old woman returned. It was plain from her drawn expression, from her shadowed eyes that she had news she didn't want to tell.

"What has happened?" he asked, the color draining from his face.

"Yer wife has refused my help. One babe has come, but he was born cursed and died with his first breath."

"What lies do you tell? Born cursed?"

"His arms were but stubs, his head not fully grown. He had naught but one eye and legs so cruelly twisted, never would they hold him. There was nothing to be done for the wee thing."

Her father stared at the woman in horror. His face tightened and he nodded once, the motion short and jerky. "And my wife?"

The woman looked down, but not before Saraid could see the tears in her eyes and the fear on her face.

"There are two more coming, and she struggles to bring them. Y' need to brace yourself for the worst."

Beside Saraid, the king took a deep, shaking breath, and she saw there were tears in his eyes as well.

The old woman led the way out of the lodge into pouring rain. It came in a deluge that made everything blurry and dark. It drenched their clothes and turned the ground to slippery mud.

As they picked their way through, Saraid saw other structures here, some built from wood, some of stone. They fanned out from the imposing round house at the center. Even through the curtain of rain, Saraid recognized everything now. It was where she and her brothers had grown up. Where they'd lived until Cathán Half-Beard and his men had driven them away and burned it to the ground.

A blacksmith stood over his fires, sheltered by his shop, watching the old woman and his leader pass with a dark look of foreboding. Saraid recognized him, too. He'd been cut down in battle three years ago. Others came out as their chieftain walked through their settlement, unmindful of the pouring rain. One by one, Saraid let her gaze linger on their faces. All of them were dead now.

Her father moved to the door of his home, of the home where Saraid had grown up, but the old woman stopped him. "Yer wife isna there," she said.

"And where would she be, then?" he asked, surprise raising his voice.

She nodded to the small stone *clochán* off to the side. The beehive-shaped structure had been built of stone by monks in a time no one remembered. There'd been a hermit who'd lived in the *clochán* before the eldest of their people were born, but it had been empty for years upon years and no one could recall it ever being otherwise.

"Why would she choose such a place to birth our child?" Bain asked, his voice crossing from confusion to fear.

The old woman clenched her jaw and didn't answer. Rain streamed over her face, turning her hair into a stringy gray mess. He strode purposefully to the door, but Saraid saw the hesitation, the dread that made him tighten his fists before he finally reached for the latch. It was locked.

"Oma," he said, his voice soft and gentle. "Oma, love. Let me in."

As his words washed over Saraid, she felt the blood drain from her face and her racing heart slow to a dull and aching thud. Oma. Saraid's mother had been named Oma. Was it possible that this was the night when Saraid and her brother were born? But she'd never known another child had arrived dead before she and Tiarnan had come into the world.

"Oma, let me in," her father said again.

"No, husband. You must trust me and leave me now." The

voice coming from the *clochán* was strained. Saraid lifted a shaking hand to her mouth.

"She has forbidden me to enter as well," the old woman said, shaking her head.

Her father tried the latch again, throwing his weight at the door as he did. "Do not make me break this door down," he warned, even as he tried.

"If you love me, Bain, you will trust me now," Oma said. "The gods are with me and they watch over our child."

"Our child?" he repeated. "It is born?"

"Soon," she answered. "I beg you, leave me to it. Women have been bearing their children alone since the times of yore, it isn't so strange. Don't listen to that virulent tongue that wags in your ear. She is the cursed. She brings the omen. I don't want her near me. Now, please. Leave me to do what I must."

"It is childbirth fever," the old woman hissed. "She doesn't know what she says."

Bain looked at her with narrowed eyes, his lashes spiky with rain. Saraid saw his warring emotions. His fear for his wife. "If she will not have y', find me another," he said. "And not a word of this to anyone or I'll have that tongue nailed to my door. Is that understood?"

The old woman blanched and nodded, but her eyes were hard and angry. "This is not my doing," she spat. "The gods are angry and this is their punishment."

Bain leaned in close until his face was only inches from hers. "Silence. Yer. Tongue."

He needed to say no more. She snapped her mouth shut and hurried away. As he watched her, his gaze drifted to the small group of people that had gathered. Saraid saw indecision flicker in his eyes and then he steeled himself, shoulders back, head high. The gusting wind blew the red of his wet mane away from his face. "There is nothing to see here," he said. "Go about yer business."

Like children, their faces turned in guilt, and without a word they did as he said. Yet Saraid could hear their whispers. Word of the misshapen monster that Oma had already birthed spread, and the people were frightened of the portent it surely signified. Saraid heard their whispers. Oma wasn't one of their own, they reminded one another. She was Saracen, a slave brought to Ireland by Vikings. Bain had bought her in the market, and within months of bringing her home, she'd bewitched not only freedom from him, but marriage as well. From slave to chieftain's wife. Who but a fool wouldn't worry about such a thing? Sure, Oma was beautiful, but who were her people? How could Bain know what catastrophe such a stranger might bring down upon them?

Mumbling their versions of Oma's tale between themselves, the people returned to their homes and the safety of their hearth fires. Only after the last door shut did Bain turn again to face the *clochán*. The man who'd seemed so formidable to Saraid when he'd first appeared now sagged against the door, his forehead pressed hard to the unyielding planks. Saraid felt the helpless rage that contorted his features. He was torn between what he knew and what he feared.

Twilight winked for only moments before dark smothered the color from the world. Soon it would be Saimhain, the night when the barriers between their world and the other would become so thin that they could be broken. It was a time when the superstitious beliefs of the people became insurmountable barriers that could never be breached.

Saraid heard a strange sound then and turned, seeking the source. It came again, a queer buzzing, the noise like fabric ripped in two. The young Bain lifted his head from the *clochán* door and looked around. He'd heard it as well. The eerie vibration raised the hairs on her arms and at the back of her neck as it became louder, more insistent.

Bain staggered back from the door with an expression of such horror on his face that Saraid nearly ran. What was it? Why did he look as though a demon from the deepest pit of hell might erupt into this world at any minute?

"What have y' done?" Bain whispered, staring at the *clochán* like he would a sea serpent slithering from the waves.

And then suddenly there came a great reverberating boom. It shook the ground and swayed the mighty oak and yew trees. Saraid held her hands out at her sides for balance as it jarred the earth beneath her feet. The doors that had so recently closed flew open, and people raced out in the deluge, telling themselves it was thunder but not believing it. The reverberating boom sounded again, and a light flashed brightly against the horizon, growing like a flame set to tinder, only it wasn't fire. It wasn't anything that could be explained. The light flared unnaturally blue and violet and then it waned and the buzzing became a sound of bees, then whispers, then silence.

"What was that?" a balding man with buck teeth and tiny ears demanded. He made the sign to ward off evil as he stared into the darkness.

Others repeated the question in panicked tones and fearful shrieks. More than one woman had tears mingling with the rain on her face. Children cried, clutching the legs of terrified adults as they struggled to comprehend what had happened. Saraid watched as Bain straightened, turning away from the shelter that kept his wife. He squared his shoulders and moved toward the frightened people, raising his hands to calm and silence them. He looked steady and sure, and his calm presence soothed. Their faces tilted up expectantly, as if he was a god himself—as if just by saying there was naught to fear, it would become so.

"Doona be afraid," he said. "There is nothing to fear."

But even as he spoke, another deafening boom shattered the quiet and shook the earth with violence. Great bolts of blue lightning streaked from the sky and hissed down to lash against trees and homes, one cracking over the *clochán* with a shriek. The people huddled together, and a bolt struck the penned cattle just behind where they stood, making the animals scream in terror. Saraid saw the stampede an instant before it began. She whipped around, looking for shelter as people raced for the homes even as the lightning hissed and struck around them. Bain stood before the chaos with a look of disbelief and the weight of the world on his shoulders.

He was shouting orders that no one heard, trying to contain the terror that spread like hot oil down a slick wall. Another flashing bolt illuminated the pandemonium of the small village that had seemed orderly only moments before. In the distance, Saraid saw something else, someone approaching. The flash left her blinded as she struggled to find what she'd seen. A man? He'd been naked, his skin so white it had seemed to glow in the flashing brightness. Yes, it *was* a man and he had a child with him, naked as well. And like the ominous storm, they were coming this way.

Chapter Twenty-one

R ORY sensed something building in the forest around them. A pressure, rising higher as he watched. He hadn't heard the voices again, but he had a sense that the men who'd spoken were not far away and there was no denying the feeling of tension coming from everywhere, deepening by the moment.

He shifted, looking down at the woman who slept curled against him, thinking again of that spooky moment when he'd thought he'd seen her standing beside her own body. But then, in a flash, the image had vanished, leaving him uneasy and wary.

Nothing like seeing things to scare the fatigue out of a person, though. Since then he'd been wide awake, watching the woods, feeling the flux of life within it. It helped him to keep his mind off thoughts of Saraid's mouth, her body, her fire. The way she'd looked at him when he'd told her about the night his father had disappeared. She couldn't know that it had scarred him deeper than any other wound could. Yet, she'd seen it and she hadn't been repelled by his shameful secret. She hadn't even been particularly shocked.

She'd peered right into him, looked at that ugly rotting tumor he'd carried nearly his entire life, and she'd changed it.

It made no sense, but somehow in the space of moments, the weight of it had left. The pain had eased.

Now she shifted in her sleep, moaning softly. Her brows came together and a tear leaked from her eye. Was she having a nightmare? After all they'd been through, who could blame her?

"Saraid," he said softly. "Wake up, princess."

Her eyes opened at once, wide and filled with terror.

"Shhhh," he murmured, smoothing the damp tendrils from her face. "It was just a dream." She stared at him with disbelief, her pulse pounding at her throat. "Easy, girl."

She took a deep breath and let it out, emerging from her nightmare by degrees, probably realizing she'd merely exchanged the sleeping version for the real-life one. Could she smell the danger that seemed to salt that night?

Rory gave her another moment before he stood, pulling her to her feet with him and brushing the twigs and barbs from her skirts. She waited like a child until he'd finished.

"You all right?" he asked at last.

She nodded hesitantly but still didn't speak. He stared into her wide eyes, wanting to chase the darkness away, wanting to tell her there was nothing to fear. He wouldn't lie to her, though. He couldn't.

"We should probably get going again," he said softly. "You ready?"

She gave him another nod, her eyes a little less wild now. "How long was I . . . did I sleep?"

"Not long. Maybe twenty minutes."

She looked astounded at that. "Y' were awake?"

"The whole time."

"Did y' see anything . . . ?"

Something unsaid dangled at the end of that question, but she didn't finish, and so he simply answered, "No. Everything was quiet."

He couldn't tell if this reassured her or not. Her distress seemed to go deeper than their admittedly dire situation.

He handed her the water flask and watched her drink. Her hands were shaking.

"You sure you're okay, princess?" he asked, frowning at the fear she seemed unable to hide.

"I dreamed," she said simply, as if that should explain it all. Maybe it did, but Rory was still unconvinced that just a dream had so completely rattled her cage.

"Do you want to tell me about it?" he asked.

"No." The word burst from her lips. "No, I don't."

Ridiculously hurt by her vehemence, Rory capped the flask, took her hand, and started walking again. Saraid came along without complaint, without a word. Rory should have been grateful she wasn't talking his ears off—or at the very least glad she wasn't prying more secrets out of him. Instead he was worried, maybe even a little disappointed. So they'd shared a few confidences and a couple of kisses. That didn't make them soul mates, for God's sake, and yet . . .

They moved quickly while above the moon inched across the sky, and their feet covered uncertain terrain. Rory's nagging thoughts chased each step until he was practically dragging Saraid behind him. He heard her gasp to catch her breath and forced himself to slow. The tension in the air had been growing with every step, and a bad feeling settled in his gut.

In a whisper, she asked, "Did y' hear them again?"

He shook his head, but Saraid picked up on his disquiet, his sense that something waited just around the corner. She followed him close, graceful as a deer ready to bound away at the first sign of trouble.

Rory had no way to judge if they were moving into the whirl of danger or away. It seemed to be everywhere at once, so he could only keep walking and hope for the best. After a while he let his focus spread outward, tuning in to the sounds of the woods, the indignation of small squirrels and rabbits as they scurried out of sight. Slowly he became aware of something else, another emotion flooding the darkened woods. Emotion, that wasn't his . . . yet he felt it in his head like he had earlier, when he'd caught the horse's fear. Felt it like it was his own.

The sensation danced along his skin and teased every nerve in his body. Awareness. A consciousness of the moon in the sky, the trail it burned, the way it pulled the sun from the other side. Knowledge of the crisp air and the whisper of winter in the fall night. Every flutter of wings on every insect buzzed in his ear, every beating heart in every animal seemed to thrum with his own.

Instinct as old as the need to survive pushed to the surface and tried to block out what he was feeling. It wasn't right, wasn't *natural* that he could *feel* the forest. But it was there, under his skin, pulsing like the blood in his veins. Pretending it didn't exist would not make it so.

He paused, took a deep breath.

"What is it?" Saraid asked softly.

"I don't know. Just a feeling."

She nodded and he forced himself forward, her hand warm in his. The need to protect her stronger than the need to protect himself. Whatever this *thing* was he'd suddenly tapped into, running from it didn't seem the best course of action. He took another breath and then softly exhaled.

There was outrage rustling in the branches, vibrating through the animals hidden in their depths. It wasn't an admonition, but a warning. *Caution.*

He slowed, pulling Saraid to a stop beside him. She glanced at his face, caught the watchfulness in his eyes, and stilled. For a moment they remained that way, waiting for something to emerge, for some sound to betray the danger that so silently stalked them, but there was nothing to see, nothing to hear.

Frustrated, Rory listened harder even as a voice in his head jeered at him. The lurking menace would not be found with eyes or ears. He took another deep breath and shut his eyes.

His skin tightened and his stomach clenched as Rory pictured his mind as a fist, and he warily pried each finger up until it was open. He turned his senses outward, remembering how as a boy he'd been able to reach with his mind and snag the ebb and flow of the very wind. Rebelling against the unnatural ability even as he used it.

It had been a long time since he'd shut down that part of himself, but suddenly the tap was there, waiting for him to turn it on, unperturbed by his neglect. His senses circled unsteadily for a moment, but it was like riding a bike—only a few clumsy wobbles and then he found the balance he needed.

His mind exploded with sensation. The wind, filled with a million molecules, filled with a million more. Each one whispered against him, each one rasped as it passed by. The trees rejoiced in his touch, branches shuddering in ecstasy, leaves shivering with delight. The animals responded in like, curiously prodding at him, yammering in a deafening symphony to be noticed. It overwhelmed him, but he steadied himself, isolated his own thoughts, curled them into a protective hold, and then tried again, inch by inch, reaching out.

There was fur and scales, feathers and hide, shiny green leaves and rough brown bark. Beneath the earth, things creeped and crawled, antennae out and reaching, tapping his signal and responding with a pulsation of their own. And then his seeking consciousness rubbed against something foreign, alien. He felt it throb with a power like he'd never known in his life, and it drew him relentlessly closer, seducing his perceptions with every pulsing breath. He felt the heat, the perfume of her skin, the beating of her heart and knew without being told that it was Saraid. Saraid, burning and writhing in deep blues and swirling purple shadows. She pulled him like she'd been doing from the first moment he'd dreamed of her.

He couldn't contain the surge she caused, couldn't keep from surrounding her with his energy. She was like mink, softer than the mind could conceive, impossible to resist, impossible not to stroke.

He opened his eyes and saw her sway and catch herself against the trunk of a tree. Her eyes were huge, her face pale. Her shocked expression told him she'd felt him, in her head, in her body. Because he was everywhere now, as thin as the air, as dense as the woods. He pulled her with him, as bewildered as she by how he did it, even as they soared higher.

Like a web, he wove his consciousness from branch to branch, seeking what he didn't know. His focus widened, sharpened. He heard the rasping croak of a frog, deep with warning. A badger lifted its head from a hole and paused its digging to sniff the shifting air, sensing the brush of Rory's awareness as it passed over. It was a giddy feeling for them both, that touch, that acknowledgment that went beyond language, beyond sound. Overhead a bat swooped from one tree to another and settled, watching, listening.

Like a line, Rory followed its attention until he heard it, too. A vibration that shuddered on the air. Men. Several of them. Their voices were low, as if they, too, feared the forest around them. He felt their anger, their cruelty. Violence barely contained. There was a harsh, brash tone in their words and a distinctive stink about the light wind that wafted past them.

"Who are they?" Saraid asked, and her spoken words suddenly brought them back to their bodies, to the spongy soil beneath their feet. They were standing closer together, their breath mingling in the space between their lips, but that net of awareness was still cast, still filling with the sounds of the forest.

"Who were those men?"

Rory held a finger to his mouth and took her hand, the heat of the touch disorienting in the mind-world he'd entered. Quietly he led her in a new direction, tracking that stench of danger. Without another question, Saraid followed, instinctively stepping in his prints, avoiding the shifting hazards that spoke to him, and through him, to her, like a guide. Not even a twig snapped beneath their steps.

The men were far off, how far Rory didn't realize at first. A part of him wondered at the impossibility of hearing them at such a distance while another part accepted it without issue.

Around him now the simmering emotions of the forest shifted and turned in his direction, following his progress like flowers follow the sun. The forest wanted him to find what had upset it. And if that wasn't the craziest damn thought he'd ever had, he didn't know what was. But it was true, nonetheless. He felt it in every bone in his body.

And there was more. Amidst his utter bewilderment there was strange joy, a mixture of intoxicating relief. It was insane and yet he embraced the new sense of this . . . this *other* world with something like guilty pleasure. The wash of emotions he shared with Saraid was sexual in its familiarity and it flowed beneath his skin, hot and silky, intimate and seductive. He knew she felt it, too—shared it, every nuance, every heated second.

They came to a point thick with gorse and broom shrubs, canopied by towering oaks and alders, yews and willows. The ground sloped sharply down to a shallow bowl and in it was a tiny clearing, barren of tree or bush, but surrounded by the earthen walls and wooded sentries. As if something here had prevented life from taking root and the forest had crowded up to its concave borders, trying to contain whatever malignance slept in the rocky earth. There was a large stone in the center of the ring and it gleamed black in the shrouded moonlight. From their vantage point above, they could see it all perfectly.

Saraid sucked in a silent but frightened breath, and Rory turned, meeting her eyes, asking the question without ever moving his lips.

"'Tis a Druid's circle," she murmured. "A place of sacrifice."

Rory had a vague notion of what this would mean to her, but it was the swelling fear of the forest that painted the true picture. In his mind, he saw the earth, rich, bountiful. Stained red with blood. Ancient fires burning at every edge of the wide circular clearing, taunting the dried foliage that crowded up to its rim with an errant lick and mocking spark. There were robed men—or women—the forest didn't know and didn't care. But those robed figures terrified every animal, every shoot and thistle, every quivering leaf.

A Druid's circle was not just a landmark or place of interest. It was a shrine and a tomb and an execution chamber all in one.

There was only one fire burning now and the torch was held by a man dressed in a tunic and short pants, like Rory. No Druids. No robed men with scythes in their hands. They were soldiers, guards at least. His father's men by their clothing, fearsome in their armory of shining chain mail over bright tunics.

Reluctantly Rory crouched behind a cluster of boulders with Saraid at his side. The powerful energy hovering around him withdrew just a bit, and he heard Saraid inhale deeply, as if it had taken that to allow her a breath of her own.

The group seemed to have stopped for more than a rest, and one man nurtured a flame from a small nest of dried twigs. As Rory watched, it caught and grew. With a grim smile, the man began to add to it until a small fire blazed bright in the darkness.

Rory began to back away, relieved that the men remained unaware of his and Saraid's presence. They'd have the advantage of moving on while the men tarried. He drew even with Saraid, expecting her to follow, but she didn't move. She seemed to be riveted to the spot, staring at the men like a mouse fixated on a swooping hawk.

He leaned close so he could see her face, but she didn't look at him, didn't turn away from the men standing in a half circle in front of the sparking fire. One of them kicked at a large bundle Rory hadn't noticed on the ground at their feet. It looked like a rolled carpet, but it wiggled and gave a groan of pain.

The men gathered closer to watch the writhing shape on the ground. From the glow of the fire, Rory could make out the coarse sack with a drawstring on top. A braid of dark hair spilled from the top.

The largest of the men pulled out a long knife and cut the bag down one seam and then jerked the free edge, rolling the contents out into the rocky dirt. The squirming mass was tied at wrists and feet, gagged with a filthy rag. It was a boy, long boned with big hands and feet that didn't fit his scrawny frame. His shoulders were narrow, his body wiry. His face was blotched, smeared with dirt and grime and streaked with tears. Even from the distance, Rory could see eyes red rimmed and blazing with rage. The men yanked him to his feet and his head barely reached the chin of the shortest of them. This made the other men laugh and jeer.

The boy was shouting something, but the gag garbled the words. Rory didn't need to hear them to know they were curses and the kid was hurling them like weapons for all the good they would do him.

"Shut the fook up," one of the men said and belted the kid in the gut. The blow took the wind out of him and bent him in half.

"Put him on the rock," the man who'd punched the boy ordered. "And hold him still."

He was a big man, full of muscle and mass, gone to fat around the middle but not soft. Rory could tell just by looking at him that he was so solid it might have been stone he wore packed there. With purpose he moved to the fire and squatted down, pulling a dagger from the scabbard at his waist. He held it out over the flame, watching it heat.

Beside Rory, Saraid gasped and clapped her hand over her mouth. Whatever the big man had in mind, it wouldn't be pretty, and Rory figured it was best they didn't stay around for the show. He gripped Saraid's arm and began to pull her back, away from the clearing. She whipped her head around, staring at him with shock.

"Go," he mouthed at her.

She shook her head furiously and scrambled back to their vantage point. What was wrong with her? Didn't she have the sense to see what the men were up to?

He moved closer. "What are you doing?" he breathed into her ear.

"'Tis Liam, my brother."

Rory frowned. Her brother? He'd met her brothers at the wedding, and this kid wasn't one of them. Then he remembered. They'd left one behind, just in case.

Saraid tore her gaze from the unfolding scene and said softly, "We have to help him." Her eyes were wide with terror and tears, and she looked at him with hope and expectation that felt like a punch to the gut.

Hell. What did she expect him to do? There were four of Cathán's men, all of them armed to the teeth. Odds only an idiot would take. He'd done what he could for her other brothers, but they didn't stand a chance of saving this kid. It would just be suicide.

He tried to pull her back, to tell her, make her understand, but she fought, as silent as she was determined, and squirmed free. She scurried to the next rock and then moved closer still to the next one.

Fuck! There was nothing he could do but stare at her retreating back in disbelief. She was a lunatic, that's what she was. And he'd be damned if he was going to let her crazy ass get him killed. But even as the angry words filled his head, he knew he couldn't walk away—not from the kid and certainly not from Saraid.

He felt the forest gathering up around him as he hesitated, felt the sting of its disappointment and shook his head at the thought. It was ridiculous imagining emotions from trees. He glanced at Saraid, crouched a few feet in front of him. There was no way to sneak up on these men because the clearing was in a depression and the only way to get to them was to slip-slide down the dirt walls. But it looked like Saraid planned to do just that.

It would be suicide, he thought, angry with himself for caring so much.

She's your wife. . . .

The whisper of a breeze through the leaves seemed to catch the thought and throw it at him.

No. She isn't, he tried to argue. But it was pointless. Now that he'd held her, kissed her, felt her heart beating next to his . . .

He cursed again as a wind came from nowhere and shuddered through the trees. In the next instant, Saraid was moving once more and he knew, stupid or not, he was going with her—but not the same way. The best chance they stood was if he circled around and came from behind.

Before he could inch forward to tell her, she darted farther away, and he knew there wasn't time to chase her down and explain his plan to her. She'd think he left her when she saw him go, but there was nothing he could do about it now. Hoping it was the right thing to do, he circled in the opposite direction.

Chapter Twenty-two

SARAID glanced back just as Ruairi disappeared in the trees. He'd left her.

For a moment, the pain of that froze her in place. He'd left her. After what they'd shared in the woods, after all they'd been through, she'd expected more. She'd begun to believe that he might truly be the man she'd hoped him to be. A man who deserved the growing admiration she'd begun to feel. A man to trust with other feelings, ones that ran too fast and fierce to scrutinize.

As she watched the leaves settle behind him, she saw what a fool she was. The hurt went deeper than disillusionment, hit her harder than disappointment. She felt it in her heart. How could that be? How had she let the Bloodletter come so close that he could touch her there?

She hadn't, she corrected, unable to lie even to herself. She'd let Ruairi get that close, not the Bloodletter. She'd been hurt by Ruairi, the man she'd begun to think of as her husband.

Cursing the tears that stung her eyes, she peered through the brush at Liam as he struggled against four men—all of them at least twice his size. He was just twelve, still a boy, though he tried vainly to hide his fear. How had they found him? And where were her other brothers? What of them? The Druid's circle was not far from the waterfall where they were to meet with her brothers. She scanned the distance, praying Tiarnan would come riding up to save Liam.

Saraid recognized the enormous man who'd struck Liam in the stomach. He was known as Scar-eye by her people because his favorite torture was to gouge out the eyes of his victims and leave their sockets as ragged holes that healed with horrid scars. Scar-eye was not likely to show mercy to her brother, no matter what his age, and the thought of Liam's beautiful blue eyes being turned to bloody pulp was enough to send her screaming mad into the circle.

Scar-eye held his blade over the fire before pulling it out to study it for a moment. Apparently satisfied, he glanced at her brother and stood.

"No," she whispered. In her fear she beseeched the gods and goddesses of the old ways, hoping they might still linger in this mystical place of the Druids.

Please help my brother. He is just a child.

A wind gusted across the clearing, pulled from a still night to whisk around the fire. It lifted sparks into the air and crackled the silence. Scar-eye jumped back to avoid being burned, but the brief show of the gods did not deter him. Saraid bit her lip to stop her cry from escaping, but she could not swallow the tears that welled in her eyes as she watched her youngest brother fight to keep his honor as Scar-eye stopped before him.

"Open his hand. The right one," Scar-eye ordered, and while Liam struggled to keep a fist, the other men forced his fingers wide. With a cold smile, Scar-eye pressed the flat of the hot blade into Liam's palm, holding it down while Liam screamed in agony, the gag still over his mouth only muffling the sound.

"Now the other," he commanded. He gave Liam no chance to recover from the searing pain before he pressed that hot blade against his left palm.

"You'll not be raising a weapon to me for some time, boy," Scar-eye said, leaning in close. "And if you don't tell me what I want to know, you'll not be seeing yer way home, either."

Liam kept his eyes shut, his mouth clenched tight.

"I don't want to hurt y'," Scar-eye said, and it seemed that he meant it. "I don't like killing children. But I'll do it if I must."

Scar-eye grabbed Liam's face in a rough grip and removed the gag. Still, Liam said nothing.

"Y' can tell me where the Book is and be on yer way, easy as that." He paused, giving Liam a chance to respond. When the boy clamped his mouth shut, Scar-eye took a deep breath and shook his head. "If y' don't talk, young son of Bain, before I'm done with y', yer hands will be dangling from my saddle for all to see. Y' won't be missing them because yer head will be hanging beside them to keep them company."

The men behind Scar-eye laughed at that, and Liam— furious, terrified, stupid Liam—laughed as well. A long, harsh laugh that silenced Cathán's men. Saraid's heart swelled with pride at her young warrior even as she shuddered in fear. "*Do not provoke them*," she mouthed to herself.

"Where is the Book?" Scar-eye said.

"Fook you."

Scar-eye's face turned a nasty shade of red. "Hold him up."

The men pulled Liam to his feet, and Scar-eye smashed his fist into the boy's face, pulled back, and hammered him again and again until Liam's face was a bloody mess. Saraid covered her mouth with her hands to hold back her scream. She'd helped her stepmother raise Liam, stepped in as a surrogate when Liam's mother had died. She loved him like he was her own.

Flashes of Liam as a child played against the backdrop of horror. She could see him splashing in the river that ran near their keep . . . racing through the waving meadows, chasing butterflies and birds . . . sitting on her lap as she told him stories of CuChulain the Hound. . . .

So many of her loved ones had died. She couldn't live if it meant losing Liam, too.

"Bain," she said under her breath. "Protect yer brave warrior. Come to me now as y' have before and bring justice on these monsters."

Again the breath of wind stirred in the clearing, turning dust into spinning circles that danced around the men. One of the soldiers, a young man Saraid didn't know, cast a nervous glance over his shoulder. Saraid watched, feeling her blood turn cold and her heart slow as her frustration grew into helpless fury. It would take more than a playful breeze to stop these men.

"Did y' hear that?" the young man asked.

But the others ignored him. Two held Liam up by his out-stretched arms. Scar-eye handed his blade to a third man, nod-ding at the fire while he continued to bludgeon her brother with fists the size of hams.

"Are y' ready to tell me where it is?" Scar-eye asked. "Or will I have to pull y' apart bit by bit?"

"We don't have yer fooking Book," Liam said. His voice cracked and his brave face crumbled. Tears streamed down his dirty cheeks. "Don't y' think if we had it, we'd use it?"

But it was clear that Scar-eye did not think at all, and Liam was weakening. He could not stand much more and neither could Saraid.

She wouldn't stay here and watch them kill Liam, and she would not abandon him while there was still breath in her body. Easing back into the foliage, she looked around, finding a small cluster of egg-sized stones nearby. Hardly weapons, but she was more than a fair shot with a stone. Hadn't she grown up with four brothers?

Her wedding gown was tattered and filthy. Fitting, she thought, considering the cursed union she'd entered. Her marriage wouldn't save her family from destruction, but her gown might help her save her brother. She pulled the skirt out and used it as a pouch, loading as many rocks as she could carry into it before inching to the edge of the basin. She wished for more than one place to hide while she volleyed the stones at Cathán's men, but she knew any hope of freeing Liam depended on speed and accuracy. She would have to knock out all of them before they caught her. Even as she hefted the first rock, she knew it was a battle she couldn't win. But she would face it bravely or die trying. Her brother deserved that much.

Perhaps death here would not be the worst fate. However misguided, she had hoped Tiarnan was right about the alli-ance her wedding was to have forged. But all his plans had frayed and come apart like strands of worn rope, and now she could only presume that Tiarnan and the others were dead.

She was alone, with no husband, no family, no clan. It would be an honor to die if it meant saving their last hope, the last hope for their people.

By now the knife was hot again, a red glowing menace, and Scar-eye took it in hand, moving this time to Liam's face. Saraid could see her brother wincing away from the heat of the blade as Scar-eye held it inches from his eye. He grabbed a fistful of hair and jerked Liam's head back. Her brother's terror rolled off him in waves, catching Saraid like a blow to the chest.

"Wonder what name they'll give y' once I dig that eye from yer skull," Scar-eye said.

Liam began to sob, and the sound wrenched all other fears away. Saraid took a deep breath, prayed that the gods would see her aim true, and threw the first stone with all the strength she possessed. It sailed through the air and caught Scar-eye just below his ear before clattering to the earth. For a moment he was too stunned to move and Saraid used that time wisely. No sooner had he turned toward her hiding place than she hurled another stone, this one bigger. It caught him squarely in the head and brought him down with wobbling knees and a shout of pain and surprise. Whether it was the gods or Bain, someone must be watching over her, for on the way down Scar-eye hit his head on the Druid stone and collapsed unconscious.

Saraid's breath came in short bursts, and fear clutched her heart. The other four men watched in shock as the giant fell, unable to fathom that someone had so easily taken out their leader with a stone the size of an egg. As they gaped, she hefted another rock and aimed for one of the men holding Liam's arms. This rock flew wide and nicked the man on the shoulder, only serving to rouse him from his stupor and make him angry.

"Over there," he shouted, pointing at the place where she hid.

They released Liam and rushed at her. She had only a moment to see her brother sag to his knees before one of the men launched himself up the basin wall and at her. He was too close to pelt with the rocks, so she took one in each hand and

letting out a cry that came from the very depths of her enraged
soul, Saraid charged, swinging her weighted fists, landing
blows that split her knuckles and shot pain up her arms. She
fought for her life, aware only that she and her brother must
win to survive. The man locked her to his body as he fell back,
down into the clearing. They landed with a thud that knocked
the breath out of each of them, and then Saraid was squirming
wildly, trying to break free.

Liam had managed to untie his bindings while the others
were distracted and now he scrambled to his feet. He was
badly beaten and she knew he'd be little help, but like her, he
wouldn't go without a fight. Kicking and clawing, she managed
to get free of the beast who'd grabbed her, but another caught
her in a bear's hug, pinning her arms. She screamed as she
slammed her head back into his nose, feeling the bones crush
and the hot splatter of blood on her neck, but he held tight,
crushing her ribs, making it impossible to draw a breath.

"Run, Liam," she shouted, feeling the whole of their history and future lay with him. He had to *live*. But a wave of
helpless frustration left her weak as she realized that he would
not leave her any more than she could leave him.

Liam grabbed Scar-eye's knife, which had fallen nearby,
wincing in agony as he clutched it in his wounded hand, and
charged with a warrior cry. While one man held her powerless
in his grasp, the other three turned to Liam, spreading out as
he barreled forward. A lucky strike caught the first man at the
throat and sliced through like butter. He had time only to
make one gurgling protest before he keeled over. Liam kept
coming, intent only on the man who held Saraid.

She shouted for him to turn, but he had the bloodlust upon
him and could master nothing over his need for vengeance. As
he hurled himself at her captor, the other two caught him from
behind and wrestled him to the ground. It was over in
seconds.

The three men stared at their two downed comrades in
shock and then rage. "Kill the boy," said one of them, stepping
forward to take the lead. He looked at the man still holding
Saraid and smiled. "Kill him. We won't need the whelp now."

Saraid watched in horror as he rucked up his tunic and

shoved a hand inside his trews to hold himself, his intent made clear when he reached out with the other hand and roughly squeezed her breast. "We'll have more fun getting what we want from this one."

Chapter Twenty-three

RORY reached the point where he'd planned to cut down into the clearing only to find a natural barrier of rock that prevented it. After wasted minutes trying to breach it, he'd been forced to backtrack until he could go around to a place where the basin wall was lowest and the forest grew to the very edge. His heart was pounding hard, and he knew too much time had passed. A sick feeling told him he was too late to save the kid. He'd heard Liam's agonized cries and then silence, knew that he was probably dead.

As he raced through the foliage, he cursed himself for leaving Saraid's side, for trying to use his brain instead of his brawn. If those men had hurt her . . . he could hardly allow himself to even consider the possibility, contemplate what he would do.

Panic surged through his veins as he plowed forward, unmindful of the branches whipping at his face. Through them he saw Saraid standing on the other side of the basin's rim, throwing rocks, bringing down a Goliath of a man and fighting like Wonder Woman on steroids. Like some primitive goddess, all wrath and wicked aim, awe-inspiring in her fury.

A few seconds more and he reached the clearing. In a blink, Saraid had been subdued and was now held by a burly, furry man with a wild mess of black hair that merged into a bushy beard. Great wily brows nearly met in the middle over deep-set eyes. A tall, agile-looking man who was nearly bald had the kid pinned with a sword at his throat.

"Kill the boy," the third man said. He was built like a brick house, solid, square-featured, battle-scarred with a fierce, mean stare. A hard man. From the command in his voice to the way the other two listened and followed him with their eyes, Rory assumed he was the new captain now that Saraid had taken out the old one.

The captain moved to stand in front of Saraid. "Kill him," he repeated. "We won't need the whelp now."

In a split second, Rory took it all in. His mind was going a million miles an hour, weighing options, discarding them. Seeking a way for the three of them to get out of this alive.

He had a weapon—but what good would it do him against men who were obviously seasoned warriors? Rory had been bouncing drunks for the past six months and he was as ripped as the Terminator. He wouldn't think twice about taking on the three of them hand-to-hand. But throw long, ugly swords and short, deadly daggers into the mix, and it was another story. He wasn't afraid for himself as much as he was for Saraid and her brother. If he was their only hope, then he'd better be sure before he moved.

But there wasn't time to be sure about anything.

Saraid and her rock slinging had been impressive, and he scooped up a couple of stones just in case. But the element of surprise was gone, and the men had a wariness about them that told Rory they wouldn't be caught by that trick again. That left him with few options, except . . . except . . .

Except he had the face of Cathán Half-Beard's son.

The realization rolled over him suddenly and completely, swamping him with all of its implications. They didn't know that he really wasn't this Bloodletter maniac that everyone thought he was.

His gut clenched painfully, but he forced himself to stand and calmly enter the circle. He was quiet, and they didn't notice him until he was right behind the bald guy who held the sword on Saraid's brother. Saraid was still trapped in the arms of the hairy bastard who probably shared some grizzly bear DNA. The site of her pinned against his sweaty chest set

Rory's blood to boil. It took everything to keep some measure of control about him.

"We'll have more fun getting what we want from this one," the third man, the captain, was saying as he reached out and squeezed Saraid's breast.

Rory fought the haze of rage that urged him to start swinging and to hell with the plan.

"Report," he commanded, startling the three of them. They spun to face him, two still holding their captives. The captain reached for his weapon, but stayed his hand when he saw Rory, armed and ready. The banked fury in his eyes made the other man falter.

In the silence that followed, a small voice of doubt whispered in Rory's ear. What if all Cathán's soldiers knew of the betrayal? What if he'd just walked into the perfect opportunity for one of them to finish what Stephen had begun?

"I said, report, you fucking idiots."

The captain said, "Caught the boy at a camp up on the hill. He won't talk, though. Won't tell us where the Book is."

The men all looked at the kid accusingly. Liam's face was bloody, eyes nearly swollen shut. Pinned to the ground by the blade of a sword, the kid watched Rory with hatred that snapped and snarled in the air. Standing nearby, Saraid watched him, too, but there was something more in her eyes, something that pierced deeper than any blade.

Surprise. Doubt. And beneath both . . . *hope.*

He tried to ignore what he saw. He didn't want her to believe in him, not in any way. Especially not now when he might get them all killed.

"Let her go," he said, and the grizzly man holding Saraid hesitated, looking to his captain before obeying. Rory stomped up to him and snarled in his face. "Do you question my authority?"

The man dropped his hands and backed away immediately. Rory pulled Saraid to his side.

He stared at her for a moment, trying to ask with his eyes if she was hurt. He could see the trembling going through her, though she kept her head up and her eyes cool. If she was hurt, she wasn't giving them the satisfaction of knowing.

Rory turned to the bald guy holding the blade to the boy. "Five of you to this scrawny runt and a woman and still you have casualties?" he said.

He showed his scorn with a sneer as he looked from the man with his throat ripped wide, bleeding into the black earth to the one Saraid had felled, the one with the knot on his forehead the size of an ostrich egg. He'd yet to regain consciousness. Rory wanted to grin at the lump Saraid had put there, but he didn't. Their survival depended on how well he played his part.

"It appears you haven't heard the news," Rory went on, his tone hard and steady. "These people are our family now. She"—he nodded at Saraid—"is my wife."

"The fook y' say," muttered the captain.

Rory strode to the man, invading his personal space until he took a stumbling step back. "I said she is my wife."

"The Laird told us—" the bald man began, but the captain cut him off with a look of rage.

"The Laird told you what?" Rory asked softly.

"He feared a betrayal," the captain answered.

If Rory hadn't known the truth, he would have believed the man. Either the captain believed it himself, or he was a damn good liar.

"No one has been betrayed," Rory told him. "We are married and we are now family."

The captain's hard eyes shifted back and forth from the kid, to Saraid, to Rory.

"Let the boy go," Rory said.

The shifting undercurrents tugged and pulled. He had to assume that at one time or another these men had followed the Bloodletter into battle. That didn't mean they liked it, though. Clearly Rory's twin had been feared, but not admired. And if Cathán had trusted these men to come after Saraid's brother, then it could be assumed they were willing to betray the Bloodletter.

And no matter how afraid they were of the Bloodletter, apparently they were more afraid of Cathán. Rory could see that etched in every tense muscle, every shifting glance that went between them.

"Why are y' out here and not at the wedding feast?" the captain asked, seeming to have just put that piece together.

"We, too, have come for my wife's brother. Now that there is to be peace."

Again, that narrow-eyed assessment moved from face to face.

Rory said, "You may either escort us back, or I will take your heads with me to show as an example of what happens to men who threaten this alliance."

The captain swallowed hard and now there was alarm in those shifty eyes.

"Let the boy go," Rory repeated.

Slowly the man holding the sword moved it away from Liam's throat and roughly jerked him to his feet. But he didn't release the kid and he didn't sheath his weapon.

"What's it going to be?" Rory asked, still watching the captain, knowing that he would be the one to call the game.

The captain's eyes twitched back and forth. He knew something wasn't right. Whether it was Saraid's tattered dress or Rory's eyes, which no longer went with a cold-blooded killer, Rory couldn't tell. But something wasn't adding up for the captain, and Rory could see him turning it over and over, trying to discern just what it was that bothered him. Finally he turned his mean glare on the bald man and nodded once.

Rory had an instant to decipher the silent message that had passed between them, but that was all it took for him to know what was coming. The bald man shoved the boy forward into Rory as he dodged away with his weapon drawn and the two other warriors came together in solidarity, shoulder to shoulder, armed and ready.

Rory spun, avoiding collision with Liam in the same move that brought him face-to-face with the hairy grizzly man who'd inched behind him. Rory had his dagger in hand and threw it in a fluid motion that came without thought. Everything was happening fast now, and there was no time to dwell on the dagger that had pierced the man's heart and dropped him to the ground. Rory danced back, keeping his body between Saraid, Liam, and the remaining two men, trying to calm the chaos in his head and focus on the fight. The odds weren't bad—nothing he hadn't faced before.

He still had a sword, but he'd never fought with one. This wasn't the kind of weapon they pulled out in the movies while shouting en garde. This was a long, heavy piece of metal, honed to a thin edge on both sides. He took it between both of his hands, feeling the weight and balance of it, shifting as the two men closed in. The bald one lunged and chopped with his weapon, catching him in the shoulder with a glancing strike before Rory could evade. The cut burned like a poker, but it didn't maim—at least not instantly. Before the man could pull back, Rory swung from low down, catching the man at the thigh and slicing deep into the muscle and tissue, stopping only when he hit bone. The sickening feeling of it filled him with elation.

The bald man howled with agony and staggered back, falling as he clutched the wound. The last man, the captain, the one who'd thought he could put his filthy hands on Saraid, moved quickly, coming round with a blow intended to remove Rory's head from his body. It might have succeeded, but for Saraid's sharp warning.

Rory tucked and rolled, feeling the blade slice through his hair, nearly grazing his scalp. The momentum of the swing made the captain stumble. At the same time, Rory saw the bald man he'd stabbed in the thigh recover his footing and lurch at Liam. He grabbed the boy from behind and in an instant, pressed a knife to the kid's throat.

On his feet again, Rory could do nothing to help. The captain had already regrouped and he moved with grace that belied his hulking mass. He lunged at Rory, swinging his sword in a powerful arc that came so quickly Rory only just managed to raise his own sword in defense and deflect it. The sound of metal on metal rang out like thunder, and the reverberation went through Rory's entire body. His shoulder began to ache, screaming at him to lower the heavy sword that was his only defense.

The captain might have been born with the long, lethal weapon in his hands so agile was he and so narrow was his aim. He twisted and struck again, and this time Rory wasn't nearly quick enough to stop it. Once again, the blade cut deep into his shoulder, shooting fiery bullets of pain down to his suddenly numb fingers.

He managed to keep hold of his sword, but he had no feeling in his left hand. Dancing away from another blow, Rory tried to clear his head, tried to think of a way to outsmart the killer that gleamed behind his opponent's eyes. But with sweat blurring his vision, blood spilling from his shoulder, he couldn't focus, couldn't think. The man leapt forward, using a foot to swipe Rory's out from under him. Rory came down like a bag of sand, heavy, hard, and spineless. His arms splayed out, the left one numb from fingertips to shoulder joint.

The bald man with the thigh wound stood unsteadily, knife still raised to the boy, but attention diverted momentarily. Overwhelmed by the magnitude of his failure, Rory had a moment to meet Saraid's eyes before he felt the pointed tip of a blade press against his throat.

"Say yer words, if y' have any," the captain told him.

Everything slowed then. Rory could feel his heart thudding painfully at his ribs, could hear his pulse as it pumped blood onto the dirt beneath him. The captain's heaving gasps, loud in the quiet. To his right, he sensed Saraid pulling in a deep breath, felt the stir of air as she dropped low. Heard the soft clunk of a rock as she scooped it from the hard ground. The captain caught the movement from the corner of his eyes, shouted "Stop her," but the words came slow, and the wounded bald man found the blade he held suddenly forced in another direction as Liam twisted, using his hand like a claw, digging into the gash on his thigh.

The captain saw the writing on the wall and turned to finish Rory off, but Saraid and Liam had given Rory the chance he needed. He couldn't hold a sword, but he still had his fists, he still had six feet, three inches, two hundred and twenty pounds of muscle, and he'd be damned if this bag of shit was going to kick his ass.

He lunged up and hard, getting under the captain's sword arm, negating the blade's power by breaching its radius. While the other man tried to adjust his angle so he could jab or cut, Rory bowled him over, catching him with an uppercut that split his knuckles and cleaned the captain's clock. He followed it with a hook that caught the captain's nose and smashed it like a melon. The other man howled, but Rory kept coming.

He grabbed the man's neck and slammed his face down to meet Rory's rising knee. The broken nose again—and then he finished with a right hook that took him down for the count.

As the captain hit the dirt, Rory spun in time to see Saraid pelting Liam's attacker with rocks, and Liam charged with a scream pitched girlishly high. The boy buried a short knife in the man's ribs, pulled it out and stabbed him again and again until at last he fell, dead.

The silence that followed was deafening. Rory swayed where he stood, sweat burning his eyes and adrenaline still flooding his system, making him feel hypersensitive and numb all at the same time.

Liam yanked free the knife he'd used against his captor, wiping the blade on the bald man's chest with icy disdain.

"Saraid," Rory said, his voice rasping. "You okay?"

There were tears in her eyes, but she nodded.

"You?" he demanded of the kid.

Liam nodded and spat blood into the dirt.

"Where is Tiarnan, Liam?" Saraid asked. "Where are our brothers?"

The kid shook his head. "I don't know. Cathán's men came up on me an hour ago." He moved over to the giant Saraid had taken out with her rocks. "Quite an aim you have, sister. But this one is still alive."

Rory watched through a haze of gray as the boy lifted the knife and plunged it through the unconscious man's heart. His body jumped in reaction and then stilled. The boy barely batted an eye. He moved to the one Rory had knocked out and repeated the performance. *Christ.* Liam had yet to grow a whisker to shave, but he killed like a soldier too long at war.

The boy turned then and stomped to Rory's side, knife raised and dripping blood. He aimed, this time, for Rory's heart. Disbelief held him still for a moment, and then Saraid was between him and her crazy brother.

"No, Liam," Saraid said, grabbing his arm and pulling him back. "No."

"And why not kill the fooking bastard? This is all his doing, sure as the rain falls."

"Can y' see into a man's heart now?" she demanded.

"Only that he hasn't one."

"People change, Liam," she said, shooting Rory a dark glance he didn't understand. "He fought them, didn't he? We'd both be dead but for him."

The boy spat again and glared at Rory. "He'll have his own reasons for that. We'd make good hostages. Y' heard them. I knew this wedding was not the peace Tiarnan thought it would be. They just want their bloody Book and the rest of us dead."

"That is what Cathán wants," Saraid said, gently urging her brother to lower his blade. "But Ruairi is my husband now. And he has fought to protect us both."

Her words opened a dam of emotion that clogged Rory's throat and dulled his pain. She spoke with a ring of pride in her voice and when she looked at him, it was not with disappointment. His left hand was still numb, but he lifted the other and touched her face, wrapped his fingers around the back of her neck, and pulled her to him.

His kiss was brief, but it was hard and fierce and possessive. She grabbed the front of his tunic and held on as she matched his emotion, kissing him with equal fervor, matching the need and heat of it, burning through the numbness and setting him on fire. Stunned by her passion, he pulled back and stared into her eyes. There was so much there, gleaming from the velvet depths, that he was overwhelmed. He didn't deserve it, but he wanted it. All of it.

"What the fook was that?" Liam wanted to know. "Yer kissing the Bloodletter. Is the whole world mad now?"

Rory grinned, as startled by the sheer joy that filled him as the kid was by his sister kissing the enemy. Her face flushed and Saraid smiled back.

"Yes, Liam," she said, facing him but not stepping away from Rory. "The world has gone mad."

The boy grunted, pointed the blade at Rory again, and shook his head. "I'd as soon split y' from gullet to groin and dance on yer innards."

The visual was there, reflected in the glittering eyes of a boy with a face like an angel. He would do it and he would enjoy it.

"Well I guess that gives us all something to look forward to," Rory answered. "But what do you say we just focus on getting the hell away from here for now? Did these guys ride?"

Liam looked to Saraid before answering. "Aye. The beasts wouldn't come near this place, though. The horses bolted as soon as they dismounted and took off into the woods."

Of course, Rory thought. It was never easy. The rush of adrenaline was spent, and now the pain in his shoulder crowded in. Riding would be rough, but walking might be damn near impossible.

"We need to get them back," Rory said.

"Did y' not hear me? They won't come near this place and they're halfway to the moon by now."

"I heard you. Which direction did they go?"

With a roll of his eyes, Liam pointed west. Rory moved to the edge of the circle, peering into the darkness, using his senses and not his eyes. He felt them, ears pricked and listening, somewhere deep in the forest. Rory gave a loud whistle and felt them stop their forward flight. He whistled again, boosting it with the last of his energy. The horses reared and turned at his call.

Liam was scowling and Saraid looked like she couldn't decide whether to laugh or cry. After a while, she said, "It's no use, Ruairi. We'll have to walk."

"Maybe," he said, but he didn't believe it.

Another few moments passed and Liam cursed, telling Saraid they should just leave the "fooking Bloodletter" behind and get away from there. Then the sound came, slowly penetrating the quiet of the circle. It grew louder until suddenly five horses thundered into the clearing. As Rory turned to greet them, he heard Liam's stunned curse, and Rory smiled again.

Chapter Twenty-four

DRUID'S circles were not to be tread upon lightly if at all. As Saraid watched the horses paw the ground, waiting for their riders, she was aware of the spirits following her, watching her, laughing at her efforts to hurry.

"Ruairi," she said. "Let me look at yer shoulder before we go."

Liam gave a gleeful snort at that, earning him a glare from his sister. He went back to scavenging weapons and other valuables off the corpses lining the circle, muttering "Watch yerself," as Ruairi moved to Saraid's side and sat on the rock she'd indicated.

Ruairi frowned at her brother, not sure if the words had been a threat or a warning. A little of both, she supposed. She approached Ruairi cautiously, her stomach churning at the amount of blood pouring from the gash in his shoulder. Michael was the healer among their people, though that role should have been hers and it shamed her that she lacked the skill for it. She'd tried her hardest to learn even the simplest of remedies, but she couldn't keep the herbs straight, or remember what treatment went with which ailment. Once Michael had stopped her just moments before she gave a deadly dose of baneberry to an injured farmer. She'd thought it would ease his pain.

"Aye and it would," Michael said with a smile. "Right to the grave."

Mortified, she'd at last admitted that she would never be the healer they all needed her to be. But if not that, then what purpose did she have? Each of her brothers possessed an innate ability that made him invaluable to the tribe. Tiarnan, a hunter and a warrior who was rarely matched . . . Eamonn, the thinker who could, in moments, size up any situation and estimate the outcome . . . Michael, who cared for their sick and mended their wounded . . . and Liam, who could track a mouse through a stone quarry, who could sit still enough to coax a fawn from the glen.

But what of Saraid? What special gift did she possess? The occasional visit of the dead? What good did that do them? What use was she to her people?

She didn't even have skill enough to stitch a wound. Something about the swollen flesh, the stench of blood and muscle torn and mutilated . . . It was all she could do not to heave the meager contents of her stomach just cleaning a wound.

Ruairi watched her with those sky blue eyes as she cut his tunic open to better see the damage. Blood had poured down his chest and embedded itself in the seared spiral there. He caught her hand as it hovered over the scar, forcing her to look at him, to meet that direct and penetrating stare. It seemed he felt her fear, her insecurity, her worry over doing him harm in her attempts to help.

He held completely still, unflinching as she wrapped his wounds, using the cleanest strips to be made from the tunics of the dead. He'd lost a lot of blood, and her makeshift bandages seemed little help in staunching the flow, but she did the best she could—all that she could.

When she'd finished, she brushed back his soft hair, pressed her cold hands against his hot face, and his eyes closed for a moment. Like Cathán, Ruairi wore his hair shorter than most men. He had the same nose as his father as well, straight and proud. He was so tall, strong, powerful—even in his weakened state, golden under the ashen pallor, baked brown by the sun. Muscular, as were her brothers, but more defined. Sculpted like a statue. His lashes lay long and silky against his cheeks, the tips nearly golden, an apt setting for the jewels of his blue eyes.

Still, Ruairi looked ashen by the time he mounted, and Saraid and Liam exchanged worried looks. He was fading by the time they found the first trickling dampness of the brook and they turned, following it as it widened, becoming a creek, then a stream, then a river. Still he gave her a smile and a wink when he caught her staring. Grateful he was still aware enough for humor, she rode on, praying Michael would be waiting and would know what to do for him. . . .

She knew these waters like she knew her brothers. She knew the tributaries led to a falls that graced the countryside like an angel rising from mist and lore. In times of peace, before Cathán Half-Beard, the vast clearing to the west of the cool pool had been a meeting place where marriages had been arranged, grievances resolved, and business conducted. Her father, Bain the Good, had built his keep not far from there, but Cathán had burned most of it to the ground years ago and driven their tribe away. All that remained was the charred husk of the *clochán* that her father's spirit had shown her just hours before.

At last they reached the place where the waterfall poured into the river. Liam stopped and dismounted, moving cautiously from the concealing woods into the clearing at the rocky banks. He would go to meet Tiarnan on foot and report back while she waited. With a silent look, he became a part of the night that moved without whisper or shadow, leaving Saraid alone with her fear and the man she'd wed just the morning before.

Relief flooded her when she saw a branch move and a moment later, Liam appeared with Tiarnan, Eamonn, and Michael following, pulling three more horses behind them. They were all splattered with blood and gore, filthy and battle scarred, but they were alive and the fates had seen them reunited. It was more than Saraid had hoped. Ruairi revived enough to sit up and take note, but his jaw was clenched with pain.

None of her brothers greeted her. No one spoke a word, and Saraid sensed the tension in the air, the anger that seemed to simmer between them. Before she could ask what had happened, she noticed that Tiarnan carried something in his arms, a body draped over his lap. She gasped when she realized it was Mauri.

"What is this?" she whispered. "What has happened to Mauri?"

Eamonn made a sound of disgust. "She was sacrificed by our fearless leader," he said, giving Tiarnan a cold glance.

Saraid glanced from Eamonn to Tiarnan and back; Tiarnan did not respond. Confused, she met Michael's eyes, but he only shook his head and, shamefaced, looked away. As baffled as she, Liam climbed on his horse again.

As Tiarnan moved to his own mount, he saw Ruairi on the horse beside hers and stopped.

"Is he dead?" Tiarnan demanded.

"Sorry to disappoint," Ruairi answered.

Tiarnan stomped forward and made as if to jerk Ruairi from the horse and throw him to the ground. Ruairi stiffened, bracing himself for another fight.

"No, Tiarnan," Saraid said. "He saved my life. Twice. I won't go without him."

"Y' won't go without him?" Tiarnan repeated, his tone low with shock. "This man? This killer?"

"Who is now my husband," she said, lifting her chin. "In word and deed. I will not leave him behind."

It was clear that Tiarnan would have liked to argue, but the weight of defeat seemed too heavy on his shoulders, and he merely shook his head and said nothing else. Ruairi watched her as she rode beside him, but she didn't look back. She was afraid to reveal what she knew must show in her eyes.

They turned sharply west, away from where their people had settled when they'd been driven out of their homes and into the wild terrain of No Man's Land. Time wore on in a blur of aches and fears and bone-rattling weariness, leaving Saraid too much time with her own thoughts. In the space of a day, opinions she'd spent her lifetime forming had been changed so drastically she hardly understood her own feelings anymore. She had accepted the impossible—that the man who wore her husband's face had changed into someone else entirely. Her feelings for him had become something she was afraid to examine.

At last they came to a cave hidden by trees and shrubs. Ruairi had been in and out of consciousness, but he managed to walk into the cave without help. There, Michael gave him a draught that well and truly put him under.

While Michael tended to Ruairi's wounds, the others gathered wood for the small fire. The cave tunneled in the back, and the smoke escaped through a series of natural flues that snaked through the hill and came out on the other side. If the smoke was seen, it would lead whoever tracked them on a merry chase and not here, where they hid.

Mauri was laid gently on Tiarnan's cloak, near the fire that was soon crackling. Now Saraid could see the blood on Mauri's gown and the bloody bandage pressed low over her breast. How had she been wounded? At last Saraid could hold her tongue no more. "Tell us what has happened," she demanded of Tiarnan.

But it was Eamonn who spoke, who told of the ride away from Cathán's hold. His eyes were cold and full of rage when he glared at his oldest brother. "There were twelve of them and only three of us. We could have taken them, though. Like men. But Tiarnan did not think us capable. Instead he used Mauri like a shield. He hid behind a defenseless woman."

"It wasn't like that, Eamonn," Michael said, his voice sharp. "Y' know he wasn't hiding. He never meant for her to get hurt."

"Y' believe that if y' want, Michael. But I know what I saw. He used Mauri just as he used Saraid. He's not a man. He's a coward, and I will follow him no more."

Tiarnan stormed across the small distance that separated them, grabbing Eamonn by the arms and shaking him.

"I did it for *you*. For the both of y'. We didn't stand a chance against Cathán's men."

"We did," Eamonn shouted back, breaking free of Tiarnan's hold. "But y' have lost yer edge, brother. No warrior uses a woman, no matter the price."

Saraid watched with shock and dismay as Tiarnan's face crumbled. He turned his back, trying to shield his pain, his shame, his rage, but his shoulders shook with the effort. The tension was sickeningly thick, the anger a flame burning within each of them.

"*I* was not used," Saraid said, her voice strong and clear, filled with enough conviction to dim the raging fire of emotions sparking from brother to brother. "I went with my head high and my duty clear. Do not point fingers in my direction or claim that it was anything but my own will. I have wed Ruairi and I believe even now that it was the right thing to do."

Eamonn cursed under his breath. "Then y' are as big a fool as he is, sister."

"And y' have never learned to control yerself, Eamonn. Quit acting like a child. This is not the time to divide and blame. We must stand together. All of us. Or we will die."

"I would rather die than live with the disgrace he has brought on us," Eamonn said. He turned and stormed to the mouth of the cave.

Saraid was torn between the need to follow and guide, the desire to mend and console, the certainty that she must stand straight and move on.

"Is Mauri's wound serious?" she asked Michael.

"No. She will live. I gave her a draught to make her sleep while we traveled."

"And his?" she said, nodding at Ruairi.

"He'll make it." He didn't sound happy about that, but relief flooded Saraid.

"Thank y', Michael," she said, blushing at the emotion in her voice, at the surprise on her brother's face. "Tiarnan," she said, her voice gaining strength as she saw clearly what needed to be done. "Go and find us food. When Mauri awakes, she will need to eat to regain her strength."

He hesitated a moment before nodding. But he did not face her, did not let her see the agony she knew was in his eyes. Her heart was breaking as she watched him gather the bow and quiver that must have belonged to one of the men they'd battled. His shoulders were stiff, his movements awkward, as if he no longer trusted his body to perform the most simple of tasks.

Alone with Michael and Liam, she made sure that Mauri slept comfortably before kneeling beside Ruairi while Michael cleaned the deep wound on his shoulder.

"What really happened to all of y', Michael?" she asked.

"Tiarnan didn't mean for her to be hurt," Michael said as he worked. "There were no other choices, and he gambled that the men would not attack if we had Mauri as hostage. It was a smart move—no one else would have thought of it. Tiarnan couldn't have known that they would attack anyway. Y' should have seen him, Saraid, after Mauri was hurt. He was like a *riastradh*—a berserker, a score of berserkers. I killed three men, Eamonn two. But Tiarnan, he cut down seven before I had pulled my blade from the second."

Saraid swallowed, picturing the bloody scene Michael described.

"Not a man was left breathing. No one to tell Cathán what happened."

His haunted eyes turned back to Ruairi, and she knew there was nothing more to tell. Silently she helped her brother as best she could. They were lucky that his horse had made it through the battle and his saddlebags were never without herbs and the fine bone needles he used to mend. He handed her a twist of an herb she should know, but of course could not remember, and told her to steep it in water that Liam had put to boil over the fire. Next Michael ground something else in the small stone pestle he was never without until the mixture was pulpy.

When he cut the remains of Ruairi's tunic free, she saw him pause as he stared at the spiral seared into his chest. He reached out and traced the pattern and then looked deeply into Saraid's eyes. There were too many questions to ask, to answer, though. With a shake of his head, he went back to work.

She kept her rioting stomach from heaving as he pulled open the grisly gash, unmindful of the agonized cry Ruairi gave. Then he sewed the inside with ten small stitches that would dissolve over time, he said, and cause no harm. Next he added the steeped herb to his pestle and ground it into the pulp before gently smearing it over the stitches. Finally he closed the wound, sewing it carefully before adding the last of his mixture on top. When he was done, Ruairi's shoulder looked like gruesome patchwork.

There was a nasty gash on Ruairi's forehead, and Michael

cleaned the blood and placed a bladder of cold river water
against the lump.

"Hold that," he said.

"Will it help?"

"It won't hurt. A prayer probably wouldn't do any harm,
either," he said.

Saraid held the cold bag with one hand and finished bath-
ing the blood, sweat, and grime from Ruairi's face and neck
with the other. His knuckles were raw and abraded, his body
bruised from head to toe, but he was breathing and he was
alive. He'd come back for her. She let that knowledge flow over
her with a secret joy.

Later, Tiarnan returned with two ducks and had them
plucked and spitted soon after. She felt hollow and weak by
the time the scent of roasting meat filled the cave. They took
a risk cooking, she knew, but they were counting on the cave's
ventilation again to diffuse the scent.

Even as she thought it, Michael, who was keeping watch,
let loose a low warning whistle. Inside the cave, Tiarnan,
Eamonn, and Saraid lifted their heads like animals scenting
the wind. Liam looked up from the fire with exhausted eyes,
unprepared for anything more.

Someone was coming, though, whether they were ready
or not.

Tiarnan pulled his sword free and Eamonn did the same, at
arms together though neither had forgotten the bad words that
had flowed between them. Saraid waited, wishing there was
something she could do besides hover between Ruairi and
Mauri.

The men were not gone for long. When they returned it was
with three others, strangers Saraid had never before seen. One
was short and built like a bull, all mass and muscle packed
onto every inch. Beside him was a pale man with blue tattoos
covering his face, neck, and arms. Saraid stared at his features, distorted by the overlaid image of a fanged snake that
turned his visage into something that was neither human nor
animal. The last man was very tall and lean. His skin was as
black as the night and his eyes looked like bottomless wells.
Red frizz covered his head like dyed wool, treated badly. They
all wore ragged tunics and patched trews, but their weapons

shone with the gleam of care and they were heavy with them. Each man wore a long sword in a sheath that settled at the spine, hilt rising over the shoulder, battle axes hung at the hip and daggers kept ready in strategic places. Still, it was clear these were not Cathán's warriors. But who were they?

When they saw Saraid, the three went down on bended knee, and the black man touched his forehead to the ground. Behind them, Tiarnan and Eamonn stood with weapons sheathed but wariness in their eyes.

"Who are y'?" she asked the three men, her voice echoing her surprise.

"I am Leary," said the short man, looking at her from the corner of his eye as if anticipating a signal. It occurred to her only then that they were waiting for her to give them leave. Flustered, she raised her hand.

"Please, stand," she said.

The men did as she'd asked, but they remained stiffly formal in her presence. "I am Leary," the short man said again. "This is Mahon Snakeface and Red Amir. We have come to serve you."

"Me?" she exclaimed.

"And the Marked One."

Baffled, Saraid looked to Tiarnan, who gave a slight shake of his head and shrugged.

"We have come to join with you, to fight with you against the man who would see our ways destroyed."

"Cathán Half-Beard?" she asked warily.

Leary spat on the ground. "That would be right."

Mahon, the man with the blue snake tattoo, looked past her. "Is that him?" he said, pointing at Ruairi. "Is that the one who defies his father?"

"How do y' know that?" she asked.

"It is written," Red Amir said softly. "Can you not read it yourself?"

"Does he have the mark?" Leary asked, putting a hand over his heart.

Michael moved to Saraid's side and nodded. "He does."

Tiarnan and Eamonn both started at that. "What mark?" Tiarnan demanded.

"The mark of the Book of Fennore," Leary said, eyeing

Tiarnan suspiciously. "In a hundred years only one man has been marked by Fennore. Legend tells us that the man who wears this mark will bring us together and deliver us to a world beyond its power."

"How is it that we've never heard that legend?" Eamonn said.

Mahon looked at him coolly. "You were born under the rule of Cathán Half-Beard. We were not."

"But that man is Cathán's son," Tiarnan said sharply. "How can the Bloodletter deliver anything but death?"

"Tiarnan," Saraid said. "He is not the Bloodletter. Not anymore."

Tiarnan threw his hands in the air. "And what the fook does that mean? First he's marked and now he's another man?"

"Yes to both," Saraid answered calmly. "I saw him change with my own eyes."

This struck each of them silent for a moment and then they all began to talk at once.

"Quiet," Tiarnan shouted. When the last rumbling faded, he looked at Saraid. "Explain."

And so she did, though it was hard forming the words, describing what had been unbelievable even to she who had witnessed it. She told them how she'd felt two men in one even as she and Ruairi had spoken their vows. When she told of Stephen and his attempt to murder Ruairi, Eamonn cursed and took a few steps away. At last she came to those moments when they'd watched the Bloodletter fade to a child and disappear and Ruairi had become whole and solid beside her.

"How is this possible?" Tiarnan demanded, glaring at the prone form on the floor.

"It is not for us to know how such things happen," Leary said. "He has been marked, and we are here to serve him."

Tiarnan held up his hand. "He is the enemy."

"No, Tiarnan," Saraid said, moving to his side, feeling a surge of emotion as she spoke her next words. "He is not the enemy. Not the Bloodletter. Not anyone we know."

"But he is still yer husband?" Tiarnan said, his tone thick with sarcasm.

Saraid's cheeks grew hot but she lifted her chin, staring her brother in the eye. "Yes, he is still my husband."

The words felt hot and heavy and filled with purpose she didn't understand. To Saraid, *husband* meant home and hearth and family and future. Was Ruairi any of those things? Could he be all of them?

She looked at where he lay in the shadowed cave. Even now she wanted to be by his side.

"Your husband, yes." Red Amir said. "This is good. This is how it should be."

Tiarnan did not know how to react. He looked to Michael, who only shook his head. Liam stood and said, "He did fight Cathán's men to save us."

Eamonn spun at that. "Which only makes him a traitor."

"A traitor to the man who tried to kill him," Saraid said.

"Do y' trust him, Saraid?" Tiarnan asked. His eyes were still dark with bewilderment, and Saraid's heart broke for the pain she saw within them. Was it just yesterday that she'd thought him brash and arrogant? It would seem she was not the only one changed by the events of the last day and night.

"Yes, brother. I do trust him."

To Michael, he said, "Will he die?" But it was Red Amir with his ebony eyes who answered.

"No. He will not die. Not today."

The declaration sent a rush of feeling through Saraid that was negated by the doubt that came with "not today." Certainly everyone died, but there was an implied portent to the tone and phrasing Red Amir used.

Tiarnan faced the three newcomers once more, but it was Michael who spoke, pushing forward, his gesture protective and hostile at once.

"So y' mean to fight with us?" he said. "Against Cathán?"

As one, the three men nodded. "To the death if we must," Red Amir said.

"To the death," the other two echoed.

"They could be Cathán's spies," Eamonn said, but no one acknowledged him.

"Are there others who would fight against him?" Michael went on.

The bull-like Leary smiled. "Oh yes. They will come."

A startled look passed between Michael and Tiarnan. At last, her oldest brother spoke. "How many?" he asked.

"Like the fish in the ocean," Red Amir said.

"Why now?" Eamonn wanted to know. It was clear he did not believe a word of this, and his simmering anger at Tiarnan had now become a blaze directed at the entire situation. "And where have they been while Cathán has tromped over our lands and our people?"

"It was not the right time to move against him," Mahon said, his eyes narrowed when he looked at Saraid's second brother, the snake image more real for the cold shimmer in them. "We needed a leader."

Saraid saw how that cut Tiarnan, but to his credit, he didn't show it. If she were not his twin, even she might not have seen the small wince, the pain in his eyes.

"And why are y' so sure that the Blood—that Ruairi is this leader?" Tiarnan asked.

"He is here to find the Book of Fennore. And he will, because it wishes him to find it. It wishes him to open its covers, ask for its gifts. Only then will it be appeased for that which it wants but cannot have."

"That which it wants . . ." Tiarnan shook his head. "What is that?"

For a moment, no one answered and a chill wind whispered into the cave, toying with the tension, taunting the fine hairs at the back of Saraid's neck. Her skin felt suddenly hot and clammy, and her stomach clenched with a feeling of foreboding so strong it weakened her knees.

Slowly, as if moving through a vat of mud, the three men turned their faces to her.

"It is said," Mahon began, his snake-face flickering in the firelight, "that the Book of Fennore is a vessel that holds a curse—a curse that prays on the greed and corruption in men's hearts. It draws to it those who would use it for their own gain and it takes from them a piece of their humanity until they are forever changed by the use."

"It's still a book—cursed or not," Michael said.

"No. It is more than that. It's a being."

"A powerful being," Leary said. "Who is trapped inside."

Mahon nodded. "It seeks a way out, but for all of its power, it can only control that which is given freely. It must have a conduit to use and it never tires in its search for one. This is how it came to be in Cathán Half-Beard's hands."

Uneasy, Saraid looked back at Ruairi. He'd told her that Cathán had possessed the Book in another time, another place. That it had pulled Ruairi into the great dark, along with his father.

Leary picked up where Mahon left off. "It is said that no man can resist the call of the Book once it has decided to tempt him. It speaks to the mind, to the heart. It comes in a time of desperation, when you would give anything for its power. It promises to fulfill every dream, every wish. But first you must ask, and in doing so, you must give."

"What does that mean?" Eamonn snapped. "Other than the whole lot of y' are crazy. It's a book. A thing. Not flesh. Not blood."

"Not yet," Red Amir said. "But this is exactly what it wants. To walk among us. To have all the power within and the freedom to go and do whatever is its will."

"Do y' know why Cathán thinks we have it?" Saraid asked softly, afraid of the answer.

"I do," Red Amir said.

His pause stretched long, and Saraid began to think he wouldn't explain. Began to wish she could call back her words, unask the question. Somewhere deep inside, her dread began to stretch and grow. Red Amir's answer would bare its teeth and make it bite. She knew this with shivering certainty.

Red Amir watched Saraid as he spoke. "Your mother was the last to call the Book of Fennore. She was very powerful and she did what no one has done before. It is, as your brother says, a physical thing. To use it, you must touch it. How else could it take? Men have searched for it in vain, never finding it, no matter that it *wants* to be found. But your mother . . . she called it. She brought it to her by will alone."

"And in doing that," Saraid said, "she brought Cathán and his son."

"Yes."

"Why did she want this cursed thing?" Liam asked, his voice young and quavering.

Red Amir's eyes were steady, and it felt as if he could see

into Saraid's mind, see the vision her father had shown her of the night when she was born.

He said, "She asked for her children to be saved, restored. Made whole."

"That's enough," Tiarnan said, striding forward. "I will not listen to yer lies. Y' will not sully the memory of my mother."

Red Amir went on as if Tiarnan had not spoken. "She gave birth to three babies, but only two survived."

"And they were horribly misshapen," Saraid breathed, remembering the old woman who had spoken to her father, hearing again the dire warning she'd given. The woman had called the births a curse, a bad omen that should not be ignored.

Tiarnan stared at her with a look of shock, but the three strangers standing before her only nodded.

"And she used the Book to save her children," Leary said softly.

He didn't need to go on. Saraid knew what came next. The children were saved, but her mother had been driven to madness and eventually she took her own life. No one had ever known why the healthy, loved young mother had become so deranged, but the whispers had always connected her sickness to the night Saraid and Tiarnan were born.

"The Book of Fennore drove her to her death," Saraid said, angry, hurt, and afraid all at once.

"That is not all," Mahon said. "Her power became the Book's power, and it saw a way to have everything it desired."

The silence that followed those words was deeper than the ocean. Saraid felt them lap against the walls of the cave and wash over the barriers in her heart. She didn't want to know anymore, but the question came to her lips and she could not stop it.

"What does it desire?"

"Do not say it," Tiarnan said angrily. "I will not hear another word of this lunacy."

The look Mahon Snakeface gave Tiarnan was compassionate, but the words did not console. "Then walk away from the truth, Tiarnan, son of Bain. Because the truth must be told."

Saraid waited, knowing what was to come. Feeling the

power of it, the dreadful certainty in what had yet to be spoken. Red Amir's eyes slowly swung to her face. His pause seemed to draw tight all of the tension inside her. The sense that what he would say next came with the weight of inevitability made her knees weak.

"When your mother called the Book and brought Cathán and his son, she gave it two boons—two gifts," Red Amir said, still looking at Saraid, though he spoke to Tiarnan. "Her immense power and also that of the one you call Bloodletter. There is a reason why he was so twisted and torn. So violent and cruel."

The four brothers looked from one to another. Saraid could see a reluctant understanding form. The Book had touched Ruairi as a child, stolen from him the very thing that made him human.

"But Ruairi's sister," Saraid said, "she pulled him back."

Leary ignored the stunned gasps from her brothers, spoke over them when they would have demanded an explanation. "This is true. And since that day it has been searching to find that power again. It has turned its eye to you, Saraid."

"Me?" she said, her voice high and strained.

"It sees that once again two boons are in its reach. It is you who has brought Ruairi back. It is you who can deliver him."

"I don't know where the Book of Fennore is. How many times must I say it?"

"But Ruairi does. And he will take you with him to find it."

"Then I won't go."

"There will be no choice," Leary said gently. "No path to follow but the one that is written."

"If what y' say is true, then what will it do if Ruairi finds it, if he takes me to it?"

Mahon paused, considering his words before he spoke.

"The entity inside will have what it has always wanted. It will take a part of you. It will feed on your power. It will tempt you to give more."

Saraid silently stared at Leary. Her power? The idea was ridiculous—her entire life she'd been powerless, dependent on her father and then her brother. She wasn't like Ruairi, who could cast his thoughts out and speak to animals, who had traveled from one world to another. Saraid had no power.

And yet Colleen's voice floated back to her. *"You do not know what you have."*

"What will it do with all of that power?" Tiarnan asked.

"The entity within will use it to escape the curse of the Book and walk among men. If that happens, Tiarnan, Cathán Half-Beard will seem the smallest of your worries."

Chapter Twenty-five

ORY came awake at once, blinking his eyes in a dark so full he could see nothing but layers of it, piled one on top of the other.

He didn't know where he was or how he'd gotten there.

He lay still, aware of the rocky floor beneath him, surrounding him on every side and from above. Aches and pains cried out from each joint in his body, from tissues and muscles he didn't know he had. His shoulder hurt like a son of a bitch, and he was certain his head had been cleaved in two. What did he drink last night? Something at the wake—but no, that wasn't right, because he'd been at the funeral this morning . . . And he'd followed the woman into the cavern beneath the castle ruins. . . .

He sat up. Agony sliced through his body at the jarring movement and spots danced behind his eyes. He steadied himself, waiting for his vision to clear, taking inventory of what ached, what throbbed, and what hurt enough to kill him.

He was stripped to the chest, wearing weird pants and nothing else. A stained bandage that was held in place by strips of different cloth circled his chest and covered his shoulder. What the hell happened to him? Gingerly he tried moving his fingers, found they responded, and felt a wave of relief.

He rubbed his eyes, uncaring that each small effort unfurled waves of torture. At last he could focus, and his gaze

went unerringly to a small form beside him. It all came back
to him in a tidal wave of memory.

Saraid.

He'd followed her . . . and found himself here, out of sync
with reality. But here was where *she* lived. Here, in this displaced world where nothing was what it should be, Saraid was
more than a dream. She was flesh. Hot satiny curves and sweet
silky scent.

And she was his.

Here, now, she belonged to Rory. Not a possession, but his
wife. It wasn't important that the title felt awkward on his lips.
It didn't matter that he'd been wearing his twin's skin when the
vows were exchanged. It made no difference that he hardly
knew her.

She was real and she was here, with him.

Saraid. A well of emotion rose up in him, complex and
mystifying. There was relief, definitely relief. But there was
more than that in it. What he felt as he stared at her sleeping
so trustingly at his side was fierce and possessive, tender and
protective.

He'd convinced himself he'd come to this time and place
because of the Book. Because of the half-baked quest his dead
grandmother had sent him on. But now he acknowledged that
was all an elaborate fabrication. He hadn't come for the Book.
He'd come for the girl. This girl, this woman who'd crawled
beneath his skin and nestled at his heart before he'd ever even
met her.

Her face was a pale orb surrounded by the shock of her
dark hair—hair that felt impossibly soft to the touch. It was
worth the pain to reach out, to stroke it. He lifted a strand,
letting it slide across his palm before smoothing it back in
place. She slept with her hand tucked under her cheek, the blue
dress that had dazzled him in the sunlight now tattered and
filthy. She had a small cut on her face, and it bothered him,
that wound. Filled him with rage that someone had hurt her—
that he hadn't prevented it.

What had he been thinking, letting her go into that Druid's
circle alone? He should have damned caution and charged in
at her side, risking anything—everything to protect her.

She made a soft noise and turned, her hand searching for

him, finding him. He sucked in his breath when her fingers trailed over his bare belly, as if to reassure herself that he was still there. The gesture roused something so hungry and savage within him that it felt like an inferno, devouring him from inside out. He wanted to roll her over, lay the length of his body against the softness of her own. Kiss her awake, kiss her senseless.

A loud snore erupted from nearby, pulling his attention away from Saraid a moment before he acted on his impulse. With a deep breath, he looked beyond her to his murky surroundings. He could make out several other shadowy forms in the dark world, and if he stared long enough, he could see the steady rise and fall of deep sleep.

He didn't know who or how many or whether he should be afraid or comforted by their company. If he and Saraid had been allowed to sleep among them, unbound, he had to assume they weren't in danger. But he was in Crazyland now, and assuming anything here could be a deadly mistake.

The air felt close and stifling, smelling of sweat and cold ash and animal. He could see the shapes of the horses against the far wall of the cave where it appeared they were tethered. To their right he saw the low opening of the cave mouth and the night, brilliant with stars, beyond.

A rough blanket lay in a ball at his feet and quietly he shook it out and covered Saraid with it, pressing a gentle kiss to her temple as he did. She sighed and shifted, but did not wake. This was neither the time nor the place for any of his other thoughts. He needed to figure out where they were and if they were safe before he did anything else.

Using the cave wall for balance, Rory got his feet under him and stood swaying for a moment, trying to find his equilibrium. A crescendo of pain pounded through him, but he stayed erect and conscious. A major accomplishment as far as he was concerned.

He was silent, both by instinct and necessity as he crept to the front of the cave. His throat was dry, his thirst a raging need, and he hoped he'd find water outside. As he passed, a big black horse with a lightning bolt between its eyes lifted its head and watched him. Rory had a hazy memory of riding him for what felt like an eternity.

At the low gap of the cave opening he found the boy Saraid had been determined to save sleeping with a sword in his bandaged hands, his head tilted awkwardly. *Liam*, Rory remembered. He was her brother and should not be mistaken for the angelic child he appeared to be. Rory shuddered, recalling the cold precision with which the kid had finished off the wounded men who'd attacked them.

Next to Liam was a leather flask, and Rory lifted it, found it held water, and drank thirstily. His body gave a sigh of relief and demanded more and Rory had to fight the desire to gulp, thinking that bringing it back up might just finish him off. Taking the water with him, he hobbled to the other side of the low opening and sat on a boulder, taking small sips and pausing to let them settle before drinking again. The air smelled sweet and damp, filled with the perfumes of life and decay. It was blissfully cool and soothingly dark.

A full moon hung low in the sky, white in the blackness with a million stars flickering around it. Huge trees surrounded the cave with branches so thick and dense, they weaved together to form a canopy. Undergrowth turned the ground into a whispering carpet of leaves and thorns and flowers, all graduated shades of gray and black. He looked closer, making out a series of shapes interspersed with the plants. *People?* He shook his head. Couldn't be, and yet . . .

He closed his eyes and opened his senses, feeling both surprised and natural as he did so. Since following Saraid into the cavern beneath the ruins, since putting the pendant around his neck and falling into whatever rabbit hole he found himself in, he'd been overwhelmed by the feeling of stretching—not physically, but mentally. As if long dormant muscles had suddenly grown taut and eager to be exercised. He didn't understand it, but their demands came like second nature.

He reined himself in, first focusing on the cave and its occupants, skittering over Saraid's sleeping brothers, amazed they were all alive. Next he found Mauri, sleeping so deeply she didn't even dream. He lingered once more on the woman who'd come to occupy so much of his mind before reluctantly pulling away to let his thoughts shush over the horses. He felt the black one shift, aware of the invasion but not disturbed by it. On the contrary, the animal seemed to touch him back, filling him with warmth and acceptance.

The other animals lifted their heads as well, and he sensed their thoughts. Felt the air moving through their lungs, experienced their desire for the outdoors, to graze. The stone floor was hard on their hooves and legs. They were thirsty. But they weren't scared. *A good sign.*

Rory withdrew and moved on, out into the forest, letting his consciousness brush against the world beyond. The shapes he'd seen before were people—men, sleeping, dreaming, thoughtlessly crushing the flowers and leaves beneath them. He didn't have a clue who they were or why they were here, but he didn't sense malice among them.

He caught a scent that turned him, making him hover like a clear vapor high in the branches of a tree. There was a black bird hopping from one twig to another. She was worried about her nest, disturbed by something she considered a threat. Something low to the ground and growling. He felt his senses hone without any conscious direction from his mind. He tunneled under the foliage and tangled vines that covered the forest floor and whisked past burrowing insects and a startled lizard. He came to a small den, hidden by deadwood and a mulch of leaves. There was something inside. He moved closer, felt the small creature scurry back and growl again.

Once more his senses shifted without him and he felt a soothing rush push forth. He surrounded the animal, coaxing it out of its hiding place. It came, though wary. Surprised, Rory saw it was canine—not dog nor wolf but a crossbreed. Young, barely weaned, and badly frightened. It had obviously been in a fight and it looked as bloody and chewed up as Rory felt.

He tried to calm it, tried to ease its fear, and the animal responded, making a small whimpering noise. Slowly Rory enticed it to come closer, felt it follow his lead through the forest. It was sluggish, favoring one hind leg that was bloody and raw. The poor animal was starving, hurting, abandoned. Rory felt kin to it.

Though he brought it every step of the way in his mind, he was still amazed when the pup emerged from the trees and stood looking at him. Rory spoke softly, using his voice and not just his mind to bring the small wolf-hound closer. The animal clawed its way up the side to the cave mouth and then stopped beside him and stared up with soulful eyes.

"Shhhh, now," Rory whispered. "You're safe."

He lifted the puppy onto his lap, and it laid his head on Rory's thigh with a soft grunt and let him stroke its matted fur.

"How the fook did y' do that?" the boy who'd been sleeping demanded, scaring the hell out of both Rory and the pup. He'd been so focused on the animal, he hadn't heard Liam wake.

The puppy jumped up, hurt itself, and yipped with pain. Before he could stop it, the little mutt had wiggled out of his grasp and back into hiding.

Liam gripped his sword with both hands and pointed it at Rory. "How did y' get out here?" he said.

"I walked out while you were taking your little nap," Rory answered, giving the kid a cold look.

Liam flushed at that, but made a threatening lunge with his sword to hide it. "I was just pretending to sleep to see what y' would do."

"Well good job, then," Rory said, unflinching. "You had me fooled."

They stared at each other for another moment. Annoyed at having something sharp jabbed at him every time he turned around, Rory demanded, "You going to use that or are you still pretending?"

The boy faltered, looking confused. He didn't answer.

"Then get it out of my face," Rory said, slapping it away. The sword skittered loose of Liam's grip and across the cave floor.

Before the boy could scoop it up, three men appeared from the cave's darkness like ghosts from a mist. Rory recognized them. Saraid's other brothers. The biggest one bent down and retrieved the sword, handing it hilt first to the kid.

An instant later, Saraid stepped from the cloaking shadows into the murky predawn light. She looked half asleep, her hair mussed, her big brown eyes drowsy. He felt his gaze drawn to her as inexorably as the puppy had been drawn to him.

Saraid looked from one brother to the next before her gaze came to rest on Rory.

"Yer alive," she said, and there was surprise in her voice. Surprise, but not disappointment, he noticed and felt foolishly better for it. The brothers, obviously, were not so glad to see him up and around.

"When did he wake?" Tiarnan demanded of the boy.

Caught between having to confess he'd fallen asleep on watch or lie, Liam stood frozen. Rory was still pissed about the punk waving a blade at him and scaring the dog, but he figured it wouldn't hurt to start making a few allies in this alien and hostile world.

"I hobbled out a second ago," Rory said. "Arrived just in time to have a sword at my throat."

Tiarnan looked from the blade Liam held to Rory and back. No one commented on the fact that the sword had been on the ground and not against Rory's neck when they'd emerged.

"What did he do?" Saraid asked, moving to stand beside Rory.

Liam looked up blankly. "Do?"

"I heard y' ask how he did something."

Slack-mouthed, he shook his head. "I just meant how he got out here without waking anyone."

It was a good volley but the kid blew it by giving Rory a doubtful glance. He had a lot to learn about deception.

"The horses need water," Rory said, distracting them with the subject change.

"And how would y' know that?" the one with the flaming hair demanded. Rory couldn't remember his name.

"It's common sense, Eamonn," Saraid said. "'Tis nearly dawn."

The logic couldn't be denied, but still both Eamonn and Tiarnan watched him with clear distrust.

Tiarnan said, "Y' keep yer arse planted right there and do not move unless I fooking tell y' to."

Since Rory was already sitting and wasn't quite sure he could stand if he wanted to, he agreed without argument.

"Who are all those men down there?" he asked, pointing to the shapes that were slowly rousing.

Tiarnan spun and looked down as well, cursing under his breath as his gaze darted from one form to another. The first glimmer of sunrise poked up from the horizon and sparkled through the trees, illuminating more of the sleeping shapes.

"When did they get here?" he asked Liam.

"I don't know," Liam said truthfully. "I never saw them."

Rory frowned. "You mean to tell me you don't know who they are?"

"The fish in the ocean," the last brother—Michael, Rory remembered—said.

"The what?"

"Friends," Saraid answered, still hovering beside him. "We were told more would come—like fish in the ocean. But we didn't expect that it would be so soon."

Tiarnan and the others ducked into the cave and a few moments later came out leading the horses. They'd taken the time to grab their weapons, and each had a long sword and several short knives. Tiarnan wore an axe in a leather holster at his hip. Rory didn't imagine he meant to go out and chop down some trees.

Cautiously they made their way down to the stream, intersecting with their visitors. The strangers bowed deferentially as the brothers went by. If they'd expected a confrontation, her brothers didn't get one.

Interesting.

Saraid moved closer and put a tentative hand against his forehead. Her touch was cool and soothing and instantly took his mind off anything but her. This close he could smell the sweet warmth of her skin as she bent close.

"How do y' feel this morning?" she asked.

"Like someone put me through a meat grinder."

"Well, it was as close to that as ye'll be wanting to come," she answered. "Y' are lucky that Michael was able to stitch y' up. He's a skilled healer."

Rory was surprised. He'd assumed it was she who'd done the fancy needlework on his shoulder.

It seemed she read his thoughts because she gave a defensive shrug and said, "I've not the knack for healing."

"What do you have the knack for?" he asked softly.

She considered this for a long time, and he watched as

emotions flickered across her face. Frustration, confusion, embarrassment. Fascinated, he wondered which would win. At last she shook her head with a look of resignation and said, "Nothing of value, that is for sure."

"I find that hard to believe." When she shot him a questioning glance, he said, "You're hell on wheels with a rock."

A ghost of a grin tugged at her mouth, but she hid it before it could go further. Rory was disappointed. He wanted to see her smile again.

She began to fuss at his shoulder, holding herself stiff and proud, as if she expected him to argue with her right to examine his wounds. She was such a feisty thing, with those snapping dark eyes, and for the hundredth time since coming here, he wanted to hold her, kiss her, touch that passion that sparked with every move she made.

As if hearing him, she looked up suddenly. Her gaze snagged on his and held for a long, charged moment while color flooded her face. He felt the heat rising from her, but he didn't let her look away, letting his eyes tell her exactly what he was picturing in his mind.

"You have a knack for other things, too," he said softly.

"As do y'," she murmured, her voice so low he thought he imagined it.

She was good and ruffled now, and he couldn't help but feel empowered by it. She'd become the center of his universe, and he wouldn't be a man if he didn't want to think he meant something to her as well. Her eyes darkened, and his blood pressure rose a couple more notches.

With a telling sigh, she dropped her gaze. "Are you hungry?"

He nodded. "Starving."

Her eyes snapped back up as her face turned red.

"I meant, that is, I mean—"

He smiled and smoothed a stray lock of hair behind her ear. "I know what you mean," he said, turning down the testosterone. "Yes, I am hungry. But I'd still trade a good meal for a toothbrush."

Uncle Frank would be so proud.

"What is it? Toothbrush?"

He used his finger to demonstrate, and her face brightened.

She spun and hurried into the cave, returning moments later with a twig in her hand. Looking proud, she thrust it at him. At his blank expression, she broke off a piece of it, peeled the ends back so it looked like a crude paintbrush, and rubbed it against her teeth.

With reservations, Rory followed her lead and found that the twig tasted minty—in a wild way. Not like the stuff that came out of the tube, but sharper, more pungent. No matter, it was a vast improvement over his morning breath. Before too long, the brothers returned from below and disappeared into the cave without a word. Giving Rory a troubled glance, Saraid followed, but she was back just as he finished with the makeshift toothbrush. He wanted to ask her about the pow-wow that had taken place but held his questions for the moment.

"What's that?" he asked instead when she handed him a fat hunk of bread wrapped around a chunk of cold meat that looked like chicken but probably wasn't. A random image of Fred Flintstone howling *Yabba-dabba-do* flashed through his head.

"It is food."

He kept his *duh* to himself as he took a bite of the bronto-saurus sandwich—tasted like chicken—and gave Saraid a thumbs-up. She smiled, but turned away.

"Don't go," he said, catching her hand. "Talk to me."

She tilted her head, glancing at him from the corner of her eye. There was curiosity in that look and something that went deeper than mere inquisitiveness. "Talk to y' about what?"

About you, he wanted to say. *About how you feel, what you're thinking, what you want . . . what I can give you . . .*

He shrugged. "I barely remember getting here."

"Well ye'd lost a bit of blood and y' were barely conscious by the time we arrived. We wouldn't have made it at all if y' hadn't called the horses. If y' hadn't spoken to them and con-vinced them to come back."

He frowned, shaking his head, as he set down the sand-wich. He took a drink of water, swallowed and said, "I don't speak horse, princess."

She sniffed and looked away, bending to prod at his shoulder again, a look of absolute concentration on her face. "I know what I saw," she said, under her breath.

He caught her hand once more, startling her as he pulled her around so she stood between his knees.

"Thank you, Saraid," he said.

"And what is it y' think I've done to deserve yer thanks?"

"You could have left me to die. If you hadn't stopped them, your brothers would have finished me off."

He circled her wrists with his hands, loving the way she felt in his grip, small boned and utterly feminine. He trailed his fingers up her arms, watching her eyes go big and round, drowning in the warmth and mystery of them. It seemed she leaned closer, and once again his thoughts spiraled down to the basest part of him, remembering the sweet passion when she'd kissed him in the forest and later, after they'd fought and defeated Cathán's men. She'd turned to him, gone willingly into his arms.

The softest tug and her hands came up to his chest and he knew she meant to push him away, but he couldn't let her do that. It would hurt worse than all his pains combined. Then, unbelievably, her hands moved to his shoulders and her mouth was only inches away. He had never wanted anything as much as he wanted to touch his lips to hers right then, right now.

For a moment her breath mingled with his, sweet and pure as the morning air, and then her lips were clinging to his, her mouth soft and lush and hot as the furnace burning inside him. He cupped her head with his hands, holding her as he brushed her mouth with his, teased her lips open. It was only a kiss, and yet it quaked through him, the feel of her in his hands, the taste of her on his tongue. It was like holding the wind, filled with sensation and seduction that he wanted to capture but could only hope to still for just the moment.

He slid one hand down her back, urging her closer still, uncaring that her brothers were just a shout away, knowing only this second with Saraid in his arms. She'd made him feel whole, and he wanted, *needed* to show her what that meant. What she meant to him.

His other hand went to her throat where her pulse beat beneath his fingers. He reveled in the frantic rhythm, the ragged rise and fall of her chest. He moved the flat of his palm down, over delicate bones and satin skin, every inch of her enticing him to want more. His hand closed over the swell of her breast and the softness, the weight of it nearly brought him to his knees. She made a sound deep in her throat that was absolutely the sexiest thing he'd ever heard.

Behind them in the cave, her brothers began to argue, and he cursed them, praying she'd ignore them, knowing she wouldn't. Then another voice joined theirs, a woman, crying. *Mauri*, he thought with one part of his mind while the rest drowned in the sensations of every touch, every breath.

Gently, lovingly, he brushed his thumb over the hard nipple in his hand, and Saraid's fingers at his shoulder flexed, unconsciously clenching as he deepened the kiss while he caressed her breast. Her grip dug hard into his bandaged wound, and sharp pain sliced through him, jarring loose a groan he couldn't stifle.

With a soft gasp she pulled back. "I hurt y'," she said, horrified.

"No, it's nothing." And he tried to bring her back into the circle of his arms, but she squirmed away and stood looking at his shoulder with wide, guilty eyes.

"Saraid, it's nothing."

"You lie," she accused. "I've made it bleed again."

She looked so ashamed, so undone that he knew any hope of distracting her was lost. With a sigh he glanced at the shoulder. She was right, it was bleeding again, and a lot. He didn't care. He'd gladly bleed to death if he could do it in her arms. Once again, he let his eyes do the talking as they traveled over her flushed face, the round of her shoulder, the lush curves below.

And incredibly, he coaxed a smile to her lips. With a scowl she was beautiful, but smiling she was breathtaking.

Before he could tell her, the voices in the cave rose again. Mauri was wide awake now and definitely not happy.

"Do not touch me," she shouted, her words hitching with emotion. "Y' are a monster, Tiarnan. Y' tried to kill me."

"No, love, it wasn't like that," Tiarnan soothed, but Mauri was having none of it.

"What happened?" Rory asked.

Saraid bit her lip and shook her head. "It is a long story that will have to wait. I must go and help," she said. "Put pressure on yer shoulder. It will stop the bleeding."

He nodded reluctantly. "I thought you didn't have the knack for healing?"

She narrowed her eyes at him, but she didn't bite back. Instead she surprised him by pressing a lingering kiss to his lips before she hurried into the cave.

Feeling ridiculously happy considering he'd been skewered like a pig and was now probably losing the last quart of blood in his body, he leaned against the stone wall and listened, slowly piecing together what had happened. Christ, he was glad he'd missed that one.

Mauri had worked herself into hysterics, and Saraid was the only one she'd allow near her. While she sobbed and accused, and Tiarnan pleaded and beseeched, Rory turned his attention back to the little dog who still waited in the foliage by the cave. It took only a nudge to bring the puppy out and onto Rory's lap. He shared the rest of his sandwich with it while the fighting inside the cave went on. When they'd finished eating, the puppy gave an aggrieved sigh, but let Rory stroke its head, and despite the ranting and raving from the cave, it fell asleep.

Tiarnan fought the good fight, but at last he gave up and stormed out of the cave. He was pale and shaken and Rory guessed as close to tears as a man ever wanted to be. He shot Rory a poisonous glare and then strode angrily down to where the men below waited.

Behind him came Michael and Liam. The younger shuffled hesitantly, looking from brother to brother, his alliances torn. From the cave, Eamonn's voice joined Saraid's in a soothing cadence. For some reason, the tone of it jangled Rory's nerves. Tiarnan was pretty much an asshole, but Rory saw that he tried to do the right thing. Michael seemed levelheaded enough, and the kid—well, he was a boy trying to be a man. It was impossible not to sympathize with him. But Eamonn . . . something about him didn't sit right with Rory.

Liam stood indecisive for another moment more. As Michael shook his head and moved away, Liam made his choice and followed Tiarnan like a well-trained dog.

Problems in the ranks. *Not a good sign*, Rory thought. But he was smart enough not to say it. He would've liked to ask for more information, find out exactly what Mauri meant when she accused Tiarnan of trying to kill her, but that didn't seem like the smartest thing to do, either.

Michael glanced his way as if noticing him for the first time. When he saw the puppy in Rory's lap, he did a double take. "And where did y' get that wee thing yer holding?"

"Found him," Rory said.

"Well he looks like he lost the same fight as yerself."

"We haven't lost yet."

That elicited a crooked smile. "No, I don't suppose y' have." He squatted down beside Rory and gently touched the puppy's head. The pup whimpered and licked him. "My sister tells us yer a changed man. What do y' have to say about that?"

"I know better than to argue with your sister."

He got a laugh with that one. Feeling better, Rory asked, "What else did she tell you?"

"Only that y' died right before her eyes, but then there y' were alive and well again. If I didn't know her better, I'd say she'd lost her senses."

"But you do know her better? And you believe her."

Michael stared at him for a long moment before answering, his gaze moving from Rory's face to his chest where the spiral scar appeared white in the morning light. "Aye, I believe her. But if I didn't, those men down there might have convinced me. It's quite a following y' have for yerself, Ruairi of Fennore."

"What are you talking about?"

"Only that they say y' are the Marked One they are here to follow."

"What the fuck does that mean?"

"They say yer touched by the Book. That it wants y'." He narrowed his eyes in a gesture that reminded Rory of Saraid. "That's what yer here for, isn't it?"

Rory could lie. He might even get away with it. But where was the point? "It is."

"Well I tell y' now, if y' let it near my sister, I will kill y' myself. Make no mistake."

"Why would I let it near Saraid?"

"*You* tell me. All I'm saying is y' should forget the fooking Book. It will bring no good."

Rory looked away. "It's what I came for. It's my ticket home."

Michael glared at him. "And what about my sister? She's yer wife, isn't she? Would y' leave her?"

Rory's jaw clenched. Would he?

"Maybe she'll want to come with me."

Michael's glare hardened to a scowl. "If y' give her over to that Book, y' will not be going anywhere, with or without her."

"What the hell are you talking about? I'm not giving her to anyone or anything."

"They say it wants her. Wants the both of you."

"They who?" Rory demanded, looking past Michael to the men below, knowing the answer already.

The fish in the ocean. That's what Michael had called them earlier. Because they moved in groups or because there were so many of them? Since he'd first tumbled out that morning, their numbers seemed to have grown.

"Who?" he repeated. "Which one specifically?"

"Not just one. There are three of them. They're yer fookin' disciples it seems."

Rory gave him a sideways look, hoping he'd see humor on Michael's face. But he was serious. And there was fear beneath the steady gaze that met his.

Biting back a grunt of pain, Rory used the wall of the cave for support and stood. Bright colors and biting agony buckled his knees. A steady throb played the "Star-Spangled Banner" in his head, but he managed to stay on his feet without keeling over or dropping the puppy. He handed the small animal to Michael.

"Any chance you can patch him up?"

"Aye," Michael said, taking the little dog with infinite gentleness. "But what are y' up to?"

Before he could answer, Saraid emerged from the cave. "Where are y' going?" she exclaimed.

She looked alarmed, and at first he thought it was his unsteady bearing that caused it. But then he realized. She thought he meant to leave her—again. Well she had good reason to suspect him of abandoning her. Hadn't he been trying to do just that since the moment he'd appeared in this time and place? But not anymore. Maybe never again.

He brushed her cheek with his knuckles and tilted her chin up so she could see in his eyes.

"Don't worry, princess. I'm not going anywhere. I've just got a little fishing to do."

Chapter Twenty-six

SARAID followed Ruairi down the sloping path from the cave to the meadow below. His steps wobbled distressingly, but he walked tall and proud as any warrior. He was big and solid, intimidating despite his wounded and weakened state. Stripped from the waist up, his skin gleamed golden brown, throwing the silky pucker of the spiral scar and the bandages covering his shoulder and arm into stark relief. Hard slabs of muscle defined his chest and torso. His skin had felt like satin stretched tight over oak when she'd touched him. A line of golden hair arrowed down from his flat belly to his trews, riding low on lean hips. A thin band of white showed above them where the sun had not touched. The sight of that flashing pale flesh did strange things to her insides.

As if he'd heard her thoughts, he shifted his blue, blue eyes to her face. The heat in his look burned over her, through her. Made the rest of the world disappear, if only for a moment. Silently he took her hand in his and held it. There was ownership in the gesture, a possessiveness that should have made her rebel but didn't. Instead the warmth of his grip soaked into her. She felt safe. Cared for. Protected.

The gathered men below noted their descent and one by one they stood and turned, watching him. Watching her. They'd seen the claim he'd made when he'd taken her hand

and she had the sense that every step he took now was somehow foretold. Everything he did, perhaps.

As he had the night before, the short, bull-like man, Leary, stepped forward. Flanking him on either side was Mahon Snakeface, expressionless beneath his fanged tattoo, and Red Amir, so tall that even Ruairi had to tilt his head to look into the black pools of his eyes.

The three bowed when she and Ruairi stopped before them, and behind them, the others followed suit. Ruairi was as disconcerted by the deference as she'd been last night. The moment stretched uncomfortably and she realized Ruairi had no idea what to do. She squeezed his hand and tried to reach out to him with her mind the way she'd done with Tiarnan in the banquet hall. At first she met only a wall of resistance, but then it gave softly, and she spoke.

Tell them to rise.

Startled, he jerked his head and looked at her. Then, with raised brows, he said, "That's enough. Rise. Stand up. Whatever."

With the formality of a royal audience, Leary introduced his two companions and then waited. She could feel Ruairi's strength waning and sent another suggestion to him. This one found its way without barriers.

Ask them to be seated.

"Apparently we have a lot to talk about," Ruairi said. "Why don't we sit down?"

The gathering parted, and Leary led the way to their campfire. Logs had been set in a circle around it. Ruairi gingerly lowered himself to the nearest, pulling her down beside him. Once he was seated, the others did the same. Leary, Mahon with his frightening snake tattoo, and Red Amir took their places across from Ruairi, so they could see each other's faces as they spoke. The remaining two logs were quickly occupied by men who were apparently leaders. The rest settled on the ground and quietly waited. The air held the hush of expectation.

They were all staring in fascination at the scar on Ruairi's chest and the amulet that dangled from his neck by a leather thong. She understood the superstition and fear she saw in their expressions. She'd felt the same when she'd first seen them.

"How do you know me?" Ruairi asked in that direct way he had.

"It is written that you would come," Leary responded, in the elusive manner of his own.

"Written where?"

All three men smiled at that. Red Amir reached down and scooped up a handful of dirt, letting it sift through his fingers. "Written in the earth and sky."

"Great." Ruairi shook his head. "Who wrote it?"

This question caused a shifting among them that made a ripple to the last man seated on the outskirts.

"This you know already, Ruairi of Fennore. Do you test us?"

Ruairi took a deep breath and slowly let it out. She felt his tension, his frustration, his resolve. But beneath it, she felt something more. Wariness and hurt from a man who didn't trust easily. A man who only recently had reassembled the missing pieces of himself.

"If you want to call it a test, call it a test," Ruairi said. "But I want answers. What does the Book of Fennore have to do with Saraid?"

Saraid's startled gaze went to his face as she realized the tension she felt was for her. His concern was for *her*.

Surprised by Ruairi's question, the trio looked at each other, and a murmur spread through the gathering.

It was Red Amir who finally spoke, his voice as dark as his skin. "To answer that I must ask another question. Do you know the history of the Book of Fennore?

Ruairi shook his head. "No, and I don't want to know. I don't care. I only want to know why it wants Saraid and why the hell anyone would think I'd hand her over."

The anger, the passion in his voice wrapped around her. She'd known he desired her. Even the Bloodletter had told Tiarnan there was desire. But what she heard in Ruairi's voice was more than that. So much more it frightened her.

"The Book has great power," Red Amir said. "It gives great power."

"That's not what I'm here for, and it doesn't answer my question."

Leary leaned forward, his massive shoulders making his head seem too small. "What is your purpose?"

"To find it. To keep the Book away from my father, I guess. I didn't get a lot of details before I left."

Saraid held her breath, waiting for him to give the other reason. He'd told her it was his "ticket" home. A home far away from her.

"Why do you wish to keep it from your father?" Leary insisted.

Ruairi hesitated a moment and then he said softly, "Because he does want the power."

It seemed that speaking those words injured him in some way Saraid didn't understand.

"He wants the power more than anything else," Ruairi finished.

No one spoke for a long moment and then in a hushed voice, Red Amir said, "You think you can destroy it."

"Yes."

The three men shook their heads. "It cannot be destroyed, not even by you, Ruairi of Fennore."

"Okay. One, quit calling me that. Two, I've had it with the double talk. Just tell me what it wants with Saraid or get the hell out of my sight. I don't have time to dick around with you."

The murmurs became a rumble of unease, but Ruairi didn't falter.

"Why does it want her?"

Mahon's snake eyes looked cold and angry, but Leary held up a hand and the gathered men immediately silenced.

"To answer, you must first know what the Book is," Leary said.

Ruairi let out a frustrated breath, and Saraid felt the anger in him. The helpless rage that came from not being able to control the world around him. She squeezed his hand, turning his head. For a moment he stared into her eyes, searching for something he seemed desperate to find. She wished more than anything she knew what it was he sought. She thought she would give it, no matter what it was. His eyes widened for an instant, and she wondered if she'd spoken in his mind. Then his gaze became heat, intimate, burning warmth that roamed her features possessively.

Red Amir went on. "You cannot see what waits ahead of you. You do not know what has been in the past."

When Ruairi looked back at the three men who sat across from them, his voice was cool, but to her toes she felt the lingering promise that had filled his gaze.

"Okay," Ruairi said with a resigned sigh. "You're bound and determined to tell me, apparently, so I'll listen. Give me the history if you have to, but when it's done, I'll expect an answer."

Leary and his two companions exchanged another pointed look and then Leary nodded. He seemed to gather up his thoughts, and Saraid found herself holding her breath, waiting. Ruairi rubbed her icy fingers between his hands and pulled her a little closer to his side.

"I am a descendent of the people born to this land, of a time before time was counted with numbers," Leary began at last. "It has been my duty to carry the story, the history of our people and the history of the Book of Fennore. I am bound by honor to pass it on so that it will never be lost."

A *seanachaí*, Saraid thought. The keepers of history were revered above all others. No wonder Leary's companions were so offended by Ruairi's disrespect.

Ruairi studied Leary for a long moment and then he said, "I am also a descendent of the people born to this land, but from a time when time is counted in seconds."

Seconds? Saraid stared at him with disbelief. Who could count the seconds?

Leary smiled. "That matters little. You are marked by the Book of Fennore. For you, time is irrelevant."

"I wasn't marked by the Book," Ruairi said, never looking away from the stout man's eyes.

"Explain."

"I did this to myself. With a bottle of tequila, a Bic lighter, and the end of a hanger. There was nothing prophetic about it."

Saraid didn't know what any of those things were, but she could not believe he had burned this symbol into his own flesh and didn't feel it was prophetic. What else could it be?

Leary only shook his head. "Have you never wondered why, Ruairi of Fennore? Why would you do this if not because the Book wanted it so?"

It was obvious Ruairi did not like the question. He scowled at the bullish man.

Mahon, speaking through the fangs of his tattoo, said, "It is told that once there lived a powerful Priest—a Druid who could commune with the gods, with the fruits of the trees, the animals who lived there, the ground beneath our feet, and the very air in our lungs. We were all one people on Éire then. All of the same beliefs. There was one king and he bowed only to the High Priest known as Brandubh, the Black Raven."

Red Amir picked up the narrative, speaking into the pause, his frizzy red hair glinting in the sun. "There came to this Priest a woman named the White Fennore. Her beauty was like that of a goddess, a dream."

Beside her, Ruairi stiffened and glanced at her from the corner of his eye. Confused, Saraid tried to make sense of what she'd seen in that fleeting look. There'd been both question and . . . fear.

"The Priest fell instantly in love with her," Red Amir went on. "She was a woman he could not resist. A woman every man desired."

The strange trio of *seanachaí* looked deliberately at Saraid and beyond them she felt all eyes follow theirs. With a mixture of astonishment and dismay, she stared back. What did they mean by this attention? She was no goddess, no dream.

And then she remembered Ruairi, his voice husky with want, telling her he'd dreamed of her before he had come here. But she was not a beauty that men desired. They feared her. Feared her ability to see death.

"The White Fennore was not just a woman, of course," Red Amir went on. "She herself had powers that the Priest had never imagined."

"What kind of powers?" Ruairi asked.

"She saw death," Leary answered, speaking to Ruairi, but his gaze lingered on Saraid's face. He knew, she realized. He knew that she was the keeper of death's secrets.

"She saw death?" Ruairi repeated woodenly. "What's that mean?"

"She knew who would live and who would die."

"Was she ever wrong?" Saraid asked, despite her vow to keep quiet.

"No," Leary said. "She was never wrong. Her gift came to her from the gods. It traveled from their hearts to hers."

Like jugglers handing off apples with a twitch of the wrist, the story was caught up by Mahon Snakeface.

He said, "She would try to change what she saw, but every effort failed. The blacksmith she saved today would only burn to death tomorrow. The fisherman she coaxed ashore in the morning would slip and fall on the way home, cracking his head against a stone instead of drowning out at sea. And so it went for years. Death, she could not escape. Death, she could not prevent."

Saraid swallowed the burn of tears in her throat. They spoke of her own despair, her own failings. Ruairi's hands had chilled and the soothing touch stilled. What was he thinking?

"Did it make her crazy?" Ruairi asked softly.

"Yes. Eventually," Mahon answered. "The High Priest, who loved her beyond anything else, urged her to keep silent about what she saw, to tell only him. She loved Brandubh as well and trusted him with her secrets and so she did as he bade. He wanted to protect her, fearing that the people would turn on her, but he was also jealous. Her gift was true and pure, but his was not so exact, and the people had lost faith in him. A terrible drought had come to them and his sacrifices, his pleas to the gods for rain, had gone unanswered."

Red Amir effortlessly caught the story and continued. "While his power diminished, the White Fennore's seemed to grow. But because the High Priest had told her to keep silent about what she saw, she suffered through each death alone. Soon it became too much for her. She begged Brandubh for relief, and so he made for her a Book. Its covers were seamlessly hewn from the skin of bear and adder, engraved with an awl made from the bones of the white stag, adorned with jewels washed in sacrificial blood and silver smelted by sacred fires. The pages were of the finest vellum, formed from the skin of countless stillborn boars and bound by threads woven from the sinew of seal. It was a thing of power before it was ever used."

The words echoed throughout the meadow, and Saraid shivered at the foreboding they caused. It seemed some part of her knew what would come next, though she'd never heard this story. Ruairi put his arm around her and scooted her closer to him. His warmth seeped into her, down to the bone, but it could not dispel her fear. That was a living, writhing thing that wormed its way through her body, clenching the muscles tight, constricting around her chest until it was hard to breathe. She looked away from the black pits of Red Amir's eyes and saw that Tiarnan, Michael, and Liam had silently joined them sometime during the tale and now listened with horror. They must see, as she did, the parallel between the White Fennore and Saraid. Two women who saw death. Two women, condemned by a gift they didn't want.

And what of the High Priest? What of Brandubh, the man who could commune with the air, the earth, the animals between? Was that not what Ruairi himself did? She had felt it when she'd flown out of her body across the forest in his care, hovering on wings that did not exist.

She glanced at Ruairi, noting the stiff set of his jaw, the lowered lashes glinting in the sun, hiding his thoughts. She wanted to reach out, to speak to his mind again. But she was afraid of what she might reveal if she opened that passageway. He was far too attuned to her as it was and even now he faced her, lifting those gold-tinted lashes, drowning her in the blue of his eyes, the heat of his gaze.

It was Leary who continued the telling now. "The Book was a work of love and power and madness. No one knows if the High Priest meant it as a gift or as a curse, though his jealousy consumed him. For now the White Fennore was a danger to him. The drought continued and people died. Though she never spoke of it, she began to make runic inscriptions in her terrible Book, and the people knew that she recorded the messages of death in those symbols. They thought that to write something down gave it power, and so they believed that she not only knew death's secrets, she shared them. She called them. She caused them."

Saraid caught her breath. *Death's secrets.* She'd always thought of the visitors who came to show her their fate as just that . . . death's secrets. On the tail of that, another thought came to her. When Colleen of the Ballagh had come to deliver her message, Saraid had said she would write it down and what was Colleen's response . . . Saraid struggled to remember. She'd said, no, because that had not gone well for them in the past.

"Still," Leary went on, "they were too afraid of Brandubh, of the White Fennore herself, to act on their suspicions. But then she saw the king's death and she could keep quiet no more. She took her terrible Book to him, showed him her runes, told him they spoke his death. The king, in his terror, had her locked away, and he called to the High Priest, who performed a cleansing ceremony, but the king feared this would not be enough, and so he ordered a sacrifice of the most sacred kind. A human sacrifice. A gift to the gods of something so prized, they would forgive whatever offense the people had committed to warrant this punishment."

"They sacrificed the White Fennore?" Ruairi said and the words seemed to come from the depths of him, emerging rough and sharp and painful.

Leary nodded. Mahon said, "But as the keeper of death's secrets, she knew her own fate. Knew that the man she loved, Brandubh the High Priest, would betray her and be the one to sacrifice her to the gods. As she was led to the sacrificial stone, she refused to release the Book. She held it in her arms as she offered her life, and when the High Priest shed her blood, she cursed him forever. All of the people who had come to watch her die were struck blind as she damned him and damned them all. Only the few who had believed she should be spared, and so did not come to see her end, were left whole. Many of the people who were blinded ran from the circle in terror, killing themselves in their panic. Others lost their minds with their sight. Only a few could retell the horror of what had happened, and even then they could only recount the moments before their sight was taken. What is known is that when it was over, all that remained of the High Priest Brandubh and the White Fennore was the Book, sealed by one of her runes."

He paused, looking at the symbol on Ruairi's chest then at its mate on the leather tie hanging from his neck. "It is said that the Book is all powerful and that it can be used, but only at a great price."

"Yeah, I've heard that before. So what did they do with the Book?" Ruairi asked.

"Three men took it to a place unknown to hide away forever. They were never seen again."

Ruairi drew in a deep breath and slowly let it out. Exhaustion shadowed his eyes, and a gold-flecked stubble darkened his face. He rasped his hands against the short beard.

"No one knows where the Book of Fennore was taken," Leary said. "It faded into legend and then myth."

"Until Cathán Half-Beard came," Tiarnan said bitterly, speaking for the first time.

"Yes," Leary answered, giving her brother an opaque look that somehow conveyed his censure. "But do not forget it was Oma, your mother, who brought the Book to our world and with it, Cathán Half-Beard."

Ruairi's head lifted at that. "She brought it from where?"

Leary stared at Ruairi long and hard, and Saraid saw the wall Ruairi tried to erect around him. She saw his guilt and dread in the shadows of his eyes. He knew exactly where Oma had found the Book—clasped between father and son in the cavern beneath the castle ruins.

"We do not know where Cathán or the Book were when Oma found them. We know only that she did. Saraid can tell you why."

Slowly, Ruairi looked at her with shock. "You knew this?"

She nodded. "About my mother, yes. Last night, when they came, they told us."

"Why didn't you say something?"

Saraid could not meet his eyes. She looked down at her clenched fingers. "There wasn't time."

Ignoring their avid audience, he took her chin and turned her face to his. His eyes were bottomless as they searched hers, and this time she knew what he looked for. He wanted the truth—truth she couldn't bear to reveal. She didn't want to see the fear, the distrust that came to all eyes that looked upon the keeper of death's secrets. But in Ruairi's probing gaze she saw only hurt and disappointment.

"How did Cathán get the Book?" Tiarnan demanded. "Y' said my mother brought them both. Cathán has always said he had it when he came and she took it away from him. So is that the truth?"

The three men nodded in unison.

"Well how did he get it in the first place?" Tiarnan said. "How did he find it?"

"He didn't," Ruairi answered, finally looking away from Saraid, leaving her bereft. "It found him. That's how it works."

"This is true," Mahon said, snake eyes steady as they watched Ruairi. "And do you know why it found him?"

Saraid's breath caught in her chest and held as she waited for Ruairi to reply.

"No, I don't," he said.

"I do not think you speak the truth, Ruairi of Fennore," Leary said.

That got Ruairi's attention. He glared at Leary. "Are you calling me a liar?"

"Does the man who claims he did not see the cliff still die when he falls off it?" Leary asked.

"That depends on whether or not he can fly," Ruairi answered.

Saraid watched the three men shift uneasily and suddenly something new occurred to her. These men had come to follow Ruairi, to serve him even. But that did not mean they had no fear of him. She could see it now as he looked from one face to another. They were all afraid of Ruairi. *Why?*

"The history lesson has been great," Ruairi said, interrupting Saraid's thoughts. "But I still don't see what any of this has to do with Saraid. You haven't answered my question yet—what does it want with her?"

"To escape the curse of the White Fennore, of course."

"Of course," Ruairi said dryly.

"That which lives inside the Book must regain its humanity," Leary said. "But when the White Fennore trapped the High Priest, a part of her was trapped as well, and she fights to keep him entombed in her pages."

"Saraid," Ruairi repeated impatiently. "What does it want with her?"

"It cannot just take her," Leary said. "She must come willingly. In sacrifice."

Ruairi turned to Saraid, his face pale, his eyes sparking with anger. "You told me you'd never seen it before. Was that the truth?"

"Yes," she said, hating the doubt she saw on his face.

"Then what do they mean?"

"You will find the Book, as you have come to do," Leary went on. "And it will work through you to get to her."

Ruairi cursed on a deep breath and shook his head.

"I won't listen to any more of this insanity," Tiarnan told them, pushing to his feet. Michael and Liam stood as well.

Eamonn had still not joined them, and Saraid could only assume he'd stayed behind with Mauri. She loved all of her brothers, but Eamonn's desire to wound Tiarnan in this way was unforgivable.

Tiarnan said, "We're going hunting. When the stories have ended, I'm sure yer bellies will start to growl."

Several men from the gathering joined the hunting party without being asked. It would take them all to feed so many mouths. They left without another word, but the look Tiarnan gave her as he walked away made her heart ache. He was afraid, she realized. Afraid for her.

After a moment, Ruairi stood, tugging Saraid's hand so she rose as well. His restless gaze roamed her upturned face for a long moment, and once again she felt that he was trying to see inside her. He wouldn't like what he found, though. What would he think when he learned that she was as wretched and cursed as the ancient White Fennore?

When Ruairi spoke, his voice was hard and deep. He looked the three men in the eye, letting them know that he meant what he said.

"You guys think what you want. I've touched the Book before. There's nothing on heaven or earth that would make me want to do it again. I'll find it, because evidently that's what I'm here to do. But I won't give it the chance to 'work through me.' I sure as hell won't let it come near Saraid."

"It may not be your choice to make," Leary said.

"That's where you're wrong," Ruairi said. "I just made it my choice."

Chapter Twenty-seven

TIARNAN led them north as the sun hit its zenith, a ragtag line of three men, a boy, two women, a prisoner—if that's what Rory was—and Leary's small army behind them. He gave the air of a man with a bigger plan, but Rory guessed Tiarnan was lost—mentally, emotionally, most likely physically. Saraid's brother couldn't stop himself from glancing back to where Eamonn rode at the end of the line with Mauri next to him. Eamonn had become Mauri's knight in shining armor and Tiarnan the villain in just one day.

From the start, something about Eamonn had irked Rory. It went beyond his aggressive and disrespectful attitude, but Rory still couldn't put his finger on the exact reason. Perhaps it was Eamonn's relationship to the other brothers. The others acted like a unit, moving with one mind, working for a greater good. Even the kid. But Eamonn seemed to have his own agenda, and when you had to depend on someone to watch your back, that was never a good thing. Now he was swooping in like a vulture, picking up the shattered pieces of his own brother's love life and capitalizing on his failures. It was no wonder Tiarnan looked like a man already defeated.

Rory didn't care about Tiarnan and his feelings—Saraid's older brother had been an asshole to Rory from the first moment, but he'd be inhuman not to feel some of the other man's pain. It was obvious he loved Mauri. Hell, that had been obvious from the first time Rory had seen the two together, gazing longingly into each other's eyes. He knew that the decision Tiarnan had made to use Mauri as the means to escape Cathán's killers had probably been a balls-to-the-wall choice—not one Rory would have ever made. Still, he doubted Tiarnan would have done it if there'd been other options. He'd gambled, thought using her would save them all. And he'd been right, at least for the time being. But Tiarnan had lost everything in that roll of the dice.

Rory glanced at Saraid beside him, thinking how deep it would cut if she turned off her feelings for him as easily as Mauri had for Tiarnan. The thought nearly knocked him off his horse.

Is that where his head was right now? Of all that had happened, of all that was still happening, was his greatest concern for this stranger he'd married, held in his arms, made love to—fierce though that loving had been—and knew not at all?

She looked upset, and he knew it was over something said by one of the Three Stooges who'd blown into camp last night. He didn't have to be a mind reader to feel the tension around her now. She'd lied to him—granted it was a lie of omission—but still it hurt more than he cared to admit. Now she was sealed up like Fort Knox, barely looking at him.

He wished he could do as she'd done—speak into her thoughts. Ask her what was wrong. But he didn't know how. He'd *never* known how. His sister, Danni, could do it, and once opened, he could communicate along the channels she'd cleared. But he'd never been able to pave the way himself. A person's mind was not like an animal's, not like soaring through the woods and brushing against instinct and emotion pure and clear. A human's mind was complex and daunting. A *female's* mind was that times a hundred.

He shifted and rested a protective hand over the puppy that lay inside his torn and stained tunic, snuggled against his belly. Michael had patched the bedraggled dog's wounds, and with a full stomach, it had only wanted to curl up someplace safe and dark to sleep. When it had wiggled its way from Rory's hands to his chest, then poked its head under his neckline and down inside his tunic, Rory had laughed. Now the animal was like a furnace there, but he didn't have the heart to move it.

He glanced at Saraid again, noting the tight line of her mouth, the small pucker of a frown pulling her brow together. What was she thinking? He let out a breath, frustrated. The Stooges told him that the other version of himself—the Bloodletter—had grown up in this place and been a victim of the Book of Fennore. Turned from a boy into a pitiless monster. It explained so much but left so many unanswered questions. His twin had lived here with his father until just yesterday when he'd died. Correction, until he'd been murdered.

"You knew me when I was a kid?" Rory asked.

Surprised, Saraid nodded. "Until y' were ten and yer father sent y' away."

"Sent me away to where?"

"To foster with a clan in the north. Most people foster their children—sons and daughters alike. If our parents had lived, they'd have done the same with me and the boys."

"Why does everyone send their kids off?"

"It's good for them. For everyone, I suppose. Brings our tribes closer together, creates kinship. Most have great feeling for their foster families."

That made sense.

"So who was this family in the north I went to live with?"

"That I do not know. They were Northmen, kin of Cathán's wife. Y' were taught about war while y' were with them and they taught y' how to fight like the Northmen do. Some think it was there that y' and *riastradh* found one another."

Riastradh. Rory tried to catalog the word and find its meaning, but he came up blank.

"What is that?" he asked at last.

"Do y' not know?" she said, surprise making her lilt more pronounced. "It is the frenzy that takes a man when he fights. They say when he has *riastradh*, he has no sense of being a man, a human. He is aware only of blood and the need to spill more of it."

Rory was silent for a moment, thinking of the red rage that had colored his world when he'd heard Saraid scream. He remembered next to nothing of what happened between the time her cries echoed in the still forest and his awaking this morning. Sure there were bits, disconnected pieces. But everything else was a strong hum that vibrated through him—not a memory, not a recollection, but a feeling he couldn't pin down.

Saraid was watching him with curious eyes and he felt stripped beneath the steadiness of it. At least she was looking at him again. After a moment, she went on, but her gaze still lingered on his face, probing, seeking.

"Others say y' were born with *riastradh* and the Northmen only nurtured it. However it was, y' left a wake of blood and death wherever y' went. I know now it wasn't yer fault and I feel bad for that boy who had his life stolen from him. It's glad I am that yer sister gave y' a second chance. The Bloodletter that lived here . . . he was not a man. He was a caged beast."

"Christ. And you married me anyway?"

"I told y'. I did it for the hope of peace."

He shook his head at the foolishness of that. She should have known better than to trust Cathán or a man who was renowned for his killings.

"Tiarnan said the Bloodletter came in person to offer for me. Y' told him y' desired me. He believed y'."

Rory stared at her, noting the way the sun gleamed off her hair, setting the reds mixed in the dark strands aflame. Her face pinked up as she gazed back at him, watching him take in every feature of her face from high proud cheekbones to round and stubborn chin. Her eyes were drowning deep, her brows a graceful arch above them. Her nose was a little long, but it balanced her other features and ended at her full and kissable mouth. Rory had known from the first moment he'd stepped inside his twin that they both desired her.

"There's no lie there," he said. "I do desire you."

His mouth went dry at the way those words seemed to travel over her skin, heating it. Turning the dark of her eyes molten. *Desire* was too mild a word for what he felt when he was near her.

Her blush deepened, and he wondered if she'd heard his thoughts.

"Is it true what y' said earlier," she began, talking fast to hide her discomfort, "that y' put the mark of the Book on yer own flesh?"

"Yes," he said, and it was his turn to look away.

He didn't want to talk about that. He'd rather talk about this *desire* thing between them. But he knew Saraid well enough by now to know she wouldn't let it go. It wasn't in her nature to move on when she knew there was more.

"Why would y' do such a thing, Ruairi?"

"I was bored."

She leaned over and touched his hand. "Do not lie to me."

The simple request carried so much weight. *Don't lie*, it said. *Not after all we've been through together. Not if you want there to be more for us to share.* It was written in those velvet eyes, and he couldn't ignore it. Yet, she had lied to him. He wanted to point that out, to deflect her investigation into the life of Rory MacGrath. He knew he could turn the tables on her with a word.

Or he could do something totally outside his experience. He could trust. He could believe that she had a reason for not telling him what the Three Stooges had said. He could trust that eventually she would tell him why.

"The Book marked me when I was five," he said slowly, drawing the words out, feeling their sharp edges as they emerged. "Inside, I mean."

Her eyes widened, but she said nothing.

"It changed who I was. Who I was going to be. Made me feel like I didn't fit in my life anymore. It took my father and left me behind, holding the bag, thinking it was my fault. Like if I'd done something differently, he'd still be there. It left me empty, torn apart." He shook his head. "I didn't realize until yesterday that I'd been literally ripped in two."

He rubbed the back of his neck, uncomfortable with this baring of his soul. Saraid watched him with those knowing eyes of hers and waited for him to go on.

"I was fifteen, maybe sixteen when I burned the mark on my chest. I guess in my own twisted mind, it was my way of lashing out. Hurting what it thought it owned."

She considered that for a quiet moment before speaking. "I can see where y' might have thought of it that way. I wish I knew how to hurt it back."

He wanted to say it didn't matter, because he was going to destroy the Book. He didn't care if the Three Stooges riding behind them thought it was impossible. He would find a way.

"It was the truth, what I said to y', Ruairi," Saraid blurted suddenly. "I never knew my mother had the Book until they told me last night."

The look in her eyes was black and tortured, and he realized with a sudden dawning comprehension that part of what had her upset was him. She was worried he thought less of her now for having caught her lie. He nudged his horse closer so that his leg touched hers. Gently he covered her hand with his and let his thumb stroke the heated pulse at her wrist. She took in a ragged breath and lowered her eyes.

"I believe you," he said. "But you need to talk to me. Tell me what's going on behind those big brown eyes."

She swallowed and shook her head.

"Come on, spill it," he said. "I told you my secret."

He smiled, dipping his head so he could see her face when she kept it lowered. He knew she caught his grin from the corner of her eyes, but she didn't smile back.

"Did y' never wonder why I wasn't already married?" she whispered.

Rory frowned and shook his head. "No. In my world you're still young for that."

Now she did smile, but it was filled with sadness. "In my world I'm quite old. Most women have husbands and children before they reach their twentieth year."

He gave a small nod. "Okay. Why didn't you? Were you waiting for me?"

He'd meant it to be teasing, but there was a throb in his voice that shook him. Christ, he had it bad for this woman. Beneath his hand, her pulse beat frantically.

"No," she said stiffly. "I was not waiting for y'."

Good to know she wasn't trying to spare his feelings. Not so great to know she hadn't been waiting, because somewhere deep inside, he suspected that *he'd* been waiting for *her* all his life.

Frowning, he said, "Then why?"

"No one would have me, Ruairi."

He looked her over, not sure what she meant by that. She wasn't joking—that was painfully clear. But what kind of idiot wouldn't *have* a woman like Saraid? She was beautiful, sexy as hell, and she was smart. There was so much courage and honor. Loyalty and integrity. The men of this time had to have shit for brains not to want that in their women.

"The men, they fear me," she said. "They fear what I can do."

And suddenly he began to see the light. He could picture the anxious faces in his father's hall. The servingwoman who'd been shaking in her shoes as she'd come close to Saraid. Even Cathán had seemed nervous when she turned those dark eyes his way. A spiraling plunge began deep inside him as he considered this.

"What can you do?" he asked softly.

Her pause stretched between them, long and filled with the unsaid. He wanted to stop the horses, get his feet on solid ground and take her in his arms. Hold her tight, let his hands do what his gaze couldn't stop doing—touch her, every inch, every sweet spot. He wanted to kiss her, pull the words from her mouth, savor her faith in him.

"I am like the White Fennore," she murmured, her words solemn. He had to strain to hear her. The shame in her tone was deep and pained.

"In what way, Saraid?"

Finally she gazed at him and the look in those warm velvet eyes drove a hole through his heart. They glittered with tears she was too proud to shed, gleamed with pain that went deeper than words could express. And over it all was the shame that hunched her shoulders and made her bottom lip tremble.

"I know death's secrets," she said on a breath lighter than the breeze that teased the leaves of the mighty oaks surrounding them.

He struggled to put a framework around her statement. Death's secrets? What did that mean? And then in his mind, Rory heard Leary weaving his tale in the morning air, telling them about the High Priest and the White Fennore. He'd said *she* knew death's secrets. And she'd died for it.

Saraid was waiting, her bottom lip caught between her teeth. Her eyes looking like they might overflow with everything she felt. She'd condemned herself, he realized. And now she was waiting for him to join her in the damnation.

"Are y' not shocked?" she said.

He shook his head, gazing solemnly back. He released her hand to cup her face, turning it so she couldn't look away.

Gently he moved his thumb over her lip, across the teeth that held it until that sweet mouth softened. "You are what you are and I wouldn't change any of it."

Now her mouth opened in surprise.

"Not any part," he said, feeling the pressure of emotion behind his words. Remembering how much of his life he'd spent wishing someone would say the same thing to him. He didn't share death's secrets, but he'd shared secrets with the Book of Fennore and at some small level, he knew what she was feeling.

"I wouldn't change one goddamned thing," he muttered, his voice husky. "But I am sorry."

She shook her head. "And why would y' be sorry?"

"It must hurt, knowing when people are going to die. That's a heavy load to carry."

A tear swelled over the dam of her lashes and slid silently down her cheek. He edged closer still so that her right and his left leg were trapped between the bodies of the animals and leaned in to press his lips to the salty trail, murmuring against the silk of her face, telling her everything was going to be okay. She turned her face into his throat and more tears followed the first in a silent release of this thing she'd held tight and painful in some dishonored place in her soul.

Her tears were not like Mauri's, not full of sound and anger, not meant for the display of her pain or fear. These were the hot, cloistered tears from a well of hurt that went long and deep. He held her in his arms and buffeted the storm of her release.

His shoulder was wet, his thighs aching from the grip he maintained to keep them both balanced and astride, but he would have held her forever if she'd needed it.

After a while she lifted her face and tried to pull away.

"I'm sor—"

"Don't," he whispered. And then he kissed her trembling lips, tasting the salt of her tears, the bitter hurt, the warmth of her trust. He wanted more—wanted to be off the horse and somewhere alone with her, where he could kiss away every pain she'd ever had, every injustice ever done to her. But there was no way to stop the world and do it.

He pulled back, looked into her eyes, and tried to say it all without a word. She gazed back with something like wonder.

"Y' are not what I expected y' would be," she said softly.

A slow smile spread across his face and he pressed his forehead to hers.

"Why is that funny?" she asked.

"Because you, beautiful Saraid of the Favored Lands, *you* are even more than I expected."

Chapter Twenty-eight

SARAID found herself falling into the blue of those eyes, drowning in the tenderness of his acceptance. She was more than he'd expected? Did that mean she pleased him? And why did that make her feel like smiling? Like throwing her head back and laughing with joy. They were still in danger. Still being hunted. Still had to face the destiny Leary and his followers were sure awaited them.

Yet the future felt less daunting now. It might even be promise she saw shimmering on the horizon.

"In fact," Ruairi said, his voice deep and soft. The heated rumble danced over her skin. "You're better than the dreams."

The words, the tone, it made her want to arch her back like a cat, stroked in just the right way. How had he taken her from tears to awareness with just a blink of those incredible eyes?

Slowly he withdrew, settling more evenly into his saddle. He must have been on the edge of falling the entire time she'd cried on his shoulder. Yet he hadn't moved, hadn't said a word. He'd only consoled her, captured her falling anguish and tossed it behind them both. Now, in this dark hour when their lives hung in the balance, when everything she knew and loved could at any minute be taken away, she felt suddenly lighter, more hopeful than she'd ever thought possible.

He handed her the reins to her horse, which she'd let fall

against the animal's neck, confident that Ruairi would, in that mystifying way of his, guide them both.

"We'll get through this, princess," he said.

"I believe y'," she murmured, trying not to think of the one question that still loomed in her mind.

"But?" he asked, hearing it anyway.

But what will happen when you find the Book? Will you return to your own time and place? Will you leave me behind?

She said none of it though and with a deep sigh, he accepted her silence, too.

Who was this Ruairi she'd wed? The man she rode beside was as much an unknown as the Book of Fennore itself. At times it seemed a little boy lurked behind his startling blue eyes, a vulnerable child lost and alone. She'd married him, expecting him to be nothing more than the monster he was reputed to be. Something feral. Perhaps tamable, perhaps not. But certainly she'd never anticipated a man with depth, with shifting emotions—with any emotion, for that matter. A man of compassion and selflessness.

That he was a man who could accept her failings and still look at her the way he did . . . like she was a woman worth fighting for . . . like she was a woman he desired more than air and water and life itself . . . it was inconceivable.

She'd trusted him with her secrets. Trusted him with her deepest shame, her deepest anguish. And she did not regret it.

She glanced at him from the corner of her eye. He gently patted the puppy who'd snuggled down next to his heat, feeling safe, as Saraid did, in his protection. As she watched, the animal moved and then suddenly it squirmed its way up and popped its head from the neckline of Ruairi's tunic. It looked so adorable, that she almost laughed, but something in Ruairi's expression stopped her. The pup gave a low warning growl.

Ruairi glanced up, flicked his gaze past her to Tiarnan and Liam riding in front. He swung on his saddle and looked back where Michael rode with the three strange men who'd come to their camp last night, trailed by the other men who'd followed.

"What is wrong?" Saraid asked.

Nervously, Ruairi shifted and looked out into the still

woods that bordered them on both sides. "Where is your brother?" he said. "Eamonn?"

"He and Mauri are behind us." She turned, searching for her brother but unable to spot him. "They may have dropped back to check that we're not being followed."

"Yeah, well, we are."

Ruairi absently smoothed the fur on the still growling puppy that had now wiggled out of his tunic and was held in one of Ruairi's big hands. She knew the touch was gentle, but the pup still growled menacingly.

"What do y' mean? They've found us? Who—"

He shook his head, his lip caught between his teeth as he scanned the shadowed forest. "I don't know who, Saraid. I only know they're close enough to scent. My money's on Cathán though, and I wager he's coming fast."

Understanding went through her. *The puppy.* Ruairi knew because the dog had sensed danger.

"Go up, tell Tiarnan. They've picked up our trail."

The sound of pounding hooves halted whatever else Ruairi might have said. Startled, Saraid looked over her shoulder to see Michael pushing his horse into a gallop.

"They've found us," he said. "Hurry."

They urged their horses forward and followed as Michael spoke to Tiarnan in a low voice, using his hands to illustrate. Saraid watched, noting the anger she saw on Tiarnan's face, the fear in Liam's eyes. Tiarnan glared at Ruairi as they stopped beside her brothers.

Michael said, "Some of Leary's men scouted out to make sure we were safe. They spotted Cathán's men less than an hour behind us."

"How did they find us?" Tiarnan asked tightly. "The Bloodletter hasn't been out of our sight. He couldn't have told them."

"Where's Eamonn?" Ruairi asked.

Tiarnan narrowed his eyes at him. "He was bringing up the end of the line."

"So he knows we're being followed?"

Michael shook his head. "No. Leary's men didn't see him when they came to report."

Tiarnan cursed under his breath.

"When was the last time you saw either Eamonn or Mauri?" Ruairi pushed.

Saraid's brothers looked from one to another. The last time she'd seen Eamonn, he'd been leading Mauri to the back of the ranks. That had been hours ago.

"Y' think they've been captured?" Saraid breathed.

Ruairi didn't meet her eyes. Still watching Tiarnan, he said, "No. That's not what I think."

The silence that fell between them was ominous and filled with something ugly, something Saraid didn't want to see.

Tiarnan said, "I don't know what yer implying, Bloodletter, but if Eamonn is missing, it's because of Cathán Half-Beard." He turned and jabbed an angry finger at Liam. "Y' fell asleep on watch last night, didn't y'? And the Bloodletter got a message to Cathán while y' slept."

Liam looked like he'd swallowed a knife. He shook his head quickly. "No."

"Quit bullying the kid," Ruairi said. "I didn't go anywhere last night. It wasn't me."

"No?" Tiarnan snapped. "Then who the fook was it? The fooking dog?"

Ruairi didn't answer, but they all knew what he was thinking. It was there on his face, in the tight set of his shoulders, in what he *didn't* say. He was thinking of Eamonn, the only one who wasn't there to defend himself. She shook her head with disbelief. Eamonn would never betray his own. He wouldn't have put his family in danger. Yet . . . she remembered how angry he'd been at Tiarnan . . . how he'd questioned every order . . . the way he'd looked at his older brother . . . she hadn't wanted to admit it, but now how could she pretend there hadn't been hatred in his eyes. . . .

Tiarnan launched himself from his saddle at Ruairi, and both men went flying to the ground. They hit with a thud that Saraid felt to her soul. Ruairi groaned as all the breath was crushed from him, but he rolled and came up swinging just as viciously as Tiarnan.

"No!" Saraid cried. "Stop it, both of y', stop it!"

In seconds Michael was there beside them, trying to pull the two apart as Liam did the same. Praying that Ruairi was wrong about Eamonn, that the two men locked in battle would not kill each other, Saraid jumped from her saddle. She couldn't get near either one of them, though, without risking a blow that one man meant for the other. Finally Michael managed to haul Tiarnan off Ruairi, while Liam did his best to keep Ruairi from following.

"Ruairi," she said, grabbing his arm and shaking it. At last he looked at her.

His face was bleeding and his shoulder wound had opened again. It would infect if it couldn't heal, and from his deathly pallor, Saraid feared it was already festering.

"My brother would not betray us," Tiarnan said, his voice hard. "And I will not hear otherwise."

Tiarnan's face was battered, too. Even injured, Ruairi had given as much as he'd taken. Tiarnan spat blood into the dirt and wiped his mouth with the back of his hand.

"Fine," Ruairi said. "Don't hear it. But it's true."

"How do y' know, Ruairi?" Saraid whispered.

He looked at her with regretful eyes before answering and she knew that he didn't want to tell her. At last, he said, "You remember how we found Liam in the Druid circle?"

She nodded, picturing how he'd soared through the forest, surveyed it all from the eyes of a bird.

"I see them," he said now.

"See them?" Tiarnan shouted. "Well fookin' point them out because I see nothing."

"And that's been your problem all along, hasn't it?" Ruairi said, shrugging Saraid off and stepping up to Tiarnan. "You can't see beyond what you want to see, can you? Well if that's the way you want to live, go for it. But I don't follow the blind."

He turned his back on Tiarnan and took Saraid's shoulders between his hands. "I saw him, Saraid. I swear it. He and Mauri are with my dad, right now. And they're coming for us."

"How many?" Michael wanted to know.

"More than a hundred. Maybe two."

Tiarnan just stared at them with blank, shocked eyes. Saraid felt the pain he could not, would not show. He had loved Mauri since he was a young man, had thought her out of his reach, and yet some part of him had always believed that someday she might be his. And when Cathán had proposed this match, she knew he'd hoped that the union of the two families might lead, somehow, to making Mauri his wife. To have that slip through his fingers, to think that his own brother might have brought the destruction of his dreams down upon him . . . it was more than any man could handle.

"If Ruairi says Eamonn is with Cathán, then it is so," she said softly. "But perhaps he's a prisoner, Tiarnan. Perhaps he went to make peace, to deliver Mauri to her father and deflect his wrath. However it is, we must act. We must trust that Ruairi has seen what he says."

The words hurt, but they were the truth. She knew how Ruairi could travel, and as much as it wounded her to consider it, she feared he was right about Eamonn. Now little things she'd dismissed before rose in her mind. Eamonn alone had stood beside Tiarnan when he'd announced the match between Saraid and Ruairi. He'd encouraged it vehemently when everyone else had been against it. Had he known what Cathán had planned? If Stephen had succeeded in killing Ruairi on her wedding night, then her brothers would have been slain as well. But if Eamonn had been in league with Cathán, then he alone would have been left alive. . . . she stopped herself, unable to even consider that Eamonn could have planned so far, so deviously.

"They've got over a hundred men," Michael was saying, interrupting the twisted road of her thoughts. "We've got forty, maybe fifty."

Ruairi cupped Saraid's cheek with his big hand. "I'm sorry, princess."

She nodded, but she couldn't speak. The pain went too deep to comprehend. If Ruairi was right, then her brother, her beloved brother, had led them to destruction.

Ruairi looked back at Tiarnan. "They're coming in two groups from either side."

"Are they coming for y', Bloodletter?" Tiarnan asked.

"No," Saraid answered. "They come for me."

The truth of that seemed to settle on each of their shoulders. If the tale Leary and his two companions had told was true, there could be no doubt that Cathán thought Saraid would take him to the Book her mother had stolen from him.

Ruairi stepped closer to her, shielding her with his body. Telling her without words that Cathán would have to go through him first. She saw the message reach each of her brothers at the same time.

"I don't trust y', Bloodletter," Tiarnan said, moving up so that he stood chest to chest with Ruairi. "And I certainly don't trust y' to protect my sister. I'd sooner sleep with a blade at my throat."

"Y' forget, Tiarnan," Saraid said, wedging herself between the two men. "I am his wife now. Wedded and bedded. It is not up to y' to trust him. It is up to me, and I do."

Behind her she heard the soft gasp of shock that slipped from Ruairi's lips. Then his hands were on her shoulders, his body burning down the length of her back. A dark red stain traveled up Tiarnan's face at her words, but whether it was shame or rage, Saraid didn't know.

"Y' expect me to take his word because of that and believe my own flesh and blood would betray me? I'd rather cut his throat now and be done with any questions."

At that, both Michael and Liam jumped in, offering their opinions on who to believe, who to trust, who to follow. Who to kill.

"Hate to break up your little tea party, ladies," Ruairi interrupted, raising his voice to be heard over the clamor, "but they're gaining on us. Why don't we table the discussion about cutting my throat and get a move on?"

Ruairi's tone was offensive, his words insultingly cavalier, but the steely look in those blue eyes subdued them. In fact she'd swear there was a gleam of respect in Michael's gaze as he turned away.

"There's a mound not far from here, a tunnel with a chamber inside," Tiarnan said, pointing to the south.

Saraid sucked in a breath as she realized what he spoke of. A fairy hill some might call it. Or a tomb for the gods, others still. Whatever it once was, it was not a place for humans to tarry—not a place to use as refuge, no matter the danger. To cross its threshold was to invite disaster.

"We can hide there. They won't find us," Tiarnan went on.

For certain, and even if they did, they wouldn't risk themselves to go inside.

She saw her own trepidation mirrored on her brothers' faces, but none spoke up. Tiarnan was their leader and they would follow him wherever he would go. He moved back to where Leary stood with the others and quickly told them what was happening. Leary gave an order and nine men on foot branched off, three to the east, three to the west. The last three went north.

When Tiarnan came striding back, he said, "We have to leave the horses. They're too easy to track."

"They'll track us no matter what," Ruairi said. "We need the speed."

Tiarnan didn't even glance at Ruairi when he spoke, his tone flat and unflinching. "Leave the horses."

"It's a mistake," Ruairi insisted.

Tiarnan looked from Michael to Liam to Saraid. "Make yer choice now. Follow him or follow me. There can be only one leader."

The note of defeat in Tiarnan's voice broke Saraid's heart. He had been tested and he had done his best, but in his own judgment, he had failed. If they turned from him now, he would be broken. She glanced at Ruairi, waiting for his response, waiting for him to deliver the blow that would destroy her brother. For an instant he met her eyes and it seemed he understood everything she was thinking.

She saw then that he knew they were headed into more danger, but their lives had become one constant treacherous path. What was one more abyss in a journey filled with them? And so he became a leader she would never have expected. He led by giving back the only thing Tiarnan had left.

Silently, Ruairi began to remove the bags and weapons strapped to his horse. With a collective sigh of relief, Michael and Liam did the same. Tiarnan hid his surprise well, but Saraid could see it there, hidden in his eyes. How close he'd been to the edge.

They took anything they could carry that wouldn't weigh them down—blankets, flasks, food. Without asking, Michael took the puppy from Ruairi's hands and slid the little dog into a bag he slung over his shoulder. When the horses were stripped, Tiarnan gave them a slap and sent them running away. The big black one with the thunderbolt on its face cast Ruairi a soulful look before following the rest. Saraid felt the heavy press of fear in her chest as she watched them vanish over the hillside.

"Let's go," Tiarnan said.

He set a fast pace, a jog that the others matched, and soon they were like shadows in the forest. Weariness was etched on Ruairi's face, but he picked up speed, running beside her as they darted through the woods and up and over the rocky hills. Leary's men spread out so as not to leave a trampled trail. After an hour, they slowed but they did not rest. Afternoon was well on its way to evening and they were exhausted, but still they pushed on.

As the soft light of dusk settled around them, Saraid began to hope they might make it. There'd been no sign of Cathán's men, and all but one of the parties Leary had sent out had reported back with no further sightings. The mound was near and she caught glimpses of it through the trees. They would have to break from the forest, but only for a short distance and then they would be safe.

Tiarnan slowed and raised his hand, signaling to everyone to stop. For a moment they waited, not even a branch swayed in the breeze. Tiarnan and Michael crept close to the forest's edge and peered out. All was still and quiet.

Then Saraid saw something move in the distance. She turned to look and there stood a man, his face bloody and beaten beyond recognition. His body moved strangely, awkwardly disjointed. He stared at her, walking through the clearing with a purpose that could not be denied. She glanced at Ruairi beside her, but he only scanned the mound, his eyes slipping past the battered warrior without pause.

So he wasn't real. Or rather, he wasn't really here. Not yet. It was his death she saw.

She braced herself as he drew near, stopping close enough to touch. His face had been pulverized by whatever had killed him. One eye was gone, the other swollen nearly shut. He was monstrous, horrifying, and she had no idea who he was. Slowly he shifted, looking at Ruairi with that lone eye before returning to her.

Saraid shook her head, wanting him to vanish. Fearing him in a way she should not. He wasn't real. He couldn't hurt her. She knew it was all true, but still she couldn't slow her racing heart or ease the hot dread that closed her throat. He wanted something, something she could never give. His lips moved and she knew he was going to speak, going to tell her about the horror that had reduced him to this state. But like the rest of his face, his jaw had been crushed and he was unable to form words. Only an inane gibberish spewed forth.

Then Tiarnan was giving the signal, and they all moved forward again. Saraid stepped past the beaten man and he vanished as completely as he'd appeared. Relief made her lightheaded, but dread made her heart beat painfully. Gingerly they picked their way out of the forest and into the late-afternoon sun. For a moment it burned their eyes after the sheltered canopy of trees.

The mound was straight ahead and Tiarnan turned, urging the others to run for it while he and Michael kept watch. There was a small creek that curved along the base and the men splashed through it and hurried up the hillside. Saraid and Ruairi came more slowly. His breathing was ragged and his pallor alarming. Blood soaked the bandages of his shoulder and down his tunic. As they started up the rocky slope, Ruairi stumbled, and his forward momentum sent him sprawling in a heap that rolled back down. She skidded to a stop beside him, found him battered and cut, a new gash on his forehead spilling blood over his face. His eyes were closed.

"Ruairi," she whispered, touching him.

He didn't move. Saraid had only a moment to realize he was unconscious before a rumbling shook the earth. She spun to see riders burst from the trees and bear down on them like a pestilent swarm. Cathán's men had found them.

She grabbed the front of Ruairi's tunic and shook him. "Ruairi, wake up. Get up, *now*!"

His eyes fluttered open but they were glazed and unfocused.

"On yer feet," she cried.

Ruairi rolled to his knees and then lurched to a stand, wiping an arm over his face to clear his eyes of blood just as Michael and Tiarnan raced back to their side. Michael shoved a sword into her hands. She had no chance to ask him where he got it. Saraid had been raised the lone sister among men—she knew how to handle a sword. Gripping it hard, she turned to meet the onslaught.

Even as he swayed with dizziness, Ruairi had his weapon

drawn. He seemed a bit stunned by the quickness of his reflexes, as if he hadn't expected the command from brain to limb to move with such lightning speed. Still, he barely got his sword raised before it was met with a downward blow from one of Cathán's mounted warriors. Ruairi's knees buckled, but he didn't fall. Beside her Michael, Tiarnan, and Liam fought and danced with graceful moves. Saraid lifted her sword and stood with Ruairi.

The sound of metal on metal went through her and turned her insides watery. Ruairi dodged and thrust again, managing to get his fist into the fabric of one of the riders. He yanked the man from his horse like he was made of straw and impaled him with his blade. Again she saw shock register on Ruairi's face, but it was fleeting and there was no time to dwell on it because another rider was on them and another. Even though Leary's warriors battled fiercely and her brothers were at her side, fighting like a unit, there were more than twice as many of Cathán's men and they had the advantage of the horses.

Saraid ducked away from a charging rider and brought her sword up to catch the man in the thigh, steeling herself for the feel of her blade slicing flesh, unprepared for the triumphant rage that filled her. She may not be a healer, but she knew that wound would cause bleeding and likely death. Another man swept down and tried to grab her. Saraid stabbed at his arm as she evaded his groping hands, but he kept coming, impervious to her glancing blade.

She fought with every ounce of strength and will she could muster, vowing that she would not go easily into Cathán's captivity. That road would lead to a fate worse than death. As she swung and parried, jabbed and dodged, she saw Ruairi and her brothers beat back their attackers, bringing them down like felled trees. Leary's men fought fearlessly as well, and it seemed that the odds had evened. There was hope. Hope that they might escape once again.

But then a terrible cry split the air, and Saraid turned to see one of Cathán's men launch himself at Ruairi, his face twisted in a mask of rage that went beyond this skirmish, beyond the feud, beyond hatred. Ruairi spun, raising his sword as he braced and lunged. But he was just a moment—just an instant—too slow and his attacker caught him low and between the ribs.

It was a deadly wound, she knew it even though she had no time to assess it, no chance to help him, because at the same moment another man grabbed her by the arms and hauled her kicking and screaming onto his horse. In one fluid motion, he disarmed her, trapped her against his saddle, and spun to charge away. Her scream was filled with terror, though she'd tried to clamp down on it. More mounted riders charged through the trees as the fight echoed around them. Ruairi had said there were two groups, she realized, and this was the other half arriving fresh and ready to fight.

There was no hope that her brothers could win now, no chance that Ruairi would live to find the Book—to destroy it. She screamed his name as she watched the man she'd wed, the man who'd seemed invincible, fall to his knees then keel over and lie still.

Was he dead? Was he? A wave of terror greater than her fear of dying stole the breath from her lungs. It seemed impossible that only days ago she'd railed at the fates that matched her to this man, because now the idea of losing him was more devastating than anything she'd ever faced before. She couldn't go on living if Ruairi were dead. She would not let it happen.

"Ruairi," she cried again, squirming with fury to be free of her captor.

"Doona worry, lass. There are more of Cathán's men than that bastard. They'll all be waiting to service y'."

His words only spurred her to kick and claw as she struggled to get free. Unable to ride and keep his hold on Saraid at the same time, the man who held her reined in his horse. Then he struck her hard across the face and clamped her in a grip so tight it crushed her ribs and stole her breath. The pain from the blow was immediate and blinding. She didn't scream—couldn't push the noise past the constricted muscles of her throat, but in her mind she cried out, opening that passageway to Ruairi.

Help me, Ruairi, I need you. . . .

Her head lolled back, the side of her face afire, and what little she had in her stomach threatened to come up. But from the corner of her eye, she saw Ruairi stir. She turned, disbelief warring with hope. Yes, his hand lifted, pushed at the hard ground. He rolled to his back, tried to sit in an awkward painful-looking motion. He was alive—a miracle in itself. He lay there for an agonizing second, chest heaving from the effort, staring at the sky, and then he shifted, meeting her eyes.

Ruairi, get up, get up, get up. . . .

She slammed her head back, feeling her captor's nose crack against her skull, and then she did it again. The man howled with pain, and his grip loosened. Saraid struggled harder, determined to get to Ruairi before someone noticed he lived. Before someone finished the job. Even as she squirmed and writhed like a snake, she kept her eyes on his, willing him to get up. To take up his sword. To fight.

He tried to lift his hand. She saw the agony of the effort in his expression and then the rage when he couldn't grip the hilt of his weapon. She willed him to be strong, to defend himself, but it was clear that his wounds were too deep and his time was short.

The man holding her caught her face in a vise grip and jerked it around to his. He held a short, sharp dagger in his hand and he pressed it to her cheek. "Keep at it and I'll cut yer nose from yer face."

She gulped, swallowing the scream that the grim promise in his eyes evoked.

"Do y' hear me, girl?"

She nodded, staring at the blade as he inched it closer. "Yer nose, yer eyes, yer ears, I'll take them one by one until yer left the hideous witch I know y' to be. Cathán cares only that yer alive."

She bit her lip hard to keep from shouting, but in her mind her screams went on and on. And then she felt something shift, something deep inside her terror. It felt cool against the inferno of fear. It moved, coating and calming, and suddenly she realized—it was Ruairi. He was inside her, telling her to hold on.

The knife hovered over her face, but beyond it she could see Ruairi sprawled on the hard rocks, covered in his own blood. He clenched his eyes tight against the pain and then he turned his head and stared back at her.

She was caught in that swirling blue gaze, feeling the vibration that rose up from below as if it had come from inside her mind—inside his mind, which had coupled with hers.

There was no sound to it or none that could be heard over the clanking of swords, the shouts of men at battle, but the earth itself began to shiver and tremble. Shadows leapt across the ground as tree branches swayed to and fro. A slithering hiss of pebbles started the slide to the creek bed at the bottom.

The tension built and she sensed her captor coming around and aware of the faint quaking. And then suddenly it was subtle no more—like a whisper turned into a scream, the blast whisked across the clearing, a throbbing wind that burned and shrieked.

Each of them felt it, felt the unnaturalness of the current. Men paused, weapons held at ready as they looked around for the source of their agitation. The pulsing drum of it increased, finding a rhythm that was not of this world but of something frighteningly *other*.

The horses shifted, nostrils flaring, ears twitching. For a moment, time ceased, and it seemed Saraid's breath had frozen in her chest. She watched as Ruairi pushed himself up until he was sitting, legs sprawled uselessly in front of him, skin leached of all color. He was a ghastly pale ghost, covered in so much blood that he must surely die. But in his eyes, there was life. Sparking, snapping, enraged *life*. He muttered something, something low and indecipherable, but once again a tremor spread out across the clearing, sizzling and hissing as it rose like a flame. The earth gave a mighty shudder, and now all semblance of fight ceased as the warriors succumbed to the dark fear that filled them.

And then everything happened at once.

The horses—all of them—began to dance and whinny. Riders swayed, trying to get control over the beasts as they hopped and pranced. It was as if the rocky terrain had suddenly become hot coals that burned. The first horse reared, clawed the air with its hooves as it let out a chilling scream. The next followed and then the next until the entire herd was up on hind legs prancing and pawing and calling one to another.

The man who held her could not keep them both mounted— not with the horse gone berserk and Saraid fighting to get free. She hit the ground with a thud that knocked the air from her lungs and rolled out of the way an instant before she was clubbed and stomped by the flaying hooves.

She scrambled to Ruairi's side, finding he'd somehow gained his feet. Ruairi gave a low whistle, and from the forest the black horse with the white lightning bolt that they'd set free hours ago came running like a dog to its master.

But all around them the other horses had become wild beasts that bucked and whirled while their riders shouted and struggled to hold on. The man who'd captured her flew through the air and hit the ground hard. His horse charged after him and with single-minded determination, began to stomp and kick, bearing down on him until he'd been reduced to a pulp.

At last Saraid recognized the man she'd seen in death.

It took only seconds and the other riders saw it all, understood by the unspoken message that passed between their mounts that if they should fall, the same fate awaited each rider.

Ruairi held his hand out and without hesitation Saraid took it, giving one glance back at her brothers to see they'd already come to the same conclusion. It was time to run while Cathán's men tried to survive the rebellion of their animals.

Run they did, though only the gods knew how they managed. The black horse Ruairi had beckoned went down on forelegs to allow Ruairi to mount. Saraid slipped on behind him, wrapping her arms around Ruairi's ribs, trying to hold tight and not injure him more at the same time, fearing this horse would go berserk like the others and trample them to death. But instead it stretched its neck and took off in a smooth gallop that felt like flying.

A glance back saw that the other horses had not ceased their crazed behavior. They screamed and reared like something nipped at their ankles. Another rider fell and was trampled gleefully beneath sharp hooves. She searched the melee for her brothers and Leary's men, but they had vanished like mist in the sun. She clenched her eyes in gratitude, praying that they would make it away and to safety. And then she held on, for the horse flew ever faster, seeming not to touch the ground at all.

It raced through the forest, following no path, no direction, dodging around trees and boulders with breakneck speed. Still seeing in her mind the mayhem of the other horses, stamping and snorting . . . killing, she held on. She'd never witnessed anything like it in all of her life. And deep inside her, perhaps most terrifying of all, lurked the knowledge that Ruairi was somehow responsible. Ruairi, like some ancient king of beasts—Adammair, perhaps—had given the command and they had obeyed. She didn't understand how he'd done it, but there was no doubt that he had.

With her face pressed into Ruairi's back, she could hear the dangerous wheeze of his breath, the frightening rattle in his lungs. She needed to get him somewhere safe to tend his wounds. She wished it were Michael on this horse with Ruairi and not herself. He would know what to do, but Saraid didn't know where to even start.

There was no time to worry about it. They'd fled the woodlands she'd known all her life and now they entered a darker, more severe forest that seemed to appear from nowhere. Ruairi had lost consciousness again, and she felt his dead weight slumping forward. She tried to reach around him for the reins, tried to stop the horse as it flew like a bird into unknown terrain. But she couldn't gain control and there was nothing she could do but hang on and pray.

Chapter Twenty-nine

SARAID didn't know where they were when the horse slowed at last, its great barrel chest heaving with its efforts to outrun the wind. The animal's fine coat was dark with sweat and flecked with foam. It snorted and shook its massive head, but gone was the frenzied look in its eyes. How it had avoided stumbling over protruding rocks and roots during its wild flight, she would never know.

They'd come to a place where the forest seemed to crowd the sky from existence and the trees and underbrush were both thick and harsh. Branches jabbed from forbidding trunks; vines, armed with spiky thorns and tangling lines, slithered at their feet. Carefully now, the horse picked its way through darkness, its ears swiveling, its breath short and loud. Birds chattered and darted through the strange twilight woods, but they silenced as Ruairi and Saraid approached and she felt them watching, tracking the horse and riders. Saraid kept her arms around Ruairi, holding him tight, taking reassurance in the rise and fall of his chest, no matter how labored. If he still breathed, he still lived.

At last they came to a steep, jagged rise made entirely of stone, and the horse stopped. Saraid looked up the stark, fearsome face of it, shaken by the superstitious chill that went through her. Spirals and strange, ugly faces had been carved into the stone like fearsome sentries. Runic writing ran the length, portending with symbols ancient and extinct. Her mother would have known what it said, perhaps. But her mother was dead and so, too, would Ruairi be if she didn't get him some help and soon.

But this was the ground of the olden—hallowed and forbidden. No place of men, and she was loath to set her feet upon it. She clicked her tongue at the horse.

"Not here," she whispered. "Go'n with y' now." She put her heels to its haunches and kicked hard, but the only response was a reproachful look from docile, weary eyes and a long, woeful sigh.

Without the forward momentum to keep him grounded, Ruairi began to list to the side and was instantly unbalanced. Alarmed, Saraid slid off, holding him as he plummeted, trying her hardest to break his fall. She succeeded, but only by becoming a soft buffer as he landed on top of her.

He was a big man and the crushing weight of him slammed the breath from her and trapped her between his unmovable mass and the hard, unrelenting ground. She tried to wiggle free, but it was like trying to squirm out from beneath a boulder. Still, she was afraid to roll him off and injure him more. The horse, it seemed, understood her dilemma. It nuzzled Ruairi's neck and ears, snorting and jostling his head until, unbelievably, Ruairi stirred. He lifted his face and looked around with glazed eyes.

"Ruairi?" she wheezed through lungs constricted and collapsed by his dead weight. She tried to push him back, for now she couldn't even catch her breath and suffocating beneath him would help neither of them.

He focused on her, frowning at her predicament beneath him, not seeming to understand that he was the cause of it.

"Y' are crushing me," Saraid managed, and at last she saw comprehension in his eyes. He levered his weight up with shaking arms and then heaved over onto his back.

Saraid sucked in great draughts of air before finally sitting up. He'd lapsed into unconsciousness again and she stared at him, feeling helplessly inadequate. *What now?* Her brothers had run in another direction. Even if they hadn't, they would be miles behind on foot. She was well and truly on her own here and she did not have the first idea of what to do. Cautiously she approached the horse, putting a hand to its muzzle. It blinked back at her, as passive as a lamb.

"Why did y' bring us to this place?" she asked.

The horse tossed its head and it seemed to point with its muzzle at something beyond the cluster of shrubs and bush. She crept closer, wary of what might await behind the cover. With a shaking hand, she parted the foliage and peered in, stunned to see a tunnel, large enough for a horse and rider, but too narrow for more than one. It was made entirely of boughs and branches, woven together over years untold until they formed a solid barrier, a wall of wood and leaf. She inched forward, afraid to leave Ruairi defenseless where he lay, but knowing she must first investigate before she tried to bring him there. As she stepped through the opening, the branches behind her snapped back into place and obscured the way out. She glanced back with trepidation that fought to become panic. Her fear of closed spaces howled through her head, demanding that she turn around and claw her way out.

But with the sudden and overwhelming darkness, there came recognition.

She'd traveled this tunnel with Bain just yesterday when he'd shown her the night she was born. He'd brought her here, moving with speed that had blurred the journey, propelling her through the tunnel before she'd realized where she was. On the other side, there would be a cove. A sheltered place with fresh water. A magical place.

At least that was what she hoped, because uncertainty rode high on her fear. If there was safety on the other side, then she would force herself to take the next step. She would do it for Ruairi.

She stared at the point where she'd entered, told herself the opening was still there, and yet trepidation clamored in her head, reminding her of all the tales of the Others—fairies, gods, impudent spirits who tricked the unwary in just such a way. Her breath hitched as she tried to quell her thoughts. But who did not know a person whose brother or uncle, cousin, or sister had stepped in a fairy ring and vanished for years only to reappear as young as the day they went missing—though fifty years might have passed. Some never came back at all. Had there been a fairy ring of mushrooms in the clearing that she'd stumbled into? Perhaps a ring so large that the eye did not at first see the pattern?

Did it matter when Cathán's men might be bearing down on them at any moment if she didn't find safety?

The tunnel curved and snaked back on itself and Saraid forced herself to put one foot in front of the other, fighting her terror as she had when the men attacked them earlier. It was impossibly dark inside and only a faint glow peeping through the layered branches and leaves kept it from closing in on her. She could do this. She *would* do this.

She had no sense of time and became disoriented, unsure of what direction she traveled or how long she'd been steadily creeping forward. She could hear the distress in her own breathing, tight and frightened, not yet a gasp but very close.

Calm yourself, she warned. She'd left Ruairi defenseless, dependent on her return. And return she would. She clamped down on her rising panic and kept moving.

At last, up ahead she saw the glow of sunshine, which could only mean the end of the tunnel. With a rush of relief, she hurried forward and out. The tunnel had brought her to the clearing she'd expected. On one side, the towering rock wall continued, forming a shelter around a grassy bay and a clear river that pooled just in this spot before continuing down into the depths of woodlands so dense they were bathed in eternal midnight. It seemed to be secluded from everything, this place, for on the other side the river cut its path through two walls of rock that protected the gentle pool and grassy glen. But growing tall and massive in between were nine trees, all bowed over the water.

Saraid moved closer, staring at the leaves, the trunks. Something fell to the pool with a plop, and Saraid saw a nut bob on the surface before a large fish neatly jumped from the water and swallowed it just as it had in the vision with her father. With a shiver of fright she didn't quite understand, she backed away from the water's edge. They would be safe here if she could just find a way to bring Ruairi through the tunnel.

It was too good to be true, and she worried that when she turned around again, the tunnel entrance would have vanished. But there it was, waiting, and she hurried back to where she'd left Ruairi, finding neither he nor the horse had moved. Emboldened by this small success, she tried to mimic the whistle she'd heard Ruairi use to beckon the horse. It took several tries, but at last she matched the pitch and the horse's ears perked and swiveled and with a snort, it came to where she stood and knelt beside the fallen warrior.

Saraid couldn't stop her surprised laughter. "Aren't y' the smart one," she said, stroking its sleek neck.

Carefully she heaved Ruairi onto the animal, but he was well and truly out and in the end, she succeeded in only pulling him halfway, scurrying to the other side of the horse and holding his arms as it rose, using its momentum to tug him sideways over its back. He groaned and Saraid caught her lip, knowing his condition was grave and being slung like a sack of feed over a horse's back would not improve his injuries. But what choice had she?

The horse balked at the tunnel entrance, but she talked in a low, soothing voice, telling it about the grassy clearing and the cool, fresh water that waited on the other side. Whether it was her steady hand as she pulled its bridle or the words she spoke, she'd never know, but somehow she convinced the horse to follow.

She worked quickly once they were through, guiding the horse to a soft place and settling Ruairi on the ground in the sheltered cove. She stripped his bloody clothes, hesitating for just a moment before plunging her hands in the cool water and rinsing the bloodied garments so she could use them for bandages. He'd been impaled through the ribs and with each breath he took, bubbles formed in the ragged wound. His shoulder had opened again and bled in a slow but steady flow. There was a knot the size of a stone on his head, and abrasions covered his face and hands. His gold-flecked lashes lay against dark circles in a grayed pallor.

There was only one bag tied to the horse's saddle by leather straps and Saraid quickly opened it, knowing it would be empty—they'd stripped the horses when they'd set out on foot—but hoping all the same. She had nothing but the clothes they wore and the knife in Ruairi's leather scabbard.

"I don't know what to do, Ruairi," she whispered, hanging her head in despair.

He was bleeding inside. She didn't have to be a healer to know that. And the bubbling wound told her his lung had been punctured. Even Michael would not be able to mend that. What hope had she to save this man now that she'd found shelter?

None, a voice whispered inside her.

But she refused to hear it. Refused to believe that she'd come so far only to watch him die in this way. If this was an ancient and holy place, then perhaps there was some of the olden spirit left. Perhaps.

Squaring her shoulders, she moved to the pool and stared into the smooth surface, remembering how Bain had taken her down, down, through to the other side. She was shaking as she cupped her hands, sending ripples across the water as she drank from them. The coolness slid down her throat and soothed. Still trembling despite her determination not to let her fear get the best of her, she splashed her face and neck.

A shadow fell over her and with a startled gasp, she spun. Ruairi stood behind her. Only it wasn't Ruairi, she realized as her shock blossomed into terror. It was not the flesh-and-blood man. It was his spirit. It was his death.

"No," she said to him. "Y' will not die. I will not let y' die, Ruairi. I need y'. Do y' hear me? I love y'."

The words stunned her, but as they settled into the serene quiet, she felt their truth. It had come like a falling star—fast and spectacular, blinding and so sudden she hadn't even understood what it was. But from the moment she'd looked into those blue eyes and seen a man as lost and unsure as herself, a man at odds with everything he was, she'd seen the first glimmer of what was to come.

She looked away from Ruairi's spirit, refusing to see him, and stared back into the water. A fragmented reflection of herself floated on the surface before the waters began to shift from some invisible force and become choppy and uneven. Now there were a hundred fractured images, eyes and mouths, noses and ears all disjointed and in disarray. As she stared mesmerized by the pieces of herself suspended in the depths, another face appeared in the splintered surface. A woman stood just over her shoulder. Slowly, cautiously, Saraid faced her.

For a moment it felt like an illusion, like she was still staring at her reflection. But the woman was more than that and
less than that, for she wasn't—couldn't be real. Her hair was
black, darker than Saraid's, more blue than red, more midnight than dawn. It fell like a curtain past her bare shoulders
to her waist. Her eyes were large and deep, wells of unknown
framed by a thick fringe of lash and a bold line of kohl. Her
cheeks were high boned, her nose a little long, but balanced
over the soft curve of lip. Around her throat she wore a golden
torque, like the one Ruairi had worn during the handfasting.
Both of her arms were bare but adorned with thick gold brace-
lets that snaked around her arms all the way up to the shoulder
where a gown of shiny gold fabric fastened at one side, leaving
her other shoulder bare. From head to toe, she glittered and
gleamed in the setting sun.

"I see you recognize me but cannot believe what you see."

Saraid did not know how to answer and so she said
nothing.

"I am Oma. I am your mother."

Young and beautiful, how she must have been when Bain
fell in love and married her. Before the babies, before her mind
had gone. Before she'd called the Book of Fennore and used it
to save her children.

"And I would do it again," she told Saraid, reading her
thoughts with ease. "For look at the beauty I brought into this
world."

She would do it again? Was this her message then? Did she
know how to bring the Book here, to this cove, where Saraid
could use it to save Ruairi's life?

"No," Oma said sharply. "Do not even think it. Never, *ever*
think it. What it will take from you, is gone forever. You do
not need the Book. *I* did not need the Book. I had the power
within me, as you do child. If only I had known . . ."

"What are y' saying?" Saraid breathed, speaking at last to
this Otherworld being who was and was not her mother.

"If I had the power to do what had never been done and
call the Book of Fennore from across the sea of time, then I
had the power to save you myself."

It could be truth, and the very idea of it shimmered in the
air between them for a tantalizing moment. It could be truth

and yet it could just as easily be wishful thinking. One thing *was* certain, though.

"I have no power," Saraid said.

"No?" Oma gave her a sad smile and shook her head. "Did you not bring this man to you? Did he not follow you to a time that is not his own?"

Saraid felt the blood drain from her face in a rush that left her dizzy. Slowly she looked back at Ruairi, sprawled in the soft, waving grasses. Had she brought him? He'd said it was true. And yet, it could have been his other self, the Bloodletter, who'd beckoned him back. The Book had been there in those moments when Ruairi had solidified and the Bloodletter had faded. How could she even think it was she, Saraid, who'd brought him when—

"Stop," Oma said. "Doubt has no place in what you must do."

Saraid stared at the breathtaking vision of her mother, seeing the beauty that had bewitched her father and compelled him to take her from slavery and make her his wife. She stepped forward, seeming to glide over the ground, and reached out with an elegant hand to cup Saraid's cheek. Colleen of the Ballagh had done the same thing, but then Saraid had felt nothing but a wished-for comfort. When Oma touched her, she felt the smooth skin of her fingers, felt the warmth of her palm and the pressure, turning her face so that she had to look into the startling darkness of her mother's eyes.

"Did you think your only gift was to see the dead?"

"My curse," Saraid said.

"A gift that I was not here to show you how to use."

Saraid's eyes began to sting and her vision was clouded by tears. This was too much, too much now in these moments when Ruairi's life was waning. "Can y' help him?" she asked. "Will y' help him?"

"No, daughter. I cannot. But you can."

Before Saraid could ask how, Oma stepped closer, using both hands to hold Saraid's face, holding her still. "Look into my eyes and feel what is inside you."

Saraid did as she was told, though fear and confusion cluttered her mind. She stared deeply into her mother's eyes, feeling herself pulled into the inky darkness, down and under until there was nothing of light left to see. And then she heard a voice that seemed to come from inside her and yet not from her at all, but from the trees, the grass, the graven stones, and the restless water. It spoke not a language but a song as familiar and unknown as the sky and earth around her.

Yes, Oma said, using not words but thought. *Reach for it. Hear its melody. It is your song. It is your power, waiting to be tapped.*

Saraid slowed her breathing, trying to do as her mother instructed. She reached with her mind, her heart, but the song only faded, trailing notes that became disjoined and jarring. She tried again, stretching, aching to hear the haunting melody. Once more, it slipped away. Frantic now, she strained, tuning every sense out, seeking the song, begging for help from the gods, the powers unseen, her mother . . . but it was no use. The harder she tried, the more elusive it became until the last pale notes faded beyond even memory.

I cannot hear it. Mother, help me.

Her mother did not answer. Instead all Saraid heard was the harsh rasp of Ruairi's breathing. Irregular, tortured. When she opened her eyes, her mother was gone, leaving Saraid helpless and alone. Still, Saraid refused to give up. She kept at it, fighting the binding quiet but nothing she did summoned the melody or the surging power back.

Numb she moved to Ruairi's side and fell to her knees, overwhelmed by the immensity of her failure.

"I'm sorry, Ruairi," she whispered. "I don't know how to fix y'." She threw back her head and cried out with rage and pain. "Tell me what to do."

What would you give to save him?

It wasn't her mother speaking this time. The voice came from everywhere and nowhere at once. Male and unfamiliar, it riffled the still night. Saraid looked, searched for whoever had spoken, afraid of who her next visitor might be. In the sudden sinking silence, nothing moved. No one appeared. She turned and looked in every direction, but there was only Saraid, Ruairi, and the black horse in the cove.

What would you give? the voice asked again, and suddenly she knew.

She felt it in her bones, in the horror that clenched her gut as hope gripped her heart. It was the Book of Fennore, the entity within. There *was* a reason why she'd come to this cove.

What would you give to save him?

Saraid breathed in the question, feeling it resonate in every part of her body.

"Anything," she answered.

The word seemed to echo, loud and strong, though she'd spoken softly. Then its answer came, reverberating from the sheer rock wall, the massive boughs of the swaying trees, the tiny scurrying of beetles and spiders.

Find me.

Saraid bolted to her feet, scanning the ancient walls, primordial trees, mystical pond. Where would it be? Hidden, certainly. By her mother? Was this where she'd brought it after she'd used it for her children? Was that why her father had brought Saraid here to show her the night she was born?

She began to circle, skirting the black pool, looking for anything that might tell her where the Book could be. She didn't know what she expected. A monument perhaps, a shrine built to house the archaic entity. There was nothing like that, though. Only dark shadows and darker stones huddled inconspicuously at every point.

Where? Where was it?

She hesitated, trying to calm her pounding heart, trying to quiet her frantic mind. She forced herself to breathe deeply, softly, silently.

It seemed she waited forever, but only a few seconds passed and then . . . she sensed it.

Her gaze moved unerringly to a place against the sheer, spiraled wall, and she knew. It was there, beneath a pile of rock that looked exactly like every other.

Certain, she bent to the mound of stones, lifting and tossing with urgency now. Each one she hurled away brought her closer. Now she could feel the low vibration thrumming through her.

Her hands were raw and bleeding by the time she'd moved the mound and found the deep hole beneath. She stared into it, seeing her face reflected once more, now on the oily black surface of the reservoir within. She glanced over her shoulder at Ruairi. He'd grown silent, and his chest barely moved at all now. He didn't have much time. Without looking away from him, from her purpose, without letting herself think about what she did, Saraid plunged her arm into the icy wet, feeling the cold in her veins, pumping with her heart as it circulated through her entire body. Her reaching fingers seemed to slide forever through the frigid world, touching nothing, sinking down, down until the frozen waters chewed at her fingertips and gnawed at her arm. And then at last she felt it. A piece of canvas. She gripped it and tugged.

The canvas held something heavy, and the silt at the bottom sucked at it as she pulled, fighting to bring it up. It seemed she hauled it from a greater depth than just the few feet of her arm's length, but at last she heaved it onto the rocky surface beside her.

The canvas wrapped around the bulky object was thick and blackened by oils and dirt and age. Deep creases marred the surface, engrained with grime. A coarse rope bound it on four sides, knotted in the middle. It was square, but not perfectly angled at the corners. Rather the edges seemed skewed and awkward, misshapen and deformed. The bundle hummed and moaned in a seesawing rhythm that jittered through her blood and fluttered in her ears. Sickened, she carried it the short distance to where Ruairi lay unconscious.

On her knees beside him, she forced herself to untie the cord and spread the canvas wide. The Book inside looked exactly as it had in those moments before the Bloodletter had become a boy and disappeared. The black leather cover gleamed with age. It was beveled with spirals, jewel-crusted, and lined with gold and silver. As old as the earth and sky, it had emerged from the water dry and undamaged. As impossible as its very existence.

The air swirled around her, a breath that came from without and shuddered through the trees, dark and insidious, scented and mysterious. Filled with that eerie vibrating hum, it rubbed against her, as sexual as it was invasive. It trilled over her skin.

What do you ask for? it questioned.

Tears filled her eyes and she brushed them back angrily. There was no place for fear here. No place for hesitation.

"Saraid."

It was Ruairi's spirit speaking. She kept her eyes averted, refusing to see him.

"Don't do this, princess. I'm not the one to save your people. It's you, Saraid. You and your brothers. You can, you *will* do it without me. Don't listen to what it tells you. It lies. It will only hurt you."

Nay, lass, the Book crooned in her mind. *'Tis only what he wants you to believe—He is like the others who would own me, seek to control me. But what do you have to fear? I am part of you. I beat with your heart. I flow with your blood. I was with you at birth. Ask me and I will give you more than you desire.*

She clenched her eyes tight, not knowing who to believe, who to doubt. Terror like she'd never imagined made her movements sluggish, her limbs numb.

Ruairi's breathing was shallow and harsh, and his flesh burned from a fire within. The ground beneath him was soaked in his blood and still it flowed from his wounds. Yet as she knelt, his hand moved ever so slightly, and she took it in her own, holding it against her breast as her tears flowed.

His eyes fluttered open, so blue against the mask of ivory that was now his face. "Don't sweat it, princess," he said, his voice a whisper she had to lean forward to catch. "Not your problem. Not your fault."

But it was her fault. She had brought him here without even knowing how she'd done it. It was she who had summoned him like the witch Cathán Half-Beard accused her of being. She had not plunged the knife into his body, but she had pinned him to this time that was not his own. She had called him here where he would die if she failed him.

Tell me what you want . . . you have but to ask.

"And what would y' have in return?" she asked the shivering silence. "What price must I pay?"

She waited, tense, fearful. Ruairi's breath wheezed and waned, and she felt death trying to capture her thoughts again, knew his spirit was waiting to emerge once more. She fought it like she had never fought before.

"What would y' have of me in return for his life?" she demanded, and this time her voice was strong. The answer came at once.

Nothing you will miss. For a thousand years upon a thousand years I have been a slave. I want only to be free.

"Free to do what?"

To live. To die.

Ruairi's hand clenched hers again, and she leaned forward. "Get out of here, princess," he said. "Go now."

Did he know she was bargaining with evil in its purest, rawest form?

Only as evil as the heart that controls me . . .

Could that be true? Could it be that the Book of Fennore was no more evil than the blade of a knife? Could it be used for good as easily as it was for bad? Why, then, did so many fear it? Why did she?

An image filled her head in a brilliant flash. In it Saraid stood on a harsh and jagged precipice, staring out at a fierce sea. Waves spewed and foamed, grinding away at a rocky shore. The wind gusted up the sheer wall and teased the fabric of her skirts, making them snap and billow. Her hair blew round her face in a dark cloud of glittering black and brown and fiery red. A man approached from behind. Tall and solid, as golden as the sun and as beautiful as the gods. He slipped his hands around her waist and pulled her back into the safe harbor of his arms. Her head fit perfectly under his chin, and she let herself melt into him, knowing he would protect her from anything. From everything.

His hands were big and they slipped up to cup the heavy weight of her breasts before gliding to pull her skirts tight around the bulge of a belly swollen with child.

A blink and it was gone, the precipice, the wind, the man . . . She looked down at Ruairi and felt the love that had been in his touch. It was a future she'd never dreamed of, and it was being offered to her now. She would give herself, but this vision implied that she would not lose herself in the giving.

"Is this a trick?" she whispered.

There was no answer, only that expectant thrumming, waiting for her to decide.

"Ruairi will live?" she tried again.

Yes, and you will live with him for as long as you choose.

With that, the lock over the Book unraveled and burst open

and the pages began to fan, back and forth, ruffling the air, whirring with purpose, with menace.

"What are you doing?" Ruairi asked, his eyes open now. "Jesus Christ, what are you doing?"

Before she could answer, his body arched in a terrible bow and he shouted in pain. Her vision blurred and her tears streamed down her face. She dragged in a deep breath, forced herself to calm, and carefully she put her hands on the Book, felt them sink into it like quicksand. She wanted to scream, wanted to jerk back, but she didn't. She held, though every instinct shrieked for her to run. She held, and did what she'd come to do. She asked for Ruairi's life.

For a moment, nothing happened, and then suddenly she was yanked from her body, sucked into a vortex, spiraling down, moving so fast she couldn't see or breathe. She felt herself break apart and become miniscule, insignificant. A wind, a breeze, a whisper. She was rushing toward an end she didn't comprehend, and then suddenly she was there, hovering over a red gash *inside* Ruairi's body. Turning, she stared at herself through the opening in his flesh, understood in a queer and unsettling way that she was both here and there.

For her entire life she'd been afraid of small, closed spaces, and now she was in a place so tiny it had no borders, no beginning or end. It was a million times worse than her most frightening nightmare. But she was here for Ruairi and she would not cower beneath her fear.

She silenced the screams echoing in her head, and some strange instinct guided her. She reached with her mind, touched the jagged flesh of Ruairi's wound, smoothed the harsh line of it, pulled the edges together, and sealed them with the burning flash of her thoughts. Her heart seized at the complete darkness that engulfed her. Would she be able to find her way out? Had she trapped herself inside him, neither dead nor alive, neither real nor imagined? Her terror became a snake, slithering through her mind, hissing that she had sealed her own fate with the act. She forced the burgeoning hysteria down and focused on what to do next.

She saw bubbles rising all around and followed them through the dark and pulsing world until she came to two sacs that hung suspended before her. *These are his lungs,* some part

of her said. She moved closer, saw the rip in one and the bubbles of air escaping. Again she reached out, touched the torn
surface, and knitted it together by thought and will. And then
she moved again, following the wake of destruction, putting
the pieces back together, seamlessly mending each damaged
part of him, ending at last with the torn and bleeding shoulder.
She stitched it all with her will, leaving the smallest of open-
ings to see out. There was her own pale and waxy face staring
sightlessly back.

She focused on the darkness of her eyes and surged forward, escaping Ruairi's body but not rejoining her own. She
hovered just over his shoulder, above the raw and swollen flesh
of the wound. He lay perfectly still, a statue of marble. Gently
she blew a hot breath across his shoulder, imagining the touch
of it against his skin, a whisper of power that mended and
strengthened. And as she watched, the two sides of the wound
merged together and became one.

Aware of the blank shell of her body beside him, Saraid
spread herself over his prone form like a blanket of mist. She
filled his nose and mouth, breathing power into his lungs, his
veins, his mind. She felt him catch his breath, heard the steady
beat of his heart as it took her strength and pulsed it back
through his blood.

And then suddenly she felt a heaving, ripping sensation, as
if a cyclone had touched down beside her. Colors blurred as it
wrenched her from his body and slammed her back into her
own.

She gasped, coughed, gasped again, each breath as painful
as the one before it. It felt like she'd drowned and was now
filled with burning water that must be ejected before she could
breathe. She crawled a few feet away and retched, spewing up
a fountain of dark malevolence that could not be human. It
floated like oil before finally soaking into the earth and
disappearing.

She sat back, looking down at herself. Every inch of her
was covered in blood, soaked in it. With a cry she stumbled to
the pool and plunged in, fully clothed, no longer fearful of
what lurked in its depths. She dunked and rinsed until the
water around her swirled a rusted brown. Shivering as much
with the cold as the shock of what she'd done, she stripped and

scrubbed with the gritty sand of the shore until her skin was raw, but clean. Only then did she emerge, legs shaking, arms weak, and spread her clothes next to Ruairi's to dry.

The Book of Fennore lay just where she'd left it, silent now. Satisfied. Quickly she wrapped it back in the canvas and tied the cord. It felt unbearably heavy as she dragged it back to the ancient wall. She didn't return it to the dark cavity where she'd found it. Instead she set it above ground and loosely covered it with stones.

Spent, she dragged herself back to Ruairi's side and curled into his heat. His chest rose and fell with an even rhythm; his skin was flushed, but not with fever. Gone were the dark circles beneath his eyes. Gone was the rattle of his lungs and the wheeze of his breath.

Numb, depleted of her last bit of strength, she let the blank page of unconsciousness rush up to greet her.

Chapter Thirty

Rory awoke in a strange place. Again.

His eyes opened to darkness and shadows, obscured moonlight and shifting shapes. He was on his back, stripped bare and laid out like a corpse beneath the starlight. Was he dead, then?

He didn't feel dead, and yet he had the sense that he should be . . . that he'd fought and lost. That Saraid . . .

Saraid. Where was she?

He turned his head quickly, and his vision swam with bright stars and violent explosions at the sudden movement, but he saw her. She lay curled into a tight ball beside him. Her hair gleamed around her shoulders like mahogany striated with scarlet. She slept deeply and without movement. The rush of emotion that filled him was at once overwhelming and strangely expected. Sometime, somewhere between those first deranged moments when he'd been neither here nor there, an invisible extension of his other half, and this moment, now, Saraid had become the sun around which he orbited. She was, quite simply, the reason he kept getting up again and again when his father's men knocked him down.

He let out a soft breath and gazed at her. An eerily bright moon illuminated her face, throwing into relief the red abrasion on her cheek, the mottled bruise with the clear imprint of a hand on her throat. Cuts and scrapes marred her arms and chest. In fact, it looked as if every inch of skin bore some sign of abuse. A slow burn started in his gut as he fought through the fog in his head to remember what exactly had happened.

Like light spilling from the crack of an open door, the events at last began to spill out. He recalled leaving the cave with Saraid, her brothers, and the strange following of Leary's men. They'd discovered Eamonn was missing and he'd fought with Tiarnan.

Hell, who hadn't he fought with since coming here?

He'd been chewed up and spit out three times—four, if he counted the skirmish with Tiarnan, which had ripped all the carefully laid stitches Michael had sewn. He remembered the blood, hot and thick, pouring from the wound as they'd run through the forest, convinced they were being chased. By the time they'd made it to the creek, Rory had felt like he couldn't take another step. And then . . . Cathán's men had found them as they crossed the creek into the clearing. . . .

Suddenly it all came back in a rush, filled with visuals and excruciating details. Some big, ugly guy had grabbed Saraid, and her scream had filled Rory with a kind of helpless rage like he'd never known before—prayed he'd never know again. He couldn't help her because a sword had sliced through him . . . the shock of it cutting through his vital organs . . . the panic of not being able to breathe . . . The blade had come from below, driving up, severing flesh and tendons, clipping his liver or kidney or both, until the tip of the blade had punctured his lung. He'd felt the breath collapse from his chest. He'd *known* his number was up.

He shouldn't have survived that.

But obviously he had survived and somehow he'd come to be here with Saraid. He remembered none of how that came to be, though, nothing after he'd hit the ground, thinking he'd finally met his end. That he'd failed Saraid.

And he'd cared more about failing her than dying.

He stared at her sleeping form, and a surge of relief went through him. Thank God she was here. Thank God she'd survived, despite him.

By degrees he stood, testing himself with each effort. Aches and pains from every joint in his body cried out in sudden clarity, but they were nothing to the waves of nausea that swamped him. Carefully he breathed in and out, willing his stomach to settle, fighting the urge to heave. He had to pause and bend at the waist, hands braced against his knees as his gut tightened.

Shock, some strangely clinical part of his mind told him. *This was shock.*

It struck him odd that it would come now, for obviously some time had passed since . . . since whatever had happened. How else had he come to be here? Stripped and sleeping beside Saraid?

But apparently his body didn't care that the danger was over. He was trembling from head to toe, weak and afraid. He braced himself, hating the last of it more than the sickening churn in his stomach. Deep breaths . . . in . . . out. Finally he stood straight, feeling better for the effort. Saraid slept on, and he waited until he could see her chest move as she breathed before taking a step away.

Feeling strangely disconnected from his own body, he turned away and looked down at himself. There was a long sickle-shaped pucker of flesh about six inches below and to the right of his heart. It curved across his ribs and trailed lower, ending just above his belly. The furrow was wide and red, but it was already a scar, already knitted flesh. Already healing.

Christ, how long had he been out?

His hand moved to the deep gash at his shoulder that should have been ragged and raw, but his fingers found instead another silky scar. Carefully he lifted his arm, bracing for the torture the movement would cause. It had felt like a hundred burning pokers were sunk into the flesh of his shoulder when he'd lifted his sword to fight. But now there was only mild discomfort, the soreness that comes from an old injury on rainy days.

He was weaker, but he wasn't thinner. He didn't have any of the side effects of having been incapacitated for the amount of time it would have taken to heal from those kinds of injuries. He shook his head, baffled. Those must have been some amazing homegrown remedies Saraid's brother had administered for Rory to have healed so quickly. The modern world of medicine could certainly benefit from Michael's secret herbs.

Suddenly another question occurred to him. Where were

Saraid's brothers now? On the other side of the stone wall, keeping watch? He tilted his head back, looking up the sheer rock face for a lookout. Nothing moved. Nothing at all.

Naked, he made his way to the pool of glittering black waters. A river flowed in and out on either end, but here in the middle it was banked and as calm as a pond. He stared at his reflection for a moment, almost surprised to recognize the face that stared back. He felt like another man, a different man.

As if in response to his thoughts, the water swirled, distorting his features.

Hesitating for reasons he couldn't quite define, he drank from cupped hands. The water was cool and fresh, slightly bitter with minerals and some other taste he couldn't define. Pleasant, but somehow unsettling. Uneasy, he warily washed his face and hands, feeling like the *Jaws* theme should be playing in the background.

With a soft laugh at himself, he sat back and looked around. The cove appeared like something from a postcard, not a scary movie. He'd never seen leaves so green, sky so blue, waters so deep and mysterious. The stone walls on either side rose sheer and undaunted, etched from earth to the towering peaks with the same spiral symbols that distinguished the Book of Fennore.

Yet for all its picturesque beauty, there was something in the air that felt . . . unnatural. There was no other way to put it.

A looming shadow fell over him, and he started, spinning to find the huge black horse with the lightning bolt on its face watching him with interest. He lifted a hand and stroked its muzzle.

"What's up, buddy?"

The horse tossed its head and snorted benevolently before returning to graze on the grassy cove.

Feeling stranger by the minute, Rory forced his fear back and waded into the water, desperately needing to wash the sweat and blood from his body, silently praying the water held nothing more sinister than a sharp rock in its bed. One of the massive trees plunked a nut into the pool, and a giant salmon broke the surface and grabbed it. Stunned, Rory stared. *That was weird.* The *Jaws* theme began once more, growing louder in his head.

Nervous, he looked across the rippling water, and one hand went to his groin in a protective motion born of instinct.

He tried to laugh at himself again, feeling ridiculous in his fear. Afraid of a fish and still water. Some fierce warrior he'd turned out to be. But he rinsed quickly, dunked nervously, and hurried out.

Shivering, he went back to Saraid and lay down beside her, spooning her silken back as if he had every right to hold her. As if he'd been doing it for a lifetime. Her warmth chased away the chill, and he pulled her closer, soaking it up. She let out a soft sigh and turned. He rolled on his back so she could snuggle against his side, using his chest as a pillow. Her hand splayed across his stomach and one of her legs tangled with his. He breathed in the scent of her hair, mint and something flowery, maybe lavender? Maybe honeysuckle. Whatever it was, it smelled good.

He could feel the press of her breasts against his skin as she breathed, and she made a small sound that set his blood on fire. How he could even think of sex when every time he'd turned around he'd had his ass kicked, he didn't know. But there it was, his recurring fantasy about this woman chasing away any fears of pond sharks, tightening the muscles of his belly, pumping blood from his brain to the part of him that required no thought.

He touched her face with gentle fingers, drawing them down the curve of her cheek to the silk of her lips. "Wake up, princess," he said softly.

The sound of his voice seemed to go through her like a shout. She yelped and sat bolt upright, her eyes wide, her body stiff and ready to fight or flee.

"Easy, girl," he said. "It's just me."

She stared at him uncomprehendingly for a long moment, and he felt a strange mixture of anger and hurt at the blankness of her expression. Who'd she expect to be waking up naked with?

"Yer alive," she breathed at last.

It was the second time she'd greeted him this way. He hoped he wasn't on the road to making it a habit.

"Evidently," he said with a crooked grin.

Her eyes looked different, and he frowned, watching her as

she touched him, running her fingertips over the scar on his shoulder down to the spiral brand over his heart to the thick pucker sealing the wound that should have killed him. As he stared, another memory tried to poke through the black crust of oblivion, but it didn't quite make it to the surface. He felt an alarming sense of relief at the solid wall that surrounded it.

What's that about?

"You okay?" he asked, brushing a stray lock of hair behind her ear.

Her lips curled, but it wasn't a smile and it didn't reach the flat blank of her eyes. "Yes."

He didn't believe her, but let it go. "Where are we?" he asked, sitting up and propping his elbows on his knees.

"I don't know," she said. "The horse took off with us and brought us here."

"What happened to your brothers?"

"Do y' not remember?" she asked, her voice rising with disbelief.

She curled her legs beneath her and hunched a little to hide her nudity, but it only made him notice it more. She was beautiful beyond words, especially like this, all warm, sleep tousled, and very naked.

"I remember fighting. . . ."

Frowning, he shook his head. Saraid shifted and made to move away. He captured her wrist, holding her still. She stared at where his fingers held her for a moment, and he let his thumb rub the point where her pulse jumped erratically, watching her face as he did. The feel of her skin seemed to send tiny jolts up his arm, but she didn't react and that blank look remained in her eyes. He didn't understand it, didn't know what to do about it.

"The horses, they fought for y'," she said softly. "They became wild. Frenzied. They threw their riders and trampled them."

Rory frowned as fuzzy images took shape in his mind. The horses . . . Christ, she was right. Had *he* done that?

"My brothers and Leary's men ran in another direction and got away. At least, I hope they did."

"But what about . . ." He touched the new scars. "Who patched me up?"

She averted her face, glancing at him from the cover of her lowered lashes. In her flashing look he caught another glimpse of that perplexing blankness. Now she tried to pull her wrist away, but he wouldn't let her go.

"Who healed me, Saraid?"

"I did what I could," she said.

"You? I thought you couldn't stitch a straight line if your life depended on it."

The chin went up. "Well it wasn't *my* life depending on it, was it now?"

He stared at her, unable to make sense of anything she said. On the horizon, the sun began to rise, breaking through the forest with long, reaching rays that speckled the cove and danced in the water. A shaft speared the twin stones framing the river and cascaded in its current. It cast her in a golden haze, like an angel.

Releasing her wrist, but only so he could tilt her chin, he asked, "*How* did you take care of me?"

She couldn't avoid looking at him now, for all the good it did him. It was like she'd been carved from marble, her skin pale, her eyes glass that reflected nothing of what she felt. "I told y', I did what I could."

Again, that glimmer of a memory prodded the fog in his brain. It was sharp and frightening. Rory wanted to turn away from it, but this time he couldn't. He needed to know what waited beneath the white banks of forgetfulness.

"Why are you lying to me?" he asked. He'd meant it to be a demand, a question she couldn't ignore or evade. But his voice was suddenly hushed, and the dread deep in his gut blossomed into something hot and consuming.

"I was scared," she whispered. "I thought y' would die."

He was up on his knees now, holding her face in his hands, refusing to let her look away. Willing that flashing warmth, the sparkling depth of her emotions to surface. Wanting to see that she cared, that she felt, that she needed him like he did her. But though her voice had cracked with feeling, her eyes stared placidly back.

Lights on, but no one home.

Rory jerked at the unbidden thought.

"I heard a voice," he said, frowning, trying to bring the

memory into focus so he could think, analyze, put together the missing pieces. "Was there someone else here, waiting for us?"

"No," she whispered.

She was trembling; he could feel the tremors coming from every part of her body. And she was lying. It was there in the pleading tone of her words.

The voice . . . he hadn't imagined it, had he?

"Saraid," he breathed. "My God, Saraid, what have you done?"

Her lips parted in a silent moan, and she lowered her lashes, trying to hide from him. But it was too late. He remembered it all now.

She'd pleaded for his life. She'd used the Book of Fennore to save him.

The enormity of it rolled over him like a giant wheel. It flattened him, demolished all but his shock. She'd made a deal with the devil, and that devil had stolen the sparkle from her eye. It had taken a piece of her, a piece he loved. A piece he wouldn't have given up for anything, especially not his own sorry soul.

His vision blurred and his eyes burned. "Why, Saraid?" he said through the thick lump of emotion clogging his throat. "Why did you do it?"

She caught her lip between her teeth and shook her head. Gently she brushed away the tear that rolled over his lashes and slid down his face, and her touch unleashed the rage of his emotions. He pulled her close, buried his face in the soft crook of neck and shoulder, and cried, cried like a child. Cried like a man.

They held each other, wordless in grief, silent in pain. Both of them pouring out the agony that would have killed them to keep in. When at last his eyes dried, he was left with Saraid in his arms and a hard kernel of rage in his chest.

Slowly he leaned back and stared into her face. She gazed back, but it was a stoic stranger looking out of those dark eyes. It was just as Leary had said. Rory had brought her to the Book—unknowingly, yes—but it was because of him all the same. And it had used him to take from her.

"No," he said. "This can't happen. I won't let it."

"It is not yer choice, Ruairi," she answered, just as Leary had.

Rory shook his head, remembering his own bold and brash denial of that. "*I just made it my choice*," he'd said. Jesus, he was such a fool.

Saraid's voice cracked with emotion, showing him what her eyes did not. "It's done."

His smile felt cold and hard, but it felt good, too. It felt powerful. Unyielding. Invincible. "You're wrong, Saraid," he said softly. He took her hand and pressed it to his heart. "You are mine. Every beat of my heart is for you. I would die for you a hundred times. I love you. Not just today, now. Forever. I love you forever, Saraid. Know that to be true."

In his entire life, he'd never spoken such words, never felt so bound by his heart, by his honor. Never known without doubt that he meant everything he said.

"And I'm not going to stand by and do nothing. Not while there's breath in my body."

Chapter Thirty-one

RUAIRI didn't give Saraid the chance to answer or to argue. He didn't give her the chance to soak in the beauty of what he'd said. He loved her. *He loved her.*

He leaned down and pressed his mouth to hers, determined to make her feel. And she wanted to—*feel* everything that was inside her.

The Book had promised it would take only a piece of her. A part she wouldn't miss. It had lied. There was still love in her heart, but it didn't swell and consume her the way his fierce declaration should have. That passion, that need—it was all subdued, muted until it was more a thought than a feeling.

The loss burned like a flame. It filled her with rage—that she still had. Anger, grief, sorrow, all of those emotions she could call up and *feel.* But joy, love, passion . . . there was only a hollow echo where there should have been heat and need and deep longing.

Ruairi's kiss was tender and sweet, desperate and enraged. She could taste his pain, his hope, his love. More than anything, she wanted to fall into it, burn with desire. He loved her. He'd vowed to love her forever.

And she felt nothing but loss. The emptiness that should have been her bursting with happiness.

No, she thought. There had to be more, had to be something she could give him back. If not, she would have chained him to a cripple . . . a living corpse who could not feel, could not share. Was this what her mother had realized? Was this what had driven her to take her own life?

Fury swelled in her breast, and she embraced it, used it now to show Ruairi that she wasn't dead inside. There was still something left of her that lived and breathed.

Whether he'd come here for her or she'd brought him through time, it didn't matter. All that was important was his heart beating against hers, his hands on her body, his lips on her breasts, her throat, her mouth, seeking a response. Seeking salvation. For she knew what he thought of himself. How it hurt him to think he'd failed her.

She raised a hand and gently traced the curve of the puckered scar on his ribs.

"I thought I'd lost y'," she murmured. "And I wanted to die."

He'd been holding his breath and now he exhaled, caressing her face, kissing her closed eyes, the hollows beneath them, her cheekbones and chin. He moved lower and she kept her eyes clenched tight, shielding him from the fathomless depths of nothingness she knew he saw there.

She wrapped her arms around his neck and pressed her body to his, savoring the feel of hard muscle, the strong arms and powerful shoulders, the way he held her like he would never let her go. She kept her thoughts on the pulse of anger beneath her skin, channeling it to heat her fingers, her mouth, the body she pressed to his. He lifted her and laid her back against the springy grass where they'd slept.

Mindful of his weight, he propped himself with one arm and stared down the gleaming length of her body. She was real and warm, and he couldn't know that inside she was anything less. She had to remember that. He could only see what she showed him and vowed that for now, at least, the dark emptiness inside her would be hidden.

Leaning forward, he pressed his mouth to the point where her ribs cradled the softness of her belly, tasting her skin and the heat of her flesh. He trailed his hand up to her breasts, following the lazy path with his lips, tongue, cupping the weight in his palms and catching the nipple of one with his mouth. He sucked and nipped, and she arched into him, urging him to hurry up, slow down, make it now, make it last. Grasping tight the flame of her anger, wielding it into something more.

He kissed her again, holding her like she was all that separated him from a soulless existence. He kissed her like she was air and water, sustenance to a life deprived of both. He kissed her with the love his words had declared, and it broke that empty shell of her heart, fractured it into a million sharp and tiny pieces. Tears might have diminished the pain, but Saraid was a dry well now, and there was only the blazing rage forging together what was left.

She kissed him back, pushing her hand through his silky hair, pulling him closer, giving everything she could. His mouth was hot and enticing, and the sensations he started rose above that numb wall and tapped into what she still had left, fanning flames that sparked and spit. He demanded that she give him everything, more than she had, more than she could. His fervor reached beneath her skin, became passion itself, replaced and restored that which had been taken from her, if just for the moment.

The feeling filled her, overflowed, engulfed. With a sound of triumph he held her tighter, giving, giving until she could take no more. She was a blaze that he danced around, never minding if she singed or flared, rejoicing at the inferno he created.

He tried to pull back, just enough to see her face, but she was afraid of what he'd find, afraid that the transformation inside wouldn't be reflected in her eyes. She couldn't bear his disappointment, couldn't tolerate her own.

He rolled to his back—or maybe she pushed him. She didn't know nor did she care. His hands slid down her spine, feeling the ridge of bones, the sinew and flesh moving and alive beneath his touch. She circled his wrists with her fingers and pulled his arms up over his head, pinning them there as she leaned forward to kiss him.

"What I gave, Ruairi, I gave willingly. I gave of my heart. No matter what happens, y' will remember that. Promise me ye'll remember that."

He couldn't promise. He wouldn't. She saw it in his beautiful eyes, understood that making that pledge would destroy the man he was.

"I love y'," she said. "I love y'."

He rolled again. This time she knew it was he who did it, and it was her arms pinned over her head. She couldn't avoid his eyes now and she saw what she'd feared—the disappointment, but only for a moment. Then it became fierce determination.

"I will have all of you again, Saraid. *That* I will promise."

She lifted her head and claimed his mouth with hers, sealing their pledge, drawing him down until there was only Ruairi and the seductive friction of lips and teeth and tongues. He tasted every inch of her from the soft underside of her arm to the vulnerable curve of her breast and the tender bend of her knee. He nipped at her belly, pressed his open mouth to her hip, and then he had her spread and exposed to the mercy of his touch. He licked and teased, sucked and rubbed until she arched her back and panted for him. He slipped two fingers inside her, and brought her to the edge and then over with a shout that surprised them both. All of her muscles contracted in a hot and tight fist and then he was moving up again, sliding his hips between her legs.

She welcomed him, opening and driving up to meet him. The hard length of him rocked her like a quake, making her forget everything but this moment, *this one moment*. Everything but his weight, his scent, his taste, fell away. There was only Saraid and Ruairi and a tension that built until it shattered her. He followed her to that explosive place an instant later, giving a muffled cry as it took him. And then he was still, his heart pounding with hers. Slowly he eased to the side and pulled her with him, not giving an inch between their bodies. She lay in his arms, yearning for the happiness she should feel, wanting to cry because the numbness had returned. Knowing that what they shared would always be fleeting and never enough.

Later she would face the consequences of what she'd done. Later she would make him understand that what was lost could not be regained. But for now she could only pretend that the morning had brought something that no longer existed.

"Y' have stolen my heart, Ruairi," she murmured as her eyes drifted shut.

He smiled and kissed her again. "Don't worry, princess. I'll take good care of it."

She knew he would try. Just as she knew he would fail. Because even what little was left, the Book of Fennore would find a way to take.

Chapter Thirty-two

TIARNAN walked with his brothers, leading, if it could be called that, the worn and ragged remains of their people. In all there were fifty, most so old they no longer had teeth, others too young to fend for themselves. In between were a handful of women, a few ungainly boys who would soon embark on the stretch and season of manhood, and a smattering of girls too young to know their allure, but old enough to see it shimmering on the horizon. If they lived to meet it, that was.

Tiarnan let out a heavy breath. Why they continued to follow him was a mystery.

He glanced at Michael and Liam, both silent and introspective. Michael absently stroked the pup whose head popped from his leather bag. They worried about Saraid, as did Tiarnan. She'd gone with Ruairi, but he had been at death's threshold. Tiarnan had seen that last, fatal blow.

He shook his head. Eamonn had yet to be found. Had Cathán's men captured him and Mauri? Or had his brother done the unthinkable? Was it possible that he'd joined with the enemy? If yes, how long had he planned it? How many nights had Tiarnan and Eamonn shared a fire and companionship while his brother plotted against him? How could Tiarnan have been so blind as not to see it? How could Tiarnan be so shallow as to believe it for even a moment?

And Mauri . . . sweet, beautiful Mauri. He'd loved her since he was a boy, since the first time he'd seen her sitting between her mother and father, plump cheeks and bright eyes. Now she hated him—as she had every right to do. He closed his eyes tightly, replaying that horrible night when he had betrayed her trust. He could see it all, every minute detail . . . the terror, the desperation. . . . her screams as the blade had found her shoulder.

It was all too much. And no matter the questions, no matter the answers, it all came down to Tiarnan and his failure. He'd vowed to keep his people safe, pledged his life to them. Yet *he* lived and so many of them were dead. Now his sister and brother were gone—lost, murdered, abandoned—he couldn't know. The only certainty was in where the blame lay. It was his fault. All of it.

Behind him Leary's men marched in a long line. More had joined in the night until now their numbers were over two hundred. Women had come, too. Fierce, armed women, some painted like Mahon Snakeface with blues and greens, strange and glittering yellows and haunting reds. Leary received these women like the other warriors, but Tiarnan, Michael, and Liam could only stare. Women fighters were not unheard of, but these women were ferocious beyond anything the brothers had ever seen.

The men and women alike followed Leary with the blind allegiance Tiarnan had once known. He hoped the other man would prove more worthy.

They'd gone north after the ambush, to where the rest of Tiarnan's people waited. As they'd come upon the small settlement, Tiarnan had seen with new eyes just how vulnerable they were here. There was no place to hide that would be safe.

Leary and his warriors had been welcomed with open arms. Why wouldn't they be? They were strong, healthy men who claimed to be friends and would fight at their side. Thus far, Tiarnan had no reason to doubt them, even when Leary suggested that they turn south in the morning and veer toward the coast.

"Why?" Tiarnan had asked.

"Because there we will meet your sister and Ruairi of Fennore."

Tiarnan didn't bother to ask how he knew, but Leary answered anyway.

"They will be looking for the Book of Fennore. It is why Ruairi is here."

"He should leave the Book where it is. Nothing would convince *me* to use it."

"You say this because you've never faced a loss too great to bear."

Tiarnan glared at the shorter man. "Y' have no idea of all that I have lost or what I can bear."

Leary shrugged. Behind him, Leary's two strange companions smiled. Uneasy, Tiarnan looked away.

Leary gave Tiarnan a quick bow and moved back into the ranks of his men. Mahon Snakeface and Red Amir followed silently in his wake.

Now they'd reached the rough and rigid shoreline, forbidding and perilous with cliffs rising up on one side, jutting boulders and sharp-edged rocks sliding down to meet the angry roll and spew of the tide on the other. The descent was painfully slow, each step treacherous enough to send them plunging into certain death. But Leary would not be swayed to stay on higher ground and move parallel to the sea. It must be the rocky beach they traveled.

After half a day of walking, Tiarnan understood why. They reached a hazardous point where the rock-strewn beach butted against the jagged black cliffs, forcing them to move in single file, rope tied around the elderly and young ones to keep them from falling and being swept out into the icy ocean. As they navigated the dangerous alley between surf and stone, Tiarnan saw a narrow cave open to his left. Leary called a halt, and as the others huddled there, his men went in and emerged with more than a dozen *curraghs*.

The oblong boats were larger than any Tiarnan had seen in the past. Each one might seat fifteen people. But they were still only leather hide wrapped around a thin wooden frame—not like the solid seafaring vessels the Northmen used. Not anything Tiarnan wanted to trust with his life.

There was a time when Tiarnan would have spoken out about it. He would have demanded to know the plan for the insubstantial boats. He would have argued that they were unsafe, that none of his people could swim, that the sea was too violent.

Instead, he kept quiet. His leadership had led to ruins. Because of him, they'd lost everything from home to loved ones. Who was he to take charge now?

"What do y' think they're meaning to do with those?" Liam asked, watching Leary's men heft the boats over their heads and carry them.

Tiarnan gazed out at the roiling sea, picturing in his mind the boats capsizing one by one and the occupants tumbling into the icy depths of a watery grave. At least Cathán wouldn't have the satisfaction of killing them.

"Aren't y' going to say something, Tiarnan?" asked Michael. "Those *curraghs* won't stand to the sea."

Tiarnan didn't answer either of his brothers. Instead he moved on, following Leary south to meet whatever fate awaited them next.

Chapter Thirty-three

RORY was quiet as they rode double on the black horse with the lightning-bolt face. So was Saraid. He could feel her fear, though, felt the same demon lurking within him. He still meant to destroy the Book he now carried in their saddlebag and kill whatever entity lived within it. But first he would find a way to get back all that Saraid had given.

He didn't know how, but he would.

His sister had beaten it once. Even though Rory hadn't used it, it had held him in the same chains that bound his dad. And she brought Rory back. She wasn't a witch, as Saraid thought. Just a girl who'd fought for someone she loved. And Rory would do no less. If he was truly marked by the Book, then maybe that gave him some special power over it. He held to that belief.

He'd survived this Book once already. It was not invincible, and he would defeat it. He would have the pieces of Saraid that it had stolen back.

"Have y' really thought this through?" Saraid asked softly, reading his mind. "Do y' not see that if y' succeed, if y' destroy it, y' will destroy yer only way home? Y' will be trapped as surely as the entity within the Book is."

He pressed a gentle kiss to her temple. "I am home, Saraid. You are my home. And I will keep you safe. Or I will die trying."

Her sigh was the only answer he got. She leaned against him, her back snug to his chest, her head lolling from side to side with the horse's gait. He felt her exhaustion, felt the grief that she tried to hide. Memories had been coming back to him all morning. Dark, buried recollections of his father. How he'd changed from a loving man who cared for his wife and children to someone hard and cold. Someone filled with anger and prone to fits of rage and violence. He'd abused Rory's mother and probably would have done the same to his children if she hadn't protected them. None of them had understood why he'd changed. What had made him go from a gentle man to a violent one. But now Rory could see it clearly.

He'd been using the Book, and it had turned his eyes flat and cold, his heart hard and mean. Where Cathán had found it or why he'd used it, Rory couldn't guess. One thing was clear, though. While Cathán was using the Book of Fennore, it was using him. At last Rory understood what Leary had meant when he said it took a piece of humanity from anyone who used it. It had done that to his father. Turned him into the monster he was now. It didn't bother Cathán to kill innocent people because he had no feelings but rage. How many times had he touched the Book before it changed him?

How much had it taken from Saraid in just one try? Would she continue to morph into something darker, more heartless? Or would she remain as she was now? Distant but still Saraid?

He thought of that night, when he was a child and had tried to stop his father. He closed his eyes, remembering the feeling of being trapped in a world black and twisted. He'd felt his father in that swirling void, felt his thoughts, his fears, but he hadn't understood them. And then Danni punched through and for a moment—for one instant, the three of them—the Book, his sister, and Rory had become one. When they were torn apart, they'd all been . . . different. He couldn't say just what made him so certain that the experience had somehow altered the Book and his sister as it had him, but he was.

Had they all come away with a piece of themselves missing? Or had they all come away with something new, something more? The idea sent a shudder through him.

If it was true and Rory had gained something from that experience, then he needed to find it, to tap into it. To *use* it.

Because of all the uncertainties inside Rory, one thing he was very sure about. He'd had his ass kicked for the last time. The next fight, he was coming out the winner.

The horse tossed its head and snorted, and Rory glanced about, suddenly alert. He sat up straighter, honing his senses as he scanned the terrain. The forest flanked them on the right, bordering the wide open land that was vibrantly green and scented with wildflowers. Nothing moved out there. In fact, he hadn't seen another soul since the battle and didn't know if that was unusual or not. What was the population of Ireland in this time? Hell, he wasn't even really sure what year it was. The date seemed an insignificant detail when people were trying to kill you.

In the distance Rory could hear the sound of the ocean rolling in to shore. Now he could smell the sea, rich with salt and brine, cold and unending. He was surprised at how the scent moved him, how time did not change it at all.

The horse snorted again, and Rory tried to discern what it was that had agitated the animal. He closed his eyes, focusing his attention, feeling what the horse felt beneath its hooves, against its coat, in the air. And there it was, a whiff that blew across the waving grasses. It smelled some of its own. There were other horses coming this way—and he'd bet the bank it was Cathán and his mounted warriors.

He tightened his perceptions, looking to hitch a ride to a better venue. Overhead a lone gannet soared and Rory sent out a line, felt it snag then carry on the wind. He looked out, seeing the world from above. Over the span of shiny feathers and spread wings he saw himself, riding steadily along with Saraid, and beyond them, an army. Hundreds of foot soldiers followed the dozens of mounted leaders. He didn't need to see the flag to know that these were Cathán's men. Apparently his father wasn't taking any chances that they would escape this time. An army that size was coming for a kill.

Christ.

He'd hoped for more time. Hoped that once they reached the rocky shore, there would be time to think. Time to figure out how they would cross the churning, sucking currents to the Isle of Fennore. More than destroying the ancient Book, the seas between the mainland and the island filled him with dread. They were not calm waters to be traversed by the faint of heart. And they didn't even have a boat.

"Where are we?" Saraid asked, waking from her light doze.

"Not sure. Close to the sea. Cathán's men are coming. Hold on, we need to ride hard to get to the beach before they do."

"Rory, we'll be trapped down there."

He shook his head. "No. It's our only way."

He didn't know what made him so sure, but instinct was guiding him now and he had to trust it. Prayed that he was right to do so.

He clicked his tongue and held tight to Saraid as they flew over the open terrain. He coaxed the animal with his thoughts, pushing it to go faster still. By the time they came to the edge of the plateau, they were out of breath and the horse was sweaty and foam soaked.

But there, dead ahead, was the sea. It crashed with great white waves, spewing spray and froth onto the rocky shore like a rabid dog. The way down was steep and harrowing. Nothing a horse could navigate. That gave him hope, but whether or not a human could manage the treacherous descent was still an unknown. They had to try, though.

Rory dismounted, sending warm thoughts to the horse, thanking him for giving his all. The lightning-bolt muzzle nudged his shoulder in response.

"Come on, princess," Ruairi said, reaching up.

She didn't argue. Instead she let him help her down. Rory quickly unsaddled the horse, pulled off its bridle, and removed the leather satchel that held the Book of Fennore. Slinging the satchel over his shoulder, he gave the horse a slap on the rump. With a soulful look, the animal trotted away, gaining speed at Rory's urging. He guided it inland, where it stood a chance of being found and taken care of.

They scrambled down the sheer drop to the sea, swapping one perilous foothold for another, slipping against the moss and slime, but somehow defying the pull of gravity that wanted to smash them like the waves against the shore. Overhead a flock of gulls swooped and swerved, catching the edgy currents and riding them into the spewing waves. Rory wished there was some way he could do the same and harness those blustering gusts and sail with them to the Isle of Fennore.

They were almost to the bottom when Saraid said, "Ruairi, look."

He jerked his head around, following her pointed finger to the beach where a lone man stood watching them. An instant later another stepped from behind the jutting boulders and joined him.

"Tiarnan," Saraid breathed. "It's Tiarnan and Liam."

Rory jumped the last few feet to the beach and reached up for Saraid, lifting her off the rock she clung to and setting her on the ground beside him. As soon as she touched down, she was moving, running to her brothers, who had now been joined by others. Stunned, Rory realized there were at least two hundred of them.

Tiarnan lifted Saraid into the air and spun her while Michael and Liam threw their arms around both in a group hug that knocked Rory's heart off beat with an unexpected longing for the familial closeness he saw in their reunion. For a moment, he could almost believe it was the old Saraid holding her brothers. But when she stepped back, he saw the flatness in her eyes that contradicted the smile on her face.

She turned to find him without pause, and took his arm, pulled him into the warm circle. Michael wrapped his big hands around Rory's neck, but only to draw him into an embrace.

"Thank y'," he said, his voice thick. "Thank y' for keeping her safe."

Rory swallowed hard. If Michael only knew the truth, he would bury his knife deep in Rory's heart and he'd be right to do it.

Liam stepped up next, shook his hand in a manly way, and gave him a curt nod. But the kid had tears in his eyes that he couldn't hold back. Rory ruffled the boy's hair and faced Tiarnan, braced for the berating that was sure to come.

But Tiarnan only stared at him through hollow eyes that seemed almost as devoid as Saraid's and said nothing.

"Did y' see Eamonn on yer way?" Liam asked Saraid.

She shook her head. Tiarnan winced and turned away.

Behind the brothers stood Leary and enough soldiers to

give Rory hope. If they had to face Cathán's men, at least the odds would be a little more even. Then the group parted and up the center came five men carrying a boat. *A fucking boat!*

Not just one, he realized; behind them there were more, over a dozen more. They were oddly shaped crafts that didn't look strong enough to float on a lake, but Christ if the sight of them didn't make his heart skip with joy.

"How did y' find us?" Saraid asked her brother.

Tiarnan hooked a thumb at Leary and said, "He knew."

A little bit of the Tiarnan Rory had come to know sparked in his eyes for a moment, but then it dimmed again.

"Will those things float?" Rory asked, looking at the boats lined on the shore.

"Float, aye," Leary said, with a meaningful nod. "More than that is up to you, isn't it now?"

Rory scowled at him. He should be used to the bull-like man's cryptic comments by now, but still he wished Leary would talk straight for once. Leary was tuned to his own satellite, though, and Rory had to hope that he wouldn't have hauled those boats from wherever they'd been to here if he didn't have faith that they were seaworthy.

Rory moved to the shoreline, looking through the gray mist out to the island, which was little more than a black spec in the distance. But it was there, as he'd known it would be. His own personal homing beacon.

"Who lives on that island?" he asked, pointing at it.

"No one does," Michael told him with a look of shock as he tucked his satchel into one of the boats. Rory had a glimpse of fur and realized the pup he'd rescued slept safely inside. "The sea is like a wild animal here. It gobbles up anyone who tries to cross."

"It's true," Leary said with a bit of merriment that struck Rory as odd, even for him. "The island is known far and wide for the sea creatures that guard it. No ship, large or small, has ever made it to shore in one piece, no matter the direction of approach."

Saraid came to stand beside Rory and on the other side, Tiarnan.

"I see what yer thinking," Tiarnan said, shaking his head. "Yer thinking y' can do what no one before y' has been able, is that it? Well look closely. You'll see the ruins of those who've tried and they had boats made for the seas."

Up and down the shoreline in either direction the flotsam of destruction littered the ground. Broken bows and oars, splintered masts and shredded sails, pieces of metal, bits of rope. All of it washed to and fro, caught in the tide pools, clinging to the stones.

Rory knew better than anyone in the bedraggled group that getting to the island would be difficult. Even his stepfather, Niall, had avoided the channel between the mainland and the Isle of Fennore and that was in a troller that had a strong engine and solid build.

"The water is freezing in case y' didn't know it," Tiarnan went on, "and none of us can swim."

Rory gave him a narrowed glance before turning back to the island. Everything Tiarnan said was true. The water was like ice, the current vicious, and the distance too far to swim even if they'd all been young, healthy, and Olympic trained. But there had to be a way.

"Will y' part the waters now?" It was Saraid speaking, a sad smile on her face.

The cold wind blowing across the ocean brought color to her cheeks and made her eyes gleam like jet. Her hair fought the braid she'd confined it to and wisps escaped to swirl around her face. She was beautiful in a way no other woman he'd ever met was. Earthy and fine and resigned to the fate he'd led her to.

She went on. "Isn't that what y' said before—y' asked me if I expected y' to part the seas and usher us all to the Promised Land?"

Silent, he shook his head. *Part the seas.* Christ, if only he could.

"Watch it," one of the men shouted, and Rory turned to see a giant stone careen down from the top of the cliff, clattering as it bounced, gathering other rocks in its wake until a landslide rained down on the beach. The gathered people scattered back, into the surf, around the bend. Then another shout rose, this one filled with alarm.

Rory craned his neck to see to the top of the cliff and discovered something worse than falling rocks. Cathán's men lined the jagged edge as far as the eye could see. Even as the realization hit him, Cathán gave the signal and arrows began to fly, slicing through the air with a haunting song that heralded death.

Chapter Thirty-four

THE first volley came like a swarm of angry wasps, black and winged and deadly.

"Forward," Rory shouted, pointing to the cliff wall, trying to hurry them under the speeding arc. "Get behind them."

He grabbed Saraid's hand, jerked Liam nearly off his feet by the front of his tunic, and launched them back against the wall. The others moved swiftly, racing to get on the other side of the arching attack, but it all happened in a blink, and the steady hiss and burr followed by a sickening *thunk* of arrowheads meeting flesh filled the beach. Tiarnan took one in the shoulder and another in the leg. Rory watched helpless as he hit the ground with a cry.

When the last arrow clattered to the stones, twenty men lay sprawled on the rocky shore, some moaning, some gaining their feet, trying to make a break before the next round was loosed. Without thought, Rory darted out of the cove and raced to Tiarnan, grabbing the man beneath his arms and hauling him up. Michael was there in an instant, taking the other side as they pulled him to safety. Leary and others did the same with the other injured men, but an instant later, the second volley plummeted and pierced anyone still in the open.

Back to the wall, Rory heaved in great gulps of air. They were trapped, just as Saraid had predicted. More rocks jumped and jittered down to the cove. He didn't need to look to know it was some of Cathán's men rappelling down the cliff, disturbing rocks that slammed to the ground.

Think, Rory. Think.

He looked up and down the flattened line of men, women, and children and found every face turned toward his, waiting, watching, praying he would perform a miracle. But what in God's name did they expect him to do? What?

He closed his eyes, tried to focus, tried to think beyond the clamor of panic in his head. There were horses up there, but none still mounted by riders. He whispered through their minds, looking through their eyes. The animals were tethered to a rope strung between two stakes. Apparently, these men knew what had happened to the last riders who'd attacked Rory and had taken precautions. Too bad Rory didn't know how he'd incited the animals to act. He could send gentle suggestions into their minds, beckon them with a whistle, or see from their eyes, but make them follow orders? How had he done that?

He frowned, considering the question. Could it be as easy as suggestion?

Trying to slow his racing heart, Rory tried. He pictured them rearing, breaking free, stampeding. The horses began to toss their heads and paw the ground. From their eyes, Rory watched the back row of fighters turn and look at them with trepidation.

Rory smiled coldly and shut off the logical thoughts yammering in the back of his mind, insisting he couldn't do what he was obviously doing. He sent a rush of alarm through the horses. They began fighting their lead lines and whinnying loudly.

"Kill them," someone yelled, and Rory saw that it was Cathán and beside him . . . Christ, beside him stood Saraid's brother, Eamonn. *The bastard.*

"Kill the horses," Cathán shouted again, and ten men pulled their swords and rushed forward.

Run, Rory urged, pushing his thoughts into the horses' heads. *RUN!*

The animals acted as one, rearing and breaking free before the first man reached them. They jerked the hastily constructed tether, pulling up the stakes, and ran with it bouncing and dragging behind them. Rory sent warning, fearful that the dragging line would snag and break their necks. He showed them how to duck their heads, how to get under the line and toss it back so that it rode across their backs. Like circus animals, they obeyed with stunning mastery.

Cathán's men gave chase, but not for long. Relieved that the innocent animals would not be slaughtered because of him, Rory slowed the last horse and looked back to the chaos.

The first wave of Cathán's men were over the cliff, halfway down by now, and the next was following. Desperate, Rory looked out to sea, flinging his consciousness ahead of him, praying it caught on something. A bird, a gull with black eyes and white feathers, snared his thoughts and sailed them out to the ocean. He urged the gull to circle above the cliff where Rory and the others huddled in fear while Cathán's men came like hot oil down from the cliff.

NO.

Even as the word shuddered through him, he caught a movement to his right. Another gull and beyond it three more. He tried to pull them together with the line of his thoughts, but they rebelled, squawking and skimming away. He circled with one and tried again, but the birds were not so easily controlled as the horses.

Frustrated, he forced his thoughts, snapping them like a whip, but now there wasn't a bird in sight, and the one he rode began to list, disoriented and faltering.

His rage swelled in him as he came back to his body. What good was he if he could do no more than ruffle feathers?

Leary was moving up the line, weapon drawn. Behind him the other warriors stepped away from the wall and moved as one. They would fight, then, the old-fashioned way.

Rory looked at Saraid, wished there was time to say everything that needed to be said. She stared back at him, her eyes flat and emotionless. But her hand reached out, stopped him.

"I love y'," she said. "Do not doubt it."

The words fell like the spray of the ocean, fine and cold, remote and unknown. Did he believe what she said or did he believe those dispassionate eyes? He swallowed hard and dropped the saddlebag with the Book of Fennore in it at her feet. He didn't need to tell her to do whatever it took to keep the Book away from Cathán. She, better than anyone, knew that already.

The first of Cathán's men dropped from the dangling ropes as he raced to join Saraid's brothers and stand against the invasion. Behind him came the rest of Leary's men and women fighters. Even the elderly and untrained women took up weapons. He prayed Saraid would stay where he'd left her. Sword in his hand, he stood shoulder to shoulder with Tiarnan, Michael, Leary, and Red Amir. Mahon was down the way, leading others Rory didn't know. Hell, even the kid was there, ready to fight. To defend.

He gave one last look at Saraid, but she wasn't looking back. Instead she seemed to be staring at something next to her. Something he couldn't see. Her eyes had widened with terror, and her face drained of color. Was it the Book? Was it talking to her? Fucking with her mind when she needed her head in the game?

He wanted to shout at her, to pull her attention away from whatever it was, but Cathán's men were on them and the fight was for the right to live.

Chapter Thirty-five

SARAID stared at Ruairi's retreating back with a hard knot of rage in her belly. To have sacrificed so much only to have him at risk once more . . . Then, from the corner of her eye, she saw her youngest brother.

Stunned, she spun. Only seconds ago he'd been between Tiarnan and Michael, sword in his hand, murderous fear in his eyes. Now it was blood on his face and death in his gaze. And she realized . . . it wasn't Liam. It was his death.

"No," she whispered, but before the word even left her lips, Michael appeared behind him. His throat had been slit, and blood soaked his tunic. The horror hadn't even registered before Tiarnan and Leary, Red Amir and Mahon Snakeface stood with them. All of them, dead. As her eyes traveled over their features, the heart she no longer thought she had shuttered to a stop.

"Sorry, princess," Ruairi said, and though she tried not to look, her eyes found his. He'd been cleaved from neck to chest, hacked to pieces by an ax that was still embedded in his flesh.

"No," she said again. "No."

The rage inside her became something hotter, greater than mere fire. It bubbled and gurgled, and then it burst, molten and flowing. All they had done, all they had survived only to die on this beach, leaving her here, alone, only half of who—of *what* she should be . . .

No.

The wind blowing off the sea razed the shore before whipping through her skirts. She took a deep breath of it, pulling it in. Remembering the words her mother had spoken. Oma said she was powerful. That she didn't *need* the Book. That she could have saved Ruairi on her own. She'd tried. She failed, and now it might be too late for Saraid, but it wasn't too late for the others.

All around her were shouts and violence, but she closed her mind to them. Closed her eyes to the death spirits that waited beside her. She pushed out, listening for that one note, that haunting song her mother had told her about . . . and there it was . . . just out of reach. She breathed deeply, this time keeping her panic at bay, not letting her fear dilute her determination. She stretched, stretched until she could pull the song inside her, letting it resonate in every part of her body. The straining notes filled her, reverberating from the sheer rock wall, the massive waves pounding the beach, the foaming tide. Without even realizing she moved, she stepped out of the sheltering cliff, ignoring the shouts from the women and children who still huddled there.

There was blood on the rocks and broken shells. Blood on the men she loved. Tears filled her eyes, and she brushed them back angrily. There was no place for fear here.

Saraid clenched her eyes, following the faint music down into the depths of herself, seeking, seeking . . . she found another note, then another, and now the song swelled around her and she could hear the euphony, the rise and fall of harmony and melody, a voice filled with vibrato wavering over the waters, through the sky.

She focused on the pitch and tone of the song, and suddenly the feel of it was everywhere. It plunged into the pit of her stomach and tightened around her gut. She was hot and cold, part of the music—a string pulled tight over the pegs and bridge. She raised her arms and she called to the dead—the dead of the past, the dead who had fought this battle already. The dead who would fight it again.

They appeared like a dream, first shadowy figures and then color and motion. She saw her father, strong and whole, and at his side was his army of warriors, men who had given their lives to save the women and children beneath the cliff. Bain saw her, gave her a gentle smile. And then he drew his sword and let loose a war cry that was music in itself.

Her brothers continued to fight, unaware that they'd been joined, but above, the men on the dangling ropes paused and scanned the shore. They could not see her dead soldiers, but they could feel them. Her father ran to meet them, grabbing the ropes and pulling himself up hand over hand. The others followed while more spread amongst the fighters on the ground, using stealth and trickery, baiting Cathán's men, giving *her* men a chance. But still, there were too many and every man Bain disarmed was replaced by another.

Once again, her power was naught in the face of reality. She scanned the rocky beach. There was Tiarnan, still on his feet, and Michael, fierce and mobile, beside him. Ruairi fought like a warrior, giving not an inch, taking as much as he could. And Liam . . . she paused, searched again. Where was her youngest brother?

She took a step forward, shaking off the hands that tried to hold her back. Where was Liam? And then she saw him. He lay crumpled on the hard beach, facedown in the wash of the tide.

Something inside her roared with rage, the feeling traveling up and out, spreading across the bloody surf, surging up the cliff's face and across the flatlands to the forest and beyond. Birds burst from the trees and into the skies, and still her rage traveled, a silent scream that echoed on forever.

Chapter Thirty-six

RORY caught a movement from the corner of his eye. A man, fighting beside him—there and then gone. Another flash, another ghostly figure he couldn't bring into focus. His opponent saw it, too, cursed and dodged. Suddenly the man's weapon flew from his hands and he screamed. Screamed with terror. Still, he reached for another knife and advanced without pause, and Rory parried, slashed, fought the man back.

They wouldn't win. Cathán's numbers seemed undiminished while theirs . . . he stared at the bloody beach. God, they were being slaughtered.

He jabbed with his sword, made a lucky hit, and brought his opponent down, but before he could fully turn, another man had taken his place. Sweat poured down his face, stung his eyes. He jabbed again, wasn't so lucky, lost his footing, and might have fallen had not something shaken the earth. He staggered, caught his balance as the other men paused. The tremor seemed to come from the very air, and it shook and tore through the battle, clawed its way up to the cliff. Birds burst into the air like rockets on the Fourth of July.

He didn't know what had caused it, but it seemed like a sign. One part of him fought hand to hand, but the other part soared into the air and rushed at the winged creatures, pulling them together with the tight jerk, not giving them a choice this time, not letting them evade. Rory spread himself out, calling them in until suddenly he was at the center of a flock that swelled and grew. Not just gulls now, but albatross, pelicans, cormorants, gannets, sandpipers, and even wrens soaring in the sky, wing to wing, a storm raging beneath the heavy gray clouds, caws and beaks moving in a cacophony that muted the thundering tide and drew the attention of the startled humans on shore.

Leary's men began to shout, and then Cathán's men turned, some still dangling like spiders over the beach, and Rory brought the birds into an arrow of their own. A deadly point that swooped and stabbed, pecking, flapping wings in rage, diving for eyes and ears and fingers that held on to swinging lines. Now jubilant shouts from below rose up and clashed with the terrified screams from those above. One man lost his grip and crashed to the sharp, stoned beach with a sickening thud. Seconds later, four more hit with an impact that crushed their bodies.

Now the birds spread, diving in like bombers, chasing the ones above, herding the soldiers like cattle. The men turned inland, running for safety, but Rory reached out again and called back the racing horses, reining them in and pointing them toward the cliffs once more. They charged into the scattering men, splitting the ranks into a dozen fractured pieces. And still the birds came, creating a wall of feathers that spun like the eye of a storm, bearing down on those who remained.

Cathán was shouting at his men, ordering them to stay together, to turn and fight, but he might as well have been telling the rain not to fall. Rory saw Eamonn, pale and terrified, watching the world tilt sideways. His eyes were haunted, his face pulled in a grimace of terror. Then he, too, broke and ran for the forest. He was Saraid's brother, and for that reason only, Rory let him go. Cathán would not be so lucky.

Rory pulled on the line that held his flock and focused the fearsome force on Cathán. It seemed the gnarled warrior felt the shift in the air, felt the eye of the hurricane center over his head, and then the storm exploded around him, chasing him to the edge of the cliff. But Cathán was smarter than the others, and at the last moment, he swerved, heading for the forest. As Rory turned to pursue, he heard Saraid screaming at him and suddenly his control snapped. The birds burst free of his rein and scattered, vanishing like raindrops in the wind.

She was bent over Liam.

"The boats," Saraid said, tugging his arm. "Hurry before they come back."

Slowly, as if emerging from a dark cave into sunshine, Rory watched the others scurry from the shadow of the cliff. They moved swiftly to the bodies scattered on the shore, checking for life among friend and enemy alike. More of Leary's soldiers had survived, but none of Cathán's drew breath. Tiarnan stood staring up at the cliff where Cathán had evaded them again. The look in his eye spoke of hatred that would last long after both he and Cathán were dead and buried.

In the sudden silence, the rolling ocean sounded loud and fierce, reminding them all that they still had one more challenge ahead.

Rory strode onto the shore, watching the monstrous tide crash at his feet. He stared out at the Isle of Fennore, feeling his destiny curl and splash with the fierce waves. It was still out of reach, unattainable. Dangerous beyond anything they'd faced so far.

But now Rory knew what to do. He knew how to part the seas.

Chapter Thirty-seven

SARAID was thankful for the numbing insulator of the Book. It kept her from breaking down, from shrieking at the horror she'd witnessed. Cathán had come very close to killing everyone she loved right here, on this very beach. With all of them dead, he would have rifled their sparse belongings and found the Book of Fennore, conveniently bundled and waiting for him. She'd always known that Cathán was a dangerous and cruel man, but just how deadly Cathán could be had not been clear until she'd used the Book herself.

Liam lay in the boat beside her. He was dying, and yet another part of Saraid died with him. Michael had looked at the long, deep gash in his chest and cried out, trying futilely to slow the flow of blood. He hadn't needed to say what they all knew. Without a miracle, Liam would die.

While the others loaded the *curraghs*, she held her youngest brother in her arms and tried to tap into that music that soared before, when she'd called the dead. But the song was as faint as a distant memory. What she'd done earlier had left her drained, weakened. She'd be no help to Liam . . . unless . . . she glanced at the satchel with the Book inside . . . it was foolish to even consider using it again. It was foolish not to consider it.

She looked at Ruairi, knowing she would have to be quick if she really meant to do this. Knowing he would be watching her once they reached the island. He would never agree to her using the Book again, of course. She would have to slip away without his seeing.

And afterwards . . . she would follow her mother's footsteps and put an end to the half-life of her existence. End whatever was left of her when the Book had taken its toll.

Ruairi stood in the frothing surf like a god of air and sea, staring out at the island he was determined to reach. Around her the others eyed him with awe, daunted by the power they'd witnessed. No man could control the birds in the sky, and so to them, Ruairi must be more than a man. They watched him with adoration and reverence that Saraid shared. She could see confidence gleaming in the impossible blue of his eyes. Acceptance of the mantle of leadership that was now so solidly on his shoulders.

It was exactly what Colleen had prophesized. Ruairi had saved her people. But he would not win against the Book of Fennore. As powerful as this beautiful man had become, she knew he could not do what he set out to do, but if she was successful, if she could get away long enough to beg for Liam's life and then end her own, it wouldn't matter. She lowered her lashes to hide her thoughts, wishing that grief had gone with her other emotions, keeping her from feeling the weight of what she planned. Ruairi would not understand why she did it, just as her father hadn't understood when Oma had taken her life. There was no way to explain, though. No way to make him believe that she had no other choices.

Ruairi turned to face the men and women who stood pale and stunned behind him. He opened his mouth to speak, but before he could utter a word, Leary, Mahon Snakeface, and Red Amir went down on one knee before him. Without hesitation the others followed until only Saraid, Ruairi, and Tiarnan remained erect. And then with a long look, Tiarnan lowered himself as well.

She could feel the surprise rolling off Ruairi, the confusion and embarrassment, the uncertainty, the doubt. Like the others, she waited to see what he would do.

After a long moment, he finally spoke.

"Get up, please. Please."

Surprised, they did as he asked.

"That island you see over there. That's the Isle of Fennore," he said, his voice ringing out as he pointed to the island across the churning sea. "In a few hundred years—maybe a thousand, I don't know—but sometime in the future, my people will live there." He looked down at Saraid and smiled that crooked grin. "Our people will live there."

They all looked from one to another, as if to confirm they'd heard him correctly, but no one questioned him until Michael spoke up.

"How in the fook are we going to get *there*?" he exclaimed.

Ruairi's smile broadened. "Well that's going to be a little complicated," he answered. "All I can ask is that you trust me."

Those words seemed to come hard for him. Ruairi was not a man who liked to ask for anything. Certainly not a man who used the word *trust* lightly.

He looked at Leary. "Let's get those boats in the water before Cathán comes back."

Saraid left Liam's side to help the fearful people who clustered around the boats, hoping they didn't see what Ruairi did in her eyes when she smiled at them. Trying to look as if there was nothing to worry over. They trusted her as she trusted Ruairi and they settled at her calm front. Little did they know that inside, she was terrified. Little did they know the Book of Fennore had taken a part of her that would never be given back and that soon she would give it more. Maybe after that, Ruairi would succeed in destroying it. Maybe he would simply hide it away for all of eternity. She couldn't know.

Leary's men held the boats still while the women, children, and elderly were loaded in. Saraid did her part, wondering how this could possibly end in anything less than disaster.

"Don't worry, princess," Ruairi said, sensing her fear. "I'll keep you safe."

Not from the Book, she wanted to say. *Nothing can keep me safe from that. Not even Ruairi of Fennore.*

When everyone but those anchoring the boats was seated, Ruairi climbed into the strange vessel beside Saraid and her brothers and looked out to the sea. She imagined she could see him casting his net, this time down, down into the cold dark waters, almost feel the frigid depths he plundered. No one in the boats spoke, not even the children. Then Ruairi looked out at the waiting *curraghs* and the expectant faces watching him.

"Hold on," he said, and the waters began to writhe and boil beneath the vessels, lifting them buoyantly, making the sea shimmer like gray green silk in a blustery wind. Leary's men exclaimed and the elderly prayed, while the children shifted to see better.

"Salmon," Michael said, his voice hushed as he looked over the side of the *curragh*. In his hands, he held the small pup. The dog yipped with fear. "It's fookin' salmon."

The salmon were everywhere, surrounding, circling, bursting from the turbulence, and flying over the *curraghs*. They hoisted the oblong boats so that they skimmed the surface of the swells, propelling them by the sheer force of their numbers for there were thousands—millions perhaps. Slowly they moved their cargo forward, past the breaking tide, across the treacherous sea while the passengers watched with an equal mix of astonishment and terror.

"Look," someone shouted, and they turned around to see Cathán and the remainder of his army standing on the beach. He sent another round of arrows at the *curraghs*, but they were too far away and the arrows fell harmlessly into the surf. The men and women cheered and jeered at him as he faded in the distance. He wouldn't give up, but unless he could call on the seas to aid him as Ruairi did, Cathán would not be able to hurt them again.

It didn't take long to reach the island. In fact, it seemed as if they flew across the waves, safe as babes in arms. But as the first *curragh* bumped the rocky beach, Saraid saw the wreckage of countless ships that had not been so lucky. Their splintered hulls littered a cove sheltered by sheer crags and a forbidding tide. The skeletal remains brought home in a way nothing else could how miraculous was their deliverance.

Leary's men pulled the *curraghs* to dry land as the people spread out. They had only the clothes on their backs and what they'd managed to carry with them through all the arduous flights from Cathán's terrorizing, but for the first time in as long as many could remember, they were safe.

Tears clogged Saraid's throat as she realized it. Turning, she wrapped her arms around Ruairi and held tight.

"Hey now," he said. "No waterworks, princess. We're not done yet."

Leary appeared at his side, like a general waiting for orders, and Ruairi surveyed the coastline like the commander he'd become. "There's a valley just to the east and woods with deer and game beyond it. Take them up. Get them settled."

Leary smiled and gave Ruairi a swift nod before moving off to do as he was told, but there were others, all needing Ruairi to tell them what to do, and Saraid knew a better opportunity would not arise. Wishing she could say good-bye, feeling her heart break with every step, Saraid took the satchel from the *curragh* and moved away before Ruairi noticed. It didn't take her long to find the cavern—Ruairi had described the jutting cliff where the castle would stand some day and she used it as a landmark, following the coast to its point. But even if he hadn't told her where, she would have felt it, the call of the place wanting its own back.

Squaring her shoulders, Saraid answered.

Chapter Thirty-eight

ORY didn't know how long Saraid had been gone. He only knew that when he turned to find her, she was nowhere in sight. None of her brothers had seen her since they came ashore. Liam wavered on the brink of death, and it was when he looked at the kid's face that he knew.

He knew.

The satchel with the Book was gone and so was Saraid.

He didn't waste time asking other questions. He ran.

The cavern was exactly where Rory had remembered, of course. Caverns didn't move. But somehow he'd feared it wouldn't be there. Perhaps in this time, it was sealed in by stones or underwater or nonexistent. He'd never known if the cave had been blasted by ancestors or formed by the hands of God and the rolling tide.

The castle was not built yet, though he could picture it in his mind, jutting out over the sea like a lord. Beneath it, the cavern was dark and cold inside, dank with the smell of dead fish and seaweed, mildew and brine. A chunk of driftwood surged with the tide inside the cavern and thumped against the massive rocks.

The cool quiet encompassed him as he moved forward, toward the back where only the surging light from the low sun streamed through. As the tide rolled in and then out, the cave brightened and dimmed disconcertingly. Still, he didn't see Saraid.

Rory looked at the walls and ceiling of the cavern as he moved deeper. In his time, spirals marked every surface like the brand over his heart, seared into solid rock by a force unimaginable. But the spirals that scarred the walls the day of his grandmother's funeral were noticeably absent now.

A movement caught his eyes, and he saw Saraid at last, kneeling next to the inky tide pool. Her eyes were glazed over, the pupils so large they absorbed the irises with their blackness. Her breath came in short, jerky bursts that seemed to scratch and burn as she released them.

"Saraid?" he said, hurrying to her side. "What are you doing here?"

But of course he knew. *Liam.* She'd come to plead for his life as she had for Rory's. She didn't even look at him when he spoke, and he knew the voice she heard wasn't coming from him—it was coming from inside those black covers, those pale pages.

He shouldn't have brought the Book with them to this island, he realized all at once. But he'd been so sure he could save Saraid and then destroy the Book, so certain that he had the power to accomplish the impossible that he hadn't considered the risk.

He'd been too rash, too cocky after the birds, the beasts, the fish rising to his command. He'd begun to believe his own press—that he was superhuman. That he could do what no man had done before.

He'd wanted her to see its destruction. To know that she need not fear it again because he, Rory—*Ruairi of Fennore*—had slain the dragon. He'd been so full of himself, so fucking convinced of his greatness that he'd condemned her without even knowing it. He'd brought her to the enemy. Delivered her to its lair.

He stood, intending to scoop her up into his arms and run from this evil place. He would come back, later, and do what he'd set out to do—destroy the malignant creation. But now, he needed to get Saraid someplace safe.

And still you do not see what a fool you are. . . .

The voice boomed in his head, staggering him before he'd

taken the first step. He felt it in every pore, every nerve ending, each ragged breath. The bundle hummed and moaned in a seesawing rhythm that felt like electricity zapping his nerves, trilling against his eardrums.

I am not a thing that has a beginning and an end. That can cease. Stupid, pathetic man, I am earth and sky. I am sun and moon. I am more than your weak mind can conceive.

The voice was fingernails dragging slowly across a chalk-board, metal screeching and grinding, glass shattering into millions and millions of sharp, piercing shards. It was all of that and none of it. It filled him with dread and hopeless-ness, terror and panic. It made him want to drop to his knees and give up, give in—give *anything* to unhear its hideous message.

But somewhere deep inside him another voice spoke, this one light where the first had been dark, fair to its foul. He tried to center on it, following it down through the acrid stench of the other's echo so he might discern the words he couldn't quite grasp.

Remember, the new voice said, and Rory thought it was his sister, Danni, speaking. Astonished, he concentrated on that, and sudden images burst in his mind. He saw again that night when he'd lost his father. The Book was held between them, and he'd felt himself sinking into it, being swallowed into its covers, flattened between its pages. Inside that hollow and hellish Neverland, there'd been many voices trapped and screaming, petrified and pleading. But above the chaos of their shrieks he'd heard a droning chant spoken over and over.

Now, in an instant of startling clarity, he remembered it. A flash of intuition told him the chanting had come from the woman Leary had told them about, the White Fennore. She was casting her curse, spinning it out like a great web, pronged with burrs that stuck in the flesh and held. Over and over it went, stretching on and on.

He tried to take another step toward Saraid, but his feet were locked to the cavern floor and he couldn't move.

With a groan of frustration, he stared at the Book of Fen-nore. It was out of the satchel, out of the canvas wrapping. Saraid knelt before it like a statue, unmoving.

The tooled and blackened cover opened and the pages

began to turn. Each was filled with spirals unending, meaningless symbols that blurred as the pages fanned before his eyes. The whir of it teased the fine strands of Saraid's hair, but still she did not move or react. Slowly, by infinitesimal degrees, the strange concentric spirals separated as the fanning pages transformed, becoming ancient runes then letters that suddenly Rory could decipher. He read, parsing the broken language into something comprehensible. Even as he began to understand, Saraid spoke.

Her voice was low and intoned with a dark echo that was not her own. Her eyes had gone black—not just the widened pupils, not just the irises. Her entire eye. There were no whites, only unearthly flat darkness between the long, lush lashes.

"Saraid?" he whispered.

She didn't hear him; instead she mouthed the words he'd read in the ancient script, speaking in that discordant voice that was not her own.

"I am the White Fennore. I am a gift of the Gods to the people, to be cherished and honored. I am that which you cannot comprehend. I am that which you fear. For your betrayal, Brandubh, High Priest of Éire, you will spend eternity and beyond bound within the pages of the Book you created for me. Banished like a vile creature, to be despised by all and revered by none."

Saraid didn't blink as she spoke. She didn't pause. Didn't see that he was afraid.

"All who come in contact with you will suffer for the evil and greed they carry with them as will you suffer. They will use you for their will, as you have used me. When the hearts of men are pure, you will then wither and fade to nothing."

Rory managed to take a step closer, reaching out to Saraid. Her hands were like ice, her fingers clenched tight.

"You may promise only what you can deliver, you may take only what you are given. If you survive, you will see me again."

Now she did pause, yet the echo of her voice sprang from everywhere and nowhere and chafed against the uneven light. The dread in Rory's gut exploded into terror.

"Saraid, snap out of it. Stop." He snapped his finger in front of her black, black eyes. Grabbed her shoulders and shook.

Her head swayed on her delicate neck, but the frozen expression did not change nor did the black eyes return to normal.

She took a breath and then spoke again, tolling that bell of doom in a tone that was not her own.

"You will not know me, but I will judge you, Brandubh the Black Raven, and you will have one chance to prove you are redeemed. This is your curse. This is your fate. Meet it well or pay my price."

The condemnation detonated in the cavern—there was no other way to describe it. The walls reverberated, the ground shuddered, and the pool of water chopped and turned in response. Saraid swayed, and then her eyes rolled back in her head as she keeled forward. Rory caught her limp body in his arms as he spun to face the Book again.

The black leather shone in the undulating light, and the silver and jewels that twined and crusted its surface sparkled with a fire of their own. Once again the pages began to fan back and forth, back and forth, while the vile vibration that wasn't a hum and wasn't a scream but something in between grew louder and louder until it seemed to come from inside Rory's head.

He wanted to turn, to flee. To carry Saraid out into the sunshine and away from this terrible *thing* that had no place in the world of men. Instead, his feet moved toward it as if compelled.

Now what he heard was Saraid's voice—her real one, though she still lay unconscious in his arms. She was sobbing as she begged for Rory's life, and he knew the Book was making him witness the moments when she gave her heart to save him. The blank page in front of him began to fill with symbols, bold and black, thick and tacky as an unseen pen scratched away the terms of the deal she'd struck with the devil.

There was her name, next to it his own, and beneath, the words she'd spoken when she'd asked for his life. Rory shook his head, denying what he didn't want to see. It was a contract. Each page of this Book was a contract. He knew it with absolute certainty.

The pages fanned again, and this time it was his father's voice, begging for money, for power, for control over a life that had spun beyond him. Other voices joined, pages upon pages of contracts filled with the tarlike ink until Rory felt his eyes burning and his heart stuttering with unfathomable pain.

He heard his own brash words: *"I'm going to destroy it. . . ."*

He'd been so sure, so confident. Had scoffed at the idea that it was invincible. But faced with this diabolic entity, he was lost. How would he do it? How could anyone?

Saraid began to cough, and her breath wheezed through her white lips.

"What are you?" he demanded of it, going down on his knees, cradling Saraid in his arms. "Stop it. *Stop it.* Let her go."

In answer Saraid's body curled in, her knees coming up to her chest. Not even the wheeze emerged now. Not a breath. She began to claw at her throat as her body arched in pain.

"Stop it!" Rory shouted again.

A blank page appeared again, waiting, invisible pen poised. Question mark dangling in the dank silence.

What would you give to save her?

Rory didn't hesitate. "Anything," he said. "Everything."

Say it. Ask and it will be yours. . . .

"What the fook have y' done to my sister?" a man's voice demanded—not in his head, but here, in the cave.

Rory spun to find Tiarnan standing in the cavern entrance, his face etched with pain and rage as he looked at the writhing woman in Rory's arms. The arrows he'd taken on the beach had been removed, but he was bloody and battered. He rushed to where Rory crouched and pulled his sister away from Rory.

"What are y' doing to her?" he demanded again.

Rory didn't answer. He was looking at the Book, spread open, obscenely sexual. Waiting for its pleasure.

It seemed Tiarnan understood. In that split second, he took it all in and he grasped what Rory had not. There was no way to win, no way to defeat something so sinister, so wrong . . . so evil.

With a cry of rage, Rory bounded to his feet, pulling out the short sword he wore at his waist and slamming it into the open spine. The Book began to shriek, trumpeting that excruciating sound that made his ears feel like they were on fire. Blood spurted and oozed from the crease, thick as oil, rank and tainted, and Rory had a moment to hope. He spun and looked at Saraid, in Tiarnan's arms now.

She bucked and writhed on the ground, black-eyed and reaching. Then she made one last agonizing effort to draw breath and stilled.

"No," Rory whispered. "No!"

He turned back to the foul obscenity and bellowed his rage, his pain, his vengeance. He lifted his knife again, and lightning shot from the cavern walls and ceiling, zapping it from his hands and turning it to molten silver at his feet. But Rory would not be deterred.

Rory reached into the Book, grabbing the pages with Saraid's name, snagging the ones next to it as well in his haste. Gripping the fistful of pages, he yanked. The pages were thick and slick, like sealskin, and they held tight, refusing to tear, but Rory was not going to give up. Behind him he heard Tiarnan's cry of anguish, and he knew that Saraid wasn't moving, wasn't breathing anymore. Then the big man was beside him, adding the weight and strength of his grief to Rory's efforts. He was mumbling under his breath, hot, angry words.

"I will not fail again."

Over and over he repeated until it became a mantra to both men. They would not fail. Sweat beaded on Rory's face and his arms shook with the strain, but then he felt it, heard it. A tear. And then . . .

The sound was like the world ripping in two—deafening, piercing, shrill beyond conception. Staggered by the power of it, Rory and Tiarnan both stood with the pieces of the pages clutched in their hands. The edges sliced through his skin, razors cutting his fingers to ribbons.

Tiarnan held the bloody pages over his head and shouted, "*I. Will. Not—*" He began to tear and shred, reducing the binding contracts to bits then tossing the pieces into the air with each angry word. "*Fail. Again.*"

Rory did the same, ripping his pages in half and half again, then he hurled them into the air.

The last tiny bit fluttered for a moment before following the others up, up to the cavern roof, where they hit the stone like rockets, bursting into flames and searing their menacing symbols into the surface where they burned and burned until the ceiling was a massive torch. The ground shook, and Tiarnan fell against him, staggering them both back. Then Rory pushed off the wall and hurried to Saraid, lifted her head, and sealed his mouth over hers, forcing air into her lungs, pausing, pressing her chest, breathing, pumping, refusing to let go, to stop trying even for a second.

Sparks showered down on them, and he slapped them out as they lit upon her tattered dress, his frayed tunic. Still he kept his lips sealed to hers. In and out, breathing, in and out.

The cave went dark and then suddenly white light exploded in a sonic boom that shook the walls and cracked the floor. Rory curled his body over Saraid's, shielding her from the stones that broke free and fell around them. It felt like the cavern was collapsing, but he couldn't see because that blinding light had turned the world into a brilliant haze that burned his eyes. He didn't know what Tiarnan was doing now. Was he still there, ripping the pages from the Book?

From the depths of the searing glare, he felt a building pressure, a harrowing suction that tore at his clothes, lifted Saraid's hair. The pull inched them forward, and desperately Rory anchored himself to a boulder with one arm, holding Saraid's lifeless body with the other. The wrenching power towed him in, lifting his feet, trying to yank his arms from the sockets, but still he didn't let go, not of the boulder, not of Saraid. He felt his shoulder rip with pain brighter, hotter, more excruciating than anything he could imagine, but he held. God help him, he held.

A shape appeared before him like a gigantic shadow show against a sheet of white. Squinting, he stared at it, watching it take shape and form, until he recognized the young face that stared back, mouth open in a scream. It was Meaghan. His half sister, Meaghan. There for just a moment, dressed in jeans and a U2 T-shirt, in the cavern beneath the castle ruins. He had only the split second to recognize and identify and then she was gone. The screeching horror climaxed with a thundering crack that must surely have split his skull, and then he felt something heaving the limp body he held. It jerked and twitched and then broke free. Before Rory could even grasp what it was, he felt the brush of it against his skin as it sped away.

What was it? Saraid was still in his arms. He hadn't let her go. Was it her soul? Had he lost her despite everything?

The deafening clamor exceeded chaos, building, building, building and then . . .

And then . . . silence.

Silence, dark and velvet. Silence, black and cool.

The blinding light was gone, leaving only the mellow glow of the setting sun, there, then not as the waves rolled in and out. Shaking, he released the boulder, crying out as his shoulder protested the abuse it had taken.

There were tears in his eyes as he gazed down at Saraid. Tears streaming down his face. She lay in his arms, still and deathly pale. Was it her soul he'd felt wrenching free, succumbing to the cyclone that had tried to suck them in?

"No," he whispered, kissing her face, her throat. "Please, no." He tilted his head back and shouted it. "NO!"

His own voice bantered around the cave, bouncing back to shame him. He turned his face to the Book, filled with a rage that he could not contain, intent on doing what he'd set out to do, no matter the cost.

But the Book was gone. Stunned, he scanned the cavern. Tiarnan was gone, too.

Had Saraid's brother taken it? Had he—

In his arms, Saraid moved. The motion was so slight that at first he wasn't sure if he'd imagined it. Afraid his mind had tricked him, he looked down. Her lashes fluttered, and then her chest rose with a deep, gasping breath. And her eyes opened.

He stared into them, the brown as dark and rich as chocolate, the whites clear and shining. Glowing with the soul of the beautiful person inside. She stared back at him, blinking, bewildered. Alive.

Rory felt as if his heart had been torn out, trampled, tossed to sea. His vision blurred as he stared into her face.

"Y' did it?" she said or asked. He couldn't tell.

"No."

Surprised, she eased herself to a sitting position and looked around. "It's gone, though?"

He nodded. "Tiarnan . . . he must have taken it. He must have figured out how to . . ."

Her eyes widened with horror.

"I'm sorry."

He pulled her to him, uncaring of the pain, uncaring of anything but the breath that moved through her lungs, the steady beat of her heart next to his. The sweet scent of her filling him.

"I thought I'd lost you," he said, and the words broke as his hold on his emotions did. He cried like a baby, holding her, rocking her, drowning in her warmth.

Her arms were around his neck, and she clung with the same feeling, the same wonder and pain and bewilderment.

"I heard y', through it all, I could hear y' calling me back."

After a moment she pulled away, touched his face, kissed away his tears.

"It's over, Ruairi. Whatever you did, it was enough. I feel it."

"You mean . . ." He frowned, not sure what she meant.

"The Book—it had a part of me, and there was this hole where that piece should have been. But now it's gone now and I *feel* again."

Stunned, Rory tilted back his head, looked at the symbols now seared into the ceiling and walls, recognized Saraid's name amongst them. Had they done it? Had he and Tiarnan accomplished the inconceivable? Was what he'd felt tearing away from her the Book's hold? The chains that had bound her?

"It wasn't just me, Saraid. It was your brother. Without Tiarnan, the Book would have won."

Her smile was soft at that, and she nodded, as if in response to a question. "That is good. Failure was too hard a thing for him to bear."

"I'm sorry," Rory said again. "I don't know what happened to him after . . . I saw him holding the Book, but then they were both gone. I don't know if he took it, or if it took him, Saraid."

"I will believe it was the first," she said, pressing a fist to her heart. "I will believe that."

They helped each other out to the beach where the sun blazed with welcome heat. He didn't take her back up to where the others waited, though. He needed to have her alone, to feel the woman he had missed so desperately. He led her around the rocky point and up to a place he'd discovered as a child. It was in a small clearing, nestled between the forest and the sea, secluded.

She didn't ask him where he was going. He figured she knew. Back with the others waited responsibility, heartache—for there was little doubt that Liam would die before sunset—and the weight of the world. But for now, there was only Saraid and Rory.

He took her in his arms and held her for a long, silent moment, letting her feel what was in his heart, what he could not voice because words were too inadequate. Tears were in her beautiful eyes, once again warm and rich with emotion. She smiled at him, and they sparkled the way he loved, filled with the fire he yearned for, the warmth he needed more than air—it was all there. All for him.

He pressed his lips to hers and kissed her softly, slowly, like they had all the time in the world. And they did. He felt it. The kiss was a pledge—a silent declaration they both breathed in and made a part of themselves. He held her close, knowing he'd never manage to get close enough to her heat, her scent, her touch. He kissed her again, losing himself in the feel of her mouth, the fire of her passion.

He'd never given himself, not like he wanted to do now. It scared him, thinking of it, picturing the surrender, the control she would have over him once she saw how completely enthralled he was, and for an instant he pulled back, survival instinct shouting for him to flee. But Saraid was not a woman like any other, and she refused to let him go. She moved as if she owned him already, branding him with her lips against his heart, her hands moving over his chest, covering the symbol burned there. She kissed his scars, opened her mouth over his throat, and let her tongue taste him as he had her.

Their clothing was tattered and torn, easy to shed. The act of removing each layer became a dance of exquisite torture. Each inch of creamy flesh drove him closer to the edge of reason, and then they were stripped. They were bruised, battered, chewed up, and spit out, but they were alive and they were whole and they were together. He pulled her down to the soft grass and took her in his arms once more, overwhelmed by how soft she was, how she fit so perfectly to the hard planes of his body. The first time they'd made love, it had been Rory who was shielded from the full force of it. The next time, Saraid had come to him through the distance of the Book. Now it was just the two of them with nothing to keep them apart.

He turned, pulling her with him until she straddled his hips, the hot wet heat of her pressing the hard length of him into his own belly. It was blessed agony that he would endure forever and do it gladly. Control was meaningless when faced with what he felt. She controlled him already, with her eyes, her lips, her courage, her heart. If that made him her puppet, then who cared?

Not me, Rory thought with a sense of helpless surrender. And he found that giving in was not the same as giving up. He found that instead of lessening, it empowered him. He was her husband, and as strange and unnatural as the word felt in his head, there was also something very satisfying in knowing it, something that flamed and sparked with elation at all it signified. He was her husband, and she was a treasure that had been given to him. One he would guard, love, and cherish.

He stared into her eyes, fell into a well of warm emotion. But the fall was soft, the splash inviting and embracing.

"I will love, honor, and cherish you," he vowed. "'Till death do us part."

"And I y', husband."

For all the sins of his life, he must have done something good to be here, now, with her in his arms.

She made noises, small moans and purrs, whimpers and pants that set him on fire. Christ, she was perfect, perfect in every way. She matched his rhythm, arching her back and hips to meet each thrust. She was the salvation he'd never thought he'd have, and he made another vow, this one silent, to protect her forever. She had called him to her over insurmountable barriers of time, and he would never leave her.

He felt her tighten around him and he shifted, moving his hand between them so he could touch her at the same time. She came instantly, with a buck of her hips and a cry that made him want to howl with pleasure. He joined her, feeling every muscle in his body squeeze tight and then expand in the rush of climax.

For a long time after, he couldn't move, couldn't speak, couldn't breathe while the sensations washed over him, and even after he could feel his hands and feet, pounding heart and light head, he didn't move. He couldn't put into words what he was feeling, but the roll and burn of emotion had hewn him, and now he was shaped in a new form.

He was changed. She had changed him, and nothing would ever be the same. He let that wash over him, felt the solid weight of it. Embraced the wonder.

With a laugh of stunned bliss, he rolled to his side, pulling her with him, as he collapsed against the soft, sweet grass. Because now that he'd found her, he at last knew his life's purpose—to live with Saraid, here or any other place—it didn't matter. They were two halves of the same whole, and what they'd shared had forged them into something that could never again be separated.

Chapter Thirty-nine

IN the weeks that followed, Saraid was torn between mourning and celebration. For so long, living had been about survival, but now they had a home where they were safe and there was no way not to rejoice in that. It was more than she'd dreamed possible. But when she and Ruairi had returned to the beach, it was to learn that both Tiarnan and Liam had vanished without a trace.

"Liam was there, in the *curragh,*" Michael said. "I felt the earth shake and turned my back for a moment—just a moment—and when I looked again, he was gone."

Gone. Just as Tiarnan was gone. Three brothers had been lost—two to the unknown—and the last to betrayal. Their absence was a hole in Saraid's heart that she feared would never fully heal. All she and Michael could do was hold tight to the belief that gone did not mean dead and the hope that one day their brothers would return to them.

Ruairi had described the horrible events that took place in the cold, dark cavern on the day he'd brought them across the seas, had told her about the strange spiral runes becoming words as he and Tiarnan shredded the pages . . . the white light, the earsplitting noise. . . . But he had no explanation for why Tiarnan had vanished or where the Book of Fennore had gone. He couldn't explain what happened to Liam. No one could.

Michael thought that Tiarnan had given his life in exchange for Saraid's. "If the Book offered Ruairi the chance to take yer place, why not yer brother? He would have done that for y', Saraid. Y' know it's true."

She did know, and it was possible. Yet for reasons she couldn't explain, it didn't *feel* right.

Still, she waited for many nights afterwards, dreading and expecting her brothers' deaths to come to her. They never did, though, and she took heart in that. Until the day she saw their spirits, she would continue to believe that somewhere, somehow, they lived.

* * *

RORY stood at the edge of the cliff where one day a castle would stand in defense of this island that sheltered them. He gazed out at the ocean alive with whitecaps and gulls, smiling at the peculiar sense of kinship he felt with the sky and sea. He turned and faced inland where one hundred and sixty-five survivors had begun the settlement that would one day become Ballyfionúir.

When he looked back, a spry little woman sat on a boulder at the edge of the cliff. She wore a white flowered shirt and polyester pants. On her feet were bright white sneakers. When she'd come before, she'd scared the crap out of him. This time, he'd been expecting her.

"Hello, Nana," he said, wishing he could hug her. Wishing she was really here.

"Sure and don't I know you're glad to see me?" she said, black eyes sparkling.

"I am. I wanted to thank you."

"I know, child. I know. 'Tis I who should thank you, I think, if such a thing really matters. You belong to this time and place, Rory. Sure I can see it. And you're happy?"

He smiled, "Yes."

"Then so am I."

He wanted to ask about his mother, Niall, and his sisters. What they had thought when he just disappeared. Were they worried?

"Don't worry, child," Nana said. "They know."

Strange as it was, he believed her.

"It's time for me to go, now."

"To heaven?" he asked, feeling very young and unsure as the words formed. Did he even believe in heaven after all they'd been through?

"*Phsst*," Nana said, cackling for a minute over his naiveté. Then, seeing what must surely have been a stricken expression, "No, not heaven but not the other place, either, Christ willing. You've done a good thing here, Rory—or is it Ruairi now?" The wicked grin flashed; the eyes sparked and gleamed. "But, I'm thinking I'm still needed on this earth."

"Here? With me?"

"No, child. It's not for you to worry about. You get busy here. Build your castle. Have babies with that young beauty you've wed. Lots of babies." She grinned wickedly.

"But—"

"It's Tiarnan's turn to carry the load now."

"Tiarnan? He's alive?"

Nana sucked her teeth and squinted at him. "*Alive* is a peculiar word, isn't it now? Who really knows what it means?"

Apparently, not Ruairi. He stared at his grandmother, dumbfounded. "Can you never just say what you mean, Nana? Do you always have to talk in circles?"

"Aye, I suppose I do."

And with that, she was gone.

* * *

SARAID found Ruairi back in the cavern, still looking for the Book of Fennore. He felt responsible for Tiarnan and Liam vanishing and thought that if he could find the Book, he could somehow undo the damage. She could have told him it was a futile search, but it gave him purpose that she sensed he desperately needed.

She perched at the edge of the tide pool and waited for him to notice her. It didn't take long. As soon as he saw her, he came to sit beside her.

"The Book is gone, Ruairi," she murmured. "I feel it in my bones."

"I know but . . ." He paused, looking into her eyes. "Have they come to you? I mean . . ."

"Have I seen their spirits? No."

"I don't think you will," Ruairi said carefully. And then he told her of the strange visitor he'd had that morning. Colleen of the Ballagh. And she'd said that Ruairi's work was over, but Tiarnan . . . he had a role to play still. She didn't mention Liam, but Saraid held tight to her hope that her brothers were together wherever they might be.

"Do you think Tiarnan has gone to the future? To yer time?"

Ruairi looked as mystified as she felt. "Who knows?"

She laughed, both elated and terrified for her brothers. She had no doubt that the road ahead of Tiarnan would be long and hard. But he was alive . . .

Or at least he wasn't dead . . .

Ruairi was giving her that crooked grin she loved so much. "Now what is going on behind those blue eyes of yers, husband?"

"Well, Nana said something else," he said, his smile widening. Saraid couldn't help herself; she grinned back.

"And what was that?"

Ruairi leaned over and lifted her onto his lap so that she straddled him, her breasts crushed against the wall of muscle and strength of his chest. Her arms circled his neck and she locked her ankles behind his back, loving the way his skin was so soft over a body so hard. She took his face in her hands and pressed a kiss to his mouth.

"What did she say, Ruairi?" she repeated.

His hands slipped down her back to cup her bottom, settling her more firmly where he wanted her before claiming her mouth with his, pulling her against him with his possessive caress. "She said," he breathed against her lips, "that it was time to start populating this island."

"Did she now?" Saraid responded, arching back as his kisses moved down her throat and his hands up to cup her breasts. "She's a very wise woman, I think."

"Aye," he answered, his mouth damp and hot through her thin gown. "Do you think we should listen to her?"

"Most certainly," Saraid said. "I think we should."

Keep reading for a special look at Erin Quinn's
newest Mists of Ireland novel

Haunting Embrace

Now available from Berkley Sensation!

ON guard, Áedán paused just inside and waited. A feeling like a soft breeze trembled around him, brushing his skin. For a moment, it seemed to leach the life from him. His legs wobbled, his vision blurred, and his head felt light and fuzzy. But just as quickly everything snapped back into focus, and he thought his imagination—his hated *fear*—had caused it.

Uneasy, he turned and surveyed the dark cocoon. Nothing moved. No slicing pain or debilitating pressure bore down on him. No vulnerability weakened his limbs. Only the steady beat of the tide and the rage of the ferocious storm broke the cloying silence. Carefully he opened his senses, testing the air, tasting the dark, seeking the danger he felt sure he would find.

Nothing. Only a vague sense of incompleteness that he couldn't define.

Relieved to the point of stupidity, he squared his shoulders and charged forward, wanting to laugh in the face of his enemy now that he had invaded its fortress. His triumphant laughter caught in his throat as he stumbled over something on the ground and nearly fell on top of it. On his knees, arms braced over the motionless form, Áedán stared in shock as recognition kicked him in his gut. A woman lay still as death on the cavern floor, her skin so pale it looked translucent, her arms and legs askew—as if she'd been dropped from above.

Meaghan.

She was so still that he thought she must be dead, and a startling sense of remorse tangled with his utter shock at seeing her again. But then she took a deep breath and her chest rose and fell.

Alive.

He did not like the relief that flooded him. He didn't care for the woman. He cared for only himself and his need to regain his power and take control of the bizarre circumstances that had brought him here. But he could not keep his fingers from brushing the soft skin of her cheek.

Meaghan.

He'd met her only days ago in the night world that belonged solely to the Book of Fennore. They'd been prisoners and allies of sorts. The world of Fennore existed in a realm most humans could not even conceive. Like heaven and hell, it was more a state of being than an actual place. But everything that had happened there felt horribly real . . . was, in fact, as real as the cold that seeped into his skin now. The world of Fennore was a nightmare that had the power to follow the dreamer into the light.

Áedán knew this better than anyone.

He narrowed his eyes at the female on the cavern floor. Could she be the reason he'd felt compelled to come here today? A mere human? Had she lured him here to trap him?

She looked frail and defenseless, yet he knew better than to forget that beneath that pallor lurked a feisty woman who'd almost broken his nose the first time he'd met her.

His gaze shifted to the full curves, the soft slope of her belly, bared where her T-shirt rucked up around her ribs. Dark, greenish bruises covered her arms, and a particularly nasty one spread upward from her hip bone, black and purple above the waist of her jeans. For a moment, the sight of her battered flesh touched off something inside of him. Sympathy? Compassion? Concern?

The alien emotions mocked him. He did not care about others, especially those who weren't of some use to him. For *eons* he'd been an entity, a thing that did not experience, did not rejoice, did not mourn. He'd lived to siphon the emotions of others, to drain them dry, make them so empty that they'd choose death over their hollow existence. But he'd *felt* nothing for them, for their plight, for their demise.

And he felt nothing for this woman either.

He cupped her cheek and let his thumb trace the soft bow of her lips. She stirred and he jerked his hand away. Her pale blue eyes opened in the darkness. She looked frightened, and with a groan, she tried to lift her head. It seemed the effort would take more than she had, but after a moment's struggle, she sat. She hadn't seen him yet, but her hands moved to tug her T-shirt back in place and smooth her hair in a self-conscious manner so unguarded that it made him pause.

She was not aware. Not of him. Not of the cavern. Not of the danger.

Leave, a voice inside him urged.

As if hearing his thoughts, she turned that clear, bewildered gaze to his face.

"Áedán," she breathed, and in the moment it took for the sound to whisper over his skin, he saw her expression change from puzzlement to recognition and then to something darker, sweeter. It surprised him even as it shocked a response from him. Her eyes widened and took on a shade of lavender that teased something in his ancient memories.

How long had it been since he'd known a woman as a man was meant to?

The stark answer filled his head. An eternity without end.

"What are you doing here?" he demanded, his confusion making his voice harsh, his infuriating fear still riding him.

Her eyes widened, wounded, and like a fool, he felt another wave of compassion. *Feck,* he thought, using one of Mickey Ballagh's words.

He leaned closer and she flinched, the small reaction like a flame held to his bare skin. "I'm not going to hurt you," he snapped. "How did you get here?"

She shook her head, and Áedán noted that her eyes seemed glazed and unfocused as she searched his features. Instead of answering his question, she placed one palm against the roughened stubble on his cheek and the other over his pounding heart. He found his own hands against the soft, rounded curves of her shoulders and told himself he meant to push her away.

He didn't, though. Instead he stood, gently pulling her to her feet with him.

When he would have stepped back, Meaghan held on to him and rose to her tiptoes, leaning into his body and brushing her lips against his in a caress as fleeting as it was riveting. Áedán froze, unprepared for the heat that licked his nerves and burned with his blood. A beast within him lifted its head and growled with satisfaction at the hot thoughts that filled him. Perhaps this woman did have use.

But he didn't understand what motivated her to touch him, kiss him, any more than he understood how she'd come to be here in the first place. When they'd met before, she'd been combative, berating him with little care for what he might do in retaliation. She'd had a wicked tongue that she'd used to lash out at her enemies. He'd expected that behavior from her now, but instead, her mouth moved over his again in a silken heat.

What game did she play?

He wanted to ask, but his brain had locked down, refusing any distraction from the sensuous slide of her skin against his. The hand on his cheek trailed to the base of his skull, and she pulled his head down, teasing his lips with her tongue—which was velvety soft, not wicked, not cruel—until he gave in and opened for her, pulling her body against the hard planes of his in the same simultaneous act of conquest and surrender. Her taste hit his senses like a whisper of hallowed memories, evoking the sultry languor of summer nights, the fragrant spice of misted fields, the perfume of female, aroused under a pale moon. . . .

Her soft curves molded perfectly against him, vanquishing any thought but keeping her there, yielding, responding, filling some hollow he hadn't known existed. She made a sound in her throat that set him on fire, made his hands hungry, his lips needy, his body parched.

It was his total capitulation that pierced the fog of want and made him hesitate.

This was not right. *She* was not right.

The Meaghan he'd known so briefly had been fire and hellion. She hadn't yielded to anyone, for anyone.

She opened her eyes slowly, confused by his hesitancy as

she tried to pull him back into her embrace. Her gaze was unfocused, her pupils so huge they'd swallowed all but a thin strip of that beguiling lavender blue at the edge. None of that fierce spirit he'd come to grudgingly respect glowed within them.

Entranced, he thought. *Bespelled*.

She fought his efforts to set her away from him, her movements sluggish, not quick and able. This woman had brought him to his knees with two quick blows within minutes of meeting him, but now she seemed barely capable of standing.

"Meaghan," he said sharply, holding her at arm's length as she struggled to reach him. *"Meaghan!"*

He gave her a hard shake and then withdrew, needing space from her heat, from her soft scent, from her closeness. His body disagreed with his decision and urged him to take her—no matter what the terms. Have her, use her. She was only human, after all.

He scowled at his own surprising reluctance, but before he could decide what he meant to do about her, she stumbled over an uneven stone and lost her balance. He lurched toward her, trying to halt her momentum, but he couldn't reach her in time. Her shriek joined the echoes of his inner turmoil as she plunged into the icy tide pool.

She burst back to the surface and stared at him in shock. Her eyes were blue again, wide and snapping with anger.

"What the feck is wrong with you?" she shouted in a shaking voice. "You fecking pushed me!"

That was the Meaghan he knew. Quick on the defense, showing anger when fear might reveal a weakness.

"I did *not* push you, Meaghan. You fell all on your own." He quickly moved to the side and reached out to her. "Here. Take my hand," he ordered.

She flashed him a furious glare and swam to the side, ignoring his outstretched hand. "I don't need your fecking help," she said, the damp and cold framing her words in a vaporous cloud that hovered at her lips.

The injustice of the moment hit his fury and perplexity like oil-soaked kindling. To think, he'd thought of *her* feelings instead of simply taking what he wanted and leaving her to deal with her own circumstances.

"I didn't push you in and you know it," he said, still reaching for her, still confounded by the fact that he hadn't already stormed from the cavern.

Her eyes held defiance and fear. Her body shook with the cold. "Don't be stupid," he said. "You'll freeze to death if you don't get out."

"I-I k-know."

Meaghan, back to her familiar stubborn and irritable self, tried to haul her body from the pool, but the freezing temperature had already made her muscles stiff and her reactions slow. She hefted herself halfway and then slipped again.

Ignoring her feeble protest, Áedán gripped Meaghan by her arms and heaved her out of the icy waters. Cursing beneath his breath, he looked at the pathetic and bedraggled female and again he felt that alien tug of compassion swiping the feet out from under him.

She didn't want his help. He should leave her and call it a good riddance.

He sat her on one of the big flat boulders and hunkered down beside her, shrugging out of his coat and wrapping it around her as he began to rub her cold hands.

"How did you get here?" he asked as he worked.

"Wh-wh-whe?" she answered.

"Where? We are on the Isle of Fennore."

At the panicked look in her eyes, he shook his head. "No, not in the world of Fennore." Not the place where they'd met, where nightmares had been the only reality available. "I believe we have arrived in the year of nineteen hundred and fifty-six. I got here five days ago."

She absorbed this in silence, still shaking from head to toes. "Oth-oth—"

"No, I haven't seen any of the others." He searched her face, looking for hints of what had come to pass since those last, terrifying moments when they were together. "What happened to you, Meaghan? Where have you been since—"

The sound of a rock scuttling into the cavern behind him drew his attention and silenced the rest of his question. He stood and faced the passageway just as Colleen Ballagh—Mickey's young wife—stepped from the shadows into the cavern, a satchel in one hand, her baby in another.

He could not have been more shocked.

She wore a shapeless brown dress with a black shawl over her shoulders and serviceable shoes on her feet. Her hair and clothing dripped damply from the storm outside, which seemed to have abated, unlike his own storming rage. She paused as she crossed the threshold to let her eyes adjust to the dark.

"What are you doing here?" he demanded, too shocked by the sight of her to temper his tone or words. *With the baby in her arms, at that?*

Colleen ignored him as she peered through the gloom, anxiously hefting her son up on her hip, making a soothing noise in her throat. Then her eyes fixed on Meaghan, and she let out a gasp.

"Jesus in heaven," she exclaimed, staring at the shivering woman. "Were you in the water? But why? It's nigh on winter, girl. You'll freeze to death!"

As if the two of them couldn't have discerned that without her help, Áedán thought. Not even a brash woman like Meaghan would have chosen to dip into the frigid tide pool fully clothed.

"She slipped," Áedán said. "We need to get her warm."

Colleen didn't even glance his way. Instead she gaped at Meaghan as if she'd never seen a wet female before. Granted, Meaghan was a sight. The jeans she wore clung to her legs and the T-shirt had become a second skin, outlining something lacy over her breasts, communicating just how cold she really was, reminding him how hot she'd felt just moments before in his arms. That traitorous feeling inside him protested at the sight of her body wracked with cold, but he steeled himself against his own baffling reactions.

Bending—for Colleen's benefit, he told himself—he took Meaghan's hands between his again and continued to rub. The gash in his palm had soaked through Mickey's handkerchief and throbbed, but the bleeding had stopped and he ignored the pain. Meaghan's breath plumed in front of her. Outside their shelter, distant thunder boomed ominously, and all three of them startled. Colleen tucked the infant closer to her body, adjusting the blanket over his head to keep him warm.

What could have possessed her to come to this cavern?

"What are you doing here, Mrs. Ballagh?" he asked again.

"Sure and didn't she tell me I'd find you here and to bring clothes, but I didn't know why, did I now?" Colleen said, still staring at Meaghan.

And with a trickle of unease, Áedán realized that she had yet to answer him, had yet to even glance his way. Was it deliberate? Was she angry about something? Colleen had never been anything but kind and thoughtful to Áedán since her husband had brought him to their door and commanded that she feed him.

"Who told you she'd be here?" Áedán asked warily. When Colleen still didn't respond to his question, he looked at Meaghan, glad to see that spark still glinting in her eyes instead of the vacant look she'd awakened with. "What is she talking about?"

Teeth chattering, Meaghan shook her head.

"It's the truth," Colleen went on, as if Meaghan had denied her claim. "She told me that I'm to go to the cavern this afternoon. 'Bring clothes,' she says. 'They might be needed.' She said I would find a girl and she might be as naked as Eve in the garden. Instead I find one near turned to ice, but I've no doubt it was you she meant."

"Who?" Áedán barked again. "Who told you?"

He stood and stalked to Colleen's side, feeling, once again, that dread coiling tight and fear tripping over his skin. But with each step, a new kind of horror overtook him. Colleen's gaze never flickered from Meaghan. Even the baby in her arms looked right through him as he stopped in front of them both.

"I don't suppose I even need to ask if your name would be Meaghan, do I?" Colleen went on, shaking her head even as she confirmed her suspicions. "What other young miss would be down here in the cold, shivering like an ice maiden?"

"Mrs. Ballagh," Áedán said, reaching out to take her arms in his hands and demand her attention. He watched a shiver go through her body at his touch, but she didn't look his way, didn't acknowledge that he was even there. Instead she moved toward Meaghan with an air of purpose, brushing him out of the way without a glance.

"I don't know how you got here, missy, or who you might

be, but I mean to help you. Let's get you out of those wet clothes and into the dry ones I brought."

In that moment, Áedán realized that he'd been right to fear this cavern.

After five days of taking meals across the table from Colleen, of working with her husband from dawn to dusk, of doing whatever menial task would help her, suddenly she couldn't see him. Suddenly she looked right through him as if he were invisible . . . as if he didn't even exist at all. . . .

He jerked his gaze away from Colleen to Meaghan, where she sat on the boulder shivering. She stared back with wide, uncomprehending eyes. So he wasn't invisible to her. The realization both comforted and terrified him. Why could *she* see him and not Colleen?

That dark and insidious feeling that had greeted him at the gaping mouth of the cavern surged triumphantly around him now. It mocked the ego that had cloaked him as he'd crossed into this den, and now he felt again that strange wobbling weakness in his limbs. The air reeked of the Book of Fennore, of the world that had been his prison for longer than he could remember.

And it whispered that Áedán would never be free. . . .

FROM

THEA HARRISON

AUTHOR OF *STORM'S HEART*

SERPENT'S KISS

=⇒◆⇐=

A Novel of the Elder Races

In order to save his friend's life, Wyr sentinel Rune Ainiss-
esthai made a bargain with Vampyre Queen Carling—without knowing what she would ask from him in return. But
when Rune attempts to make good on his debt, he finds a
woman on the edge.

Recently, Carling's power has become erratic, forcing her
followers to flee in fear. Despite the danger, Rune is drawn
to the ailing Queen and decides to help her find a cure for
the serpent's kiss—the Vampyric disease that's killing her.

With their desire for each other escalating just as quickly
as Carling's instability spirals out of control, the sentinel
and the Queen will have to rely on each other if they have
any hope of surviving the serpent's kiss . . .

"A master storyteller."   —Christine Feehan,
                              #1 *New York Times* bestselling author

"Thea Harrison has created a truly original urban fantasy
romance."   —Angela Knight, *New York Times* bestselling author

penguin.com

M879T0411